Camera (

"Lavie Tidhar's *The Bookman* is
read in a long time, and I read
James P Blaylock

"An emerging master."
Locus

"*The Bookman* is without a doubt the most enjoyable, fascinating and captivating book I have read in a long time."
Dailysteampunk.com

"Fast paced adventure with tons of sense of wonder. I loved the author's style and I found the book's narrative energy high with smooth transition from one episode to another. Just big time fun, *The Bookman* is highly, highly recommended."
Fantasy Book Critic

"Kim Newman, Alan Moore, Lavie Tidhar: what do they have in common? The answer is a superb ability to throw the actual history of the Victorian age up in the air alongside the popular fiction of that era and allow the whole lot to fall down together in new and interesting shapes."
Cheryl Morgan

"A steampunk gem. Fantastic."
SFFworld.com

"A boisterous mix of steampunk, Victoriana, mystery, travel story, thriller, adventure, partly coming of age story. And it pays homage to fictional and real persons who belong to the Victorian era. It brims over with allusions and cameos. This is steampunk in 3D! Highly recommended from the bottom of my heart."
Only the Best SciFi & Fantasy

BY THE SAME AUTHOR

Osama
The Violent Century
A Man Lies Dreaming
Central Station

and in the Bookman Histories
The Bookman
The Great Game

LAVIE TIDHAR

Camera Obscura

ANGRY ROBOT
An imprint of Watkins Media Ltd

Lace Market House,
54-56 High Pavement,
Nottingham,
NG1 1HW
UK

angryrobotbooks.com
twitter.com/angryrobotbooks
Eye of the lens

First published by Angry Robot in 2011
This new edition published 2016
The short story "Titanic" first appeared in *Apex Magazine*

Cover by Sarah Anne Langton
Set in Meridien by Epub Services

Distributed in the United States by Penguin Random House, Inc., New York.

ISBN 978 0 85766 600 0
Ebook ISBN 978 0 85766 601 7

Printed in the United States of America

9 8 7 6 5 4 3 2 1

To Elizabeth, always

Even if my readers are too well informed to be interested in my descriptions of the methods of the various performers who have seemed to me worthy of attention in these pages, I hope they will find some amusement in following the fortunes and misfortunes of all manner of strange folk who once bewildered the wise men of their day. If I have accomplished that much, I shall feel amply repaid for my labour.

– Harry Houdini, *Miracle Mongers & their Methods*

PROLOGUE
The Emerald Buddha Massacre

The young boy huddled in one corner of the house, half-reading a wuxia novel and half-keeping watch on the night. The night was very still. Outside only the barest hint of wind rustled in the coconut trees, and the air was thick with humidity and the promise of rain.

There were few lights.

Mr Wu's Celestial Dry Cleaning Emporium stood on the very edge of Chiang Rai, stooping like an aged uncle on the border between city and jungle. Mr Wu was standing behind the counter, rolling a cigarette. His hands were liver-spotted and shook a little, dropping bits of loose tobacco on the counter. It took him three tries before he managed to light the match. The cigarette glowed like a firefly in the dark.

On his stool, the boy was reading about heroes and villains. There was a girl, a beautiful assassin, and a man she had to kill, travelling a great distance to find him. There were others like her, all seeking the man they had to kill. The boy's name was Kai. He was reading by the light of a fat, half-melted candle. He put down the book and listened. Somewhere in the distance thunder sounded. The light from Mr Wu's cigarette traced unpredictable orbits in the darkness. "You stay here," he said to the boy. Then he went to the open door and stepped outside, into the night.

Kai listened but could hear nothing. He put down the book, assassins and chases abandoned for the moment, and stood up. Quietly, he too went to the door. He peered outside.

A thin yellow moon cast strips of light and shade on the street, bands of yellow light cut in stark relief with hard lines of darkness. Kai could see Mr Wu standing just outside, looking up and down the street, waiting–

Mr Wu dropped his cigarette and ground it with the heel of his shoe, the dying smoke expiring in a shower of embers. Kai's head snapped up. A line of shadowed figures was coming slowly down the abandoned street.

They made no sound. He could not see their faces, could discern nothing about them but their being there, as suddenly as if they had materialised out of nowhere. Kai's heart beat hard and fast inside his chest, and his palms felt sweaty. Mr Wu, framed by the moon, a small, slight figure, was motionless outside. The dark figures approached slowly, walking a single file. Lightning streaked the sky far overhead, for just a moment, and Kai counted the seconds until the thunder erupted. The storm was still far, but was coming closer. He watched the approaching figures. In that one brief moment of illumination he saw they were cowled.

He would have thought them monks, but no monk he knew wore black. Their robes stole the night and made it their own. He could tell nothing about them, could see no faces or eyes, nothing to tell him who or what they were.

He had noticed one thing, though: they did not come empty-handed.

When the cowled figures came close they halted. Above their heads the sign for Mr Wu's Celestial Dry Cleaning Emporium stood dark. They halted before Mr Wu and Mr Wu made a stiff bow in their direction, his hands joining together before his chest: a mark of respect. To Kai's surprise, the monks – if that's what they were – returned the gesture, their hands rising higher than Mr Wu's had, showing him the greater respect. Why?

The monks spread out before Mr Wu. Four of them came forward then. They were carrying a heavy-looking crate suspended between them on thick poles of bamboo.

They lowered the crate to the ground. There was another strike of jagged lightning high above, and the thunder came much quicker this time. The storm was approaching fast.

Mr Wu made a jerking movement with his head, aimed at the crate. He said, "Open it." His voice sounded raw.

Two of the monks brought out wrenches. The others fanned out around them, facing the street. The crate made keening sounds as it was opened, nails groaning, wood splintering. Mr Wu said, "Careful, now."

There was another flash of lightning and in its light Kai thought he'd seen, for just a moment, another figure moving in the distance, between the trees. Then the crate was fully opened and he turned to look and forgot everything else.

The moonlight hit the figure inside the crate. The two monks with the wrenches moved back. Mr Wu came forward and knelt down beside the broken crate. A scaly, inhuman face – the face of a giant lizard – stared out of the crate. It was made entirely of jade, apart from its eyes, which were giant emeralds. Mr Wu reached into the crate–

The silence was broken, too quickly, the sound foreign and unexpected. Kai had heard it only once before, but he knew it instinctively.

Gunshots.

One of the monks dropped to the ground. His robes seemed to grow even darker. Mr Wu turned his head, startled. He saw Kai and his eyes opened wide. The monks shot out across the street, dark shapes moving without sound, like characters in Kai's wuxia novel, like Shaolin monks or other kung-fu secret masters, only the sound of gunfire was growing more intense now and it was coming from the forest and the invisible shooters were finding their targets with deadly accuracy.

"Get inside!"

Mr Wu, sheltered by the monks, reached into the crate and pulled out the statue. Kai stared at it, fear momentarily forgotten. It was beautiful – though perhaps that was not quite the right word.

Majestic, perhaps.

Or strange.

A lizard carved in jade, with shining emerald eyes. Sitting cross-legged, like the Buddha. For just a moment he thought he could hear it whispering, a tiny voice in his head, then it was gone and his father was carrying the statue in his arms, back into the relative safety of the Emporium. Kai watched the monks – and now there were people coming out of the jungle, several figures the colour of foliage, and they carried guns. The black-clad monks attacked them. He watched them, mesmerised – they seemed to almost fly through the air, jump off walls and onto the attackers. The fight spread out across the street. One of the green-clad men killed two monks before a third sailed above his head, landing softly behind him and twisting the man's neck – almost gently, it seemed to Kai – and the man dropped down to the ground, a leaf falling from a tree, the gun tumbling out of his lifeless hands.

A slap shook him out of it. The jade statue was inside the shop and so was Kai's father, who grabbed him by his shirt and dragged him away from the doorway. He said, "I told you to stay inside."

Kai said, "I did." His father shook his head. He said, "You must leave. I didn't know–"

"What is it?" Kai said. His eyes were on the statue. The statue seemed to be regarding him, perhaps with amusement, perhaps with indifference.

"It's a–"

Another burst of fire from outside, and it was followed by an explosion of thunder. Rain began to fall outside, great billowing sheets of it, and lightning flashed again and in the light all Kai could see, like a series of frozen tableaux, were the two groups of men fighting, hand-to-hand, in a street full of unmoving figures lying on the ground, the pavement slick and red with blood and rain. He felt sick, for just a moment. Then there was another sound, so soft he almost didn't hear it, a surprised sound, air escaping a throat, and his father went down on his knees before the jade figure. Kai screamed. His father looked up at him, and blinked. A dark stain was spreading over his crisply ironed shirt. Kai fell down beside him, holding him. His father's voice was soft, the hiss of escaping air. He said, "Kai..."

Kai said, "No." He may have said it several times. His father's lips moved, though no sound came. Then, "Go."

There was nothing else. Kai shouted but his voice was swallowed by the storm. When he let go his father was lying on the floor. His hand was resting on Kai's wuxia novel, the cheap yellow pages growing dark with blood.

Kai looked outside and the green-clad figures seemed to be winning, and they were coming closer and closer, and the few remaining monks were now standing before the entrance to the shop, holding them back – but for how long?

Go. The voice had been his father's. Now it echoed in his mind, and he looked up and for a moment it seemed to him the jade statue was staring at him, no longer amused or indifferent, speaking in his father's voice. Go.

Kai looked down at his father and knew he was dead. There were gunshots outside and another monk dropped down. Kai screamed again, defiant or afraid he didn't know, and stood up and with the same motion grabbed the jade statue. It was surprisingly light.

He headed for the back of the shop. Through rustling clothes and the silence where steam had, until recently, been, through the silent presses toward the back door. They might be waiting there too but he didn't care; his mind was filled with rain and thunder and blood and he burst out of the back door into the narrow alleyway beyond. Then he ran, the statue held in his arms, the rain dripping down his black hair, making his clothes heavy. There were more gunshots behind him but he never looked back. He ran out of the alleyway and down the road toward the trees. He knew the men would come after him. He ran until the forest was there and then he ran through the trees, no longer thinking, the thick canopy holding back the rain, his feet sinking into dead leaves and mud. Running, falling, rising, going deeper and deeper into the forest, until the sounds all died behind him.

PART I
The Murder in the Rue Morgue

ONE
A Woman With a Gun

There was a crowd of people outside the house on the Rue Morgue, making the place easy enough to spot. Rue Morgue – the unfashionable side of Paris on display, like dirty laundry hanging on a clothesline. Soot-blackened bricks, the smell of rotting rubbish and fresh excrement in the street. Eyes staring out of windows. A neighbourhood where no one wanted to get involved with the law – and yet: a crowd of spectators, eager for a corpse and some entertainment.

The hansom cab had some difficulty navigating the narrow street. The woman inside the cab tapped her long, sharp nails on the windowsill. They were painted a deep shade of black.

There were gendarmes stationed outside the house, doing a bad job of keeping the spectators away.

That was soon going to change.

The cab stopped. The horse on the left raised its head, neighed once, then added its own contribution to the street's refuse. A couple of urchins turned and giggled, pointing at the fresh, steaming pile.

The door of the cab opened. The woman stepped out.

What did she look like?

Six foot two and ebony-black, a halo of dark hair around her head. Strong cheekbones, pronounced. Her arms were naked and muscled, and there was a thick gold bracelet encircling her left arm. She wore trousers, some sort of black leather, and that might have been shocking, but the first, and then only, thing you noticed about her was the gun.

She wore it in a shoulder holster. A Colt Peacemaker, though there was little that was peaceful about the woman. When the people of the Rue Morgue discussed it, later, they decided it was a coin toss, whether she would shoot you or merely batter you to death with that gun, using it as a bludgeon. They decided it would have depended on her mood.

The crowd moved back a pace, without being asked.

The woman smiled.

You could not see her eyes. They were hidden behind dark shades. She stepped toward the gate of the house. The two gendarmes snapped to attention.

"Milady."

She barely acknowledged them. She turned, facing the crowd. "Go home," she said.

She watched the crowd. The crowd, collectively, took another step back. She said, "I'll count to three," then smiled. She had very white teeth. "One."

Her hand was stroking the butt of the gun. She looked momentarily disappointed when the crowd, in something of a hurry, dispersed. Soon the street was quiet, though she could feel the eyes staring from every window.

Well, let them stare.

She turned back and, ignoring the two gendarmes, went through the gate into the house.

The apartment was on the fourth floor. She climbed up the stairs. When she arrived the door was open. A photographer was taking pictures inside, the flash going off like miniature explosions. She went inside. The corpse was on the floor.

"Milady!"

She smiled, without affection.

Flash.

The Gascon was lithe and scarred, and he still carried a sword on his hip as if a sword was any use at all. He said, "We are perfectly capable of solving this murder without interference."

She arched an eyebrow. It seemed to sum up her opinion of the gendarmes and their investigative abilities. The Gascon said, "Why are you here, Milady?"

She smiled. He took a step back and, perhaps unconsciously, his hand went to the hilt of his sword. She said, "I have no interest in who – or what – killed him."

"Oh?" Was it relief in his voice – or suspicion?

"The why, though," she said. "That's a different matter."

Flash.

The light was blinding. She said, "Give me the camera."

The Gascon nodded at the man. The photographer began to protest, then looked at the woman and decided that, perhaps, he should do as he was told after all. She took the camera from him and smashed it against the wall. The photographer cried out. "Get out," the woman said. The photographer looked at her, helpless, then at his boss. The Gascon was not looking at him. The photographer opened his mouth to voice a protest, caught sight of the woman's gun, and made a wise decision.

He left. There were just the two of them in the apartment now. "Who owns the place?" she said, though she already knew.

"A Madame L'Espanaye," the Gascon said. "And her daughter."

"Where are they now?"

"My men are trying to find them as we speak."

She said, "Your men." There was no intonation in her voice, but somehow it made his face turn red. Again he said, "You have no need to be here."

She said, "Oh?" She still hadn't looked at the corpse. She moved to the window now, stared out at the night. The window was open, and the ground was four stories below.

"I understand the door was locked from the inside?" she said.

The Gascon said, "Yes. The gendarmes had to break it open."

"And yet no one could have climbed in through the window," she said.

He said, "Perhaps..." and there was the faint hint of a smile on his face.

"You have a theory," she said. It was not a question. And now she turned to him and he wished he could see her eyes. "The man was the lover of the young Mademoiselle L'Espanaye. He was living here with the two women. Perhaps he became affectionate with the older L'Espanaye. Perhaps the younger one didn't like it. Or it is possible they got together and since blood is thicker, as they say, than water, they decided to get rid of the man who came between them. Either way, once you locate the missing women they will confess – murder solved, case closed. Correct?"

The Gascon had lost the smile. And now the lady nodded with apparent satisfaction. "And you could devise some clever scheme to explain how the murder was committed – perhaps a trained ape had climbed four stories into the locked room, the window left open especially for that purpose? Or, much simpler –" and she was almost done now, close to dismissing him, and he both knew and resented it – "the door was never locked from the inside. What do you think?"

He was standing by the door. She turned her back on him. When she turned again he was standing away from the door. Had there been a key in the lock before? If so it was no longer there. She nodded. "Or perhaps the man committed suicide. Regrettable, when a man takes his own life, but not unheard of." She tapped her nails against the wall. The Gascon stared at them. She said, "Yes, I like that one best. Leave the women out of it. A suicide, nothing more. Not worth attention – from anyone. I hope you agree?"

"Milady," he said. The pronounced lines around his eyes were the only outward signs of his displeasure. The woman smiled. "Good," she said. "Write your report and close the case. Another speedy result for our dedicated police force. Well done."

He nodded. For just a moment his head turned and he looked at the corpse on the floor, and a small shudder seemed to run down his spine. For just a moment. Then he turned his back on the woman and the corpse and the case and walked away.

TWO
The Corpse

Now that she was alone at last she stood still for one long moment. The air in the room was hot and filled with unpleasant scents. She still did not look at the corpse. She glanced around the apartment – cheap furniture, a print on the wall, incongruously, of Queen Victoria – blood. On the walls, on the rickety old sofa, on the floor – the stench of it strong in her nostrils. A drop of blood had hit the lizard queen's portrait and ran down it like a tear. She went to the window.

Looking down at the Rue Morgue, shadows moved far below, spectators robbed of their moment of excitement. How easy would it be to keep a lid on what had happened here? To the smell of blood, add machine oil, foliage, rot – the smell of a jungle somewhere far away and hot. This last did not belong in this, her city.

Her city. She remembered days running in the alleyways, hunting for scraps, hiding from the urban predators. Had it ever been her city? She was not born there and, later, had not lived there, yet here she was. She glared at the lizard queen's ruined portrait, deciding the blood added, not detracted, from the painting. She remembered the lizards' court. Her second, unfortunate husband had often taken her there. His death…

She wouldn't dwell on it. The barest hint of wind coming

through the window, and she realised her face was wet, that the atmosphere in the room had made her sweat. Looking down – was that a shadow moving up the wall, climbing cautiously, some animal well used to shade making its slow and careful way up to this place of death? She watched but could not be sure. She turned away from the window, taking a last deep breath of air fresher, at least, than that inside, and looked at last at the corpse.

That first glance only took a moment, and she turned her head, breathing hard through her nose. She closed her eyes, but the image of the corpse was waiting for her in the darkness behind her eyelids, and she felt the room begin to spin. She opened her eyes and looked again, and this time she did not look away.

A man lay on the floor at her feet.

One side of his head had been caved in. What remained of the face seemed to belong to a man hailing from Asia, though it was hard to tell with certainty. His skin had taken on a waxy aspect. He was lying in a pool of blood, the fingers of one hand – his left – curled into a fist, the other loose, one finger stretched out as if pointing. She half-expected to see a message scrawled in blood, on the floor or the wall, some cryptic riddle to lead her to the man's killer, but there was none, and it would have made no difference either way since she was not overly concerned with who killed him, but only of what they had taken from the man after his death.

The head wound was ordinary enough. She let her gaze wander further down, past the neck, towards the chest and stomach… yes. She knelt beside him, feeling sick. And now her hands were on him, studying the gash in his corpulent belly. The skin was hairless and the belly-button pronounced, and the man looked pregnant, even in death, as if his stomach had contained a womb and a foetus inside it – though there were none there now.

He had been gutted open, with a long, sharp knife. The

flaps of his stomach looked like the torn pages of a book. She took a deep breath and plunged her hand into the corpse, searching, knowing even as she did it that she would find nothing but intestines and blood.

And now there was a sound coming from the open window, a small rustle as of a creature of some sort trying to enter without being noticed, and she turned.

A shadow was perched on the windowsill. She stared at it, her bloodied hand going to the knife strapped to her leg. The shadow on the windowsill moved and gained definition, an impossible apparition that would have frightened the residents of the Rue Morgue to death.

She said, "It's about time you showed up." She brought up her knife and suspended it above the corpse, then plunged it in. Perhaps something still remained inside the man. She had to make sure.

When she looked away again the shadow had moved from the window and came crawling towards her. For a moment they were a tableau – corpse, woman above him with bloodied knife, a crawling, enormous cockroach symbolising death approaching or fleeing, she couldn't decide which. The mechanical cockroach whistled plaintively. The woman said, "That's hardly an excuse."

The thing whistled again, and the woman said, "Well, you're here now, at least. See if you can find anything."

The cockroach approached, feelers shaking. As it came closer the faint whirring sound of gears could be heard. It was about the size of a small dog. Its feelers moved and another whistling sound came out of its matt-black body, and the woman said, "You're the forensic automaton, Grimm, so why don't you tell me?"

The automaton she had called Grimm crawled closer to the body. The woman stood up, cleaning and sheathing her knife, and looked down. Probable cause of death – strike to the head with a blunt instrument. Mutilation inflicted post-mortem –

the killer or killers knew what they were looking for and had come away with it.

She watched the little automaton crawl over the corpse. It buried its head in the man's glistening belly, its legs pushing it deeper into the corpse until it almost disappeared inside, making little whirring noises all the while. She walked back to the window and breathed in the air from the outside: air that carried nothing worse with it than the smell of smoke and dung and rotting rubbish.

THREE
A Spark of Electricity

After a while she went through the deceased's effects. They were few enough. Grimm was still studying the body. Right now its pincers were busy digging deep inside the man's head, and bits of brain dulled their colour when they emerged. The lady had examined the man's clothes but had come to no conclusions. The clothes were not new nor were they foreign.

The man's pockets were almost entirely empty. She found a handful of coins, a packet of loose tobacco, almost empty, and a matchbox to go along with it – no identity card, nothing to suggest who the dead man may have been or where he came from. She looked at the matchbox – the cheap print on the cover advertised a tobacconist in Montmartre. She put it in her pocket.

Grimm was still working on the corpse, emitting little whistles and clicks which she ignored. There was an Edison player on a table by one wall. She approached it but could find no perforated discs. She searched the apartment thoroughly then.

Madame L'Espanaye's room first – distinguished by more Victoria prints, aerial shots of the Royal Gardens, commemorative china plates, a chipped coronation mug – the woman was obsessed with the royal lizards from across the Channel. Les Lézards. Her mouth made a moue of distaste.

Madame L'Espanaye's interest in lizards evidently did not extend to her wardrobe, which was full of frilly, lacy, pinkish-dirty, oversized gowns and negligees. That interested the lady a lot more. In the back of the wardrobe she found a box and inside the box a bottle of Scotch whisky, Old Bushmills, expensive and, if she recalled correctly, a lizardine favourite. It was three-quarters empty. Beside it was a roll of bank notes. They looked new. She ran her thumb through them, then put them in her pocket. Curiouser and curiouser.

There was a dresser with a vanity mirror and plenty of rouge and white paint, and she could almost picture the senior L'Espanaye in her mind. She went through the drawers and found a small-calibre gun at the bottom-most one on the left, and it was loaded. The bed was large and unmade, the sheets rumpled. In the small adjacent washroom she found several bottles of pills and grimy walls, and when she ran the tap the water was brackish.

She scanned the bedroom again but found nothing else of interest and moved on to Mademoiselle L'Espanaye's room. The daughter's was almost bare, the bed dominating the room, a single chair by the window, candles, many no more than stubs, standing like fat monks around the room, their wicks dead. She tossed the room and found nothing: it was as if no one had lived there and if they had, they'd left nothing behind them.

Conjecture: the two women shared the master bedroom, and the dead man had been using the daughter's room.

Grimm whistled from the other room, and so she walked over and stared down at the man's corpse, which looked even worse now than it did before, thanks to Grimm. "Traces of what?" she said.

The automaton spoke in Silbo Gomero, a technical compromise on communication that was also an assurance of confidentiality, since there were not many speakers of the whistling language, in Paris or elsewhere. The language had come from the Canary Islands, adopted by the Spanish who settled there and finally modified by Grimm's makers using a simplified French vocabulary. Grimm whistled again, and the lady said, "That doesn't make any sense."

Grimm whistled, more insistent now, and she said, "What do you mean, watch?"

Instead of an answer the mechanical insect crept closer to the corpse and extended a pincer toward it, gently touching the man's flesh. The lady watched. A small blue spark of electricity passed between Grimm and the dead man.

The corpse twitched.

The woman watched, her hand going to the butt of her gun without her being consciously aware of doing so. Grimm retreated from the body but it continued to twitch – and now its one remaining eye shot open.

The woman took a step back and her gun was in her hand and pointing at the corpse – she watched a dead foot kick, and the finger that had been pointing at nothing was rising now, impossibly, and the dead man was pointing directly at her, his face twisted in a mask of grotesque agony, accusing her…

The bullet took out the remaining eye and bits of brain exploded over Grimm and the print of the lizard queen. The pointing hand fell down, lifeless again. The body shuddered, once, twice, and finally subsided. The woman reholstered her gun and said, "Get rid of it."

Grimm began to whistle then, apparently, changed its mind. It approached the corpse again, pincers extended like surgical saws. Together, woman and automaton worked to erase the crime that had taken place there, tonight, and as they worked, dismantling the lifeless body into its separate components, she wondered why it was left the way it had been – were they interrupted, or was the dead man himself a message scribbled into the stones of the Rue Morgue for her to find?

FOUR
Outside Rue Morgue

When the work was done she left Grimm to dispose of the body parts – the giant insect secreting quicklime, squatting over the man's dismembered corpse digesting one piece at a time. She looked through the apartment again – there had been no sign of a struggle, and she thought it was a reasonable enough proposition that the two women who resided here had merely been absent – by chance? Or were they paid to make themselves scarce? She thought she'd be able to find them – assuming they were still alive...

A locked-room murder. The apartment was four stories high. Well, Grimm had managed to scale it easily enough. And the window was open... The how of it scarcely interested her. The who, though, had become something of a priority.

She washed her hands in the foul-smelling water in the sink, watching it turn red and pink and disappear in a gurgle down the drain, taking the dead man's blood with it. She dried her hands thoroughly and returned to the room and was relieved to see Grimm was almost half-way there. When it sensed her it turned, its feelers shaking, and emitted a burst of high-pitched whistles. The lady nodded, then said, "Take the samples to the under-morgue when you're done."

She went back to the window, glaring out at the city below. Night was settling in and, if she guessed correctly, the Madame and Mademoiselle L'Espanaye would be hard at work. She pulled out the matchbox she had found on the corpse and looked at it again.

Montmartre.

She put it back abruptly and turned away from the window. Why was the name of the tobacconist familiar? She said, "I'm going for a walk."

Grimm whistled, a sad lonely sound that followed her as she walked out of the door.

Below, Rue Morgue was deep in shadow, its residents hiding behind their cheap walls. Windows were shuttered, as if excitement had given way, suddenly, to fear.

Good.

She walked alone, and the soft sound of her moving feet was the only break in the silence of the street. She watched the shadows, her hand on the butt of her gun. She was not disturbed.

She decided to walk for a while. She had always liked the city best when it was dark and silent. As a child she–

She turned at the sudden sound and the gun was in her hand and the shadows shifted and then eased back. She smiled, without humour, and walked on.

She thought about the dead man. He had carried something inside his own belly, a foreign object that had somehow been inserted into his flesh, and valuable enough that it had been ripped out of him savagely and carried away. The man had no identity, as yet, and neither did his killers. And as for his cargo…

She thought about Grimm touching the corpse, that little spark of electricity that had set the dead man rising. She had to conclude that, though he was human on the outside, his inside may have been a different matter. Well, it was of little concern right now. No doubt the doctor would be engrossed by Grimm's samples, down in the under-morgue…

She passed out of Rue Morgue, breathing a sigh of relief,

though the entire neighbourhood was the same, dark and dank and dismal. She headed for the Seine, finding her way with ease through the narrow, twisting streets. The old city morgue used to sit at the end of that street, she remembered, lending the road its name. Thoughts of the corpse niggled at her. She had seen plenty of bodies but nothing like the one Grimm was busy erasing from existence.

After a while the streets became wider and more prosperous. She found an open café and went inside, into the gloom of candles and smoke. She ordered a coffee and sat down by the window and glared at the night.

The door of the café banged open, then shut, and a shadow slipped into the seat opposite her. She raised her eyes and stared at the smiling Gascon.

"Milady," he said. "What a pleasant surprise."

She glared at him. The Gascon signalled to the waiter, mouthed, "Coffee."

Ignoring her.

"You followed me," she said.

"Surely a coincidence," he said, and now his smile hardened. "Of all the places–"

"What do you want?"

The Gascon shrugged. And now the smile melted away, having never reached his eyes. "That murder is mine," he said.

"What murder?" she said, and was pleased to see the flicker of anger that passed over his face.

"You wouldn't," he said.

She sipped her coffee. The hot liquid revived her. She stared at the man evenly, waiting him out. He looked away first.

"The Republic has law," the Gascon said at last. "You can't cover up–"

"Can't?" she said. And now she stood up, dismissing him. "Stay out of my way," she advised. "And forget about the Rue

Morgue. There is nothing there for you now."

He looked up at her. She examined him, feeling a vague sense of unease. Why was the Gascon still pursuing the case?

"I can help you," he said. His voice was soft. She smiled, showing teeth, and walked away without answering him, her back to him all the answer she needed to give, and the door banged shut behind her.

FIVE
Across the River

She could have taken a coach or one of the new baruch-landaus but instead she walked, not feeling an urgency any more, but wondering what it was that had been surgically inserted into the dead man's belly. It was not a case of murder, she thought, but theft. She found the Seine and followed it for a while, watching the ruined Notre Dame cathedral growing larger as she approached, a wan yellow moon rising above it. Lizard boys hung around the broken-down structure at all hours: hair shaped into ridges over otherwise bald domes, skin tattooed into lizard stripes, tongues forked where they had paid some back-room surgeon to split them open. Dangerous, yes, but predictable.

She crossed the river, looking down at the Seine snaking its way through the city, a lone barge still floating down it at this late hour, carrying pails of garbage, and she thought – there were a hundred different ways to disappear forever in this city.

She walked away from the river, into the maze of never-ending streets, her feet sure on the ground, knowing their way, the ground like taut skin stretched over the body of a giant lizard. She thought the dead man must have come into the city very quietly, but not quietly enough – had slipped in and found the apartment in the Rue Morgue, thinking it was safe – he must have waited, must have made contact with person or persons still unknown, and waited to conclude the transaction – for she was sure that's what it was – but had somehow faltered. Or not. Perhaps he knew all along how he would end up, a gutted fish in a Parisian market where everything was for sale.

She walked for a long time, her long legs carrying her easily, swiftly, along the ancient narrow streets. She knew them well. As a kid she had run through them, had lain in wait for the apple cart owner to turn away for just one crucial moment – for a dark shadow of a girl to swoop and make a grab and run away, laughing. She had looked through rubbish piles for clothes and food, and hid in the abandoned places, the tumbledown houses where others roamed, the animals in human guise who preyed on those who had the least of all… a far cry from the home she could no longer remember, the place where she'd been born, so far away, where the sun always shone, where her mother had come from, the same mother who had died so quickly here, in this new land of white men and gleaming machines. She had first killed in a place just like this, a dark alley where a man was bent over a child – a boy who was a friend, as much as the other small humans on the street could be called that – and she had snuck behind the man and cut his throat with her knife, feeling nothing but a savage satisfaction, and the boy – he was still alive – had staggered away from under the corpse and down the street, clothes drenched in blood, some of it his own. She never saw him again, and there had been other predators, other animals on the streets of this most glorious Paris, city of equality, fraternity and liberty, this city of the Quiet Revolution.

The streets gradually became brighter, lamps alight and places of business still open: night business, for she was approaching Pigalle. There were people on the street, women leaning at corners, two men fighting in an alleyway, drunks spilling out of a nearby tavern, the sound of music and shouting and dancing from a building nearby, a brasserie serving buckets of mussels with bread for late diners, glasses of beer – faces leering at her until they saw the gun and turned away, eyes suddenly, carefully empty. She saw a man's pocket being picked by a small child and two gendarmes watching without comment. The man never noticed but the gendarmes did and when the child tried to run they were waiting for him, counting the money, taking out their share. This was her world, had been her world, and she still felt more comfortable here than she ever had at the lizardine court or the embassy balls – though that was merely a different kind of throat-cutting and pick-pocketing, done on a different scale.

The little boy ran off, and the two gendarmes disappeared through the doors of a bar. She walked on. Closer to Montmartre now, and the streets grew quieter, the ruined church on the hill above casting down a faint eerie glow. She walked a short way up to the small square where a couple of restaurants were closing, and into the all-night tobacconist's that only recently had sold a box of matches to a dead man.

SIX
The Immaculate Mr Thumb

Thumb's Tobacco was well lit and empty. Behind the counter were orderly rows of the tobacconist's merchandise. Hanging on the walls, startling her for a moment, were posters advertising The PT Barnum Circus – The Greatest Show on Earth! A tall black woman, muscled and scantily clothed, holding a pair of guns, was featured on one. She looked at it for a long moment and bit her lip. The Ferocious Dahomey Amazon! screamed the notice above her head. She smiled at last, and shook her head, and looked away. Then she looked over the counter and a pair of eyes stared back up at her.

The eyes rose to meet hers – and now she knew why the name had sounded familiar, as the eyes blinked recognition and a wide grin suddenly split the small face they came with.

"You!"

She nodded, unable not to return the grin as the small man behind the counter straightened up, climbing onto a stool so that he stood with his upper body above the polished wooden top. "Cleo–" he said, and she shook her head, No. "It's De Winter now."

"I haven't seen you since–"

"It's good to see you, too, Tom," she said.

The Vespuccian man was dressed immaculately in a child-sized suit, a pocket watch hanging on a chain from his pocket.

"Since you left the circus," he said.

"It's been a while."

"I have your publicity poster," the small man said proudly, gesturing at the wall.

"I saw," she said, not following the gesture. Looking at him.

"Last I heard you were in England," he said. He rubbed his thumb and finger together. "Married to some lord."

She said, "He died."

The grin grew larger. "They tend to do that, don't they?"

She let it pass. For now. She said, "Last I heard you were in England."

He shrugged. "Had to leave in a bit of a hurry, didn't I."

"Why doesn't that surprise me?"

The small man shrugged again.

"Still fomenting revolution?"

"Nah, mate," Tom Thumb said, "I'm legit now. Out of the revolutionary business. Minding my own business, for once, and liking it that way."

"The quiet life," she said.

He nodded, watching her carefully, no longer smiling now.

She said, "I find it hard to believe."

Tom Thumb shrugged. Believe what you want, the shrug seemed to say. See if I care. And now she smiled, and the little man shrank a little from it.

She took out the box of matches from her pocket, played with it. Tom Thumb watched her fingers. "You smoking now?" he said. "You never used to."

She flipped the box over, not answering him. Printed on the cover was Thumb's Tobacco, Montmartre. The painting showed the front of the shop, a little figure just visible behind the glass. She threw it across the counter at him and he flinched back but caught it.

"One of yours?" she said.

He looked at it, put it down on the counter. "Got my name on it, hasn't it?" he said.

"It does, at that," she said.

"So?"

He was watching her warily now, caged but not yet knowing why. Or maybe he did... maybe he'd been expecting her, or someone like her, to come eventually to his shop.

So... "Popular shop?" she said, looking around her at the empty space.

"Doing OK," he said, using the Vespuccian expression. It almost made her smile – she hadn't heard it in a while.

"That's a nice suit," she said instead.

"Thank you."

"Must be expensive."

"Oh, you know..." he said.

"And that watch. Gold?"

"This old thing? Nah. Just looks like it."

"It certainly does. Looks new, too."

Tom Thumb stared at her, expressionless. "You a copper now?"

It was said less as a question – more an accusation.

"We've all got to make a living," she said. "Don't we, Tom?"

"I'm making a living," he said. "I sell tobacco."

"So I see."

"Well, it was nice seeing you," he said, "Milady. Now, if you'll excuse me, I have a lot of work to–"

She reached across the counter and picked him up. He said, "Wha–"

"I'll dismiss you," she said. "When I'm done with you. OK, Tom?"

She dropped him. He glared at her, smoothed his jacket where she had grabbed him. Suddenly he grinned again. "Come see the ferocious Dahomey Amazon!" he said. "Remember? I used to love your act. Got your publicity poster right there–"

"I know, Tom. I saw it."

"Yes, well, we're old friends, you and I, aren't we? There's no need to get rough."

"I hope so, Tom."

She waited him out. He stood, watching her – she could see him thinking. She didn't hurry him. At last he said, "Sit down, I'll make us a brew."

Sit down, I'll make us a brew. As if they were back at the circus, and the last show had finished – everyone winding down, but not yet ready to let go – the rush still there, the shouts of the crowds, the smell of sweat, and smoke from the torches, roasting peanuts and piss from the animal enclave... sawdust. Sometimes she really missed the smell of fresh sawdust.

It always became less and less fresh as the evening progressed.

She said, "OK."

SEVEN
Imports & Exports

Tom Thumb made coffee. He put a coffee set down on the counter between them – sugar cubes, small jug of milk, a couple of pastries, cups and saucers and spoons.

She took hers black and drank it through a sugar cube. "It's not bad," she said.

"It's from–" he said, and then he hesitated.

She said, "You selling coffee now?"

"Amongst other things."

"What sort of things?"

"Cleo–" he said, then checked himself, almost saying her full name, the way she was billed back in the show. "Fine, fine! Milady, then."

She waited.He said, "Is this going any further, or is this between us?"

She thought about it, said, "It depends."

"On what?"

On a corpse that was no longer there... She said, "I don't care what you do. I'm just trying to find something that's missing."

"What sort of something?"

"I'm not sure yet."

He shrugged, letting it go. "Fine," he said. "What do you want to know?"

"I want to know who bought that box of matches from you."

Tom Thumb looked exasperated. "How the hell should I know?"

"He was Asian."

She saw him noticing the was. And now his eyes narrowed, and his hand played with the pocket watch, releasing and closing the lid, working it.

"An Asian man who needed a place to hide out in..." she said, "Where did you say your coffee comes from again?"

"I didn't."

"But you were going to."

"Was I?"

Open, shut, open, shut. She took another sip of her coffee. "Leave that alone," she said.

"Lots of Asians in Paris," Tomb Thumb said at last. "Indochina. Siam. Doing business. So what?"

Making a connection, and she threw him a line: "You selling opium?"

... and he bit. Tom Thumb shrugged. "A little. Not illegal, is it?"

"No," she said. "But this isn't a smoking den, so what, you deal bulk?"

He didn't answer.

"Got a contact over there? Sends you stuff over?"

No reply.

"Coffee, for instance?"

"It's good coffee," Tom Thumb said. "Good opium, too."

"What else does he send you?"

Nothing from Tom, staring out through the window into the night.

"People, sometimes?"

Tom, still staring out at the night. Thinking. How much could he tell her? She knew that look.

"People who need somewhere to hide, for a little while?"

Tom turned to her. No smile, eyes calm like grey skies. "Is Yong Li dead?"

And now she had a name. "Yes."

Tom said, "Damn."

I have a little shipping business *(Tom Thumb said)*. Import/ export, with this guy in Indochina on the other end of it. I buy coffee, tobacco, now and then opium for those who like that sort of thing – all legit. So maybe I don't pay customs every time, you know? And maybe sometimes, just sometimes, I ship some stuff East.

What stuff? You know. Stuff.

You don't know?

But you want to.

It's nothing serious, Cl – Milady. Milady de Winter, huh? Seriously? Think I met Lord de Winter once, back when I was still living across the Channel. Whatever happened to–

Fine. Yes. Arms. Sometimes. And literature.

What do you mean what literature? How should I know?

I'm more of a drop point, now that you press me on it. Don't think I'm the only one working for this guy. So sometimes they drop off little packets for me – mostly paper. I don't know what's in them though.

Did I look? No.

Fine, maybe I did a couple of times. Didn't make much sense, though. Technical stuff. Like, you know those Babbage engines? That's what some of it looked like. Technical specifications. Once this mechanical beggar came into the shop, a proper derelict, could barely move, one of those old people-shaped ones, moving one leg after another, you can hear the motors inside they were so loud, doesn't say a thing but drops off this box – I open it, it's got an arm inside.

No, a metal arm. Real artwork. Only, I open the box, this arm reaches out, tries to strangle me. After that I didn't look again.

Yes. I'm getting to that. So, we do business, you know, mostly legit, a little bit of it under the counter – don't you dare make a joke – only sometimes there's people need to get from here to Indochina don't want to be going through the usual channels. I don't ask questions. Usually I know to expect them. Then off they go with the next shipment.

Got his own ship, ships, I don't know.

Sometimes he sends people over. No papers, half of them don't speak the language. I mean, any language. Don't know what they want. If they need it I arrange a safe house, somewhere to put them, lie low for a while. If not then *poof* – they disappear into the city, I never see them again.

Where the safe house is? You don't think I'm going to tell you, do you?

How did you know?

Oh.

So that's where you found him. Poor bastard.

He came in about a month ago. Nervous little guy, fat belly, gave him lots of problems, cramps, I don't know. He kept holding it, almost looked pregnant. I put him up for a couple of nights. Nice guy. Taught me this drinking game–

I don't know where he was from. Don't know what he was doing here. I don't ask questions. A couple of days later L'Espanaye tells me the place is free, I send him over.

The mother, yes. She's the one I've been dealing with. Wouldn't mind dealing with the daughter though, if you know what I mean.

Right. Sorry.

No, never saw him again. Didn't think I'd hear about him again either, until you walked through my door.

The poor bastard.

He was a nice guy.

EIGHT
Tattoos

She finished her coffee. Tom Thumb lit a cigar. She watched him – trimming it first, then using the matchbox that came from a dead man's pocket. Tom blew out smoke. She said, "Do you have any idea what he was carrying?"

"Ask no questions," Tom Thumb said, "hear no lies. That's my policy."

He knew more than he was telling her. She was sure of that much, at least. But Tom Thumb wasn't going anywhere. He'd been going nowhere for a long time. She said, "And the name of the man you deal with? The one in Indochina?"

Tom shrugged. "Never asked his name."

She let it pass. "What does he do, exactly? Beyond selling you coffee?"

"No idea."

But she had an idea.

"You've always been a revolutionary," she said. "What were you doing in England, Tom?"

"Minding my own business," the little man said. He blew smoke towards her and she smiled and reached over and pulled the cigar from his mouth and put it out on his hand.

Tom screamed.

"I'll come back," she said. "When you're feeling better."

She walked away, thinking of the dead man, but thinking

of someone else now, too – a man somewhere in Asia, a man with no name. He would be a very careful man, she thought – cautious, a planner. And ruthless – she thought of Yong Li lying on the floor of the apartment in the Rue Morgue with his stomach cut open where someone had opened it before and hid something inside. Was Yong Li meant to have died in Paris?

Somehow she didn't think so. No doubt Tom would be in a hurry to send word back, and that was all right – she wanted to know what they would do.

She was still thinking when the shadows moved around her. She ducked but even so the blow caught her on the side of the head, knocking her out of balance. They were very quiet. There were four of them that she could see, dressed in black, faces masked and covered. She backed away. None of them seemed to be armed.

She pulled out her gun.

Too fast – one of the shadows rushed her, aiming an impossibly high kick at her gun hand – no time to think – her finger was on the trigger and she pressed and the gun went off, an explosion of thunder in the silent street, and the man fell back, half of his head missing.

One of them came at her again from the side, and she felt a savage blow to the head – the same place – and dropped the gun. Her mouth filled with blood. Her eyes stung with tears of pain. Another kick took her in the ribs. She lashed back, going back in time years, when the streets were her home. Her leg caught one of the assailants on the shin. She rolled, kicking again from below, dropping one – but he gracefully turned his fall into a jump and came back at her, another kick throwing her back – but now the gun was close. She picked it up, almost blind, and used it as a club, all discipline forgotten, and caught the man in the face, hearing bones breaking, delighting in the sound. She flipped the gun around and shot him in the knee.

And now the other two shadows were retreating, disappearing as if they'd never been there. The lone remaining assailant lay on the ground clutching his leg. Still no sound. She was impressed.

She was breathing heavily now, and she needed to pee. Her head echoed with pain, and her side burned. She went to the man, from behind, the gun ready to discharge, and pulled off his black mask.

An Asian face, and somehow she was not surprised. Not unhandsome – young, clean-shaven face, mouth clamped shut to stop him from screaming. She smiled at him and shot his other knee.

This time he did scream. She grabbed his head. "Who sent you?" she said. "What do you want?"

He spat in her face. She back-handed him. Wiped away blood, some of it his, some of it her own. "Tell me."

"The key," he said, and then he smiled. His face was a death mask. "See you in the other world," he said, and then he bit hard on something in his mouth. She smelled bitter almonds, watched his face relax, and now his eyes saw nothing, and she let him go.

She was left standing there, breathing heavily, her head ringing, two corpses on the ground beside her. He had spoken perfect French, she thought. And in a Parisian accent. She searched him, then the other man. Nothing on them. But she did find something.

Both men bore identical tattoos on their left wrists.

NINE
Notre Dame de Paris

She copied down the tattoos, then left. A little down the road, finding a dark corner, she squatted, feeling relief as she peed. As she was walking away she could see the first gendarmes coming up the hill. There was a swelling on her face, and her ribs hurt. Still, she thought – she had come off lightly, and she wondered why. They could have taken her out easily enough with a gun, or even by themselves.

A warning, then?

Again, she walked, the distance clearing her head slowly. It was a long night and dawn was still far away. She had a lot to do.

For one thing, she needed to see the doctor.

A sense of revulsion, but she knew she had to go down there. And he might have something for her by now.

She walked back towards the Seine, gliding through shadows, avoiding the few passers-by on the streets, late-hour drunks and those who preyed on them, knowing everyone else was ensconced behind locked doors. Everyone who could afford a lock, or a roof…

Blessed be the Quiet Revolution.

Gaslight, reflected in the surface of the Seine. The bookseller stalls closed for the night, their gaunt owners sleeping inside the little makeshift stalls, wrapped in words for warmth and comfort. Fat lot of use it did them. She remembered the stories about the assassin they called the Bookman, and the confused reports coming from across the Channel for a while, three years back, that said England had a new, human king, stories that quickly ebbed away and finally disappeared. Victoria was still on the throne, the lizard queen, though it was said the balance of power had shifted, that the British had had their own Quiet Revolution, human and automata joining forces – she had not been back there in a long time, not since her husband's…

Dark thoughts for a dark night. She crossed and came to the ruins of Notre Dame, eerie in the gaslight coming from the banks of the river. The ruined cathedral glowed the bright sickly green of the lizards' strange metal, and in the tumbled-down structure she could see figures moving stealthily, and fires burning. Lizard boys and night ghouls and tunnel rats… She walked through them and they shied away from her, knowing her for what she was, recognising in her what they saw in themselves.

She walked past fallen gargoyles, their heads staring in bemusement into the sky, past toppled columns and the remnants of a giant bell. It must have been magnificent, once…

It had been built by Les Lézards, long before the Quiet Revolution – a potent symbol of the power beyond the Channel, that some said had come from the stars… She had heard the stories of Caliban's Island, of Vespucci's ill-fated journey when he awoke the slumbering creatures on that far-away island – but that's all they were to her, stories, and of little concern to her.

She had had her own ill-fated journey on the seas, the one that had brought her here, just as it did all those other migrants, the Mexica and Aztec and Kampucheans, Zulu and Swahili and Nipponese, some curious, some eager, and some without hope… Migrations went one way and then the other, the poor of Europe heading out to the same kingdoms from which others came in the opposite direction, ships crossing in the night, across the seas. As she had come here from faraway Dahomey, that great kingdom that was once, so long ago, her home.

Now she was no longer sure what she was, where she belonged. Serving the Quiet Council, hunting down such cases as belonged in the files no one ever saw, the ones kept only in the under-morgue... Something inside her longed for a journey, to be somewhere far away. A place without cities, without gaslight and smoke and steam, away from the complex incomprehensible schemes of humans and machines. Instead she walked through Notre Dame until she found the hidden door and spoke to it, and the door opened for her and she walked inside, and down.

Down into the under-morgue.

TEN
Into the Catacombs

The tunnels stretched for miles under Paris. She knew them well enough, but thought it was impossible to know them all. They were not empty. There were people down here, too. Hers was not the only entrance, and there were plenty who came here and some who made it their home.

Tunnel rats, grimy and dark with the stench of the sewers about them, those who hunted in the refuse of the city for whatever they could find. There were treasures and bodies buried, it was said, in equal measures in the catacombs... There were vast old cemeteries, dumping grounds for ancient skeletons, an entire city of child-sized coffins from some long-ago plague. There were the old mines, depleted now, but still worked sometimes, in secret, by those poor and desperate enough. There were times when sections of the under-city collapsed and caused holes to appear in the above-ground world – disrupting lives and traffic and offering a glimpse into what lay just below the city, its dark underbelly – these had to be covered up quickly. There were trains down there, mines, sewers, cemeteries, streets that once lay in the sun above-ground, long ago... She walked through the tunnels and watched its denizens. In a room branching to the left four old men sat around a fire, roasting a rat on a wooden stick. They toasted her as she passed them, and she noticed the man holding the bottle they were drinking from had lost several of his fingers.

She passed orderly piles of skulls and the entrance to a sewer where children were chasing rats, making no sound as they hunted. She saw their faces, briefly, moving from light to shade – grime-streaked, serious, intent – children in body only, with a childhood that had drowned long ago in these same sewers.

There were lights, here and there, in this under-city of permanent dusk. Camp fires, stationary, and bobbing torches. The glint of a knife, too – and other metal.

She came across the first of the automatons past the sewer entrance. Once it had been human-shaped, from whatever factory or lab had made it, one of the discarded, now lying there, a broken-down old machine, staring at her with eyes that couldn't be read. It was impossible to say if it could see, if the eyes still functioned. Some had lain there unmoving for years, were finally picked apart for what might still work, might fetch a few coins from the dealers in such things. It was another difference between here and across the Channel. There, they did not have many automatons, the bias running deep, enforced by the lizard queen and her get. It was rumoured they were afraid of such machines.

Not so here. Vaucanson's Heirs, they were called, these derelicts – the product of another time, a vision of the world that was brighter and cleaner than the real. The new machines were slicker, different somehow. She had heard they had begun to build themselves.

Not in the under-city, though. She threw the beggar a coin and it snatched it from the air, surprising her. "Thank you," it said, the voice a scratchy echo of a long-dead recording. She walked on, somehow disturbed by his response. There were others like it down in the catacombs and they banded together when they could, fighting off those who would break them down for parts. The gendarmes never came down into the under-city. The law here was not of the world above, and so the Quiet Council found it useful, and had appropriated a substantial area for its own secret purposes. But she was not there yet.

She walked past a brook, the water surprisingly clear, a hidden river under the city that had been forgotten long ago by those above. A family was washing in the thin stream, a man and a woman and three children, their few possessions lying on the bank beside them.

She came to a crossroads and went left, when she had the feeling of being watched. She walked a little further then turned and glided into shadow, her gun out, waiting, tense, when a voice close to her ear said, "Hello, Milady."

She said, "Damn," and reholstered the gun. "It's you."

"I saw you walk past," he said, by way of an explanation. "You on Council business?"

"I'm always on Council business," she said, and he grinned, a sad grotesque expression in that ruined face. "You should marry," he said. "Again."

"I like the freedom."

"Free to roam the underworld? What sort of freedom is that?"

She looked at him and knew that what was for her a rare freedom was to him a prison, and one he could not escape. She shrugged, acknowledging a point.

"So what's happening, Q?" she said. "Have you got something for me?"

He frowned, said, "Let's you and me walk a little way."

They walked side by side, the tall woman with the gun and the squat hunchback beside her. She never knew his history, only that he had come from a place near Dahomey, Dugbe it was called, but whether as a child or a man she had no idea. He never referred to his origins. He haunted the catacombs, trading in favours and knowledge the way others traded in stocks and shares.

"There's been rumours," he said.

"There're always rumours," she said.

"And more than rumours," he said, "there have been people down here, moving like shadows through the under-city. Strangers, with a lighter step than I have ever heard."

"Oh?" she said, her interest quickening, and he said, "The way assassins move. They are searching for something."

"Do you know what?"

"No," he said. "All I know is that you should be careful. The under-city is dangerous – well, more dangerous than usual."

"I can take care of myself."

"Yes," he said, looking at her bruised face, and she grinned, and he grinned back. "I can't help the way I look," she said, and the hunchback, his grin dissipating like smoke, said, "Neither can I."

"I know," she said, and reached out, squeezing his arm. "Q, if you hear anything else–"

"I'll find you," he said. Then he grinned again. "Unless that policeman finds you first."

She said, surprised: "The Gascon?"

"I think he likes you," the hunchback said, his grin holding. Then, curiously, "What is it between the two of you?"

She sighed. "It's an old story," she said. Then, into his silence, "He was a friend of my first husband."

The hunchback nodded. "Just look out," he said. "Be careful of the shadows."

"Always," she said. He half-turned away. "I better get back," he said. "Esme will be waiting."

She watched him go, and felt a momentary pang of envy.

ELEVEN
The Under-Morgue

She walked on, and into a dead end – a tunnel sealed with a solid wall, leading nowhere. She spoke to the wall, then put her hand on one of the stones and pushed. A small door swung open and she went through it, the door shutting noiselessly behind her.

Welcome to the under-morgue.

The first thing she always noticed was the smell. It made her want to retch.

Formaldehyde was a part of it. Ammonia, oil, burning coal – there were steam engines deep underneath, below the bedrock, hungry beastly things always feeding, always moving, and the smell seeped through. There was also manure, fresh, and the scent of rot – the smell of growing things and dying things commingling in the under-morgue, the Quiet Council's secret domain: she always thought of it as the place they kept to throw away the dirt and guts and blood, the refuse the rest of the world didn't need to see. She looked around her.

The cavern opened before her, larger than the largest ballroom. Gaslight globes glowed on the walls, but the place was always in gloom despite them. The gardens in the distance – she shuddered, thinking of what grew there – and the cages nearby, the cages where they kept the–

"Milady!"

Straight ahead was the lab area, and a figure in a dirty-white smock was coming towards her, smiling happily in the wan light. His face was not unhandsome, though almost comical in the thick lips, the small but pronounced nose, the mess of hair, eternally shocked, that stood above his head. He carried an assortment of pens in the front pocket of his smock. His teeth were bright and his eyes brighter – insane-bright, as she thought of them.

"What happened to you?" he said as he came closer. The smile was replaced with a concerned look and she sighed and said, "Hello, Viktor."

"We must fix you up!"

"No," she said, a little too quickly. And, "I'm fine."

"Nonsense! Come with me."

She followed the scientist along the hard floor of the cavern, toward his open lab. Viktor favoured steel. There were steel desks and towering banks of instruments, gauges and blinking lights and enormous switches, all set into steel cabinets twice her height. There were steel surgical instruments and steel beds, an entire operating theatre lying there – thankfully unused, for once.

There were refrigeration units, powered by the hidden-below engines. When they arrived at the lab area it only took Viktor a moment and when he turned back to her he was holding a syringe in his hands and she almost shot him. She had the urge to shoot him every time she came there.

"It's a rejuvenation serum," he said, proudly. "Still experimental, of course, but..."

"I just want a cup of coffee," she said. Viktor's face fell. "This will revolutionise medical science!" he said.

"I have no doubt it will."

"Of course," he said, putting it carefully away, "I still need to iron out some of the more unfortunate side effects..."

"You do that," she said.

"Coffee," he said. "Coffee, coffee... where did I put that machine?"

"You now need a machine to make coffee?" she said.

"Milady," he said, turning to her with a curiously serious expression on his face, "we must show respect to our machines."

"I wonder if they are indeed ours," she said, but softly, and he didn't seem to hear her. "Or if we're theirs, and don't yet know it..."

"Aha! There it is." Viktor had found a (steel, naturally) machine in one corner and pulled down a lever. There was a crack as if of lightning, and a gurgling sound could be heard. "Won't be a moment. Milk?"

"No, thank you."

He spoke French well, but with an accent. He had once been a baron, for what it was worth. He always insisted on Viktor. He was as egalitarian as if he had personally fought in the Quiet Revolution.

And just as dangerous.

He brought her a cup of coffee – china, mercifully, and not steel, in that at least – and took one for himself. "Are you sure you don't want me to do something about your face, at least?" he said. "Your poor face. I could hasten the healing process considerably–"

"It's fine," she said. "Honest."

"A modification of my own based on the early Hyde formula," he said. "Really, it's perfectly safe."

She let it go.

He took a sip from his coffee, made a face, and looked at her. "The Council is very concerned," he said.

"About my face?"

He shook his head, fighting off a half-smile. "About the missing object. I take it you haven't found it."

"Yet," she said. He nodded. "Of course."

"No," she said. "I haven't found it. Yet. It would help,

perhaps, to know what it is."

He shrugged, expansively. "What does it matter? You need not worry about what it does, only that we have it, and not–"

She watched him. He blinked and looked away. "Not who?" she said.

"Well, anyone else, obviously," he said, sounding a little irritated. Sounding like he had given away more than he was meant to.

She watched him over her coffee. The scientist could not sit still. Already he was fidgeting, the coffee a distraction, conversation an effort. Wanting to go back to his work, his knives, his electricity... She said, "Was Grimm here?"

"Grimm!" Viktor beamed at the name. "Yes. He dropped off the samples. Fascinating. Fascinating!" Happy again, he abandoned the coffee and wandered off to a long work table where test tubes, a microscope and various instruments lay in apparent disorder. "Fascinating!"

"So you said."

"I am going to have to run more tests."

"Naturally."

"But I can tell you–"

"Yes?"

"I have not seen such a thing before."

She thought of the man's ruined corpse on the floor, of Grimm reaching over, sparking it alive with electricity. "What is it?" she said.

The scientist fiddled with a pen, opened and closed his mouth. "I don't know," he said, finally. Then, with more defiance – "Yet."

"Yet," she agreed, smiling.

"Perhaps–" he said.

"Yes?"

"I think the thing inside him may have affected him. The tissue samples are suggestive..." He fell quiet, thinking. "You should be careful," he said.

"People keep telling me that, recently."

He smiled, ceding her the point. "The Council wants to see you," he said.

"Who's there?" she said, and his smile dropped when he said, flatly: "All of them."

TWELVE
The Quiet Council

Stone arches, dim light. The Council convened in what may have once been a wine cellar. The smell still lingered, of old vinegar and smoked cedar wood. The entrance was through the under-morgue. She had to pass the cages to get there. The things in the cages stared at her as she passed. Every time she tried not to look, and failed.

What do you want to know about the Council? The Quiet Council, the secret council, those lords and ladies of the underworld? Human and machine, revolutionaries after the revolution had come and gone, quietly. Picture them sitting there behind their half-moon desk, looking down at the Lady de Winter as she entered, as she stood before them. Glaring up at them, a wilful child, but useful. Useful, particularly, in this curious matter of the dead man on the Rue Morgue, and of the thing that had been inserted into him and then, so savagely, taken out. A missing thing. A trifle, nothing more. And yet, a cause for some anxiety.

"Milady de Winter." The Council spoke through the Hoffman automaton. Built by Krupp, rumour had it, and long ago, and based on an obscure Teutonic writer. The voice, full of hisses and scratches, had a thick, heavy accent. "Please to make your report."

She stood and glared at them for a moment longer. So much

anger, so much passion so tightly controlled! A street child, a circus girl, a lady, a killer – the last one first and foremost.

She gave them her report. The murder in the Rue Morgue, the Gascon, the corpse, the search of the apartment, Tom Thumb, the shadows, Q's warning – she missed nothing and the Council listened with a grave silence, faces hidden behind shadows.

"And so?" the Hoffman automaton said at last, when she had finished.

"And so I came here to see what results were–" she began, but Hoffman interrupted her.

"What results?" the automaton said. "What results indeed, Milady. I see no results."

A murmur of agreement. She stared up at them, silent. "The nature of the corpse is not your concern. Your only task, child – your only purpose – is to find that which is missing. That which was taken. That which we want."

Another murmur of agreement spread around, waves on the surface of a pond.

"Results we want. And you bring none to us."

She said nothing. They noticed her hand go, perhaps unconsciously, to the butt of her gun. There were some smiles at that. A charming young thing, very spirited. Too attached, perhaps, to her projectile weapon.

"Where, for instance," the Hoffman automaton said, "are the two women whose apartment it is?"

"I have not located them yet."

"You did not try!"

"I am only one person. I can't do everything."

"Perhaps you should be replaced, then."

She shrugged, waited him out, a small smile playing on her lips.

The Hoffman automaton made a curious sound – a cross between a cough and a spit. She waited for it to readjust its sound.

"Perhaps you could tell me what I'm looking for," she said.

"That is not your concern!"

"Does that mean you don't know?"

Silence.

The Council observed her, woman-child, this tall and deadly woman sworn to serve the Republic. Sworn to protect it, and that she does, but the danger from the East is great, greater than they had anticipated.

And now she was turning the questioning on them.

"Who is Tom Thumb working for?" she said.

Silence, full of scratches.

"And who are the people also looking for this thing, this object borne inside the man all the way across the seas?"

"Let us see the impression you obtained," the Hoffman automaton said. "The tattoos."

She stepped up to him, sensing the others shying away, further into the dark. A council of masks, hiding from prying eyes. What were they afraid of?

"Is it the lizards you are so concerned with?" she said.

"They are always a concern," the automaton said.

Was that relief, detected in his words?

The East. Indochina. What was there? A part of the world distant and filled with mysteries of its own. The Hoffman automaton took the sketch from her and studied it.

"Imperial assassins," it said.

What?

"So she is after it too," it said, the voice low, barely above a murmur.

Victoria? The lizard queen on her metal green throne?

"It is as we suspected," another voice said, deep within the shadows.

"And yet."

She waited, but there was no more, not for a while. Then, "Proceed with the investigation. Report back to us. Find that which was stolen."

"I still don't know–" she said, but the automaton cut her off: "You are dismissed."

She walked off then, leaving the Council to its devices.

Would she live? She was very good at not dying. They conferred amongst themselves. Perhaps another agent in the field – no, too dangerous. And already it was spreading, the grey–

THIRTEEN
The Little Grey Cells

Back in the under-morgue, she helped herself to the medicine cupboard and cleaned her face. She felt fatigued, knew the long night was not yet over.

She was not angry at the Council. It was the way they operated, seeing her and others like her as chess pieces and little more, to be moved on the board according to formulae and calculations she could not even imagine. They would keep her in the dark, using the power of her ignorance to bring out that which was hidden even from them. If there was such a thing.

Viktor was at his lab, muttering to himself, bent over his microscope. She walked over to him. "What am I not being told?" she said.

He blinked. "That covers a lot of ground," he said.

"You seemed," she said, and then stopped, putting her thoughts in order. "Almost dismissive, earlier."

"What do you mean?" But he looked flustered, a fish hooked and watching the ocean disappear away from him.

"Of the corpse. You said you've never seen anything like it before–"

"Yes?"

She smiled at him. He took a step back.

"I think you were lying."

He tried to outstare her and failed. "That's absurd," he said, but his hands were fluttering, the fingers working as if independent from the body, and she thought – he wants to tell me. Poor Viktor, all alone in his underground lab, no one to share the excitements of science with... "Have you seen such a thing before?" she said.

"Well," he said, still being evasive, knowing, she thought, that it wouldn't fool her, "naturally, in my line of work... reanimation of the... as it were... the effects of electricity on the human... such as... scientifically speaking..."

"Viktor," she said, speaking patiently, as if to a child. "Scientifically speaking–" She smiled at him, trying to make it a nice smile, trying to reassure him. He was a nervous little man, afraid of crowds, torches, pitchforks and milk. "You have, haven't you?"

He didn't answer. She moved closer to him, towering over him, knowing the effect she had on him and using it. "Viktor, Viktor," she said. "My poor little Viktor..."

"Milady, I..."

She ruffled his hair. He whimpered. "What are you trying to tell me, Viktor?"

"The... the tissues... you see, they're –" then, with more force – "I can't," he said. "Council business, Milady. It's Council business!"

"Out there," she said, "in the dark streets, out there in the night few dare to walk – out there I am the Council, Viktor."

She looked down at him, then at his workbench. On the tabletop – was it flesh, a fold of skin? Grey and sickly – and moving. She listened back to what he said. "The effects of electricity on the human body," she said.

He looked up at her, his eyes bright. Dying to tell her, she thought. "I know the effects of electricity on the human body," she said. "It does not make a man walk again, or open his eyes and point with a dead finger. It does the opposite. It kills."

"My research indicates a high probability of eventual re–" he said but didn't finish. She smiled at him. "Is this it?" she said, pointing at the grey matter.

"This? Oh, this is just a–"

"Electricity does not do that to the human body," she said. "Am I correct, Viktor?"

His fingers, interlacing, releasing, tapping air.

"But what if the body is no longer human?" she said, and he jumped.

"More coffee?" she said.

"Thank you," he said. "I think I've drunk enough."

"You are tightly wound up," she said. "Perhaps you need a rest. I know a castle–"

"Please," he said, raising his hands before him like a shield. "No more castles."

"Yes," she said. "I too find them overrated."

"It's the draught," he said. "And the heating bill's always enormous."

"Tell me about that body, Viktor. You have seen such a thing before, haven't you? I know you have. You want to tell me about it, don't you? You don't want me to get hurt, do you, Viktor? You don't–"

"Please," he said, and she knew he was hers. "Show me," she said.

He took her to the far side of the cavern. Past the cages again, and turning her eyes away from the figures inside. Viktor's experiments, following from the works of–

No. She walked past and they came to a large metal door set into the rock. The under-morgue proper. When she put her hand to the door the metal was cold to the touch. Viktor played with a pad by the door and it opened with a faint hiss. Tendrils of fog ebbed out, as if reaching for them.

"Follow me."

She did. They went inside. Ice-cold, steel walls, icicles hanging like nooses from the ceiling. Inside: rows of metal cabinets pulled open, holding corpses in various stages of decomposition on their trays. Men, one woman, two children. The children looked almost identical, a boy and a girl with china-white skin turning grey.

Viktor looked expectant. Waiting for her to make a connection... It took her a moment but the colour began to dominate her view and she said, "Grey."

He said, "Yes."

She came closer, examined the hand of the boy. The grey had spread down his arm, in patches, looking oily, looking... she wasn't sure. She reached to touch it and Viktor's hand held her back. "Don't," he said.

He went to a table laden with instruments and returned with a prod. When he pressed the little trigger a burst of blue electricity sparked at the end.

"Watch," he said. There was something almost fond in his voice when he said, "Watch the grey cells."

She watched.

He put the end of the stick to the boy's dead hand and pressed the trigger.

She watched. The electricity singed the skin. She watched the grey shapes on the boy's white skin.

Nothing at first.

Then...

The grey spots, she realised, were slowly moving.

FOURTEEN
Post-Mortem

How to describe it? The grey moved along the boy's frozen corpse as if it were alive. It looked snake-like. It looked reptilian. It looked like mercury and it looked like shadows. That was it, she thought. Like grey shadows, growing on the boy's dead skin, animating it. Shadows bellowing across naked arms and chest, along closed eyes and china face. She said, "What is it?" and her voice was very small in that cold, hushed place.

Viktor said, "We don't know."

She said, "Where does it come from?" and he said, "That, Milady, is what the Council hopes you could tell us."

She stared – and now the boy's left hand was twitching, the fingers closing, slowly, slowly, into a fist, and she took a step back when – there! – his eyes sprang open and the corpse stared at her, cold-blue eyes not seeing, dead eyes animated by a grey shadow that should not have existed, a wrong thing, unnatural and yet–

"Stop it," she said.

But Viktor was no longer applying the electricity.

"The effect lasts for some time independently of the trigger," he said. "The cold slows it down. The main reason we're keeping them in here. You did well, by the way, disposing of the corpse. It would have been… inconvenient if the deceased began to walk down Rue Morgue post-mortem."

She almost laughed. She felt a little hysterical. In one moment the investigation went from something understood – something within her remit, within the world as it was, as it should be – into something else entirely, something alien and unknown. "When did it start?" she said.

The little scientist beside her shrugged. "Who knows?" he said. "We began grabbing them as soon as the reports started filtering in. I have no doubt we missed a few."

"How long?"

"Two years," he said. "Possibly three."

"Years?" she said. She had to get some fresh air. The boy was moving now, his entire body shaking, the head moving in a silent no. "Open the door," she said.

Viktor, too, seemed happier once they were outside, the door safely closed behind them.

"Is it–" she said, and hesitated.

"Infectious?"

She nodded. Viktor said, "Not so far, but..."

"But what?"

"It seems to be spreading."

Moving grey shapes. It was as if, having viewed the corpse (and now she realised, too, that she had come in close contact with the dead man in the Rue Morgue, skin-to-skin, and did the subtle grey shapes leap from one to the other? Were they even now working their way into the fabric of her being, into her cells and bone-marrow, into her bloodstream and brain?) she was now seeing the world in a skewed fashion, the night world of black shades transformed into a half-light place, inhabited by moving grey shapes... She blinked but they would not go away, houses and windows and lamps at strange angles, footsteps in dust and clouds flying low.

Like the shadows of another world, she thought, and the night felt colder, clammier somehow.

She had left the catacombs on the left bank of the Seine, exiting through an Employees Only door of a hotel on Rue de la Bûcherie. She felt a sense of urgency now, a need to find the missing women, to begin to answer the questions that were growing, sprouting like grey-capped mushrooms all over her post-mortem investigation.

Who were the black-clad assailants in Montmartre? Who had killed the man called Yong Li? Were they the same people? It seemed unlikely – unless they already had the object in their possession and wanted to discourage her from pursuing them. She had asked the Council and Hoffman had said, "Imperial assassins."

But which empire? Was the lizard queen behind the murder? Yet all the threads were leading East, away from these cold European lands…

Her carriage was waiting for her. A black unmarked vehicle, its mute driver ready with the horses. She could have had a baruch-landau, a horseless carriage, to take her through the narrow streets of Paris. She preferred the horses. Like canaries down in a mine, the horses could warn her of danger before it was there.

"Pigalle," she told the driver. He nodded, without expression. A large man, with stitch marks on his forehead, around his skull. One arm was shorter than the other. One of Viktor's creatures, who only came out at night. The man was dressed in a black cloak and a low-hung hat. Just another shadow in this city of shadows, unremarkable, invisible to all but the few like itself. She settled back in the carriage and felt the streets pass without looking at them, listening to the city as it entered the deep-end of night.

She had questioned Viktor but he could tell her nothing more – couldn't, or wouldn't, but either way the result was the same. He'd shown her the cultures growing in his test tubes, grey swirls sprouting, forming shapes almost like an alphabet, carrying a meaning hovering just beyond her reach. And that was it.

One last exchange: "Who was the agent in charge?"

Viktor: "I'm not sure I'm at liberty to–"

Grabbing him by the neck, her fingers closing on his throat – "Just a little squeeze, Viktor, and who'd put you together again?"

"Tômas! It was Tômas!"

Him? That mask-wearing murderer, that phantasm, shape-shifting like a thing from a British Penny Dreadful, changing his clothes, his hair, the colour of his eyes – at will, it seemed – second only to Holmes of Baker Street in his capacity as master of disguise – but without the Great Detective's honesty, his morals, a blank slate, Tômas, a creature of the gutters, a killer and one who enjoyed the killing, and yet–

A valued agent of the Council, who knew well the value of such men.

"A body-snatcher?" she said. "A suitable job for him."

"No doubt," Viktor agreed, croaking the words. "Well, I won't keep you."

She released his throat, left him to massage it. She saw the look in his eyes, knew its meaning. What makes you any different?

I don't enjoy the killing, she wanted to say, but didn't. Perhaps, she thought, she feared it wasn't true.

FIFTEEN
Place Pigalle

She let go of Tômas – for now. She would find him, later, and she would extract the truth from him, however much he threatened or fought. She had dealt with worse than him, before. And she let go of Viktor, too – cooperative Viktor who was still lying to her, still keeping her from the truth – she knew him, could read it in his shifty little eyes. He was only telling her what the Council wanted her to know, no more, no less. She was the Council's creature – well then, she would follow the scent blindly, and do as she was told – for now, for now…

They were, all of them, the Council's creatures: serving the greater good, whatever that was, per the calculations and machinations of these strange, artificial beings. Viktor in his lab, Fanto – Tômas with his robberies and secret murders and body-snatching – even Q, gentle Q who lived underground and kept his misshapen eyes on things – the Council's eyes, leased, borrowed, sold.

She settled back and the coach rattled on. To Pigalle, the one place guaranteed to be lit up this time of night. She had already passed through it once tonight. But then it had been too early.

At that moment she missed Grimm. He was back in the under-morgue, and she had not even seen him – not stopped to check on him, that metallic, insect-like creature, another denizen of Paris' secret world. Yet faithful. Faithful and–

No. Let go of Grimm. Let go of it all, the half-light, half-life of the catacombs, their smell clinging to her leather coat. Her ribs ached and her face felt swollen. She opened the window of the carriage, let the comforting smells of the upper city in, the smoke and manure and the curses and songs, the lights in the distance, growing closer – Pigalle, the place of merriment and drunkenness, of dancing and whoring and knifing, of carousing and robbing and killing.

Her kind of place.

And now there was a sound penetrating the night like a knife – a woman's scream, high-pitched, terrified – terminating so suddenly that the silence ached, and she was out of the carriage and running before the mute driver could bring it to a halt. Running, towards the dark mouth of an alleyway, Peacemaker out of its holster, running and knowing all the while that it was too late.

She burst into the alley and saw a shape on the ground, a dark pool around it, and a shape standing above, turning to look toward her and she ran–

A grey misshapen face, moonlit despite the darkness – a skull as white as moon rock, eyes in which the tendrils of galaxies swirled – the mouth open in a silent hungry grin–

Man, beast, spirit, ghost – the knife a solid real object, too late – it slashed the woman lying on the ground. She fired, the gun making a loud noise in that small confine. Stars above, half-hidden by the city's perennial smoke. Stars looking down. The crazed grinning face turning to her, a crack in that elongated skull – the mouth opening, snapping at her, snap, snap! and she fired again.

The figure on the ground moved, groaned. The creature took another hit from her gun and only grinned harder. Then – shouts behind her, the whistles of gendarmes. The creature waved a paw – a hand? – a sickle moon –

goodbye, goodbye, and–

Jumping – floating? – a shapeless grey cloud scaling the wall of the alley. A hiss in the night, a wordless promise, we'll meet again, my lovely.

Soon, she answered him, firing all the while at the retreating grey shape, knowing it was useless. Soon, I hope.

And it was gone. The night was ordinary once again. A woman lay by the alley's brick wall, amidst the rubbish of the adjacent restaurant – mussel shells, discarded, rotting meat, an empty turtle shell crawling with fat black flies, pools of rancid oil staining the ground like blood.

Place Pigalle. A shout and feet running behind her, stopping abruptly. Violent sounds – it took her a moment to realise it was someone being noisily sick.

Other, unhurried footsteps coming. She crouched down by the woman. Elderly, her dress revealing wrinkled skin, coarse-painted face, the sagging breasts rising and falling still, though almost imperceptively, with the body's last intake and outtake of air.

Slashed. "Tell me," she said, whispering to the woman. Watching tendrils of grey crawling over her wrists. The woman's eyes looking into hers, black eyes, as dark as a starless, moonless night.

"Door," the woman said. The single word a whispered puff of air. "Door. K... key."

She said, "Where?"

The woman, dying: "Every... where."

The eyes, closed now. The heart, the engine of the body quit. Remembering Viktor's lectures. Blood circulation stopping, brain functions terminating one by one. A silent machine, beginning to decay, impossible to fix. Nothing more nor less than death. She thought of doors, and keys.

Behind her, footsteps stopped. A hand on her shoulder – gentle. A familiar voice: "We'll find who did this."

Not looking up at him. "You won't."

"Milady…" the title whispered, an exasperated sound. And something else… but what?

"Why do you always have to turn up like this?"

An English expression came to her mind and she began to laugh. "Like a bad penny," she said. "A bad penny–" laughing, the laugh becoming sobs. The Gascon's hands on her shoulders, drawing her up: "Hush, we'll find her killer, we'll find–"

Lady de Winter, calming slowly against his shoulder. Whispering: "You'll find shit."

SIXTEEN
Microcosm

She was sitting at a bar that had no name, drinking coffee laced with cognac, sugar and cream. Opposite her sat the Gascon. Gazing at her, in a way that she found disconcerting. Her first husband had been a noble, renouncing his title but not his ways. This happened after… the Gascon had been his protégé, for a while at least. They had both done wrong – to others, to themselves. To each other. The Gascon was stirring a spoon of sugar in the black depths of his coffee. A quiet bar, and quiet conversations carried in dark corners. Absinthe drinkers, artists, working girls at the end of a shift, and all she could think was: a lock and a key.

To what? To where? And why?

The Gascon: "What do you want us to do with Madame L'Espanaye's body?"

She looked up at him. Not smiling, neither of them. For a moment she felt comfortable with him. They were both being professional, for once. She said, "Is that who she was?" and her voice was raw.

The Gascon nodded. His eyes were deep-set, surrounded by black rings. She wondered what she herself looked like. "We have been attempting to track her down," he said – a slight note of apology in his voice. Going against her orders. "Unfortunately, we came too late."

"Yes," she said. "I know how that feels."

In the silence between them the dead woman pirouetted. Three years before, across the Channel, there had been a murderer who favoured the knife. But he had been a lizard boy, or so it was rumoured, just as they said the British had a human king who had returned from exile. Perhaps this hidden king of theirs had killed the lizard boy who had preyed on Whitechapel. Fairytale stories, she thought. And then she thought of the shape that was not a shape, the elongated skull grinning at her, the knife flashing, her bullets catching the creature again, again, and making no impact.

As if it existed in more than one place at once.

An odd thought. She pushed it away and drank her coffee – alcoholic, sweet. Warmth returning to her body – she didn't know that it had gone. And now she was shivering.

The Gascon said, "Milady–" and then fell silent. He reached out a hand and covered her fingers with his own. To her surprise, she let him. "Did you see the attacker?" she said.

He shook his head. Not a no, not a yes. A frown, a flicker of unease: "It was too dark. I cannot be sure what I saw."

She nodded. Wrapped her fingers around the glass. Sailors in one corner of the bar. A short-legged boyish man who looked vaguely familiar, staring into a glass of absinthe in a separate corner. The Gascon returned his hand to his side of the table, took a sip of coffee, lit a cigarette. "The body," he said.

Grimm will take care of it, she thought. "Leave it by the entrance to the sewers," she said. "And let no one touch it."

"I saw shapes," he said abruptly. The cigarette sent out blue-grey smoke to hover between them – the victim replaced by her killer. "Swirls of grey moving on her arms..."

"You saw her killer," she said – not asking, a simple statement. He stared into her eyes. "I don't know what I saw," he said.

And there it was – his failure. A miracle world, she

thought: where a lizard queen sat on the British throne, a shadowy assassin killed with books, where a corpse could be impregnated with an unknown device, where grey shapes flittered like the shadows of another reality... a fantasy? A world of science, rather: a world in which machines spoke and made plans, where stars were real, enormous things, full of potential, and promise, and threat – for who knew who, or what, lived beyond their own world, what other beings inhabited that vast realm beyond the Earth? Not angels, not gods, no burning sword or Garden of Eden. Science was the art of confronting the world as it really was. That it was strange there was no doubt. Humans continued to scheme and war and make love, to make mistakes and become confused and angry and murderous and loving, a vastly tiny microcosm, like Viktor's cultures in his test tubes in the lab. To refuse to see what was beyond did not negate its truthfulness.

She said, "I know what I saw."

"Then you are lucky," the Gascon said, and smiled, and for once there was nothing sarcastic in the expression, which was a little wistful, perhaps. "You always know what you see, Milady."

"I see what is there," she said, simply, and let it rest. She pulled out her gun and began loading it with bullets. The Gascon smiled again, and now it was back to business as usual, softness melting between them like a mirage. "And a bullet is always a cure for mystery," he said.

She smiled back, cold again, and said, "That's right."

Though it wasn't. There had been something familiar about the creature in the alleyway, some markers she was missing... but the bullets hadn't killed it. Why?

She didn't know. She said, "Thanks for the drink," and got up to leave.

The Gascon, still sardonic: "Where are you in such a hurry to?"

Lady de Winter: "I have to find the younger L'Espanaye. Or

have you forgotten her?"

His smile, mocking, growing larger. "I have not."

"Oh."

"Would you like to speak to her?"

"I thought I told you to leave this investigation alone."

He shrugged. "So you did. It must have slipped my mind."

"Where did you find her?"

"Working the adjacent alley," he said. "We were on our way for the mother when–"

"How is she?"

"Complaining. Apart from that she's keeping quiet."

"Complaining about what?"

"The competition."

She let it pass. "Where are you keeping her?"

"The station by the cemetery."

"Then let's go."

He mock-saluted her, rose from his seat. He left a handful of coins on the table top, stubbed out his cigarette, and offered her his hand – which she ignored.

SEVENTEEN
Broken

Along Boulevard de Clichy, the nightlife bright still in these early hours, bright lights and glimpses of naked flesh, like sordid promises. Drunks outside, drunks inside. Music, competing. Past the Moulin Rouge and the turning windmill, past the mouth of the cemetery – gaping, dark – into the station house, cheap stale coffee, cigarette smoke, urine from the cells, vomit, someone crying quietly, a couple of manacled men in flamboyant dress chatting across a desk.

The young woman behind the table in the interview room looked worn out. Her youth had been scrubbed from her, leaving oddly old eyes in that still-unlined face. She glared up when they entered, said nothing. A cigarette was smouldering in an ashtray on the table that looked as if it had never been cleaned.

"Mademoiselle L'Espanaye?"

"Who the hell are you?" Turning to the Gascon, a plaintive tone – "Why did you bring her here?"

He gave her his customary shrug, open palms facing up, and sat down in a chair.

"She don't look like no whore. She looks like–" Mademoiselle L'Espanaye examined her opponent critically, concluded – "like a machine is what she looks like."

Snorting. "Losing all our business to the bloody machines."

The Gascon, in a whispered aside – "I'm afraid she's rather single-minded about her topics of conversation."

Milady, not bothering to whisper: "That's going to change."

Mademoiselle L'Espanaye scratched her head. A strand of red hair fell down on her face and she blew it away irritably. "Machines, machines, machines. Make them look a little like women and the punters suddenly think they're better?"

"Mademoiselle L'Espanaye," Lady de Winter said. The woman gave her a dismissive look, said, "What do you want?"

Milady, standing up, kicked back the chair – the gun, newly loaded, exposed in its holster. Observing the young woman taking it in. "I'm going to ask you some questions. You are going to answer them." She gave her a slow, measured smile and watched the woman swallow. "Clear?"

Mademoiselle L'Espanaye, turned to the Gascon, a plea in her eyes. The Gascon looking elsewhere.

"Clear?"

Mademoiselle L'Espanaye, a little girl voice. "What do you want to know?"

"I want to know why there was a dead body in your apartment."

Watching her. Did she know? From the woman opposite, no visible reaction. "What are you talking about?"

Too cocky – as if she knew something they didn't, and was enjoying it.

Well, that was about to change.

"His name was Yong Li," Milady said. "And someone gutted him open with a knife. Was it you – or was it your mother?"

Ah – reaction. "You leave my mother out of this!"

"Tell me about him," Milady said.

A shrug. The eyes hostile, still taking her measure. She sat down slowly, faced Mademoiselle L'Espanaye. "I'm waiting."

"Don't know what you want me to tell you." Sullen. "Sometimes we take on lodgers. To help pay the rent, see. Even a shithole like Rue Morgue costs. Don't know nothing else."

She'd had enough. "We have your mother next door," she said. "Would you like to see her?"

She had gone back to the alley. A guard on the street, no one inside. In the shadows, Grimm, slowly working, summoned by the mechanism inside her bracelet. She stroked his head and said, "Leave me the face. And one of the arms."

An old wedding ring on one finger.

Transported what remained of the head back to the station, the gendarmes cursing her, but quietly. "And don't touch it!" she'd said. "Whatever you do, don't make contact with the body."

"What have you done to my mother? You let her be!"

The Gascon murmured something inaudible. Milady, reaching over, a graceful hand to assist the younger woman. "Come with me."

Mademoiselle L'Espanaye, brushing away her hand. Following her nevertheless, a tough child-woman – let's see how tough you are, she thought, but said nothing as she led her out of the door and to the next room – opening the door for her, waiting for her to step inside–

Eyes to adjust to the dim light, time to put together the pieces on the table, the ruined face, one eye staring into nothing, a loose arm with an old ring on a finger that would never move again, time to comprehend their meaning, time to–

She caught the girl as she fell. Gave her a moment, stood her up. Forcing her to look. A small voice, choked, broken, polluted water running over pebbles – "Mother..."

A shake of the head. Inaudibly – "No. No!"

Milady, holding her, a silent command – look.

The girl looked. A head, an arm – was sick all over the floor. Milady held her all the while.

"And now we talk."

EIGHTEEN
The Clockwork Room

And now she hated her. Hated her, yes, but feared her more. The woman behind the table was afraid, terribly afraid – of her? Only a part. And the rest?

"Tell me about the man in your apartment."

She talked.

The safe house – Tom Thumb – the arrangement – "We slept in the same room, my mother and I, and the guest –" she referred to them as guests – "in my room, unless, you know."

A pause, waiting. The girl smoking a cigarette as if it were a life line of oxygen and she was drowning. "Unless I liked him."

Always men. Not many – perhaps ten, twelve in the past three years. All via Tom, "That horny little midget, I wouldn't give him the time of day –" some staying a day or two, some weeks. "All Asian?"

No. One African, a couple of Europeans from the East, one Vespuccian man who said he was a Sioux, whatever that was. Never any visitors. Stayed inside, until other arrangements had been made, and then they left.

"And Yong Li?"

He was a nice guy. On that she seemed in agreement with Tom Thumb. He liked to drink but was a polite drunk. He had a good singing voice. He never made advances, even though–

"I wouldn't have minded, you know. Even with that stomach of his..."

"Tell me about his stomach."

If she thought it was odd she gave no sign. "He looked pregnant," she said. It was odd. She saw him naked, a couple of times – "Coming out of the shower. He had a scar running down it. His belly protruded so... he used to touch it, stroke it as if there was something living inside. He walked funny. Carrying around that weight – we used to make jokes about it. Mother–"

A wait as she cried. Lit another cigarette from the one glowing in the ashtray. The smell of it mingling with puke, the girl's body odour. The Gascon silent beside her, as if he had fallen asleep. But she knew he was listening.

"Did you kill him?"

"No!" Looking at her, the hatred returning. Then, eyes softening – "Is he really dead?"

"When did you leave the apartment?"

They left as usual, with night falling. Heading off to Pigalle, to work – "Girl's got to work, right?" staring at her, defying her, but no longer having the heart for it. "We left together, Mother and me. Last I saw of him he was asleep on the couch. That's all I know, honest."

Only she was lying.

"Where was he meant to go once he left you?"

"I don't know."

"Did he go out? Did he meet anyone?"

"I told you, none of them ever–"

Faltering. Milady's eyes never leaving the girl's face. Daring her back – dare to lie to me again.

"You went out with him?"

Only once! It wasn't meant to happen, the rules were very clear. She woke up – it was about a week before – and saw him pacing the floor, looking nervous and excited. The window was open. There was something in his hand, a note perhaps, but when she looked again it had disappeared. He said, "There is a place I want to visit."

"So he spoke French?"

Yes, very well, though with an accent.

"Where did he want to go?"

A blush, startling on her face. An angry expression. "The Clockwork Room."

Recollection – a building on the other side from the Moulin Rouge, down a side street, no sign outside, windows blackened – known by reputation.

"Tell me about the Clockwork Room."

Mademoiselle L'Espanaye did.

Picture a place of gleaming chrome and burnished leather. A place of polished brass, muted carpets, the smell of pipe tobacco and expensive cologne, the tinkling of a piano player. Picture men in smart evening wear, congregating in their masks. Imagine champagne flutes, the bubbles twinkling in the glass, the hum of machinery, cries – of pleasure, or pain, it's hard to say – echoing, sometimes, from the upstairs rooms. Hosts and hostesses move throughout the room mechanically, touching a hand here, a shoulder there, refilling glasses – sexless creatures, as beautiful and perfect as a blueprint made flesh.

There are not only men amongst the clientele. Women, too, of high society and money to spare, seeking excitement, wanting the new, come here, their faces as masked as those of the men. And there, in a corner, dressed in full regalia – a rare lizardine diplomat, exchanging hushed conversation with a government minister, the lizard's tongue hissing out, tasting the air, savouring – one likes to think – the atmosphere of this place.

The Clockwork Room.

A long curved bar, and behind it a man-shaped automaton

effortlessly mixing drinks. On the walls, anatomical drawings – pipes and organs, wheels and breasts, tubes and male appendages. There in the corner, a habitué of this place – a short-legged artist drinking absinthe and drawing, in love with these marching gliding perfections, these machines built for love.

There are many designs, and the artist wants to capture them all. There are many designs, for women and men, even for lizards – and who wants to enquire too closely as to the sexual reproduction habits of those majestic, alien beings? But someone must have. Or perhaps it is true what they say, and machines now design themselves... Every now and then one masked member of a party might break from it, ascend upstairs, up the wide curving staircase, and disappear into one of the private rooms, where love is enacted, perfected, a clean and sterile thing, a union, however temporary, between human and machine.

To this place, then, came the curious man from Asia, this Yong Li, and his escort both reluctant and excited. For to enter the Clockwork Room one must have money and influence both: and yet this little unknown man with his distended swollen belly is welcomed without question by the two liveried guards and allowed entry along with the girl. Inside, and to the bar – pressing a gleaming brass button on the menu, and the girl watches, fascinated, as the bartending machine mixes cocktails, pipes running in and out of its body. Like a great spider it seems to her at that moment, and she turns away from it and watches the hosts and hostesses, their naked metal flesh and skin like wax and eyes of glass, and she feels repulsed by them, and resents them for stealing away an otherwise honest trade – and yet excited too, and the man beside her touches her lightly on the arm, brushing her suddenly raised fine hairs and says, "Perhaps you could go upstairs, for just a while. I have conversation to make."

"Is that what he said?" Lady de Winter asked. "He had

conversation to make?"

"That's what he said."

"It's an odd choice of words."

Mademoiselle L'Espanaye shrugged. She looked around the interrogation room, perhaps comparing it, in her mind's eye, with that other place. Finding the room lacking. Perhaps.

"So then what happened?"

Not so quickly. She had looked around the room, recognising – or thinking she did – many prominent people. She drank a glass of champagne. Yong Li lit a cigar, for once, rather than his cheap loose tobacco from the pouch. He, too, scanned the room.

"As if searching for someone?"

Yes, that was the impression that she'd had. But she saw no one approaching him, no one signalling to him, no one even noticing this man and this woman standing at the bar. Not an entirely uncommon sight, couples coming to the Clockwork Room, add a little spice to a jaded palate–

"Let's get back to Yong Li."

Mademoiselle L'Espanaye, staring at Milady. Expressions fleeting on her face, hard to read – the eyes, so hard one moment, softening with tears the next. "You'll find him, won't you?" she said.

Lady de Winter, nodding. Their eyes locked together, something passing between. A promise. "The one who killed my mother?"

"I will."

NINETEEN
Projections

"Tell me about the room. Did you notice anyone out of the ordinary?"

Mademoiselle L'Espanaye, laughing suddenly. "At the Clockwork Room?"

Lady de Winter, conceding. "Anyone who caught your attention, then? In particular? Who may be relevant?"

No. Or rather... of course, she had been watching the royal lizard, it was hard not to, everyone did, even the sophisticates pretending not to care. A rare appearance in the Republic–

Lady de Winter: "Do you think he was there for Yong Li?"

Mademoiselle L'Espanaye, surprised. "He never indicated... it would have been too public – a meeting like that–"

"And yet discreet," the Gascon murmured, besides Milady. Both women turning to look at him, a little surprised to find him still there, perhaps. He gave a smile through hooded eyes and said, "Not much comes out of the Clockwork Room. A very quiet place."

Milady de Winter, beside him, tensing. Was that a veiled message to her? The Council...

"After all, such a place needs powerful patrons to survive," the Gascon said, turning his eyes on her. "To stay in business..."

And now she thought – machines. Listening, perhaps, these unobtrusive subservient automatons, perhaps ignored – at peril?

She filed it away, for now. And yet…

Mademoiselle L'Espanaye, biting her lower lip. "There was a fat man. With the lizard."

Milady and the Gascon exchanged glances. "What did he do?"

"Nothing. But…"

The Gascon sighed.

Milady: "What did you do then?"

And now the girl blushed. Her bluster gone, she said, "I went upstairs. There was a room… Yong Li had settled the bill in advance."

Pipes and moving parts, water and soft brushes, warmth and cold, moving about her, settling her down, touching her–

"And there was something else," she said. "I noticed it, later. When I was… when I was done. Coming out of the room, at the end of the corridor, a room unlike the others, the door black and half-open, for just a moment. I saw shadows flickering on a wall, light and shades, moving shapes. I couldn't make them out, and then the door closed. It was only for a moment."

Shadows flickering, light and shades – the girl: "Like a camera obscura."

A projection. Milady de Winter, adding it to her list. "And Yong Li?"

"I waited at the bar. A man spoke to me. He said some of them still preferred human to machine. I said, after the last hour, I wasn't so sure I did – we laughed, he bought me a drink. Yong Li came down half an hour later. He was holding his stomach again, in pain. We left."

Lady de Winter, reaching across the interrogation table. Her hand on the girl's, black on pale white – "I'll find him. I promise you I'll–"

The girl, softly: "I know."

A change between them.

"So what do you want to do?" the Gascon said.

Leads, possibilities, branching off into unknown paths – but which to follow? She said, "She mentioned an artist."

"Henri," the Gascon said thoughtfully. "Yes."

"You know him?"

"Who doesn't? If a house has ill repute Henri will be there, drawing. For a while you could find him nearly every night at the Moulin Rouge but I did hear he was rarely to be found there now. Henri..." Looking up at her, suddenly troubled. "He was at the bar earlier. Where we found the body."

A short man – an adult body with stunted child's legs. She'd noticed him, yes – "We should talk to him."

If the Gascon noticed the we he gave no sign. But between them, too, something had changed – a mutual acceptance, as momentary as it may be – two professionals agreeing to work together, to put aside, if only for a while, their differences. Nothing to be stated in words, but there nevertheless–

"He isn't hard to find."

"And the Clockwork Room–" She yawned, and suddenly couldn't stop. Outside the window, the first rays of sunlight could be seen. All the coffee in the world, she suddenly thought, won't be enough. The Gascon said, "You can't do everything."

"I have to," she said, knowing there was a curiously plaintive tone in her voice. "There is no one else."

"Get some rest," he said. "You can sleep here, if you like. I'll clear a room. There is nothing to be done now that the night is ending. Even murderers have to sleep."

"I'm not so sure..." she said, puzzled, and yawned again. And, giving in – "I'll take the coach."

•••

Morning was rising around her as the silent coachman drove her home. The morning's sounds, the morning's smells – fresh bread and greengrocers opening their shutters, the cockerels crowing, the traffic picking up – coaches and baruch-landaus, newfangled bicycles, above the last of the night's airships going back to depot, having delivered the night mail.

Back at her apartments, no servants, no living thing – in the drawing room she paused. Grimm, curled up in the unlit fireplace, munching slowly on a lump of coal. She smiled and stroked him, briefly, and tiredness overwhelmed her. To her bath, drawing it herself, adding salts and scents and lying in the water, almost falling asleep… Washing away, gradually, the night's sights and smells and sounds, the night's death, its cargo of misery. Rising, naked, from the bath, not bothering with a towel, she went through the door into her room and fell to bed, and closed her eyes amidst the silken sheets. No dreams, she thought. Please, no dreams. Holding on to a pillow she fell asleep.

INTERLUDE
Jungle Fever Boy

Kai ran through the thick forest, heading deeper and deeper into the trees. Exhausted, fear kept him going – fear, and the voices that shouldn't have been there.

The voices guided him. Here and there he could see signs of people – a hidden bird-trap up in the canopy, a long-necked bamboo basket with bait inside – the bird would crawl into it and be caged. There, a hint of cultivation through the trees – avoid.

Would they be chasing him? He knew they would. They were. He had to disappear, to get away as completely as possible and never return. His life, the voices murmured helpfully, was over. His life as he knew it.

Which meant what, exactly?

Think of yourself as a wuxia hero, the voices suggested, though perhaps that was not so accurate to say. They didn't speak so much as hint, conjuring images, scents, markers to their meanings which Kai's mind translated into speech. A young wushu warrior. The evil faction had just killed your master. You are escaping, vowing revenge. Into the forest, where all things are possible, where young boys since time immemorial went to become men.

Or, a part of his mind whispered, you're going crazy.

Jungle fever.

He saw mosquitoes hover but somehow they never bit him. He stopped by a brook and drank and lay, exhausted, against the thick, mottled trunk of a tree. In his mind he kept seeing the silent assassins with their loud guns, the black-clad monks fighting them – and losing.

So much for the powers of wushu.

Machines, the voices murmured. In his mind – guns. The voices: yes… machines have power.

Then I will use that power, Kai said, and found that he couldn't rise, could not bring himself to run again. He lay by the brook and listened to the frogs. I will become a gun, if that's what I must do.

For now, the voices said, you need to rest.

When he closed his eyes the darkness wasn't absolute. He lay there, holding the grotesque statue still in his arms, this green jade lizard with its emerald eyes: it felt warm in his hands, against his body. Behind his eyes the darkness swirled in lazy eddies, lines and circles flashing and disappearing, forming into a vague grey vista of a world. He fell asleep holding the statue, and his dreams were filled with menacing hulking shapes and he cried out, and then the voices were there, soothing him, and he was walking through a grey landscape, as if through a thick mist beyond which everything was ill-defined. Somehow, it was peaceful.

It was only when he woke up that he cried, and then he did it soundlessly, still afraid, though the voices murmured incomprehensible things about perimeter scans and body heat signatures and checksum routines returning satisfactory values.

When the fever did take hold of him he thought he was going to die – not in glory, like a wuxia hero, but in pain and fear and horror, like a bit character, like the peasants who always got killed by marauding attackers or simply for being poor and unimportant. He felt hot and then cold and he shivered, holding on to the jade statue for warmth but not really feeling it, the cold coming from inside him. He sweated and he moaned and he voided his bowels and threw up, too sick to get up so that the contents of the last night's dinner lay inches from his face, driving him to be sick again even when there was nothing left.

The voices recommended drinking plenty of water.

At some point he slept, fitfully, waking with every unfamiliar sound, afraid they were coming to kill him, but there was never anyone there.

He dreamed about his father, the steam presses at their shop, the smell of freshly laundered clothes. He dreamed of vegetables in oyster sauce and was nearly sick again, in the dream, though he usually loved the dish. The idea of food was nauseating. The voices, for some reason, agreed with him.

The voices accompanied him into the dreams. Like old uncles, unable to shut up, narrating stories from so long ago no one knew or cared any more. In sleep he walked through a grey haze, a land of crazy jagged shadows, straining his eyes to see beyond the mists that seemed to always hover, like a screen, before his face.

The voices talked about prime numbers. They seemed excited about numbers, and he had the feeling that, just as he was walking through this alien landscape, the voices were walking through his own mind and sampling the little world inside, like a group of travellers on a self-important sightseeing mission.

He slept and woke and crawled to the stream and tried to drink the water. He felt parts of his body acutely then, strange pains in his arms, in his legs, cold and heat travelling across his torso, like ants – but they were not ants.

He did see ants. He lay and watched them walk in a long single file, an army of ants, but when they came near him they neatly avoided him, forming a crescent moon around him and disappearing into the undergrowth beyond. His entire world shrank to the stream, the tree he lay against, the seemingly endless army of patient marching ants. Beyond that world were only nightmares – his father's corpse, the silent assassins, the endless grey mists behind which were voices.

We can help you, the voices said, talking about diagnostics routines and recalibrating bone structure, cell augmentation and establishing a two-way interface.

Help me do what? he said, or thought he did, forgetting he mustn't acknowledge the voices or he would have to acknowledge his own madness.

Whatever you want. Power, riches, love, fame, revenge.

Make me, he said, and closed his eyes, feeling the currents running up and down his body, the fever growing stronger inside him, consuming him until his mind was a grey and endless fog – make me into a gun.

PART II
Chinatown

TWENTY
Shaolin & Wudang

One moment she was asleep, and in the next her eyes opened, staring at the darkening room. Listening. The house around her, familiar sounds, but trying to discern – what?

There. The creaking of a beam where one shouldn't have been audible. Listening. There it came again, and now she had no doubt – someone was creeping along her own version of a nightingale floor.

She reached for her gun. It was never far.

And now she waited.

Footsteps, so cautious as to be inaudible – but for the sounds of the house, as known to her as the streets of her childhood, every sound a warning, and lack of sound an even greater mark of danger – sleeping in the tenements, abandoned houses, in places where the rats formed an advance guard, where every footstep out of place spelled threat and risk. Early on she learned to always have at least one avenue of escape – and never assume a place was safe.

The world wasn't safe. She waited, her finger on the trigger of the gun.

When they came through the door they were very quick and very quiet and she fired twice.

They moved so fast!

It was impossible to escape a gunshot – wasn't it?

And now they weren't there at all.

Two bullet holes in the wall. Two black-clad shapes–

She tensed, the gun steady, trained on the dark doorway. A voice from the darkness, in English – "We only want to talk."

The accent strange, a voice from somewhere distant in the Lizardine Empire's domain. She said, "You have a strange way of going about it," and rose, still slow, waiting for the opportunity to fire.

"We… apologise."

"Show yourselves."

To her surprise, they did. Two robed, hooded figures, the cloth black, the faces under the cowls impassive.

Young. A girl and a boy, their arms raised before them, empty – and now they did a curious thing: they put their hands together before them, palms touching, and bowed. "Milady de Winter," the girl said, "we wish only to talk."

"Then why break in?"

They hesitated, exchanged glances. "We tried to knock," the girl admitted, a small smile playing briefly on her face. "There was no answer. You have no servants?"

"We are all but servants of the state," Milady said, and was gratified to see the two looking confused. She gestured with the gun. Neither of them, she noticed, had in any way acknowledged her nakedness. Though come to think of it, the boy did look a little nervous… "Turn around," she said. "Go to the lounge. I'll join you in a few minutes."

Again, the bowing, the joined palms. "We shall wait," the girl said. The boy said nothing. She grinned at him, and he blushed.

Good.

They did as she told them. She closed the door and went to her bathroom and ran the water. The shower revived her. She dressed, applied a touch of make-up. It was early evening, she saw. Outside the windows the light was waning, night returning to the world.

When she entered the lounge they were standing there, faces turned toward her. The room was spacious, large windows letting in the last of the day's light. Sofas, chairs, a few things collected in her travels, statues from Dahomey, a warrior woman with a spear standing in one corner, a poster for Barnum's Circus on the wall, next to the late Lord de Winter's portrait. She lit a gas lamp, sat down, crossed her legs. "Who are you?"

Hesitation. And now the girl said, "I am Mistress Fong Yi of the Yunnan Shaolin School."

Milady: "What?"

The girl, confused, looking again to her companion. "I am Ip Kai of Wudang."

Milady: "What?"

A sigh. Milady said, "Just sit down."

They did, settling into the sofa opposite. "We represent an association of societies. I did not expect that you would have known of them. Our masters are somewhat... private."

"We're from Qin," the girl said.

"Chung Kuo," the boy said.

"The Middle Kingdom," the girl said.

"China," Milady said, in English.

"Right," the girl said.

They smiled at each other.

"And we're here because of something that was stolen from us many years ago," the boy said.

"An object of some value to us," the girl said.

"And which we have been tasked with guarding."

The girl, looking apologetic: "It's a job."

Milady: "Tell me about it..."

"Our masters have recently learned that the object was..." She searched for the word. The boy said, "Active."

"Active. Yes. There is great danger–"

"There is always great danger," the boy said. The girl shrugged and snapped something in what Milady took to be Chinese.

"And you believe this – object – has now been smuggled into Paris?"

Yi shook her head. "No. But something has."

"A part of it, perhaps," Ip Kai said. "Though our masters were not clear on whether that was even possible. However, they sent us to investigate."

"But you're – you're kids!"

"I could kill you with one finger," the boy said – not boasting, a statement said quietly. Milady said, "I'd like to see you try."

The girl, Mistress Yi, spoke to him again in Chinese. "What did you say?" Milady asked.

"I told him to stop boasting."

Again, they smiled at each other. The boy looked irritated. Yi said, "We are trained in certain clandestine forms of the martial arts. These are coupled, or have been, with the power of this object. It gives us a certain... edge."

Like dodging bullets? She was going to say it was impossible, then thought of the killer in the alley, the way he had taken bullet wounds as if they were mosquito bites. "I'm listening," she said.

The girl shrugged. "We have not been able to find it. Yet. And now there are others searching."

"We wanted," Ip Kai said, "to establish where you belonged in this hunt."

"We were surprised by your involvement."

"Well, perhaps not surprised. We thought someone like you would become involved–"

"You are not police."

"Yet you have authority."

"The object must be destroyed, Milady de Winter."

For the time being, she would give them no answers. "Can you tell me what it is?"

They exchanged glances. "We don't know," Yi said.

"We believe it was implanted into the courier's stomach by

his master," Ip Kai said.

"We must all have masters," the girl said with a sigh.

"It has to be destroyed," Ip Kai said. In one fluid motion, both he and the girl stood up.

"Perhaps," the girl said, "you could pass that along to your Council."

And then – she wasn't sure how – they were gone.

All this – for a message? There were others searching, the girl had said… but how many? One thing was sure, she thought sourly, rising. Pulling the cord that would ring, down below, for her silent coachman to arise. While she slept, others had combed the city.

And had been unsuccessful, she thought.

And though they were looking still, yet she had one advantage, she thought, and she smiled slowly as she left her house.

She was Lady de Winter.

TWENTY-ONE
Moulin Rouge

The coach took her back to Pigalle. It was early still. On the Boulevard de Clichy people were strolling, and did so casually. It was too early for the night trade. She went into the same bar she had been to the night before and ordered coffee, a plate of food. She scanned the room but did not see the short-legged artist.

He had been at the Clockwork Room when Yong Li went there… and he had been right here when Madame L'Espanaye was brutally murdered on the other side of the wall. She did not believe in coincidences. Her food came and she ate, an omelette with mushrooms and cheese, fresh bread, a salad, rounding it off with a croissant and jam and another coffee. The bar was half-empty. She signalled to the man behind the counter.

"Henri?" he said. "He's not been in tonight. Probably still asleep."

"Comes in regularly?"

"Here? Not often. To tell you the truth, he doesn't often have money. And I don't think much of his paintings. Sometimes he gets people to buy them, for drinks. Not me, lady. I've got taste."

"Where can I find him?"

The man shrugged.

She paid and left. She went down the street – bars, cafés, nudie shows, the mechanicals, hostesses, the freak show, the torture room, brasseries, the Moulin Rouge. The artist was in none of the places she tried. No one knew where he stayed. No one seemed to care. She saw some of his early artwork hanging, here and there. Vivid, energetic pictures of can-can girls, bill posters of the kind Barnum would have liked, an alive sort of art that changed, suddenly, at the last address.

She went into the Moulin Rouge.

That ridiculous windmill, turning lazily... doormen, stripped down to the waist – big guys. Wearing masks – green mottled faces with great big bug-eyes. She said, "What the hell are you supposed to be?"

The doorman on the left, West African accent overlaying his French: "Welcome to outer space."

She stepped through the doors.

The music hit her almost physically.

The sound of pistons, the whistle and blow of steam. The drumming of coal being shuffled. A manic sort of sound, rhythmic, wild and yet ordered. The screech of train wheels on the track.

Welcome to outer space–

The room was black. Stars covered the ceiling. Bug-eyed monsters slithered throughout the room. On the stage, a mechanical girl. Steam billowing around her. A girl made of metal, with a silver face. She stared – not an automaton. A girl made to look like one. And now the dancers, more of the green masks, green flesh, writhing on the stage, green breasts and steam and stars.

Welcome to outer space–

She stared. Even though it was early the room was busy. There was a tentacled machine behind the bar, arms moving like a carousel, serving drinks. But again, not a machine, only the semblance of one. She approached the bar and the machine separated, bare-chested boys behind the façade. She thought of L'Espanaye's description of the Clockwork Room. The Moulin Rouge, it seemed, was mocking it.

"What can I get you?"

The man behind the bar had a nice smile. A boy, really, good-looking and knowing it. She said, "I'm looking for Henri de Toulouse-Lautrec."

"Not seen him." Leaning over. "He doesn't come here often any more."

But he used to, she thought. She wondered what had changed, and why the artist was no longer frequenting his old haunts. The boy behind the bar said, "Moon Rocket Punch–" looking into her eyes.

"Excuse me?"

"That's your drink."

"I don't know what that is."

He grinned. For a moment the group of men behind the bar came together again, the tentacled alien swirling, and then a glass was before her, a long tall shape filled with a purple bubbling brew.

She took a sip. It wasn't bad.

"Do you know where I can find him?"

"Have you tried the thirteenth?"

Girls approaching the bar, taking a break. Bare breasts painted silver for the one, green for the other. They lifted up their masks and asked for drinks.

"What's that place in the thirteenth Henri likes?" the bartender said to them. "This lady wants to know."

"Not here for the show?" the green-skinned girl said. "You should."

"Henri," the silver girl said. "He was born with a glass in his hand."

The green girl: "More like a pipe in his mouth."

The silver girl: "I thought he only got into that recently."

The bartender: "Once he started hanging out with these Chinamen."

"China women, more like–" the green girl said. They all giggled.

"Try the Speckled Band on Avenue des Gobelins," the green girl said. "He won't do Pigalle before midnight."

"And he doesn't come here any more," the silver girl said.

"The cheat."

"We're not good enough for him any more."

"Have you seen his new paintings?"

"Machines, he doesn't like girls any more–"

"Oh, I don't know about that–"

She took another sip from her glass and was surprised to see it was almost finished. The bartender beamed at her, then leaned over and said in a low voice, "I'm free later if you want–"

She smiled, and for a moment was tempted. Then she thought of the dead Madame L'Espanaye and the smile went away and didn't come back.

The bartender shrugged. "If you change your mind..."

The girls downed their drinks and rushed away – there was a bellow of thunder and the stage darkened further, and now narrow beams of light were piercing the darkness, illuminating the outline of a giant globe hovering in mid-air on stage, a miniature world with continents and seas, rotating: a green and silver world – and now, by some clever illusion, it seemed to drift away, shrinking, becoming one more star in the dark heavens–

And now something like a rocket appeared in the darkness, moving against the background of stars–

An unseen voice: "Welcome to outer space."

Cheers, then silence.

And on the stage the lights picked out a lizard. Cries from the crowd. A royal lizard standing there, one of Les Lézards – only this, too, she realised, was an illusion – a human girl, but made, cunningly, to look like one of the reptiles. And now she sang:

"Across space we travelled for aeons untold..."

The lights picked out others like her in the background, dressed in fantastical uniforms – a strange, multi-legged creature hiding in one corner–

"For a world to call our own–"

"A world like yours–"

Boos, hisses from the crowd–

"To take for ours–"

A beat – the crowd expectant – the lizard girl turning face-on to the audience–

"But we took a wrong turn, and of all the nations of the Earth, we got the English!"

Cheers. Laughter. And now the lights came on, bright and many-coloured, the rocket shot off into space – a loud explosion – a burst of stars – and the dancers filled the stage, the sound of pistons filling up the air–

"Let's hear it for the fabulous lizard girls!"

And the can-can started, green legs flashing naked in the lights. Lady de Winter finished her drink and stood up.

Outside the night was ordinary and for a moment she was tempted to go back and see the show. She had heard the story being told – some said the lizards were not native-born to Earth, had come from an unimaginable distance, from outer space, had fallen down and slept on Caliban's Island for untold centuries before Vespucci found them–

But these were stories, nothing more. The lizards were not her concern.

The silent coachman was waiting for her. She climbed into the coach and said, "The thirteenth arrondissement."

TWENTY-TWO
Toulouse-Lautrec

There was a multitude of alphabets on the shop fronts, signs she couldn't read, lanterns, the smell of cooking unfamiliar, soy and rice vinegar, frying ginger, frying garlic, chilli – men and women sitting outside eating noodles from large bowls of soup, the strong smell of dried fish everywhere, in the windows dark-red pork and ducks on hooks, on a street corner a juggler playing with fire. Barbershops, tea houses, a bathhouse, dogs, cats, children, scrolls of elaborate calligraphy, bamboo baskets with chickens inside, a woman selling dried roots, bodies pressing against bodies, Milady de Winter striding through the crowd a head taller than most, searching for the Speckled Band.

She found it down a narrow avenue – a dark front, a sickly-sweet smell wafting from the open doorway, a woman made up in the front, bowing as Milady approached, the eyes checking her out – expertly. "Madame, please welcome," the woman said. Her eyes said she knew exactly what Milady was – not missing the gun, the posture. Her eyes said Milady was a problem she wished would just go away. Milady smiled and showed white teeth, the woman nodded and the smile remained fixed. Tried, nevertheless – "We pay already."

"I'm looking for one of your customers."

"We don't want trouble."

How many times had she heard that before? She said, "Then don't make any," and strode past, and into the Speckled Band.

A low-ceilinged dark room, low couches, girls gliding between patrons who lay comatose, long pipes held in lifeless fingers. The girls lit the pipes, dark resin releasing vapours that travelled through the pipe into the patrons' mouths. Opium, that great export of the East – though most of it came from the lizards' colonies in India, stamped with the lizardine government's seal. She scanned the room, saw him–

Henri de Toulouse-Lautrec lay on a divan, a pipe resting beside him, a glass of absinthe on the low table before him. His eyes closed, his little chest rising and falling steadily. She went over to him.

"Wake up," she said.

There was no answer. The woman from the entrance materialised beside her. The other girls – and patrons – did a good job of not seeing her there. "He is deep into the dream," the woman said.

"What does he dream?" Milady said, and the woman shrugged. "This," she said, throwing her hand in an arc, taking in the walls. Milady looked.

The walls were covered in paintings.

They began conventionally – the paintings she had seen before – can-can girls in vibrant colours, caught in motion, lively and alive. Changing, gradually, as the colours muted, and she saw women/machine hybrids, gears and pipes protruding from an abdomen, a belly, eyes on stalks, arms of metal, becoming gradually less and less human even in shape, until the wall had become a chart of bizarre unsettling machines, cogs and wheels and gears and moving pistons, all the while the suggestion of sex, not man, not woman, but there all the same, machines mating with other machines.

She followed it further, past a corner and to the next wall where the colours muted again, even metal rusting, and the wall was grey, the machines disappeared, and the paintings depicted a world as seen beyond a mist, a blackness where alien stars shone in strange configurations, where giant machines floated in space, in a ring around a bloated red sun…. "He sees beyond, now," the woman said.

"Beyond what?"

The woman shrugged. "Beyond this world," she said. "Into another."

She felt uneasy and didn't know why, exactly. "Is it the opium?" she asked. The woman said, "It helps, but no. It is him."

"Can you wake him up?"

"You shall have to wait. Would you like a cup of tea?"

Flawless Parisian French, all of a sudden. Milady grinned. "Sure."

She waited as two of the girls came and lifted the minute artist, carrying him away to an adjacent room.

She followed them there, drank tea, grimaced, watched the little artist come around. It took less time than she had expected.

He sat up – so rapidly it startled her. His eyes opened, and he said, "Let me back!"

She waited. His eyes were still unseeing. The artist's hands closed into fists. "My pencils!"

The girls hurried back to him, already carrying his equipment, no doubt used to this ritual. Henri took a sketch pad and selected a pencil. His hand moved rapidly over the paper. A crazy sense of scale – enormous structures floating in space? She watched. She had few doubts now. The artist's face was contorted. His eyes were staring elsewhere, beyond the room. He still hadn't noticed her. He finished the sketch with one last savage line and collapsed on the seat. "More," he said. Then, his eyes flickered, opened truly for the first time, and he looked around him in confusion. "Where is my pipe?" he said, his voice that of a reedy child.

Milady had brought the artist's opium pipe with her into the room and now held it before her, the artist's eyes drawn to it, to her. "There is no pipe," she said.

"Wha–"

She held the pipe in both hands and as he watched she broke it in half.

"Tell me about your friend," she said.

"Who the hell are you?"

But he looked frightened now. "We saw each other last night, didn't we?" she said. "I want to know what else you saw."

"I see nothing."

She snatched the paper from his lap. "And this?"

He shrugged, but looked uneasy. "Dreams, nightmares. Nothing more."

She smiled, and he flinched. "Tell me about Yong Li."

"I've got nothing to say to you."

She smiled. She went out of the room and returned with a fresh pipe and a ball of opium and she put them the other side of the room from him and then went and sat down again. She watched him watching the pipe. She watched him thinking about it. When he did move it was surprisingly fast but she was ready for it and a bullet travelled faster than a man and the pipe exploded in his face and he howled. She kept the gun in her hand, not quite aiming it at him.

"I'll get you a new one," she promised. "Sit down."

He hesitated, standing there like a caught animal. "Sit!"

He went back and sat down. He looked at her and there was naked hunger in his face.

"Tell me about your friend," she said again, soothingly. The gun was in her lap but she didn't need it. "Tell me everything, and they'll make you a new pipe."

His eyes burned, but he slowly nodded.

"I met him at Thumb's," he said.

TWENTY-THREE
Yong Li

When he began talking it was in a rush, the words tumbling over each other. The first thing he said surprised her. She said, "At the tobacco shop?"

"Yes."

He was a friend of Tom Thumb's. Two little men with big appetites. He knew Tom was dealing with Indochina, because sometimes Tom gave him back gifts – "A little opium here and there. For medicinal purposes. I am not a well man–"

She waited.

"So then, about a month ago, I went into the shop and Tom introduced me to his new friend. Yong Li. He was a nice guy–"

The same words Tom had used. And the girl.

"So… I don't know how to tell it. There was just something about him. An aura. I could sense it but couldn't see it though I knew it was there. I knew I had to paint him. Do you know of the Eastern religions? He was like the Buddha, with his glistening large belly, his smile. His eyes saw further than humans can see. He was a man deeply changed by some experience in his past. And that scar down his belly – I was fascinated by it. I was attracted – not to him, exactly, but to what he – what he had inside him. A difference. I didn't know how to describe it. I drew and sketched and painted him, trying to capture that essence. It was a thing of no discernible colour. A grey metallic – but not metallic, either, not exactly – it was as if his essence was hidden behind mist, and try as I might I couldn't penetrate it."

He sighed, his eyes clearing, and called for one of the girls and asked for his drink. The girl looked at Milady, who nodded. The girl went and fetched Henri his drink.

"Tom is supposed to meet me here," he said suddenly.

She turned sharply, looked at him. "Tom?"

"We sometimes get together–" He blinked, said, "I think, maybe, not tonight. I was mistaken."

She filed it away. The artist blinked again, focused on her. "You look like the girl in the poster on Tom's wall," he said suddenly. "The girl from the circus. I could paint you."

"And I could shoot you," she said, "so why don't we table both for the moment and concentrate?"

He shrugged, a small smile appearing for the first time on his face. He was getting some of his energy back, she thought. He was almost bouncy. "It would be a pleasure to paint you."

She smiled too, and said, "It would be a pleasure to shoot you–" watching him lose the smile. She nodded. "Tell me about Yong Li," she said.

He was drawn to the Asian man. But when he returned to the shop Yong Li was no longer there. He had gone – "To a safe place, Tom said. He had an… appointment in Paris, but not yet, and Tom had to keep him safe until then."

"So what did you do?"

"I was disconsolate! I had to find him!"

Softly: "And did you find him?"

Henri did. He had asked Tom, but Tom refused to divulge Yong Li's location. So he watched. He saw Mademoiselle L'Espanaye go into the shop – he knew her vaguely, one of those faces you see around – but his suspicions were aroused. He listened outside and heard the Asian man discussed. He followed her, to her work and then to her home. He came to the Rue Morgue. He watched the windows in the night, watching for a sign of the man who gave him glimpses of another world.

"What do you mean, another world?"

Another world, he said. An alien world, just out of reach, yet so close he could almost touch it. He needed to see it, sense it, feel it... He wanted to draw it, but could not see it clearly. Only glimpses, flashes in the mind. "It was after I met him that I began to take the opium with some intent," he said. "It allowed my mind to relax enough for the glimpses to become more than glimpses. A vast endless space where great shapes floated, moved – but with intent! They were aware, they were watching, and they were coming closer all the while. It was as if Yong Li's wound, his scar, was the closed door to another world, but things slipped through – like a keyhole where you put your eye to it you could see to another room."

He engineered a meeting with the man. He knew he had to go outside sometime, if only for his foul rolling tobacco. He bumped into him by chance, and Yong Li was delighted to see him.

"He did not enjoy being cooped up in that place," Henri said. "He said the women were not clean. That Europeans were filthy and did not wash, and their smell was bad. He was quite rude, really, but I guess you have to make allowances. I think he was just in a bad humour, from being held there all this time. He was very glad to see me."

"So what did you do?"

Henri looked surprised. "We got drunk," he said, as if the answer was obvious.

"Oh."

"And then I painted him."

"I see."

"He wouldn't discuss it with me," Henri said. "But I think he was glad because I could see what he saw. I think it was very hard for him. He would touch his stomach and grimace, as if he were in pain. But it was not a physical pain. It was the pain of seeing that you did not wish to see."

But Henri wished to see. He found that by touching the man's naked stomach the visions in his mind became clearer. He became obsessed with trying to capture more clearly what he was seeing. He sensed a great presence there, and a great danger too, beyond the wall of mist. They met in secret, he and Yong Li, when the two women were away. Once he came up to the apartment, but Yong Li did not like that. So they met in a bar, and talked, and drank – "He didn't like the opium. Alcohol helped him not see, but opium had the opposite effect –" and Henri drew.

"Then he told me his time was near, and he could unburden himself and go home. And then he told me we could not see each other again – it was becoming too dangerous. I was disconsolate!"

"Disconsolate," she said.

"Yes! I did not know what to do. I was mad! But I promised him I will stay away."

"Did you kill him?" she said. The artist opened wide, shocked eyes. "Kill him? How could I kill him?"

She thought of the body ripped open, as if someone had reached inside... "To open the door he was keeping locked," she said.

"Never!" He looked flustered and she knew she had something.

"You thought about it, didn't you?" she said.

"I... that is not... I would never!"

"What did you do?"

"I waited. I stood outside all night, but he never came down. I came here and took much opium, but my link was fading, it was becoming harder to see."

She waited. "The Clockwork Room," she said.

Yes. There came a night when he saw Yong Li go out. He

was accompanied by the younger L'Espanaye woman.

"So I followed them," he said, shrugging. "What else could I do?"

"You followed them to the Clockwork Room?"

He used to be a regular there, he explained. He loved the place, the smell of oil, the hum of the machinery. There was something about it, he realised later, that was a little bit close to the other world he could – almost – see. He couldn't quite say what it was... When he saw that was their destination he went ahead, came inside through the back entrance, and was already at the bar when they came in. If Yong Li noticed him he gave no sign. But he knew that he did.

"What was he doing there?"

He described the evening – the girl looking overwhelmed by the place – Yong Li at the bar – the girl going upstairs to the private rooms. He watched Yong Li all the while, waiting for the man to come to him, but he never did.

And now she sat forward, waiting, for this witness, this drug-addled, short-legged artist who could fill in for her the missing time at the Clockwork Room.

"Tell me," she said.

TWENTY-FOUR
Taken

They were waiting for her when she left the Speckled Band. Dark-clad shapes moving in the street outside, ringing her – onlookers studiously not looking.

They were Asian, and that came as no surprise. They stood in their semi-circle and regarded her. She looked at their faces. Only a couple were unscarred. She said, "Black never goes out of fashion."

One of the men, older than the others, stepped forward. "You are to come with us, please," he said.

"Or else?" she said.

For a moment, the man looked confused. "Or else what?" he said.

"You're supposed to say *or else,*" she said, "and then tell me what you'll do if I don't come with you."

"Oh," he said, nodding. "Thank you, yes. Come with us or else we'll kill you and throw your body into the river, please," he said.

"Well, since you put it so nicely," she said. She looked back at the door of the Speckled Band. It was shut.

"I can't say I'm that surprised to see you," she said, speaking to the one who seemed to be their leader. "Whoever you are."

He smiled, only a little. "You have been busy," he said.

"Work," she said. "You know how it is."

He nodded, without a smile now. There was something in him that she responded to, a similarity to herself. A professional, she thought. She said, "Shall we?" and the man said, "Follow me, please."

It was the most polite kidnapping she had ever experienced. Walking in the midst of the black-clad men she had the surreal feeling she was going to a funeral. She hoped it was not her own.

There were people everywhere in the street, most of them Asian, all assiduously looking away when they passed. For all purposes she and her little group were invisible. The smells of cooking engulfed her as before.

She noticed they did not appear concerned about her gun. They led the way through narrow side-streets and she saw a building rising in the distance, a façade decorated with lizardine gargoyles, enormous chimneys rising above it, belching smoke and steam. She knew what it was.

The Gobelin factory.

They came to a door and it opened from inside. They went into the building. The corridor was long and brightly lit and smelled of cleaning material. They followed it for a while and came to an elevator. It opened and she was motioned inside. She went in and was followed by the leader and two of his men. The other remained outside. The leader pressed a button and the elevator ascended slowly.

She knew about the factory. Viktor had worked there for a while, he had told her that once. It was once owned by the Gobelin family. Now she wasn't sure who owned it. They used to make garments there – one of the first places to use the Daguerre looms, machines that automated production... It had been a natural step for the factory to–

The elevator doors opened. They all filed out. Another white, clean corridor. They walked down it and came to a door. The door opened onto an antechamber. There was a sofa and a small table and the leader said, "Would you like some tea?"

"Do you have any coffee?"

"Please," he said, looking pained. "It is not good for you."

Apart from the two items of furniture the room was bare. The walls were very white. It was very clean. There was a set of doors at the back of the room. They were closed. She sat and waited and the leader waited with her, standing, while one of his men went and fetched a pot of tea. Then there were just the two of them there.

She poured some tea into a small china cup and sipped it. "Jasmine?" she said. He nodded with seeming approval. "Very beneficial for both spirit and body," he said.

She said, "Do you have a name?"

"I am Colonel Xing of the Imperial Secret Service," he said.

She said, "It's not secret if you tell me about it."

For a moment she almost thought he would smile. It passed.

"Do you not serve your Council in a similar capacity?" he said.

"A lot of people seem to know a lot about me, all of a sudden…" she said.

"You are an interesting woman," he said, and this time he did smile. "It is only natural…"

She tilted her head, looking at him. "There are no secrets between the likes of us," he said.

"Right."

They smiled at each other.

"What are we waiting for?" she said.

He didn't answer that one. She sipped her tea. They waited.

The doors opened at the back of the room almost without her noticing.

It was impossible to miss the woman standing there, though.

She was very old, and half her face was metal.

"Milady de Winter?" she said. "I am Fei Linlin. Please, come inside."

TWENTY-FIVE
The Empress-Dowager's Emissary

"Madame Linlin–"

They were standing in a room overlooking the city. They were high up in the Gobelin factory. Below the streets of Chinatown snaked, covered in lights. Beyond was the Seine and the whole of the city. Just outside the window were two enormous gargoyles, lizard-shaped, split tongues out, reptilian mouths open as if to catch the rain.

"I hope my men were not rude–"

"Colonel Xing was very polite."

"That is good."

Madame Linlin lit a cigarette. It was inserted inside an ivory-coloured holder. She took a deep breath and exhaled smoke. She was very old and looked a little like a dragon. Her eyes were large and bright. One eye was set in a human, wrinkled face. The other was in a half-globe of smooth metal. Milady noted that, and wondered. The woman knew she was looking and didn't seem to mind.

She was small, and now she went and sat behind a large desk, her back to the windows, and looked even smaller.

And strangely powerful.

She had the feel about her of a woman used to wielding power. Her eyes examined Milady and there was nothing personal about it: it was the way a merchant might study his wares, deciding how much they were worth and what best use to put them to. "Please, sit down."

Milady remained standing. She looked out of the window at the city, returned her gaze back to the old woman.

"Who are you?" she said.

"I told you my name."

Milady inched her head in reply and the woman smiled. "But you want to know, of course, what I am."

"Yes."

"I am the representative of the Empress-Dowager Cixi," the woman said, equally simply. "Of the Empire of Chung Kuo."

"China."

"Yes."

"I thought–" She did not know much about that far-off, mysterious place. "I thought you had an emperor."

"We do."

"Ah."

"Sometimes it is best to – how shall I put it," Madame Linlin said, "to help matters from behind the throne, as it were. An emperor, after all, is an important soul, a ruler with many tasks. He must be seen. He must be worshipped. He should not be burdened with–"

"More practical matters?"

"Exactly."

When the woman smiled it was with only one half of her face. The metal side never moved at all.

"What happened to you?"

The woman shrugged, not taking offence. "I was injured in service," she said. "Our scientists are not without knowledge."

"I did not know you had–"

"And we try to keep it that way," Madame Linlin said, a little sharply. "Oh, the lizards tried to invade us, not once but twice. They were repelled. I suspect that, sooner or later, they will try again. The lizards and their humans, those English on their tiny island. Do they really think they can take us? No, my dear. We know much that we do not tell, and learned much beyond that. Just as we know how to deal with this great Republic of France, should your metal-minds ever think to make the same mistake."

"You are being very forthright."

"I am not a diplomat," Madame Linlin said, and again she smiled that half-smile. "We work behind the scenes, you and I, do we not?"

Milady let it pass. "What is it you want?" she said.

"Won't you sit down?"

"No, thank you."

"As you wish."

She blew smoke into the air. Its smell was sweet, and a little cloying.

"I want the same thing you want," she said. "I want the thing that was hidden inside a dead man's stomach."

Milady glanced at her. Fei Linlin smiled back at her. The cigarette-holder was clamped between the teeth of her human half-face. "You know who he was?"

"His real name was Captain James Wong Li," she said. "Also known as Iron Kick, also known as Yong Li, Li Fong, and half a dozen other aliases. Born in Hong Kong, which is a small island given to the lizards in concession –" her half of a face expressed disgust, but the expression quickly disappeared – "hence the English first name. A Tong member, a bandit, later captain in the Imperial Guard."

"Everyone said he was such a nice man," Milady said, and Madame Linlin shrugged. When she did, there was the barely audible sound of gears.

"I have no doubt he was. He was also ruthless when he needed to be, and very loyal, until–"

"Yes?"

But Madame Linlin did not seem eager to pursue that line of conversation. "I am being very open with you," she said, "because I want you to understand what is at stake. Our goals are similar, or we wouldn't be talking. The missing object is dangerous. To Chung Kuo and to France."

She thought about the killer in the alleyway, the inhuman face – thought about Henri's drawings, remembered Madame L'Espanaye's last words–

"Door," the woman had said. The single word a whispered puff of air. "Door. K... key."

She had said, "Where?"

And the woman, dying, said: "Every... where."

"What is this object?"

No answer, and she said, throwing it to the older woman – "A key."

Madame Linlin looked taken aback. "Yes..." she said.

"Why was Yong Li here?" She thought about it for a moment. "Did you send him? You said he was a captain in your–"

"No."

There was a moment of silence, stretching between them. "No," Madame Linlin said at last. "He... Some time ago he changed his allegiance. He defected – to serve the Man on the Mekong."

"Who?"

"An enemy."

They regarded each other. Milady waited. The strange old woman watched her too, her eyes uncertain. At last she said, "The man who sent him here."

Interesting... And now Tom Thumb's mysterious contact in the East was gaining a little more of a shape. "Why was he sent here?"

But she thought she already knew.

She said, "Les Lézards."

And Madame Linlin, stubbing out the remains of her cigarette, said, "Yes."

TWENTY-SIX
Fat Man and Lizard

There had been a fat man at the Clockwork Room that night. That was what Henri had told her at the Speckled Band. A fat man standing with the lizardine ambassador. Very fat, with a prominent forehead, a prominent nose, and deep-set eyes that seemed to miss nothing – deep-set eyes that had fastened onto Yong Li as if they had been expecting just such a man.

That the fat man was with a royal lizard was significant. Yet he did not seem to Henri to be an assistant, an aide-de-camp or a servant – he had the manner about him of a man not easily fazed, and when he turned to speak to the tall lizard beside him he did it with what Henri could only describe as an indulgent smile.

The fat man had moved slowly and drunk little, and seemed to pass through the room attracting surprisingly little notice – "And my attention was on Yong Li, you understand, not on the fat man."

"I understand."

And now she remembered that Mademoiselle L'Espanaye, too, had noticed a fat man…

"When I saw Yong Li going up the stairs to the private rooms, naturally I followed him," Henri said. "There was a room at the end of the corridor and the door was closing behind him and I went to it and knocked. A voice said, "Who is it?" and I said, "It's me, Henri, let me in."

The door had opened then, and the Asian man stood there, his face stricken. "You must go, now!" he said. Both his hands were on his belly, not patting it but – "Like he was holding it in, trying to stop it from bursting, you know?"

He'd said, "Quick! You must go. You must not be seen."

"But why? What are you doing?"

"For your own sake, man! He's coming!"

The door had slammed shut. Henri was left alone in the corridor – and as he looked from door to staircase he heard footsteps climbing, slowly but with an even step, up the stairs.

"I don't mind telling you I was unsettled," he said. "But, you see, I know the Clockwork Room well."

And so he opened one of the doors lining the corridor and stepped inside, shutting it behind him just as the footsteps had reached the top of the staircase and began coming down the corridor, towards that last room.

"There was a woman in there – oh! I knew her very well. A very famous novelist. I had been to her salons several times. But she did not see me. No – she was inside one of the clockwork engines of that place, and it was working at her – I would have liked to have sketched it."

"That's nice."

"Yes, well… she did not see me. And so I was safe."

He heard the footsteps coming closer. When they came to Henri's door they paused – "I don't mind telling you I was worried" – but finally moved on. Henri had opened the door then, just a crack. He saw the fat man disappear into the last room, the one holding Yong Li. The door had closed shut behind him.

"I should have left then. But I needed to see."

And so he left his hiding place, machine and novelist and all, and tiptoed to the last door, the unmarked one. "I peeked through the keyhole," he said. His eyes grew very large then, and his hands shook. His head sank back against the cushions. She was losing him, she knew then. "What did you see?" she said – demanded. But the little artist's eyes were no longer seeing, and the expression on his face was filled with both fear and longing. "I saw it," he said. "I saw it."

His eyes closed, and his breath came softly, scented with the sweetness of opium. "What did you see?" She slapped him, but it made no difference.

"I saw their world," he said, and he smiled, a small, child-like smile, and then he spoke no more. She tried, but could not rouse him, and at last she left him there, to dream his grey dreams.

"We believe," Madame Linlin said, "that Captain Li was in Paris to meet secretly with a representative of the lizards' secret service." She grimaced, a disconcerting sight as one side of her face remained metal-smooth. "His name is Mycroft Holmes. His influence is far-reaching. He is very dangerous."

Milady almost laughed. She had no doubt Madame Linlin was just as dangerous. And no doubt she occupied a similar position to this Mycroft's in her own country's service. She said, "Why did Yong Li – Captain Li – not meet them across the Channel?"

"In the lizards' own domain?" Madame Linlin shook her head. "No. Paris was a sensible choice."

It did, Milady had to admit, make sense. Yong Li's master had something to – to sell? To trade? – with the lizards. He had chosen the one place they could not move openly in. "What does he look like, this Mycroft Holmes?" she asked, waiting for the answer to confirm her own thoughts.

"He is a very fat man," Madame Linlin said, with some distaste.

"Ah."

"You know of him?"

"I think," she said, "that he had indeed met with Captain Li."

"Yes. My people have not been as diligent as they should have. We have not been able to locate him in time."

"Did you kill Yong Li?"

The old woman smiled, then shook her head. "No. It would have made things simpler if we had. And you and I wouldn't be talking."

"Do you know who did?"

The smile disappeared. "No. We need to find out, and we need to retrieve the object. It must be destroyed."

"I need to know what it is."

The old woman shrugged. "It is a piece of something which should not exist," she said. "A legend, a folktale."

"I am tasked with finding it," Milady said. "For my own people."

"It must be destroyed."

"That is not my decision."

The woman shrugged. "We can make our own arrangements with the Council," she said. "It is the lizards we are most concerned with."

"Are there others from… from Chung Kuo looking for this object?"

The old woman looked at her sharply. And now she extracted another cigarette and fitted it into her holder. "You have encountered others?"

"I am merely asking."

For the first time real anger came into the old woman's eyes. "There are secret societies," she said. "They are little more than criminals. Bandits." She muttered something under her breath. "Colonel Xing!" she called, and in a second the man was there. She spoke to him in what Milady took for Chinese. The man nodded, his face expressionless. In a moment, Madame Linlin had switched to French. "Please escort Lady de Winter safely out of the building. We have concluded our little conversation."

"Have we?" Milady said. The old woman smiled her half-smile, not mistaking the threat in Milady's voice. "Only for now, I'm sure," she said sweetly.

"Only for now," Milady said, returning the smile.

She turned to Colonel Xing. "Shall we?" she said.

"It would be my pleasure, please," he said.

TWENTY-SEVEN
The Goblin Factory

She was not happy about the old woman's involvement – not happy about the direction the investigation was taking. She had a feeling she was being used, and she didn't like that either. She had the feeling she should shoot someone, but she resisted it, for now. Colonel Xing, at least, had good manners.

They did not take the elevator down this time. Instead he led her through another corridor and through a secure door and suddenly she was standing in a vast, cathedral-like space, and all around her were the goblins.

They were not the creatures of European folklore. They were… she wasn't sure what they were.

In the middle of the great open space of the factory stood a large pool filled with boiling, liquid metal. Figures moved down there, human-shaped and small, and she suddenly realised just how large the building was, how high above the ground they were on this level.

And the pool was very large.

There were machines down there, enormous machines, the sound of their engines filling up the space, blocking all other sound. Steam and smoke rose through enormous metal pipes all the way to the ceiling above her head.

When she looked down she could see a heap of arms.

There was another one, of legs.

Hanging from the walls, on every available space, were the goblins.

They were mute, unmoving. They came in many different shapes. Some looked almost human. Some looked aquatic, some avian, and several looked very much like...

Like royal lizards.

Down below, a human figure flicked a giant switch and sudden lightning flashed in the great hall of the building. Milady shivered. The lightning caught between two giant balls of metal and continued to pass back and forth between them, growing in intensity all the while. She looked away from it.

A hand touched her, gently, on her arm. Wordlessly, Colonel Xing motioned for her to follow him. She did, over to an observation platform jutting from the side of the surface they were on. When they had stood inside it, it began to descend.

She watched the goblins – the automatons – if that was what they were. She wasn't sure. She had never seen so many, and there was something about them that did not recall to mind those few beggars in the catacombs, or even those ancient beings on the Quiet Council. These had a definite... martial feel to them.

The makeshift elevator took them down slowly.

Past faces staring out – not the rubber-flesh skin of human-like automatons, not the crude machine faces, like a caricature of the human, such as belonged to the truly old ones.

No. These were smooth, smooth masks and faceless, making no pretence, no attempt to deceive as to what they were. Here was a silent army of machines, and as they went down she could see more being made, down on that vast factory floor, where human shapes in masks and protective clothing moved along a moving belt, assembling parts...

Did the Council know about this?

Colonel Xing led her through the floor. She felt the heat

rising from that pool of toxic metal and, skirting it, saw an area set aside that resembled Viktor's place in the under-morgue – surgical tables, bright lamps, refrigeration units, scalpels... She turned away from it and a moment later they were outside.

The night's air was cool, wonderfully cool after being inside. She felt as if she had been trapped inside the belly of a giant monster and had at last been spat out. She had been sweating, she realised. The doors, when they closed behind them, had shut out the constant sound of the engines, but she could still feel them under her feet, tiny tremors in the ground.

And now she understood the smoke that was constantly, endlessly belching out of the chimneys. She said, her voice too loud in her ears, "What are they for?"

"You know what they are for."

"Whose?" she said, and he began to smile, then stopped. "Anyone who'd pay," he said, as if the question surprised him – as if it were evident.

"Does she own it?"

He looked surprised, again. "No," he said. "The Shaw brothers bought it from the Gobelin line, years ago. They did the conversion. It's their factory now."

She didn't ask who the Shaw brothers were. She was just happy for the silence.

"I hope we meet again," Colonel Xing said, and smiled. He smelled nice, she thought suddenly. "I will see you again, please."

She said, "What will you do now?"

"Wait," he said. "See."

"See if I find what you're all looking for?"

"Unless we find it first," he said.

"Where have you been looking?"

He said, "There is a large community from Asia in this city. Chung Kuo, Siam, Kampuchea... Perhaps some of our own people are involved. Many of the –" he used a word she didn't know, realised it, said, "the secret societies, they operate here too. Wudang, Shaolin, the Beggars' Guild... they too are searching, I think."

"Have you been keeping an eye on the British agent?" she said, and he looked at her, alert now, and said, "Yes, that too."

"Where is he staying?"

He told her. Then, very formally, he shook her hand. Then he grinned and, unexpectedly, kissed her on the cheek. "Goodbye, Milady," he said.

She nodded, and he smiled again, and disappeared back into the building.

She touched her hand to her cheek.

She didn't know what to think.

She walked away, into the night and the streets of Chinatown.

TWENTY-EIGHT
The Unfortunate Demise of Tom Thumb

There was a body floating in the Seine and it was Tom Thumb's.

There was a metal taste in her mouth. She stared at the small corpse. Tom's eyes were open, staring up at the stars. The current carried him gently. Milady said something – she wasn't sure, later, what it was. Tom had been slashed open with a knife. Grey swirls were forming on his skin, moving disconcertingly, at odds with the current.

She ran down to the embankment, pushing people out of her way.

She fished the little man out of the water.

Tom Thumb lay dead on the stones, a pool of red water forming around his body. Milady knelt beside him.

Backtrack.

Connect the dots.

She'd left the Goblin factory and had been thinking as she walked.

Some things did not ring true in Fei Linlin's account.

For instance, who had attacked her in Montmartre?

She remembered the tattoos on their arms.

She remembered back to the under-morgue:

The Hoffman automaton took the sketch from her and studied it.

"Imperial assassins," it said.

What?

"So she is after it too," it said, the voice low, barely above a murmur.

She had thought, at the time, he had meant Victoria. But what if he meant the Empress-Dowager? And yet now, as she thought about it, it seemed unlikely. Another Asian faction, then? It was getting hard to keep count.

"The secret societies," Colonel Xing had said. "They operate here too. Wudang, Shaolin, the Beggars' Guild... they too are searching, I think."

Yet she had spoken to those from Shaolin and Wudang, and they seemed to have the same objective as the others. Everyone wanted the missing object – or almost everyone...

What, she thought, if there were other factions, other secret societies at work? For all she knew there were hundreds of factions in that huge, secretive empire of Chung Kuo. And some might have a different agenda – and she wondered again what this object was, what its importance really was – and why it was sent to Paris, and for whom.

The lizards. And it occurred to her the one faction not looking for the missing object was the one which had already, so it seemed, seen it. She decided she needed to have a word with the fat man from across the Channel, this mysterious Mycroft – and soon.

And she was still thinking when she found herself along the river and, looking down, discovered her one-time friend floating face-up in the dirty water of the Seine, dead eyes staring at her accusingly.

Tom Thumb looked very, very dead.

And now that she was crouching beside him she felt the press of the crowd lessen, and two small figures appeared by her side–

"Milady de Winter," the girl said.

"Mistress Yi..."

"Milady," the boy said, dipping his head.

"Ip Kai... I wondered when you two would show up."

She felt tired, and angry, and she looked down at Tom Thumb's dead face, remembering him from all those years before, from the circus, the shared times – knowing he was a rascal and a rogue but liking him nevertheless – losing touch, as one does, hearing he had gone off to England, had become involved in revolutionary politics – being surprised to see him here in Paris, but knowing he was still involved, still walking on the wrong side – a short but busy man, a short but busy life, leading to–

She almost screamed.

The grey circles along Tom's body moved more rapidly. It was almost as if a storm was picking up across his skin. And now the corpse blinked.

She stared into Tom Thumb's eyes, and saw broiling grey clouds forming.

She felt rather than saw the two beside her step away. They didn't speak. She said, softly, "Tom, can you hear me?"

There was something behind those dead eyes. But she wasn't sure it was Tom – and the sudden realisation was chilling.

The eyes focused, and that was eerie. They looked at her face. And now the mouth opened, and a wet, bloated tongue licked wet lips, the gesture strangely obscene.

Then it spoke.

The word came out with a whisper of foul-smelling air. "Waiting..." it said. The body was crawling with grey spirals, currents washing over the corpse. Milady moved back from the body and her hand twitched on the handle of her gun.

Though what use was a gun against something that was already dead?

"Soon..." the voice whispered, and the lips formed into something resembling a smile. Then the eyes closed, and grey activity ceased, and it was only Tom Thumb lying there, and his throat had been cut with a very sharp knife, and Milady stared and thought, my, how the corpses are piling up.

She knew the killer must be close. She was disturbed by this grey plague that seemed to be slowly creeping up everywhere, something alien and strange and disturbing, but it had not killed Tom Thumb. Someone had, and she meant to find him.

TWENTY-NINE
The Grey Ghost Gang

"Yes," Ip Kai said, sounding surprised. He was looking at the sketch of the men's tattoos. "There are opposing factions to us. The Five Poisons Cult, the Sharks Sect, the Blood Sabre, the Ancient Tomb Sect, the Demonic Cult… but this I have not seen." His lips curled in a grimace. "Its meaning is clear, at least," he said, with evident distaste. "They seek that which lies beyond the gate."

Milady grimaced too, at that. It'd been another long night, she had another death on her hand, and was no closer to locating the missing object – nor did she feel much inclined to, any more.

Tom Thumb's death had made it personal.

She didn't know where the object was but she knew a killer was out there, hunting down everyone who had come near it. A killer who knew her, and wanted to send her a strong, clear message when he dumped Tom Thumb in the Seine, ensuring the corpse would float past her at the right time. He could be out there right now, in the shadows of Chinatown, watching her, waiting…

She needed a way to kill something that couldn't be easily killed.

There were several options.

But now she sat with Mistress Yi of Shaolin and her

companion, Ip Kai of Wudang, in a small but comfortable tea room decorated with spread-open fans printed with images of the Great Wall and the Forbidden City and so on, and lanterns, and it was empty apart for them, and the old woman who seemed to run the place brought her a coffee, not tea, without being told.

And so things were looking up – though not, admittedly, for Tom Thumb.

And not for Milady's peace of mind, either.

"I have seen this before," Mistress Yi said, examining the sketch, and her face was troubled. "It is the emblem of the Grey Ghost Gang. But they have not been seen for many–"

Her eyes widened.

She was looking past Milady.

Milady knew something was wrong–

She felt the window explode a split second before the glass burst.

She ducked and glass fragments showered her, and she could feel a sudden pain in her cheek, a shard of glass cutting her–

She swore, a burning fury rising inside her, and coupled with it was a wild, unconstrained joy.

She was finally going to shoot someone.

"The Grey Ghost Gang!" Mistress Yi said, and followed it with something in Chinese that sounded like a curse.

When Milady looked up the gun was in her hands and dark shapes were streaming into the room. She fired and watched the first one drop to the floor, a flower of blood spreading on his chest. They were dressed in black, of course they were dressed in black, and she knew with absolute certainty that, if she only looked, she'd find a grey tattoo on the man's arm.

Mistress Yi leaped into the air. Milady had never seen someone move the way she had. She bounced off the wall and spun and kicked, and her foot connected with one of the attackers' heads and knocked him out flat. She landed but it only lasted a fraction of a second and she was airborne again, spinning, her legs catching two more of the attackers–

And Ip Kai had joined her, moving like a ghost, appearing behind two more attackers – there was something in his hands – like tiny needles – both went in simultaneously, into the men's necks–

And they both fell. Milady fired, and again, and watched another man fall.

How many were there?

"Get out!" Mistress Yi shouted, suddenly very close. She threw a metal star, lightning-fast, and another man dropped down. The small tea room was fast filling up with the dead. "The back door! We'll hold them!"

Milady said, "Later," and rose. She had a second gun strapped to her leg and now it was in her hand and both her hands were full and both her guns were loaded and she fired, left, right, left, turning with each shot, moving forward to catch as many of them as she could–

A kick connected with her legs and swept her down to the floor and she roared, the guns forgotten as she found her feet and rushed her assailant, grabbing his head with her arms and she twisted–

There was a sickening sound–

She reached for the Peacemaker on the floor, the other gun lost, and held it by the barrel and used it as a club and bashed a man's head in–

Something cut her arm then, deeply–

Ip Kai was flying through the air and his bare hands were weapons–

But there were so many of them, so many more coming in to replace the fallen–

"Get out, damn it!"

And then Mistress Yi was there again and somehow the small girl was dragging the much larger woman, away from the fighting, towards the back of the room–

"We'll. Hold. Them. Off!"

And threw her through the kitchen door.

The desire to fight left her suddenly. She scrambled to her feet (noticing the kitchen was empty, the door to the back open wide) and went through the door, fast.

Behind, a dark alleyway that was very empty.

Why would they be chasing her?

She didn't have the key.

A key. A key to what? None of it made any sense. She thought of what the girl, Mademoiselle L'Espanaye, had told her. What she saw in the room at the end of the corridor, at the Clockwork Room...

Shadows flickering on a wall, light and shades, moving shapes. "Like a camera obscura."

A projection. Not a key, but a – what?

And she thought – perhaps it was showing what is behind the door.

She had to find the fat man.

And she had to talk to Viktor again.

And to the Council.

But first, she needed a new gun.

THIRTY
The Toymaker

She was not pursued and she was thankful for that. She sensed her time in Chinatown was coming to an end and was not unpleased. Her arm still stung from the cut it had sustained, but she was fine otherwise. She hoped Yi and Ip Kai would be, too. She needed to go down to the catacombs and there was a way down nearby, a way that would lead her under the river, and luckily – or perhaps not, depending how you felt about it – it was through the Toymaker's shop.

When was she last there? Two, three years before? And that was on Council orders. This was not her part of town and the Toymaker wasn't someone she looked forward to seeing – usually.

Now she needed him.

The Toymaker had been a magician, and he had been a builder of automata; and for a time was very well known. His name had been Jean Eugène Robert-Houdin. He had once been known as "The heir of Vaucanson", he who had been the father of the Republic.

That had all been a while back. Before the incident with the Eve, and the subsequent scandal...

The Toymaker's shop sat on its own in a pool of darkness by the river. Clocks were set on the otherwise impassive façade, clock-faces showing the time around the world, staring at the passers-by as if challenging them to step inside. To do so, they seemed to suggest, would be to challenge time itself.

There was no sign to advertise the Toymaker's craft. A single black door was set into the building and it was closed.

But the Toymaker seldom slept...

The door had no handle. Milady knocked, and somewhere inside an ominous martial music rose like a waking dog.

All suitably orchestrated. She banged on the door and shouted, "Council business, open up!"

The door swung open without a sound. And now that she could see into the inside of the shop she saw nothing but darkness. Yet there was a sense of intelligence inside, of hidden eyes watching, and the faint sounds of movement could be heard – if she concentrated – of gears and wheels, as unseen shapes flitted away in the darkness.

She came inside. The door closed behind her.

"Show yourself," she said.

"Milady de Winter," a voice murmured, close to her ear, "what a pleasant surprise."

It had startled her.

Which had been the intention.

"Houdin," she said, and the voice said, "No!" and then, more quietly, "Not any more."

He had built her Grimm. He had built many things. Once, he had been head of the Council...

Not any more.

"I need something from you," she said, into the darkness.

"That is always what brings them to my shop," the voice said. Farther now. "Always they want something. My only desire had been to build that which resembles the human. Tell me –" the voice said, moving even farther away – but then, one could never trust the source of the voice, as she had no doubt machines could replicate it across the dark space, only one of the magician's many tricks – "if it acts like a man and sounds like a man – how do you know it is not a man?"

"As I recall," she said, "it was not men that were your problem."

A short, dry laugh. And now lights sprang into existence across the shop, illuminating–

He stood at the far end, dressed in a black suit and a top hat. A white handkerchief was in the breast suit of his pocket. In one hand he held a cane. His face–

The shop was filled with mechanical toys. Trains began to run suddenly across what seemed like miles of miniature rails, climbing walls and descending mountains of furniture. Airships glided in the air, black mechanical things resembling insects. Toy soldiers marched towards her, guns raised. On the wall, the only clock was half-melted, frozen at the time of–

"I tried to save my child," he said. "That was all."

"She could not be allowed to–" she said, but he was not listening.

When his wife had died giving birth he had enlisted Viktor's help. The two of them had created something–

In the secret records of the Quiet Council it was referred to as The Affair of the Bride with White Hair.

There had been several dozen victims before–

The old magician stepped forward. And now she could see his face, and wished she couldn't.

The man was wearing a mask. It was not like Madame Linlin's face, half-alive, half-metal. His was the mask of humanity, a shifting rubbery façade such as was used for one of his automatons. It could pass for human – in the dim light. If one did not look too closely, and saw the ripples on the false skin, the way the eyes moved across the face, the dance of the shifting mouth…

She said, hiding a shiver, "Is this your boy?"

A smaller figure had appeared beside the magician. Like Houdin, it too was dressed in evening dress and top hat, with the same white handkerchief, the same cane. But the figure was very still, with the frozen countenance of the dead.

"Say hello to the nice lady," the magician said, speaking gently. The little figure moved forward – and now she caught the look in the magician's eye, saw the glee there, and the anger. He knew she was repulsed, and both enjoyed and was angered by it.

"Shake hands," the man said, and the little boy reached out a hand, mechanically, and Milady shook it. The hand felt soft and smooth – would always feel soft and smooth. It would never grow, never change – and now it held her hand and pressed, and there was strength beyond a boy's strength in it, the little hand beginning to crush the bones in her hand–

She cried out and the magician hissed a command. The boy released her hand and turned around. His hair was black, cut short at the back. It would never grow, never fade.

"What do you want?" the magician said.

"There is a killer in the city," she said, and the magician laughed. "There are many killers in the city," he said. "You should know. You're one of them."

It had taken all their efforts to halt the man's creation. The bride with white hair did not go quietly…

But it had been her work that had finally terminated the creature's "life".

She said, "This killer is different."

"I see," the magician said with a strange, sing-song voice, "a long journey in your future, and a tall dark stranger."

"I didn't come to have my fortune told," she said. "I need a weapon."

"You are going to need more than a weapon," he said, in the same voice. "You are going to need to become a weapon."

It was told that, in the darkness and isolation of his shop, he had perfected machines that could read the future in numbers, predict events and patterns of history beyond even the abilities of the famed Mechanical Turk. And yet he told her nothing…

"I still have my sources," the old man said. "I was once of the Council, and that is not something abandoned lightly. I know about your killer. I know more than you do. I–"

"You've seen the corpses," she said. Thinking of the corpses in the under-morgue, the shifting greys…

"Are they not beautiful? So beautiful… I wish to find where they are going, where they had gone. But the door is not here, it is far away."

"Tell me what you know."

He laughed. The silent boy beside him never stirred again. The magician ruffled the boy's hair and said, "It would take a lifetime and you would be none the wiser at the end of it."

She said, "You know who the killer is." Watched him as the left eye drooped downwards and trailed across his face. He reached, unhurriedly, and put it back. "Will you find him," he said, "– or will he find you, Milady?"

"I need a weapon," she said, and the old man seemed to droop, the fight – if that's what it was – going out of him. "Of course," he said. "I was told you would come. I have it ready."

"Told by whom?"

He shrugged. "The Council."

She felt suddenly trapped in a web of lies. Deceit – she was being led along a path she didn't choose to follow, her every stepped marked in advance by machines more powerful than could be imagined. The old man, as if reading her mind, said, "Sometimes I wish I had no part in it. Our children always supplant us, don't they, Milady? It is the way of the world…"

He spoke to the boy. The boy turned and, without a sound, disappeared into the darkness. "The children…" the old man said.

"He could have grown to be a man, one day," she said. "I'm sorry."

She said it every time and they both knew it made not an ounce of difference.

"Let me give you your gun," the old magician said.

THIRTY-ONE
The Code of Xia

She went into the underworld through the Toymaker's shop. The wide stone stairs were wet with moisture and when she finally reached the dark floor she knew she was under the Seine.

The gun was with her. It was a strange contraption, more similar to a blow-pipe. She had five bullets. The bullets were grey. The grey moved as if it were alive upon the metal. "Whatever you do," the Toymaker said, "never touch them with your bare hands."

Wearing thick gloves, he had loaded the weapon for her. "I don't know if it would kill him," he told her. "But it might just slow him down."

Which was not all that reassuring.

She walked in the darkness under the Seine. Gradually, lights came on, small fires burning – for even here, in the secretive tunnels below the river, there were lives, the refugees from above-ground, those who had nowhere else to go but down into darkness.

She paused there, under the river, imagined she could hear the tug-boats passing overhead, the fish swimming. The British had their whales in the Thames; the Seine, so it was said, had bloated corpses.

She thought about Tom Thumb. She had no doubt he was

not killed for his involvement, or rather, not entirely: he was killed as a message for her.

The killer knew her. And she thought – he does not want the missing object. His goal is different than that of the rest.

There were many searchers, she thought. The Shaolin girl, and the Empress-Dowager's emissary. Herself, of course. But not the killer.

And not, she realised, the lizards. Or, if they were, they were doing it very quietly…

There was the Grey Ghost Gang… She did not understand the world she was entering. Mistress Yi had tried to tell her, a little, on their way from the riverbank. She spoke of Wu Xia, which meant something like Honourable Fight. She spoke of the Code of Xia, of warrior monks without regard for whoever sat on the Imperial Throne in – the Forbidden City? – but only for righteousness, and for–

There was an ancient object that these societies had been guarding. Yet it was – stolen? Had somehow disappeared? – and this all came back to that. The object gave the adherents of Xia power, of sorts, something the girl called Qinggong – The Ability of Lightness. She had seen them fight with the Grey Ghost Gang–

It was all too much. None of it concerned her. Only the killer did. She walked on under the Seine and the ceiling dripped water as she passed.

The denizens of this subterranean world were all around her. Shadows fleeing from shadows… A girl holding an eyeless doll stared at her as she passed. Milady knew that if only she turned to the girl, the girl would flee – just as she herself would have done, at her age. It could have been her standing there – it had been her. A metal beggar shuffled past in a series of click and whirrs. Through a natural opening in the rock face she saw two lizard boys, moving away as she spotted them. She wondered if the killer would come for her here, in this twilight world. She hoped he would.

Instead, it was a beggar who came to her.

She had crossed the river and the tunnel branched ahead. A lone, elderly beggar was sitting cross-legged against a wall. He had long white hair, a black eyepatch over his right eye, and he was dressed in a loose-fitting robe, like a monk's. His eye was closed, but opened at the sound of her footsteps.

An Asian man, but then more than several of the underworld's denizens here had escaped from the above-ground Chinatown. His eye was very bright. His mouth curved into a smile and he said, "Milady de Winter," with only the trace of an accent.

She stopped. The man remained serene. "I had hoped you would come this way," he said. "We have much to talk about."

"Not again," she said, and his smile grew wider. "You think there are many of us searching," he said. "And you are right. You have entered the world of the Jianghu, Milady." The smile faded a little. "It is a dangerous world."

"Which world isn't?" she said, and the man nodded. "Please," he said. "Sit down with me. We will not be disturbed."

She said, "Jianghu?"

"The followers of Xia," he said. "Beings like yourself, Milady."

"I follow no code–"

"No code but the one that matters," he said. "You are Xiake – a follower of Xia, whether you know it or not. Though you lack the skills of the initiates – of those of the Wulin – nevertheless you are one of us."

"And you are?" she said.

"Please, sit down, for just a moment. The night is ending, and the day is near, and you are tired. The one you seek will not reveal himself this close to dawn."

And now he had her interest. But – was dawn so near? She suddenly realised how tired she was. Time had slipped her by, and she hadn't noticed.

"Please," he said, gesturing with his hand, and she nodded, and came closer. When she sat down, opposite him, the old man nodded approvingly. "You move in the way of a cat," he said.

"I'll take that as a compliment," she said dryly, and he laughed. "Who are you?" she said again.

"My name is Long," he said. "Master Long. Here, I go by Ebenezer. Ebenezer Long. Are those enough names for you?"

"You have others?"

"I have many names. Names are... fluid. What, after all, is in a name? You yourself have had several, have you not?"

"Master Long..." she said. "You seem very well informed."

"I have been around for a long time," he said.

"And you are from – what?" She tried to recall the names. "Wudang? Shaolin?"

He laughed. "As much as I belong," he said, "you could say I am of the Beggars' Guild."

She said, "Just how many guilds do you have?"

He shrugged. "Over the centuries there have been hundreds. Some change, some disappear. New ones are formed. We are all of us of the Wulin, the followers of that which is now lost."

"And which you are all trying to recover?"

"Indeed. Though it is not here, in Paris, that it lies. What came here, I suspect, is only a fragment of the object called the Emerald Buddha – though its outer casing is made of pure jade, not emerald, despite the name – an object which should not have existed and, though it does, should have never been activated."

"You talk as if it is a kind of machine."

He said, "Oh, it is most certainly that."

So the object had a name. And what had been surgically inserted into Yong Li's belly – was that a fragment of this thing? She said, "What is the Emerald Buddha?"

Master Long said, "That is a good question. I am not sure I

know – that anyone truly knows."

Riddles upon riddles... She said, "So what do you know?"

"It is the pure jade statue of a royal lizard," he said. "Pure on the outside, at least. Its eyes are emerald. Its inside had never been examined, though not for lack of trying. It was found..."

And there, in the darkness of the catacombs, he told her a story.

THIRTY-TWO
Master Long's Story

The Emerald Buddha was found one day by a boy walking along with his camel in the desert. The desert was a great one and the boy loved it. He loved the wide open expanse of sky, the endless horizon, the always-shifting nature of the land. There were sand dunes that rose into the sky and when the boy slid down their sides on his back they made a deep, rumbling sound, as if the sand itself was talking. There were low-lying, evergreen hills, and a place where, between two mountains, a river snaked in frozen splendour, and you could walk upon its surface and, reaching the end, drink ice-cold water as it slowly melted… There were rivers and lakes, and places where nothing grew. There was everything in the desert.

The boy came from a migratory people. For untold generations they had wandered the desert, through harsh summers and brutal winters, through extremes of heat and cold, pitching their great tents wherever they went, their horses and camels and cattle with them. They made alcohol from the milk of the camels, and drank it on the long nights. The camels were double-humped. The boy's camel – his first one, and his alone – was an ill-tempered beast, but the boy loved him for all that. The boy's family were passing through one of the most arid parts of the desert, and the boy had become fascinated by his grandfather's stories, which told of a place far away where the bones of giant creatures jutted out of the sand. They were of some enormous beasts that had walked the world long ago, when the world was young.

The boy had decided to see them for himself.

He had packed food for the journey, his crossbow and his spear and his knife, and plenty of water, and he took his camel. The caravan of migrating families moved slowly; he knew he could easily catch up with it, sooner or later. He could read the maps of the desert, and had travelled this road, back and forth, ever since he was born and even before, as an embryo in his mother's womb.

But he had never seen the giants' bones.

He saw the small bones of many other creatures on his way. To die in this part of the desert meant to remain forever in the spot where the sun had finally caught you. There were skeletal camels and skeletal cows and, once, a grinning human skull on top of a pile of stones. Where his people passed they had assembled these places, mounds of stones that lay all across the desert, and when they passed them they left small presents there for the spirits of the place – offerings of food and drink, blue ribbons of cloth tied to twigs jutting from the stones – and sometimes their dead.

The boy found the place two days after having set off. The story his grandfather had told him was true. It was the silent graveyard of giants.

For a long time he walked amidst the bones, marvelling at how impossible they were. Enormous creatures, with skulls the size of boulders, with ribcages as large as houses. He had been warned by his grandfather that the place was sacred: he must take nothing he might find.

And the boy was happy to merely look – until he saw the flash of green light in the sands…

Some time in the distant past, he saw, the ground here had been disturbed. A small crater lay further away from the giants' bones, and the sand had fused into a sort of greenish glass. He walked over to it, for it was not the glass he had seen.

Something was buried in the sand, in the centre of the crater. Something that flashed a beautiful jade green.

"Those who tell the story of the Emerald Buddha tell it differently," Master Long said. "It is said it was made in India, many centuries ago, and had since travelled widely across the civilised world – around Asia, I should say – always claimed, never resting. From India to Ceylon, and from there to Burma, and from Burma to Luang Prabang, and to Siam... The king of Siam lays a claim to it, and so do half a dozen other emperors and kings, from the Forbidden City to Angkor Wat. It is a statue of jade in the shape of a royal lizard – and here lies its mystery, and the wrong at the centre of the tale. For how could an Indian artificer, however talented, fashion a statue in the shape of beings not seen in the world at that time?"

She tried to imagine it, and fear took hold of her. The lizards had changed the world when they were awakened by Vespucci all those years ago. They had claimed the British Isles for their own, and set about conquering the known world, assembling to themselves colonies and protectorates as if they were blocks in a child's game. How long had they lain dormant on Caliban's Island before being awakened? And where had they come from?

From space, if the stories were true...

"Stories," Master Long said, "are true for what they tell us about ourselves more than for their own internal truth." He smiled, though it seemed to her there was mostly sadness in the expression. "Let me tell you about the boy..."

What it was, he didn't know. And yet it seemed to speak to him, a babble of voices rising in his mind, saying unfathomable things.

Testing language modules... initiating geo-spatial surveillance... mind scan initiated... complete... audio-visual reconstruction activated... long-range scan returning negative... help us, boy! We are in the sand.

Something hidden, something talking to him, confusing his thoughts. The camel watched him for a while without much interest, then wandered off in search of shade. The boy tried to dig into the sand but it was hard as glass. He tried to smash it but it was strong. And all the while the voices spoke, an insane babble of them, promising him untold riches and eternal life...

"The boy was young then, and had dreams of glory," Master Long said. "Of riches beyond compare, and dusky maidens, of conquest and victory and admiration and glory... but I suspect that, even without it, he would have liberated the statue. For nothing but curiosity, Milady. It is what makes us human, in the final count. More than love, more than hate, more than dreams of immortality or glory – it is curiosity that–"

"Killed the cat?"

"What?" He looked at her, then shrugged. "Quite."

The boy's hands were bloodied, the nails torn, the knuckles bruised. Still he worked. With knife and spear until they broke, and then he used rocks, smashing them against the ground again and again, unheeding of the need for food or drink or shelter.

The voices spoke their insane babble: Biological life form unrecognised. Checksum negative. Biological energy levels low. Initiating molecular restructuring. Feasibility study incomplete. What is this place?

The sun burned him. The camel was nowhere to be seen. Time held no meaning to him.

Only the thing in the ground.

At last, he managed to dig a small hole. Underneath, the sand was soft and he cleared it away and pulled out his prize.

A green monster of a lizard stared back at him.

"It was not yet jade, you see," Master Long said. "That came later, and the eyes. What the boy saw was a lizard, yes, but it was slimmer then, without the camouflage of human workmanship. It was an alien thing, something he did not – could not – understand. It was made by tools and beings unknown and, I think, perhaps unknowable. It was made of a strange green metal–"

She thought of the green metal the lizards had brought with them from Caliban's Island. Master Long nodded, as if reading her mind.

"Was it some tool of the lizards, unknowingly discarded? Had it come with them from their home and fallen down to Earth? It is possible. Other things have materialised that should not have been. It is said the Bookman himself was once a creature of the lizards... has been said, and very quietly, at that, these past three years."

"There had not been a Bookman assassination in all this time," Milady said. Master Long nodded. "Three years since the Bookman was last heard of. Three years since the revolution on the British Isles. A lot can happen in three years, Milady de Winter."

And she thought – the grey manifestations had began less than three years ago – began, perhaps, just after the time of the upheavals...

The boy held the statue in his arms, cradling it as he would a baby. When he went looking for his camel he did not find it, though the skeleton of a camel lay nearby. He could not remember when he had last eaten or drank, but the voices spoke to him and comforted him and offered him nourishment.

He held the statue and began to walk across the desert, searching for the caravan of his family and his friends.

"But he never found them," Master Long said, and there was infinite sadness in his voice when he spoke. "Time had passed differently in that place of old bones in the desert, and when the boy returned to the world, the world had irrevocably changed.

"He never saw his family again."

THIRTY-THREE
Lord of Light

The silence lay between them, as heavy as a gun. She said, "How long ago...?"

He said, "It is only a story. It happened long ago, in another time and place."

"I hardly knew my parents," she said, not knowing where the words came from. "I came on the ship. My father died in the war–"

"Which war?"

She shrugged, a helpless gesture. "It was not an important one. It did not justify having its own name."

"Most wars are forgotten," he said. "And most of the dead."

She said, "My mother was with me on the ship... I remember the waves crashing against the hull. I remember being very sick. She was with me... Then, one day, she wasn't there. And then we arrived in this new continent, this new alien world, where people had pale skins and spoke an alien tongue. And I was alone."

"But you survived."

She said, "I had to."

Master Long stirred. She had not realised how still he was – as still as an automaton, she thought. He said, "And now you work for them."

"For the machines," she said. He looked at her for a long

time. "The world may have been a very different place," he said at last, "without the presence of either lizards or thinking machines... Whether it would have been better or worse, though, I cannot say."

She let it pass. She said, "What happened to the boy? From your story?"

He smiled, though there was sadness in it. "Centuries later," Master Long said, "the boy's people conquered Chung Kuo, the land of the Han. Then they fell back into their old ways. They still roam the desert, still raise camels and cows."

"And the boy?"

"It is said," Master Long said, and smiled, and his single eye glittered, "that he journeyed for many years, beyond a mortal's life, and found at last an isolated place in the high mountains and stayed there. And though he grew up he never grew old, and he communed with the Emerald Buddha, and learned much that was hidden, and practised wushu and Qinggong, the way of light..."

"What was his name then?" she said, and the old man shook his head. "Who can remember?" he said. "It is told that a man who was not exactly a man had lived in the mountains and there, over the years, others had found him, and came to learn with him. It became a monastery, of a sort, and its name was Shaolin. But these are only legends, and there had been many such places over the centuries, followers of the Emerald Buddha – for it is told that the Buddha is asleep, and had been for thousands of years, but that one day it would wake and change the world. I once spoke with a woman who told me there are many worlds, all lying close to each other. It is said the Emerald Buddha is a key, a way to open doors between the worlds. The orders of the Jianghu were formed to guard it, to keep it sleeping. There is great danger when two alien worlds meet."

She thought of what he said and they sat together in silence, the tall Dahomey woman and the short Master Long.

"What happened three years ago?" she said.

"The Change," he said. "Yes... you ask good questions, none of which I have answers to. Perhaps the fat man you are seeking can answer that one."

One moment he was sitting down. The next he was on his feet, and offering her his hand, though she did not see him move. "But it is too late now, or too early. The sun is climbing once again into the sky, and you should sleep."

She took his hand. He pulled her up to her feet. "I have to keep going," she said. "I have to find–"

"The answers will wait," Master Long said. "They have waited long enough, after all. Rest, and tomorrow you shall have your answers – though at what cost even I do not know. But we will help, as much as we can."

"An old magician told me I would be..." She swayed on her feet. She was suddenly so tired she could barely stand. "I would meet a tall dark stranger and go on a long journey... Are you that stranger?"

Master Long laughed. "I am not exactly tall," he said.

"And he said..." She swayed again. Her eyes were closing, the darkness closing in. "He said, a weapon won't be enough. That I should... I should have to become a weapon. What do you think he meant?"

But there was no longer any answer, or if there was, she could not hear it. Her eyes closed and wouldn't open again, and she felt herself sinking into the blackness, into a thick and dreamless sleep where nothing came.

INTERLUDE
The Other Side of the River

Days became nights and nights blended into days, until he could no longer distinguish the periods of light and dark or the changing of the seasons. The world Kai walked in was shifting around him, changing in unexpected ways. It was a twilight world, an autumn world, where the bright green of rice gave way to the murky colour of a flooding river. It was like walking through perpetual mist, through low-lying grey clouds.

The statue still spoke to Kai, but more and more he felt that the statue's attention was turned elsewhere. The statue spoke of energy burst source unknown subsystems brought online, and about trans-dimensional shift parameters aligned and about proximity cluster confirmed, bipolar transfer engaged and, last and unexpected: home.

Home was something he no longer had. Chiang Rai disappeared behind the mist as if it had never existed, the steam-filled shop and his father at work and Kai playing with the other kids in the road and reading wuxia novels by candlelight – all gone, washed away by rolling grey mists.

He travelled on foot, became used to the thick jungle, knew to avoid the poisonous plants and the lairs of bears and snakes and tigers and the isolated homes of the Karen people. He knew where to find their traps and knew how to make his own, which fruits to eat and which to leave. He avoided roads and whenever he saw elephant prints he hid, afraid of riders nearby.

At last he came to the big water. Mekong, he thought, the word rising in him like a lone bubble. The river was wide and filled with water to the banks and it rained every day, lightning lashing across the sky like a whip, the thunder like cannon fire echoing all around him, the sound of war. He walked along the bank in the direction of the mountains.

There were people using the river, of course. There were villages with bamboo huts standing on stilts above the water, and fisherfolk in canoes or wading through the shallows with nets. There were children playing in the water and there were barges and cargo boats travelling in both directions, many of them Chinese, like his father, and some of them from Siam, like his mother had been. And many others, too – dark men from the mountains and light ones from the lowlands far away, and Europeans – he had once seen one, an exotic creature visiting the town of Chiang Rai. There were steamboats, too, and he marvelled at them, delighted with the way they moved and churned the water, these great hulking beasts that belonged to the king of Siam. He hid when boats passed and he stole food from the villages if he could, and caught fish and small birds and animals. All the while he was going somewhere, but he didn't yet know where.

One day he stole a canoe and crossed to the other side of the river.

It was during a thunderstorm. The statue liked the storm. Somehow, it acted as an attractor for the lightning, yet it never hit Kai, nor the statue. The lightning struck all around them, him and the statue, and it was as if they were encased in a bubble, and it glowed in blues and greys, crackling with electricity, and the statue would talk of utilising natural energy sources and renewable power supplies and reinforcing multi-dimensional boundaries. When he crossed the river he was very scared, though the fear was different now, the fear was like a polished stone that he held in his hand, a force that could be transmuted into pure power, be made into a cold hard fury and be controlled. When he crossed the river it was as if the two banks would never meet, as if he had left one behind him while the other kept receding away in the distance. The current was very strong and soon he was being borne along it without control, his choices reduced to none. He let the current take him where it would. On the river, the two worlds, the two banks seemed impossibly distant from each other, the outlines of two separate worlds. In one was laughter and sunlight and new shoots of rice, ginger and jasmine and dry cleaners and steamboats and love. In the other was… what? The unknown. The statue longed for it – a darkness, and strange stars, and massive structures floating in the inky black…

How long he drifted on the river he didn't know. He drank the water of the Mekong and caught fish with bare hands, and ate them raw. Boats came and went but never seemed to see him. When the storms came he huddled in the small canoe and the lightning danced around him, and the statue glowed as if satisfied. Then, one day, he came around a bend in the river and saw a city.

PART III
The Man in the Iron Mask

THIRTY-FOUR
The Woman in the Mirror

Drippety-drip, drippety-drap the sound came, light fingers tapping on the window, a low wind blowing pipes of poisoned darts, the darkness pulsing like a heart, drippety-drip, drippety–

Splat.

Her eyes opened.

She was lying in her bed.

She had no recollection of how she had arrived there.

Outside the window it was raining, and the wind was howling a mournful tune. When she got up she half-expected more assailants to come through the door but the house was hushed and empty. She went into her drawing room and Grimm was there, curled up in the fireplace, and she stroked him, and the metallic insect turned its head so it rested in the palm of her hands. Its skin felt warm. The hiss of a tongue touched her palm like a kiss.

She knew she was close to the killer. She had missed something, she thought. But she knew he was close, that he was hunting her just as much as she was hunting him. For the moment, the question of the missing object did not occupy her as much. Also, it seemed obvious to her that when she found the killer, she would find this object, this key. Had it been used already? She thought of the killer, a grey grotesque shape in the dark of an alleyway. The corpses Viktor showed her in the under-morgue… yes. It had been used, and if not this one then another like it. And something had come through from the other side… or something here had been corrupted.

When she stepped into her waiting room there was an envelope on the table. She tore it open. It contained a ticket to a ball, to take place that evening at the Hotel de Ville. An appended note was stamped with the Council's emblem, and a handwritten scrawl said, *"British ambassador and entourage to attend – V."*

She was going to a ball. Wasn't there a children's story about this sort of thing? She smiled, though the expression felt grim on her face. She didn't feel like dancing – she felt like shooting someone. Some thing.

She had a feeling it would not be long before she had her opportunity.

She watched herself in the mirror. The long coat trailed down almost to her feet, the gun in its shoulder-holster, the other gun on her hips. She wore a dark scarf and a silk blouse and her black leather pants, and when she looked at herself in the mirror she saw a tall dark woman with eyes reflecting grey. Her nails were a dark red. As a final touch she put on her old hat, from the Barnum days, her time in the ring. Low-brimmed, it shaded her eyes. The horse riders of Vespuccia wore those when they rode the trails, on that massive open continent where the buffalo roamed…

She went back to the fireplace and Grimm rustled awake. "Stay close to me tonight," she murmured, her hand on its head, and the creature blinked in acquiescence. The gold bracelet on her arm would let Grimm know where she was. And now she stood up, ready to face the coming night.

The ball, yes, but first–

•••

The silent coachman dropped her off at Place Pigalle. She looked around for watchers, saw none, knew they would be nearby. She had begun to realise her role in this investigation, her real purpose there. No one cared if she caught the killer, the Council least of all. No – she was there to bring them all out, rather, all the silent watchers – bring them out into the open so they could be seen and studied and made known. She passed the cemetery on the way to the gendarmes. Something seemed to call to her from inside that factory of graves. There had been stories... She walked away and into the station, and almost ran into the Gascon.

For a moment, their bodies had almost collided. She felt the warmth of him, his tautness, no fat on him, a wiry man as driven as she was–

The Gascon pulled back. She could not read the look in his eyes. He examined her slowly, from head to toe, and shook his head. Around them a silence fell like snow. "Gunslinger," he said at last. She smiled, touched the brim of her hat in acknowledgment. "Inspector," she said. "What do you have for me?"

"Very little," he said. "I heard you found another corpse. You seem to have a knack for finding people dead."

She said, "Tom was a friend."

He nodded. "Mademoiselle L'Espanaye is safe," he said. "My men have tracked down the killer's escape route." He hesitated. "It seems he had made his way to the cemetery – beyond that we lost his tracks."

Somehow she was not surprised – and now she said, "What happened in the cemetery?" and watched his face. Yes – the question hit him hard. "What makes you think anything happened?"

She thought of the corpses in the under-morgue. And now she said, only half-guessing – "Have any graves been robbed in the past two years?"

The Gascon stared at her, not speaking. "And you can offer

me a cup of coffee while you tell me," she said, and he slowly smiled. "Yes, Milady," he said.

When they sat down the man seemed to relax a little. He said, "Yes, there have been. We've kept it quiet – as much as possible. Rumours got out, naturally."

"Naturally," she said, without inflection, and he gave her a sharp look before catching himself. He shrugged, ceding her the point. "There is a... caretaker in the cemetery," he said. "But he would not speak to us, and I'm afraid we can't press him."

And now he watched her, waiting – "Who is it?" she said, and his smile was predatory when he said, "What he is might be a better question, Milady."

THIRTY-FIVE
Ampère

No one knew much about André-Marie Ampère. In life he had been a scientist, obsessed with the study of electricity. When his wife died he was distressed to the point of confusion. She had once heard Viktor speak of him – in reverence. He was born, had lived, and died – only he hadn't, not quite...

There were simulacrums in the world, and that was only natural. There were machines that could almost pass for human, and humans who, one thought, too closely resembled machines. It was told the Bookman could remake the dead, reassemble them into living things once again... and perhaps Ampère was one of his creatures, though who could tell? He was born and lived a man, he died – and now he lived, if such a word could be used, alone and undisturbed in the Montmartre Cemetery, in a small stone building beside his very own grave.

What was he? A copy of a man? A machine? A ghost?

She did not believe in ghosts. "Did you search the Clockwork Room?" she said. The Gascon nodded. "We found nothing. Whatever meeting was arranged there, they did not leave anything behind."

She did not suspect that they did. She would confront the fat man soon enough, she thought. But now she had the traces of the killer and she was going to follow them, wherever they may lead.

"Ampère was one of the Council, once," she said.

"When he was still living?" the Gascon said.

"No."

"Ah."

She knew he did not like the machines. Few people did, though they accepted them, lived with them, and to a large extent let them decide their lives. And so she said, "I'll go alone."

He said, "No–" but she knew the fight wasn't in him. "As you said, he won't see you. I have the authority–"

Knowing that was another thing that made the Gascon unhappy.

It had stopped raining, and the night air felt cool and fresh. And she liked cemeteries.

They were peaceful places. They were humanity's way of acknowledging change, of laying down the past. The dead did not rise again. They were absorbed into the earth, became, in time, something new, the dying bodies recycled and reused. Cemeteries were quiet and filled with a sense of space and quiet purpose.

Though now she could see one part of it was not so quiet. And it was still raining where she was going, though it was a strange, localised storm...

The graves rose all around her, elaborate houses for the dead, though the dead could no longer appreciate them. And there – a miniature castle where the storm hovered, lightning flashing, again and again as it hit a metal pole rising from the turrets.

Gargoyle-faced edifice... And now she saw they were not, as was common, lizardine, but something different. And she wondered what Ampère really knew, and had he ever been east, for they were shaped like grey and faceless ghosts.

She walked through the drops and reached the door and

banged on it. She heard movement inside. She could see how this place would have appealed to the murderer – but she did not expect him to be there. She waited and Ampère opened the door.

He was dressed in black, as if in mourning. Whoever fashioned him had done a good job. He moved without stiffness, and his eyes looked very life-like. The face was unlined, and she knew it would never age. Though the machine might run down, one day...

He said, "Milady de Winter?" His voice was scratchy, old, incompatible with the face. It occurred to her he might have built himself, once upon a time, and the machine kept adding new parts but could not change the voice. She wondered if there were jars of moist artificial eyes in his pantry, different colours for different occasions. She wouldn't look – it was altogether too likely.

"I've been expecting you. Please, come inside." He gestured at the sky, the storm. Lightning flashed above them. "I've been working."

"I can see."

She followed him inside. "Though I am retired from the Council my work still concerns–" Then he stopped, and the machine allowed itself a small, wan smile. It looked very natural. "I'm afraid I can't help you," he said.

And machines could lie so much better than humans ever did...

"How long have you lived here?" she said.

"Over fifty years. Ever since I – ever since my predecessor died. He constructed this lab for me and paid for it along with his tomb."

"You research electricity."

"I research life," he said, and smiled again. She did not return the smile and the machine she was talking to dropped it. "I study the fundamental powers," Ampère said and she said, only half-listening – "Why here?"

"Why not? It is quiet, isolated. I am seldom disturbed."

"Until the dead began to rise?" she said, and he didn't move. "When did it begin, two, three years ago? Was it something you noticed, or was it something you made happen? Tell me!"

"Milady," he said, "your accusations are quite baseless."

What if there had been another key? Another transaction from the Man on the Mekong, as Fei Linlin had called him? Another fragment offered? She said, "Viktor showed me the corpses. But I don't think they were the only ones."

"Viktor and I are not in the same line of work," he said.

"Are you harbouring a killer?" she said.

"What?"

"I need to know."

"What I do," he said, "I do for the Council."

And now the suspicion she had been trying to avoid voicing resurfaced. She said, "He has to be stopped–" and watched Ampère take a step back, then stand very still. "He is killing the living, now," she said.

"He always did…" The words were a whisper.

"Tell me."

The automaton shook itself awake. "Go," he said. "I–"

"No."

Lightning struck the roof, the sound echoing through the dark hall of the miniature castle. "I have to go," he said. "I have to finish the work – come back to see me. I will tell you what you want to know–"

And now a sound rose from the back of the hall, coming from behind a closed door, and Ampère glanced back and then at her, and moved to push her out. "You must go. Hurry! Come back to see me when the night is deep."

A growling sound, growing louder. "Go!"

She took out her gun in one swift motion and put the barrel against his neck. The automaton stood still. "Make sure to be here when I come back," she said. Then the gun was gone, an act of magic, and she stepped out of that dark dead room and into the cool air outside. She had the feeling of unseen eyes watching her. She walked away from the castle and the lightning cracked behind her, filling up the sky with violent blue electricity.

THIRTY-SIX
The Lizardine Ambassador

And so Milady de Winter went to the ball.

Out there, beyond the windows of her carriage, the silent watchers watched. She could sense them there, these intrusions into an orderly world. Xiake, Master Long had called her – a follower of Xia, whatever that meant. A code beyond government or law, the way of righteousness.

She did not feel very righteous. She felt tired, consumed by three days of not eating properly, of running around chasing shadows, of being kidnapped and assaulted and watching people die before her, and not knowing why. Outside the Hotel de Ville there were carriages, hansom cabs, baruch-landaus, liveried footmen and lounging drivers, the usual Parisian crowd gathered to watch festivities to which they were not invited. There were roast chestnut sellers, newspaper boys, booksellers from their little domain by the Seine, beggars, portrait artists, photographers, and the air smelled of the mix of chemicals from the baruch-landau vehicles and the steaming manure of the more traditional horse-drawn cabs. The air smelled of chestnuts and caramelised peanuts; and lightning flashed overhead in silence, the thunder too far away, as yet, to be heard.

She stepped out of the carriage and the silent driver with his stitched-up face drove away.

Photographers – and now she recognised one of them. He tried to walk away when he saw her coming. She grabbed him by the arm and saw his face twist with the unexpected pain. She said, "What are you doing here?"

It was the photographer from the Rue Morgue. The one whose camera she had smashed against the wall. It felt like months ago. It wasn't.

He didn't speak and the pressure on his arm increased, Milady finding the nerves, her long fingernails driving into the man's flesh. And now he said, "He sent me! Let me go!"

"D–" no, she would not say his name, "The Gascon sent you? To take pictures of the guests? Why?"

His face was pale. He did not relish being there. He said, "He thinks... he thinks..."

She let go of his arm. He rubbed it, shying away from her. "He thinks the killer might make an appearance?" she said, and the man nodded.

"Clever Gascon..." she whispered, and then she smiled. The photographer melted into the crowd. Very well. She wondered what the Gascon knew, or what he guessed at. She went through the gates and up to the building.

The Hotel de Ville – municipality building, mayor's house, the beating heart of the urban metropolis of Paris. The Seine was nearby, carrying ferries, rafts, fallen flowers, fish and the occasional human corpse. The smell of it wafted through the air and was replaced, as she stepped through the doors into the Hotel de Ville's ballroom, by the stench of expensive perfumes, canapés, polish, engine oil and something she could not quite discern until she turned and found herself, suddenly and without warning, beside a tall royal lizard.

Les Lézards. She had never expected that, and it always came as a surprise to her, no matter how many she had met before in the English court: their smell was different. She couldn't quite describe it. The ambassador (for that was who it must be) smelled of the warmth of rocks in the late afternoon, of swamps and – very faintly – of eau de cologne.

He was tall and – she thought – elderly. He towered above her, green-skinned but for bands of colouration that ran across his body, and his tongue hissed out as if tasting the air. He was dressed in an expensive, understated suit. His tail looked formidable, like a weapon. And now he turned to her and said, "Milady de Winter, I presume?"

She nodded, trying to remember him from the court and failing. The ambassador took her hand in both of his, bent down gracefully and kissed her – the tongue flicking out again, the touch of it like electricity against her skin. When he straightened up he seemed to be smiling.

"You were married to Lord de Winter?" he said. "A most charming man. Often we went hunting together at Balmoral."

The Queen's remote estate, in Scotland – so the ambassador was high up in the lizards' social order. Which wasn't surprising–

"His death was most unfortunate," the ambassador said.

"Yes…" Milady said, and the ambassador again seemed to smile. His tongue flicked out again, disappeared back into the elongated mouth. "And so you have returned to the place of your childhood? It must have been a pleasant childhood indeed."

She thought of the small girl running in the night, of the abandoned houses where predators roamed… "Very," she said, giving him a smile full of teeth. They were playing a game – and she thought it was no coincidence, the ambassador standing just there as she came in. She wondered if he really had known her husband, or whether he was merely reading out of her dossier. Well, perhaps it was both. "Sometimes when I was hungry I'd catch geckos and roast them on the fire – you had to stick a sharpened wood branch into them to stop them wriggling."

"Indeed." He reared back, looked down on her. And now there was nothing friendly in his face at all. "You have been luckier than your husband, it seems..." he said. "Be careful that your luck doesn't run out."

She moved her coat aside, just a little, and saw his eyes fasten on the gun. "I'm always careful," she said, and the lizard hissed.

"Ambassador," a voice said, close by, and she turned, startled, for she had not heard the man approach. "You must meet this absolutely charming mechanical–"

She had not heard the fat man approach. And now she watched him stir the lizardine ambassador away, towards an ancient man-shaped automaton on the other side of the ballroom... She followed him with her eyes and for just a moment the fat man turned back and winked at her.

THIRTY-SEVEN
The Electric Ball

The ballroom was filled with revellers. Metal globes hung from the high ceiling and lightning flashed between them back and forth – a Tesla invention, if she recalled correctly, but one that seemed ill-suited for a night's entertainment. She looked around her and realised something had been missing from her invitation: it was a masked ball.

She should have expected that.

The lizardine ambassador, of course, was bare-faced. And the automatons' faces were masks all by themselves – though some, she saw, had joined in the spirit of the event and wore elaborate mechanical masks that changed expressions in a sequence or randomly, it was hard to tell. The humans, most of them, were masked. She saw chieftains from Vespuccia in their elaborate headdresses and what she knew to be war paint, short men armed with decorative shields from the Zulu kingdom accompanying a young woman, Indian rajahs with diamonds in their hats, Aztec priests in their garb – the cream of the diplomatic circle of Paris, all gathered here for the electric ball.

She looked around for someone from Dahomey but the place was too full and besides, she had left the place too long ago. Her links with the old country had been severed one by one, and now none remained, and she was a citizen of–

Of what? of the Republic? Of the lizards' court? She belonged to all of these, and none. Perhaps she really was Xiake, a member of the secretive world Master Long had called the Wulin. She didn't know where her loyalties truly lay, but she knew what was right, and she knew what she had to do. What had to be done.

And the Gascon was right, she thought. Somewhere in the throngs of masked women and men the killer, too, was dancing.

A band of automatons was providing the music from a dais at the back of the hall, a player piano and a steam-powered orchestra. The lightning crackled overhead without thunder, electricity jumping from one spinning globe to another, casting odd shadows onto the dance floor, like a fractured mirror. And there – dancing together, a handsome young couple, both masked with the faces of some sort of fantastical animals – Mistress Yi and her shadow Ip Kai? She watched them as they circled the room, holding each other, moving fluidly with the dance, and yet – she could sense their awareness, the way they watched the room. And now she thought – there are many watchers here tonight.

They were not alone.

Here and there, the Gascon's men, trying and failing to blend, shouting gendarmes in the way they stood, the way they watched – the way they drank, for that matter. And now another familiar body waylaid her, and for a second time this evening she was taken aback.

He was young and very beautiful, with his bare chest and his mask of a tiger, and he swept her up in his arms for a dance. "Remember me?"

The voice and the physique… "The bartender at the Moulin Rouge?"

"I hoped we'd meet again. You are very beautiful."

"So are you," she said, meaning it, and he laughed. "I would like to make love to you," he said. She had to smile. He carried her effortlessly, a born dancer, and she said, "Perhaps when all this is over…"

"The ball?"

"Not exactly…" She gently pushed him away and he twirled back and bowed. "At your service, Milady," he said. Then he danced away and into the throng, and was soon engulfed in the arms of another woman.

… who was familiar, also. A woman who needed no mask, for she wore one as a matter of course. Madame Linlin, who danced with the young man for a minute, then turned to speak with a minister and his entourage – the old lady making an appearance in an official capacity, then? Milady couldn't spot Colonel Xing, which told her nothing. She suspected he, and at least some of his men, where somewhere in the crowd.

Well, well… this ball was certainly turning out to be more interesting than she'd thought.

"Milady!"

She stared at him. "Viktor?"

"Wonderful party!"

The scientist had replaced his habitual smock with evening wear, a jaunty black hat sat at an angle on his head, and his mask was that of her coachman, the stitched-up face of a monster. "What the hell are you doing here?"

"Dancing!" the scientist said. "They gave me the night off."

"The Council?"

"Shh!" He made an exaggerated sign, finger to his lips. And now she could smell the alcohol. "I'm off-duty."

"I thought you preferred the company of the dead," she said, and he shrugged. "The dead don't dance, and they seldom drink."

She let it pass, said, "Who's on in the under-morgue?"

Viktor smirked. "You think someone's going to rob the morgue?"

Something cold slid slowly down her spine. Something was wrong, and the Council… She did not trust the Council.

"Have you seen Tômas?" Viktor asked. There was something a little too casual in the way he said it, and it gave her pause.

"Tômas?"

Viktor had told her, hadn't he? Memory returned. Tômas had been in charge of the body-snatching duty, retrieving the grey-infected corpses. Tômas the cruel, the master of disguises, Tômas who they called the Phantom – and now suspicion bloomed. She thought about the Council. What were they planning? And she thought – I am their bait – but who are they hunting?

"I shall speak with you later!" Viktor said, too brightly and, turning, hurried off after a troupe of green-painted, scantily clad dancers.

The lightning flashed and flashed overhead. Something in Milady wanted to forget the currents, forget the other world, the murders, the futile chase for a thing that had no right to exist. Drink, she thought, and dance, and be merry – but she wasn't sure she remembered how. Find that beautiful young dancer...

Then she thought of Tom Thumb lying on the Seine's bank with his throat cut, the grey swirls moving on his skin as if they were alive. Alive and hungry, she thought. And–

The killer must be amongst the crowd.

But which one of the masked creatures was he?

THIRTY-EIGHT
The Fat Man

"Drink?"

She swirled round – and found herself at last facing the elusive fat man. "Mr Holmes," she said, and the man smiled. Unlike the rest of the crowd, he was not wearing a mask. "Always a pleasure to be recognised," he said, though she thought a hint of irritation had crept somewhere in there. And, "Please, call me Mycroft."

"Mycroft," she said. "In our line of work it doesn't pay to be recognised too often."

"Yet who could fail to recognise such a beautiful woman as yourself, Milady de Winter?" he said, and she smiled back, the boundaries stated, the chess pieces aligned.

"You are British Intelligence?" she said. He shrugged, and she said, "They say it is an oxymoron."

His face wore a pained expression. "Please," he said. "Let us not engage in hostilities."

"Yet," she said. "Is that what you mean?"

"I'm not sure I follow..."

"Are we heading to war?" she said.

"You and I, Milady? Never."

"Britain and France," she said. "Lizard and machine. Is that what this has all been about?"

"Please," he said. "Relieve me of my burden–" handing her

a flute of champagne which she accepted but did not drink. "The white man's burden..." she said, and he laughed. "I want to know how Yong Li died," she said, watching him carefully. The fat man's face became carefully blank. "I am not familiar with that name..."

"The man you met at the Clockwork Room," she said. "The man who showed you an impossible thing, the pictures of another world. Am I correct so far?"

"I'll admit I'm impressed," Mycroft Holmes said. "I take it from what you say that Captain Li is dead?"

"Please," she said. "We can speak candidly, here."

The fat man took a deep breath, let it out slowly. "Very well," he said. Around them dancers moved, the music played. The harmless lightning flashed overhead.

"Did you kill him?"

"No."

She nodded slowly, approving. "A straight answer," she said.

"Then I shall be candid further with you," Mycroft Holmes said. "I do not know who killed him. It was not... it was not our work."

"Did he show you what you wanted to see?"

"What we wanted to see?" He made a helpless gesture with the hand holding his almost-empty glass. "I did not want to see what Captain Li had to show. But to close one's eyes, Milady, does not make unpalatable things go away."

"And what," she said, "did you see?"

Mycroft's face a sudden grey cloud...

Imagine a camera obscura, Mycroft told her. Imagine a box of wood through which light travels. An image is projected onto a screen. Imagine a series of such images, flickering like grey shadows on a wall – what do they show? They are not reality, are not, perhaps, even an accurate representation but something else, an obscurity of form that hides rather than reveals. What do you see? What lies beyond, in the source of the light, beyond the images revealed?

"I saw the future," he said, very softly. The silence, grey

and featureless, grew a gulf between them. "You saw another world," she said.

"Yes. Almost within reach…"

She said, "What do you intend to do with such knowledge?"

"What will your own Council do?" he said. And now she had to consider him, looking down at the fat man, thinking – "But what makes you think the Council is aware–" she began, and he interrupted her. "Please, Milady. Let us not play games. This was not the first approach made, nor the last. A door has been opened, and it lies – for now, at least – in the east. What may come through it is a worry and a danger – but what may be gained by passing through it to the other side, now, that is another matter altogether…"

"Could you take control of it, though?" she said, and saw she had hit a spot with him. "You will try," she said. "And so will we…"

"And so will the Chinese," he said. "Unless we can all work together…"

"Is that likely?"

"No," he admitted.

"You would try to use it?" Another thought struck her. "Or close it?"

He smiled, and there was nothing pleasant in the expression on his face. "That is the question…" he said softly. "Would you excuse me? There is someone I must see…"

"Of course," she said, and he nodded to her. "Please remain well," he said. "It would be a shame…"

He turned away before she could reply. It did not entirely surprise her to see him, moments later, chatting quietly to Madame Linlin on the other side of the hall.

This was how matters of politics and diplomacy were decided – how lives were added and subtracted, wars decided upon, like this – in a ballroom full of music and dancing and drink, in a civilised manner – in the manner of people who decided others' death without risk to their own.

And what would be the end result?

THIRTY-NINE
The Phantom

She waited and the dancing grew more frenetic around her, the drinks liberating the crowd, the dresses twirling, the music loud, the masks slipping as the humans celebrated – what? The air was thick with cigar smoke and a hint of opium, with spilled wine and the combined sweat of so many people. She needed fresh air. She turned to leave. She stood by the cloakroom and it was quiet there, and a little cool air came in from the outside, refreshing her.

A step beside her. She turned and saw a man wearing an iron mask, the way prisoners were once masked.

"Milady de Winter," the voice said. It was a familiar voice. He was dressed as an automaton, the iron mask covering his whole face. His hands were encased in gloves. "Tômas," she said. And now a dormant suspicion became more than that…

"Milady."

"What are you doing here?"

"Drinking, dancing – watching the fools for an easy mark. The usual."

She watched him but the iron mask never smiled. She thought about the man she knew, the man he'd been – a murderer, a thief, but human. The thing she had met in Place Pigalle was no longer that.

She said, "Let me see your hands."

"You wish to become intimate?" And though she couldn't see it she could hear the leer in his voice. She kept her voice level, said, "I need to see your skin."

"Many women have told me that," he said. "But you, I never expected–"

Before he finished speaking a gun was pointing at him. "Now," she said. Suspicion turning to understanding, but horrified – she had not thought of another Council agent...

"You want to shoot me?" he said, and his voice was low and husky, and he bent towards her and put his forehead against the muzzle of the gun. "You did before..."

And now she noticed how elongated his skull seemed–

She reached for his hand, tore away the white glove–

His hand rose up, freed. She saw the grey swirling on the metamorphosed skin–

His hand closed to a fist and swung at her. His knuckles were like metal, and he knocked her back and there was blood on her cheek. She fired, point blank. She felt him sag against her–

And rise again, laughing, a wild inhuman sound – and now he reached for her, and a tongue licked her cheek, tasting her blood, and his voice said, close to her ear, "And all the time you thought you were hunting, it is I who has been hunting you..."

She fought against him but couldn't break free. "And now I am tired of the game," he said. "Now I wish to enjoy the rewards of winning..."

His hand grabbed her by the throat. She watched the grey swirls climb up his wrist and onto his fingers. "The Council set you to catch me?" he said. "Me! Did they really think a girl like you could stand up to what I've become?"

He shoved her, hard, and she stumbled, gasping for air. "I'll give you," the thing that had once been Tômas said, "one more chance. It will be... how do the English say? It would be sporting. Come and get me. I'll be waiting for you, Milady de Winter."

She raised the gun and fired, and fired, and fired. There were screams in the distance. The man in the iron mask laughed and ran, his gait that of a strange lithe animal, jumping impossibly off the walls of the hall and out through the open door, where the rain was falling down. He ran through the crowds and they scrambled away from him, and there were more screams. She ran after him, firing until there were no bullets left, not heeding the crowds.

Far away, the figure that had been Tômas turned to face her. He had pushed up his mask, and now she could see him for what he was, a grey, wolf-like thing, that grinned at her with wet teeth in the thin moonlight. "Catch me if you can..." his voice came, like a whisper, on the wind.

Then he was gone.

There was a commotion in the hall, and now she saw the watchers coming outside, and now she knew why the Council truly set her to find Yong Li's killer. She was their bait, to flush out the Phantom – but not only him, all the other watchers too. The Council had used her twice, to identify the other players and draw out their rogue agent – two birds with one stone, and she was the worm. Outside the gates she saw an old Asian man with one eye, sitting in the shadows. Ebenezer Long, watching. She went to him and dropped a coin into his begging bowl, and his serene face smiled up at her. "The darkest hour," he said, "is the one before dawn."

"Spare me," she said.

"We will protect you," he said, "if we can."

"I won't hold my breath."

She turned away from him. There, on the steps, watching. Viktor, still holding a drink in one hand. He had known, and hadn't told her. The Council had set her searching, in ignorance, counting on her to stir up events. Whether she lived or died mattered little to the machines.

"But you would do the right thing," Master Long said. "You always do, Xiake."

Then he, too, was gone, a whisper on the wind.

Her hand closed around the other gun, the one she hadn't used, the one she should have used: the Toymaker's gift. She would use it, and she would destroy the menace that the Phantom represented. She would hunt him down, out of compassion, and put a bullet in his head and watch him die.

She knew where he would go.

And now her sense of urgency was gone, replaced with a cold expectation. She summoned her coach and it came. The crowds had gone, the music had died behind her in the hall. A fearful, expectant hush...

"We're going back to Montmartre," she told the silent coachman.

She watched the lights of the Hotel de Ville recede in the darkness. They would all be mobilising too, she thought. All of them who wanted the key, the thing that was stolen when Yong Li died. The Council must have been furious when their own agent turned on them. When the other world reached out and touched him, and remade him in the process, a key of their own to open this world...

She sat back and closed her eyes, and her fingers tightened around the gun.

FORTY
Rise of the Jade Grey Moon

The thunder still rolled over Montmartre Cemetery; lightning continued to flash above the caretaker's miniature castle, and the night was dark and full of menace. Or so it felt to Milady. She listened out for bird cries but heard none. The cemetery was silent, the graves almost unseen but for when the lightning illuminated the headstones. Such an elaborate façade, she thought, for a depository of dead things... They were all gone and finished with, the men and women who lay there. Their minds had gone, and what was left crumbled slowly, flesh peeling, blood draining, only the bones remaining – but they, too, would turn to dust. Only the headstones remained, names and dates inscribed in stone, signifying nothing.

She wondered how many of the grey-infected corpses had initially come here. And where had the initial infection come from? Did the Man on the Mekong, Tom Thumb's mysterious contact in the east, send other keys, other couriers? How long had the Council known – and how long had the lizards?

She made her way through the graves slowly, her gun drawn. She was watching for the Phantom. She remembered the first time she had met Tômas. Down in the under-morgue, a young man with an unremarkable face, a face that could transform – with a hint of rouge, a false moustache, a wig, an expression, into someone else's face. He had been a murderer;

a blackmailer; a thief and a robber; the Council found him highly useful and had recruited him – where and when she never knew. Just as she had been recruited, when she first came to their notice, before her travels in Vespuccia, before Lord de Winter – before her first husband, even. A brat in the under-city, who did what she could to survive... They had liked that. They had fashioned her, in their way, into a gun.

Now she hunted a comrade; another like her; and yet nothing like her, she thought. She stalked toward Ampère's castle. As she passed a large headstone the lightning flashed and she saw the name inscribed there.

André-Marie Ampère. So it was true, and the man's simulacra had made its home right beside its one-time owner.

She came to the door. When she knocked there was no answer. She kicked it open. "Ampère!"

No answer, but something moving in the darkness. Lightning flashed and the light came through the open doorway and she saw the thing on the floor.

The automaton had been sliced open, its insides showing, gears and wheels changing even as she watched, becoming a strange, grey mist. And, as if prompted by the lightning, a blue electric light began to glow around André-Marie Ampère, spilling out from his insides. The automaton's mouth moved, but no words came out. She stepped closer.

"I take it Tômas has already paid you a visit," she said. The thing on the floor groaned. Grey clouds spilled from its insides, and now she could see what she had missed before – there was a fragment of a green stone embedded into the automaton's stomach, the smoke and the light falling from it, growing...

Awakening, a voice said. She took a step back. It did not quite speak. Somehow the words were in her mind. Lights, flickering. Static pictures, hovering in the mist. A camera obscura, she thought. But this was more. And it was real.

Home...

There was more than one voice. They sounded... lonely?

She stared into the automaton's belly, where a sun was rising in dark space, illuminating... what?

A vista of impossible structures, floating in space...

"What are you?" she said.

Worlds within worlds... old beyond time... we are ghosts, nothing to be frightened of... for ourselves, we want nothing.

She took a step closer to the corpse; and now she was standing directly above Ampère. He was no longer moving. The machine was dead.

"Awakening," she said, echoing them. "Why? Why now? Or..." Not now, she realised. "Three years ago. What happened?"

A sense of a vast intelligence turning over her question, tasting it, polishing it like a stone, examining it in a dim light. No answer. Then, A signal. Chrono-spatial; anomaly; awakening; birth; child; like us not us; close – we must find it!

"I don't understand."

In the place you call... A vast mind rifling through a catalogue of names and meanings, searching. Oxford.

"What happened there?"

Again, the words dizzying her, the voices swallowing her, and she found herself bent down, her face so close to the dead machine's open belly, where the jade-green flashes seemed to shape themselves, suddenly, into the shape of a key... Birth. Multi-form intelligence infant anomalous same same different dimensional representation insufficient–

"You don't know..."

A shriek of anger, a sense of waiting, and she reached out to the fragment of jade, compelled to touch it–

Her hand froze above it. She thought – the Phantom had put it there. He had killed Ampère. He had set it for her, to touch. What would it do?

And she thought – it would make me like him.

"No," she said. The voices silenced. The Colt was in her hand without her knowing it. She fired – again and again.

FORTY-ONE
What Transpired at the Montmartre Cemetery

The grey mist dissipated. The electric corpse twitched and shook, sparks and smoke rising from Ampère's chest. His eyes bulged out, then fell altogether and rolled on the floor, leaving two empty sockets behind.

A lifeless figure lay at her feet. The room was dark, and outside the storm had abated, the clouds slowly dispersing.

She turned away and was sick.

After a couple of minutes she felt better. She didn't know what lay inside Ampère's castle, and didn't want to find out. She went outside and closed the door behind her.

Clap.

The sound jerked her head upwards. She scanned the night, saw nothing.

Clap. Clap. Clap.

"Tômas."

"Milady. Is it true you killed your first husband?"

"Show yourself."

"And your second?"

She turned, round and round, searching for him. Where was the voice coming from? Her gun was in her hand. The other gun was still safely hidden in her coat, and she didn't dare reach for it...

"We are not unlike, you and I."

"Don't flatter yourself."

"I was flattering you–" he laughed. "I want to show you something."

"Then come out and show me."

"All in good time, Milady. All in good time." The voice circled around her, invisible, unseen. "I have seen so much. There are no words to describe the things I've experienced. I have seen the universe, Cleo."

She had not been called that in a long time... Tom, she thought. Tom Thumb had called her that, the last time she saw him alive.

"I saw the stars of deep space," the Phantom said. She searched for him but couldn't find him. "The swirling galaxies," the Phantom said. "I have seen suns explode and life flourish where no life should be... And I have seen the lizards."

"Oh?" she stopped, stood still. Was that a branch cracking underfoot?

"I have seen rings in space, enormous structures, and dark ships like whales sailing between the stars. I've seen worlds beyond the world, I've seen wonders such as I can't–"

She turned and shot. A silence, then a low, husky laugh. "Good try," Tômas said.

"You could return with me," she said. "We can try and find a cure. Reverse you–"

"Reverse me? I am beyond human, Cleo. I am the next step. I am better than all of you."

"You're insane," she said.

"And you're a fool," he said. "Do you think the Council would be grateful to you for destroying their key?" He laughed again. "It is of little consequence. It was but a fragment, a small thing. I am a key unto itself. And there is a door, too... a gateway in Asia, and its gatekeeper selling tickets to the highest bidder – who do you think that would be? France? Chung Kuo? Perhaps the Sioux Nations? Or the fat-bellied lizards and their human servants?"

"Why do you care?"

Circling again. Was that a shadow, moving? She fired, and the shadow dropped back. "That almost hurt," he said. Then he was closer, very suddenly, and she fired with the gun while reaching for the other, the one with the grey-metal slugs–

And – "I don't," he said, and he was very close. She saw him then, illuminated in the moonlight, a steely-grey monster, naked now, grey swirls like living tattoos on his skin. That elongated skull, and the row of teeth that opened in a hungry smile… "I've waited a long time for this, Cleo," he said, and then he seemed to be everywhere at once and she could not reach the gun, her hands would not obey her and she tried to turn – too late – and felt an explosion of pain erupt in the back of her skull. She fell to her knees, tried to raise her gun arm but weights were dragging her down now, down into black and murky depths from which she couldn't rise… Her hands fell to her sides and there was pain again, a lot of it, and she fell sideways, and into a dark abyss where no dreams came.

Movement. Her head was aflame. Pain spread out like molten silver throughout her body. She was being carried. His hands were on her like a vice. She was dangling from his shoulder, her head almost grazing the ground. She saw tombs pass by, upside down. "Lovely Cleo," he said. "Soon, now…"

She passed out again, mercifully.

And awakened, to see the stars overhead, no clouds, no rain (she would have prayed for rain, craved water). The pain in her head was a dull constant sound, a hammer hitting a distant anvil.

Notre Dame de Paris. In the ruins shadows fled from the Phantom and its prey. She stirred, trying to – trying to – she had a–

His hand on her neck and she could no longer breathe. "Into the under-city we go, we go," he sang to her. "You and I, how pleasant it will be..."

The fingers pressed on her throat and squeezed; she couldn't breathe...

Darkness again.

Going through the passages of the under-city, going through the catacombs... She thought she saw Q, hidden in a corner, watching her sadly. She tried to whisper to him, but no words came. Past fires and beggars and lizard boys, past the sorry denizens of this sorry dark world. "Not far now, my love..." he whispered, and there was pain, there was so much pain, and she sought escape in the cool and empty darkness, diving inside it, her last thought a wordless cry, an old prayer: Please don't let me wake up again.

FORTY-TWO
I am Pain

"Why the cemetery?"

"All those lovely corpses… my little garden of the dead. And that fool Ampère to store them and study them and keep quiet about my little indiscretions. You spoiled my little arrangement…"

"The Council put you on body-snatching detail–"

Sounds in the dark, metal sliding against metal, and she tried not to think of that. "They didn't count on you getting infected yourself?"

"Oh, I think you'd be surprised," he said. Flames, burning metal. She bit down hard, trying to focus. "I suspect they wanted to see how it would affect me. Not just me, Milady de Winter. Another part of my job was to bring them test subjects. Little kids from the street, old women, old men, a whole cross-section of society – as long as no one would miss them. Little kids…" he said. "Like you'd once been."

She thrust against the restraints, wanting to get at him, and he laughed. She was strapped into one of Viktor's operating tables. They were in the under-morgue, and it was locked up tight, and there were only the two of them.

"I didn't mind," he said. "I liked it. It gave me…" He sounded thoughtful. "New abilities," he said. "I no longer needed to serve the Council. The new me had no one to serve but itself."

"But they sent you to get Yong Li," she said. He snorted. "That sad little man... I merely reversed the operation he'd already undergone. He was a little like me, and glad not to be, I think. He was grateful for my knife."

"But they sent you. To get the key."

"Yes..." he said, not sounding certain.

"But you wouldn't give it back to them."

"I was happy," he said. "In my little garden. I was going on a long journey, you see. To another place."

"What happened?"

"The key was not enough. It was like the hole in a camera obscura – enough to show the image coming through, not enough to cross over. No, the gateway is only one and it is far from here, in Asia, where the fragment came from. I will be going there soon, to meet the Man on the Mekong."

"Does he have a name?"

"He might have had one, once. What do I care for names? I shall cut his belly open and walk through the doorway."

"You're insane."

"No," he said. "I am pain."

He turned to her then. He was wearing his iron mask again, and one of Viktor's white smocks. He looked down on her. He had stripped her down to her underclothes. Her coat lay crumpled in a corner. The gun, she thought. The gun must still be there.

It would not do her any good. It was as far as if it were the other side of a vast ocean. And now she could smell the burning metal, and above her the Phantom raised a red-hot cleaver. She strained against the straps but it was futile. Fear blossomed inside her like a fever. "The heat will cauterise the wound," he said conversationally. He had tied her up with her arms spread out, and her legs. A strap pressed her forehead down, another choked her neck. She couldn't move. She couldn't escape.

"Please," she said. "Please. Don't do it."

When she looked at his hands she could see the grey swirls intensifying, moving in the red glare of the knife. "Don't–"

The cleaver, a butcher's tool, came down hard.

She had screamed. For a moment, joyfully, she lost consciousness. But it returned, too soon, far too soon, and then she cried, and the pain was horrifying, it was everywhere, everywhere but in one place.

He had cut off her right arm, just below the elbow.

And now he showed it to her, waving it in front of her face before throwing it away across the floor. She cried, she couldn't help it. She begged him to stop, or tried to. The sounds that came from her mouth were barely human.

"No more questions, Cleo? No more investigating, no more mystery-solving? I'm disappointed. You must have so much you want to ask me still."

She screamed. He said, "That's not a question."

The next time she was conscious he was pulling a needle from her arm. "This will help," he said.

He'd picked up a surgical blade. One of Viktor's. He played with it in front of her eyes. She could no longer think. Her whole being was fear, as pure as an animal's. She shook and tried to move away and there was nowhere to go. "Perhaps… an eye?" he suggested.

She tried to shake her head. She moaned. She tried to kick. Her whole being was shaking uncontrollably. "So I could see you better with it, my dear…" he said and laughed.

He reached for her and stroked her hair. His hand was very close to her eyes. She closed them, praying to whatever gods or spirits there were to hear her, but none came. His thumb stroked her closed eyes. "Left… or right? What fearful symmetry you have, Cleo."

Then he pressed, and pressed, and pressed, and the pain was worse than before, and she knew she was dying.

•••

"Look," he said. There was a bloodied ball in his hand, and he was waving it before her. He had just injected her again, she didn't know with what. One of Viktor's potions... to keep her alive.

"What is a human?" he said. "How much can we reduce while we remain? Legs? Hands? Eyes and ears? What is left when all the outside appendages are taken out?"

Her one eye moved rapidly, uncomprehending. He threw the eyeball at the wall. It slid down, and there was a circle of blood where it had hit. "That is what I wish to find out, Milady. I am so glad you've agreed to help me."

She whimpered. She was reduced to nothing, a burning darkness, a sun flaming with pain. To live was to hurt, to suffer. Somewhere in the back of her mind Milady still existed, beyond the wall of torment, but she was dormant, hidden well behind, a tiny presence in the mindless pain.

"I want you to see what I see," he said, earnestly. Somehow that was more frightening than anything that had come before. His hand disappeared, returned...

Something green. It shone with its own internal light. "A fragment of a fragment," he said, and giggled. She tried to speak, to say, "No, please, please please don't don't d–"

His hand came down. His thumb pushed into the open socket of her empty eye.

She screamed.

"Another injection?" he said. He sounded irritated now. She felt a needle slip into her neck, then all feeling stopped.

"There," the Phantom said. "That's better, now."

His thumb, pushing... There was a scraping sound. No pain, but the feel of something hard moving, grating against her skull. "Soon," he said. "Soon you'll be able to see. Really see. It is a great gift I give you, Cleo."

She shivered. He ran one finger, lightly, down her cheek. "Hush now. Can you see? Can you see it yet?"

"You're crazy," she said, or thought she did, and he laughed.

"What shall we do next?" he said. "Hmmm?" He seemed to give it some thought. In her head the alien object felt as if it were reaching inside her, as if a larva had been planted in her eye socket and was now emerging, questing out…

The Phantom said: "An ear, perhaps? Or a leg? Not your tongue, my dear. I like to hear it when you voice your opinions – and you are ever so vocal…"

The cleaver again. When had it come into his hands? The man in the iron mask never smiled, never changed expression. "This is so much better than with corpses," he said softly. Then the blade came down again, above her knee.

FORTY-THREE
Grimm

Awakening. Pain. It came and went in waves; she rode them, cresting higher and higher. Thinking: no more no more no more please please please no more kill me–

Blinking her one eye. Darkness. Silence. The monster was hiding, was waiting to pounce. Please please please don't–

Calling on old gods of a place she had long forgotten and never believed in. But a child believes. Once again she was that child; alone and afraid in the dark, in the city, hiding from predators, fearing every footstep. Knowing they were coming, that you couldn't run forever, that sooner or later it would happen, and they–

His voice, in the distance. Speaking, the corresponding voice echoing strangely. Communicating with someone through a Tesla set, the little part of her mind that was not yet insane thought.

She couldn't move. And the pain was a part of her now.

Her leg was gone. So was her arm. She was no longer strapped in, in those two places. There was nothing left to strap in.

Something moved in the darkness and she almost screamed, but wouldn't, no, she wouldn't give him the satisfaction.

Only it was not the Phantom.

A familiar shape. Slithering quietly, cautiously, along the cold stone floor.

A familiar insectile head. The quiet hiss and whirr of gears.

Grimm.

She closed her eye. When she opened it Grimm was still there, moving towards her. It raised itself up. Grimm's soft metal tongue hissed out, touched her skin like a kiss.

"Oh, Grimm," she said, or tried to. "Oh, Grimm."

Grimm's mouth found the first of the leather straps. Grimm's tongue licked it, and the leather hissed. Her little familiar was eating the straps. "Hurry," she whispered. "Hurry!"

The next time Grimm's mouth moved a drop of acid fell on her hand. She bit her lips until the blood flowed. She would not make a sound.

Beyond the small area of the surgery the voices were fading and she knew the Phantom would be coming back. "Hurry," she said, and then, with a final hiss of Grimm's tongue, her body was free, and her arm.

With a clumsy hand she loosened the neck strap, then the head. She was clawing, panting, desperately fumbling with the remaining strap, the one that had held bound both of her legs, and now…

She fought the strap and tried very hard not to look at the empty place where her leg had been.

She heard his footsteps. Grimm slithered away. Then she was free. She tried to stand and of course couldn't. She fell down on the hard floor.

The Phantom appeared. "What are you–?" he said, and then he laughed. She dragged herself forward, one-armed, her one leg kicking. Slowly she progressed, her one eye fixed on the coat lying a few feet away.

"You are like a strange new creature," the Phantom said. "And I have created you. Crawl, little fish. Where are you going?"

She kicked, and pushed, clawing her way one inch at a time, leaving a slimy trail of blood against the stone. He was striding towards her then, not hurrying, enjoying the wait.

She was almost there.

And then so was he, and he kicked her, and her ribs flamed in pain and she rolled from the impact–

Her body found the coat–

And there was something hard inside, a metal pipe, the Toymaker's curious gun–

The Phantom's next kick found her head, broke teeth. Blood filled her mouth. She could barely see – his ghostly outline was above her, descending with a flash of metal–

A knife, descending–

She fumbled in the coat, one-handed, reaching for that inside pocket, and her fingers closed on the smooth cylinder of the gun–

The knife was coming down very fast–

She rolled, or tried to. The knife grazed her face, sliced a part of her ear–

She couldn't release the gun from the coat!

The knife rose, began to come down again–

She watched the expressionless iron mask and the blade, afraid, unable to think–

The knife whispered as it cut through air, towards her, and–

She fired, blindly, through the coat's material.

There was a burning smell.

The knife clattered to the floor.

The Phantom took a step back, and then another. He looked down.

On his chest, an explosion of grey. The moving shapes resembled nothing, suggested everything. They were volcanoes and hurricanes, earthquakes and floods. The grey flooded him, and she fired again, and he stumbled and fell to his knees.

He looked at her through the iron mask. He raised his arms, examined his hands. His fingers were melting, and he screamed. The grey engulfed him, like molten silver, burning.

The gun dropped from her fingers and she fell back, knowing she was dying, welcoming it. To die would be to never again experience pain. Dimly she was aware of Grimm beside her, Grimm's dry tongue on her cheek. "Oh, Grimm," she said, or wanted to. "It had all been–"

Then her eye closed, and she knew nothing else.

FORTY-FOUR
The New Translation of Lady de Winter

Darkness, cold, a blessed silence. She could no longer feel her body. Was she dying? Had she died?

A sense of calm, so wonderful. But something else, intruding. A feeling as though she was moving.

Or being moved.

She blinked an eye. She saw faces above her, as distant as moons. No longer afraid – she felt wonderful, in fact. So wonderful… She giggled, or tried to.

Voices, from an immeasurable distance: "Close to death– nothing we can do– the drugs won't work forever."

She could not distinguish between the voices, could not tell who was speaking. She tried to tell them she was fine, really, she was, but they wouldn't listen.

"Build– radical surgery– she wouldn't thank you– need her– go to– ridiculous– shock alone would–"

She could hear the words but they made no sense. She giggled again, then felt the world disappear.

… and reappeared again. The sense of moving intensified. Sounds in the distance, the motion of water, and she thought – we're crossing the Seine. Voices, speaking far away: "Why is she not dead?"

Another: "Injected."

"With what?"

The second voice was Viktor's. "My own modified Hyde formula."

"She should have died of the shock. And loss of blood." The voice, too, familiar. Colonel Xing – why were the two of them together?

"The Hyde formula is... rather special. It was very clever of him to use it. A great compliment to myself, really."

She would have shot him if she could.

"Still, even at the factory, I don't know if–"

"I know it well. I am sure we can–"

Across the river, and the air changed, and she smelled Chinatown. They're taking me to the Goblin factory, she thought. "Make me into a goblin," she said, and giggled, though no one seemed to have heard her.

"It would have been better to let her die."

"We need her still. She is our tool. She has always been our tool."

"People are not implements," Colonel Xing said. "We are not – utensils."

"Then I shall make her into one," Viktor's voice said, complacently.

The smell of tar. The smell of oil. The smell of machines and hot metal. Flashes in her mind of a phantom figure raising a knife. The smell of burning flesh... a hand on her head and she screamed. A voice: "Quick, give her another shot!"

Pain, penetrating into her neck. The flashes dissipated like a bad dream. "How do you say, please?" Colonel Xing, the tail-end of a conversation.

"A translation," Viktor's voice said. "Like a saint. Our Lady of Vengeance."

The hum of machines, the bellows of steam, the air thick with humidity and very hot, and now they were doing something to her leg.

But she no longer had a leg.

She couldn't see them. She tried to scream, tell them to stop, but no one heard her.

"She will be a child of the new age," Viktor's voice said, faint and far away.

"A monster–" Colonel Xing.

"We are all monsters," Viktor said cheerfully.

Then blackness. Then light. Another pain, this one in her arm. She could feel her leg – both her legs. It was a strange sensation. They were doing something to her arm.

"Not much I can do for the eye..."

"She would look fetching with a patch."

"The arm, now, is another matter again–" from Viktor.

"She will kill you if she could."

"So would many others. But she will obey the Council."

"We shall be late to the meeting."

"I do not trust the lizards."

"I do not trust the Jianghu. We have no choice."

"The what?"

"The Shaolin–Wudang coalition."

"You have strange customs."

"As do you."

"True. Can I trust you?"

"No."

"I didn't think so. Ours is a mutual distrust, yet we must work together..."

"We shall send our own people after him."

"As will the lizards. As will all the others. Of course. But you have tried before?"

"Yes..."

"And failed."

"Yes..."

"I heard Krupp is going to the meeting."

"The weapons man? The German?"

"Yes, and yes. Next year will be a hunting season..."

"You take too much delight in your work."

She felt her arm. The arm she'd lost. She tried to move it.

"Careful!"

"It's not loaded."

The bite of a needle again, and a numbing coolness.

"You are too fond of the needle, too."

"Stop telling me my business, colonel."

"She deserves better."

"We all do. Now step aside."

"Finish it."

"I would if you gave me the opportunity."

Her arm. What were they doing to her arm? It didn't hurt but the sensation was terrible, unnatural. "Careful, damn it!"

"She's stronger than I thought!"

Her arm broke the straps then, hit something – someone – and she heard a scream, and then a dull thud.

"Hold her still!"

Hands on her, and she struggled – she could smell their fear and didn't know why. They forced her head back and she kicked–

"Damn it, do it now!"

There was a sharp pain like an insect bite in her neck and her whole body went limp. They had given her another shot.

"Finish it!"

She tried to speak and couldn't. The world spun away. Then there was only darkness.

INTERLUDE
Kai Wu Unrolls His Mat

For a long time after he had arrived in the city the voices were quiet. He had gathered a little of their history. They were weak, their vessel inactive for long periods of time. A human presence revived them, gave them strength, but only for a while. They were, he thought later, when he had learned of Tesla waves, a little like a man turning a dial in the hope of finding a working band. But their attempts were futile. They spoke of transdimensional calibration and quantum effervescence and chrono-spatial matrices returning negative values but mostly what he felt from them could only be described with a human term, and that was loneliness.

He knew that feeling well.

As time passed he became accustomed to the city. It lay in the conjunction of two great rivers, one of which was the Mekong. Above it towered mountains, high forbidding cliffs and thick forests where bears and tigers roamed. The city had many temples and a royal palace and a king, and was a vassal of Siam, but they spoke a different language, which was Lao.

Also spoken in the city were Chinese; Hmong; Karen; Hakka; there were many dialects and tongues and many different people. There were mountain people and lowlanders, Siamese merchants and Chinese traders, and here and there the people called franag or falang or Europeans. Once he saw something he had thought impossible – a lizard taller than a man, and walking upright, and dressed in clothes. It was dressed like a prince, was escorted by a retinue of farang and Lao. He had thought it one of the Emerald Buddha's illusions, but later found out it was not so, and that such beings did exist, and were very powerful.

He washed in the river and ate when he could. In the dry season he helped the farmers plant seasonal gardens on the banks, and build bamboo bridges across the river. He carried sacks of rice and flour for the Chinese merchants, interpreted for the Siamese, stole from the Hmong when they had something worth stealing. He learned the city, came to know its tiny stone alleyways, its hiding places and its night places, roaming from beyond the half-island of the rivers' confluence into the lands beyond.

The statue gave him lightness; he could see in the dark and leap across walls, could spin and kick and duck and run faster than any other child. He could pass unseen even in a crowded place. It was what the wuxia novels had called Qinggong.

There weren't many books but there was one Chinese merchant who sold fishing nets and tackle and sundry small items from Chung Kuo and he had a small library, and when Kai did small jobs for him he let the boy borrow a book, in lieu of pay. And so he continued to follow the adventures of the Shaolin monks and the Wu Tang Clan and the Beggars' Guild and their enemies, of assassins sent after evil emperors, of lovers fighting impossible odds, of the Wulin and Jianghu and the eternal battle between right and wrong.

Few noticed him. For a while he had the sensation of being watched, closer than was usual, by a decrepit old beggar whose single eye seemed a little too bright, but when he sought him out the man was gone, and no one could recall seeing him before or after. For a while he worked at the palace, cleaning up the elephants' dung, sweeping floors, watering the flowerbeds, helping the cooks or the gardeners or the monks. He was, in the words of one of the novels, unrolling his mat. He was settling in, making the city his home. For a short time, he was happy.

As he grew older he began to notice changes in himself. His skin grew thicker, coarser, a metallic grey. One day, scrabbling in the mud, his hand returned and a fingernail had fallen off. Another became loose the next day. He felt the change sweep over him, his old body shedding itself for something new. "What is happening to me?" he asked the statue.

There was a faint sense of amusement. You asked to be made into a gun, the voices said.

"I changed my mind," he told them, and had the mental impression of a shrug.

It is too late to undo what has begun.

His face, too, acquired a metallic sheen. It did not spread evenly, only affected one side of his face. The fallen nails were replaced with thicker, sharper versions, their colouring metallic, grey, and he felt as if he were a ghost that still, somehow, had substance.

You could be anything you want, the voices told him. You could be king of all this land.

"I want my father. He died for you."

He died for an inaccurate belief, the voices said. It is unfortunate. Your race does not have the – *a concept, divorced from words* – to comprehend us, make sense of what we are.

"What are you?"

A shifting series of wordless concepts, images, and he said, "What do you want of me?"

We wait, the voices said.

"For what?"

A sign. There is another in this world now. A child, but it is – and then a void, a gap where understanding lay.

He didn't know what they meant about the child. But he understood being alone.

Too long… the voices said.

For months after that he did not speak to the voices. He tried to be human, to eat and to drink and to think like a human. He watched the puppet shows that were popular at that time. He drank rice whisky (he was old enough now) and had his first hangover, though it passed swiftly. He watched the sun set over the river and the mountains. He gambled with the Chinese, and lost, and read the mulberry scrolls in the monastery's library, finding hints of a story about an impossible statue that spoke and drove people mad. For several months he became a monk, and wore the saffron robes, and felt peace.

He thought himself safe.

He was wrong.

Perhaps, he thought – much later – the statue itself was sending out a signal of some sort. Perhaps in its search it was also broadcasting – and it was possible others had devised some sort of machine that was able to pick up that signal. He had hidden the statue, though the statue could hide itself quite effectively. Kai had a little bamboo shack on the bank of the river and the statue was safely buried in the soft earth under the woven mat. And were anyone to find it, they would not see the Emerald Buddha – a flash of light, perhaps, like water moving in a stream, and as if in a dream they would turn away, their mind fogged by grey impenetrable clouds.

And yet they came.

The black-clad men. Chinese, and well trained. He was in the hut, watching the flow of the river, when they came. They had surrounded the hut. It was twilight, the sun had almost disappeared. There was chill in the air. They had guns.

There were four farangs with them.

He fought them. Desperation made him bold. Qinggong made him lithe and light. The change wrought in him made him strong – terribly strong.

But there were too many of them.

As he fought them he thought of his father, the silent attackers in Chiang Rai, men like these; he lashed out and his nails took out a man's throat and he watched the blood flow on the black earth. He leaped and descended and two more men were down.

"Don't kill him," he heard someone say.

Instead, they went for him with nets.

The nets were connected somehow, by a long wire, to an engine the men had brought with them. It belched steam and its cogs moved and current came through the wires and fed into the nets. He tore at them, but they were made of metal, and he couldn't break it. They caught him with long rods and ran electricity through the metal and made him scream.

"Search the hut."

"Yes, Manchu."

So their leader was a Manchurian. He swore at the man, telling him he'd kill him, and the man laughed. By then Kai was pinned back, caught in the webbing of their trap, and the electric current ran through him and pain blossomed everywhere.

"Little thief," the Manchu said. "You have been very lucky."

Two men returned from the hut. He saw, amazed and frightened, that they held the Emerald Buddha in their hands.

Help me! he shouted, mentally, at the statue.

The voices seemed distant, more confusing than usual. Probability cluster skewered – approaching crisis point – geo-temporal coordinates suitable – confusion – executing long-term projection analysis–

He said – pleaded – They would use you!

Design flaw – not tool – interference pattern–

He said, Use me. I will help you. I will serve you.

The Manchu approached the statue. He ran his hand lightly over the jade surface. "The Empress-Dowager will be pleased…" he said.

One of the farangs said something in one of the farang tongues.

"If I let her have it," the Manchu said, and laughed again. "Can you meet the price, Mein Herr?"

A blond, blue-eyed man, with skin darkened by the sun, said something in a language Kai didn't understand. The man sounded angry, but the Manchu just smiled. The blond man spoke again, sounding angrier still–

"No?" the Manchu said. "Very well." Then, as quick as a Wulin, a gun appeared in his hand and he fired. The farang fell to the ground, blood gushing from his chest. The other three farangs jointly took a step back, and the Manchu smiled.

"Or maybe I shall keep it..." he said. "Yes... it is a most attractive proposition..."

The three farangs exchanged glances. But they did not challenge the Manchu.

And now the man approached Kai. "Why were the Wulin transferring the statue to your father?" he asked conversationally. "Who did he work for? Who was he?"

"He was my father," Kai said.

"Why would they risk transferring the object?" the Manchu said. "What change were they expecting?"

"I don't know."

"Look at you," the Manchu said. "You are no longer human. You are nothing, dirt not fit for the poorest sweeper to brush away. I will enjoy dismantling you, piece by piece, in my lab. I'll find out what makes you tick–" and he took out a timepiece from a pocket and held it up. "You are a clockwork device," he said. "Nothing more. A machine made to serve another."

"My name is Kai," Kai said.

"You have no name. You are clockwork."

He made a gesture. The electric current increased suddenly and Kai screamed. The Manchu beamed down at him. "You are nothing," he said. "But I am fascinated–" and he bent down, peering at Kai's terrified face.

"Knife," the Manchu said. One of his men hurried over,

placed a silvery blade in his hand.

Expense – waste – preserve – energy resources low – the boy would serve – the time is near–

Help me!

The first cut opened the side of his body. The Manchu reached into the gap, and Kai screamed as he felt the man's long-nailed fingers rooting inside him. "What are you made of...?" the man murmured. Slowly, he cut along Kai's arm, ran his finger along the cut, rubbed the thick blood between his fingers. "What has it made you into? You could be valuable to me yet..."

He was killing him, Kai knew. Slowly, methodically, and as a display for the others. Dissecting him the way a scientist would a frog, to see what secrets it held inside.

The next cut opened up his belly and for a moment he lost consciousness. When he opened his eyes again the man's hand was inside him again, and the man was wearing a pair of spectacles high on his nose. The pain was horrific, and the electric current was humming loudly, the very air vibrating with the current.

The man cut him, here, here, there, slowly at first, then with increasing fury. "What are you?" he roared at one point. "Why are you still alive?"

Kai didn't know. He wished he wasn't. But the man kept opening him up, kept cutting him until–

The power – most primitive – coal generator – can draw – will it be enough?

He felt the voices reaching out to him.

Make me into a gun, he whispered.

This has hurried the process...

He felt his body somehow manipulating the electric current, drawing it into himself. The Manchu jumped back. "What are you fools doing?"

"Sir?"

"Turn the machine off!"

Shouts, confusion – "It won't stop, sir!"

He was drawing in the power and the power was burning through him, burning him, but it was being controlled...

The power coursed through him and he felt himself changing–

He tore the webbing, as easy as spiders' webs. The men were firing at him. The bullets irritated him. He killed five of them before they realised he had moved. The others tried to run away. He pursued them, caught them, executed them. Several tried to run to the river. He let them. They would not come out alive.

Of the three remaining farangs two tried to flee and he tore out their throats. The last one standing tried to bargain with him. He could understand the man's language now and only wondered why he couldn't before, it was so simple. The man said, "I am authorised to offer you anything you desire. We shall give you papers, an estate, servants, wives, power. Join us."

He growled. The man stumbled, but straightened. "We can help you," he said softly. "We have scientists, people who could study you–"

"Like he studied me?" he roared, and the man nodded, once, as if at an acquaintance he had long been expecting to see. He stood very straight when Kai killed him.

Then there was only the Manchu.

PART IV
At the Insane Asylum

FORTY-FIVE
Charenton Asylum

She woke up to the wails of the insane.

A cold, stark room of bare stone: darkness outside the window, lights down below – she was on a hill, the windows barred, the door closed – locked.

The lights of Paris in the distance.

At least, she hoped it was still Paris.

Where was she?

What had happened?

Recollections trickling into her mind slowly, torturously. Weren't the Chinese said to have a special water torture?

The Chinese…

The Goblin factory.

What had they done to her there?

Darkness. She had been strapped to an operating table, and the Phantom was above her, and a butcher's cleaver came down–

His thumb pressing against her eye, the pain erupting like molten gold–

And something pushed into her, grating against the bones of her eye socket, and–

Like larvae, hatching, reaching out–

Something had settled inside her eye socket, something almost alive–

Her hand rose, but where her eye had been she encountered only a smooth, unbroken surface. Panicking, she grasped at it – it came away from her skin.

An eyepatch. She stared at it in her palm, traced the smooth leather with her thumb. She raised her other hand and the motion took her by surprise, a smooth metal appendage almost hitting her in the face.

Instinct made her close her fingers into a fist. But there were no fingers, and when she did and made to turn them, like a key, there was a burst of noise and the window exploded outwards, shards of glass falling away down to the grass.

High-toned screeches from outside, a cloud of dark shapes bursting upwards.

Bats.

The screams intensified beyond the walls. Milady paid them no mind. She stared down at her hand. She could see the arm reaching down to her elbow, but where her elbow had been the human arm terminated, and something else continued...

A cylinder, metal-smooth and light and strangely familiar...

Running footsteps beyond the door, a key rattling in the lock. Cool air blew in from the broken window and she thought – I did that, and felt satisfaction.

The door opened. Two women in nuns' habits. A syringe in one woman's hand.

Milady, smiling grimly – her new arm raised before her, aimed at the women: "Don't come any closer."

All she had to do was tell her brain to close her fingers, and turn...

Her beautiful new arm: they had given her a Gatling gun for the fingers she'd lost.

And someone had left it loaded.

She laughed then, and the two women backed away a step.

"You are very ill," the one with the syringe said. "This will help..."

"Stay away from me."

The women glanced nervously at the window, at Milady's extended arm. The Gatling gun – her Gatling gun – shone in the pale moonlight coming in through the window.

And now the women seemed to decide to obey.

Good.

"Where am I?" Milady said.

Flashes of memory – the under-morgue, the Phantom with his knife raised high, descending, descending…

She pushed herself away from the bed. Standing – both legs seemed to work fine.

What had they done to her?

The two women exchanged glances, didn't speak, and she knew they were no nuns–

A thin stiletto blade sliding out of the second woman's sleeve – the other ready with the needle – "Don't even think about it," Milady said. She tried bending. She was almost entirely naked, she realised – dressed in only a patient's cotton shift. She could see her leg.

Her new leg.

Metal had replaced flesh. She couldn't feel it – but it held her up, and when she tried to move the leg obeyed her, moving as it would have done before.

Even better than before.

"Where am I?" she said again.

The two women exchanged glances once more – the knife flashed – Milady's hand jerked once, twice, and the nun's habit was stained red, the knife cluttering to the floor. The screams beyond the door rose higher, a cacophony of laughter or rage, it was impossible to tell. Milady said, "Fly, little birds–"

The two women fled, the knifewoman holding her wounded arm against her chest.

She could stand. She could shoot. What more could she ask for?

The fragment of jade embedded in her cranium seemed to

thud in her head. Suddenly dizzy, she sat down hard on the bed. When she closed her eye – eyes? – the room disappeared–

Was replaced with mists, and voices whispering, and she seemed to be flying, cutting through the mists like a blade, heading towards–

She opened her eye – eyes? – she could no longer tell – and the mists were gone, and she was back in the empty room. She found the eyepatch on the bed and put it back on, and the thudding in her head quietened down. A wardrobe by the window, and she went to it. Her clothes hung there, pressed and cleaned. She dressed, one-handed and clumsy, put on a long black trench coat – felt complete again. Her dark shades were in the pocket of the coat – she left them there. This place was dark enough.

Quiet now. The wails had ebbed. Presences beyond the walls. She had a feeling she knew where she was. Somewhere she had never wanted to visit–

Black leather against her skin – inside the wardrobe was a mirror and she looked at herself – Milady de Winter, her face thinner than it'd been, an eyepatch like a pirate's over one eye, a machine gun in place of an arm.

She almost laughed. If only Barnum could have seen her, he would have offered her a job again in a second. She wondered what A– her first husband would have thought, if he saw her. Then she decided she didn't particularly care.

Voices whispering beyond her new eye. She could see through the jade, she realised. Eyes, then. But what she could see…

The Phantom's thumb pressing on her eye, the pain exploding in burning hot waves – the jade fragment pushing in, adjusting itself to her eye socket, sending out exploratory tendrils… no. She shook her head and the past disappeared. She was alive. That was what mattered now.

The door had been left open. She stepped through it.

A long corridor. Doors set in equal intervals. The cries and shouts came from beyond them. Cells, she thought.

A home for the insane.

She walked down the corridor. Grilles set into the doors, little observation windows. She peered through one:

A hunched man by the window, humming to himself. She did not recognise the tune. He had a jar in one hand and a spoon in the other, and he was laying a thin layer of powder on the windowsill.

Sugar, she thought. Flies buzzing around the man – she could smell him even from where she stood. As she watched the man, still humming, he put down the sugar bowl and the spoon and snatched at the flies. She stared, repulsed, as he caught and swallowed two in rapid succession. Milady drew back, but as she did the man's head snapped to the door and he hissed. She took a step back. The man's face appeared in the observation window.

"Have you come from him?" he said. "I have been waiting. I have been good. I have been hoarding flies to catch the spiders to draw the birds." He hissed again. "Their taste is in my mouth." His dark eyes looked into hers. "Help me," he said.

Instead she stepped away and heard wails rise from that cell, and the sound of a heavy body crashing, again and again, against the door, and a voice said, close in her ears: "He is beyond our help, but you are not. Come with me."

She turned, and her new gun arm was raised, but they had crept up on her and had come ready: a group of the nuns, with guns in their hands, blocking the end of the corridor, and standing close to Milady – too close – was the man who'd spoken.

"Lower your gun," the man said. "Please." His jowls shook when he spoke. He was the fattest man she had ever seen, and the most ostentatious. He wore fat rings over fat fingers with fat rubies and topaz and blood-dark emeralds set in the yellow gold, and his clothes were satin and lace and silk, and a hungry smile was stretched wide across his face, where fat red lips parted to reveal a fat red tongue. Not quite alive, she thought. But a semblance of life so remarkable it could have only been the work of the Council.

"I am Citizen Sade," the man said, and smiled. "Welcome to the Charenton Asylum."

FORTY-SIX
Citizen Sade

"Would you like to see some of the others?" the fat man said. She had thought Mycroft Holmes was fat, but Sade eclipsed the other man entirely, the way the Earth eclipsed the moon. "We do have such a wonderful collection here. They do… excite me."

Her gun arm was still raised. She said, "Step away from me."

"But of course." He raised his hand placatingly, and smiled, the smile as fake as the rest of him. "What am I doing here?" she said.

"The Council felt you should be kept out of sight, for a while," Sade said. "Until you recuperated sufficiently." He hadn't moved away. And his nuns were blocking her way… She said, "Well, I am recuperated."

"Of course. I will inform the Council…"

"I will go now."

The smile disappeared. "I am afraid that is not possible."

She tensed, getting ready to fire – the fat man said, "Wait."

She waited. He said, "Perhaps we've started on the wrong foot, as it were. We did not expect you to wake so soon–"

"You've been keeping me sedated," she said.

"On Council orders! Your body had suffered severe trauma. It was deemed prudent you were kept… comfortable."

"I'm still waiting," she said.

The fat man sighed. "I shall send word to the Council. In the meantime, why don't you come and wait in my chambers? I can assure you, they are most comfortable."

She watched him, his silent nuns behind him, and knew she was outnumbered. Slowly, she lowered the gun arm.

"Excellent," the man said. "Come! You look like you could do with a drink."

Not waiting for an answer, he turned – his wide back providing a tempting target.

The cries of the insane rose around them. She followed Sade down the corridor. He said, "They are disturbed by your presence here. You seem to upset them."

"Tough."

He laughed, a thick, gluttonous sound, but made no comment. He waddled as he walked. The corridor was long, the doors all barred. She peered into rooms as she passed: in one, a man sitting bound to a chair, a wide, grotesque smile carved into his face – Sade said, "One of the Council's men – he had an accident with a vat of chemicals. It altered his face and loosened his mind, the poor soul."

Howls came from another cell, animal sounds raising a chill up her spine. Looking inside she saw a young man with long, wild, matted hair prowling on all fours, growling when he noticed her. "Raised by wild animals," Sade said. "I am trying to teach him to speak but, alas..."

All the while the silent nuns watched her. At the end of the corridor Sade walked down a flight of stone steps and Milady followed.

Sade's quarters lay at the end of a second, shorter corridor, thankfully bereft of inmates. She could still hear their cries, but they were more muted here. "Please," Sade said. "Come inside."

When he pushed the wide doors open it was onto an opulent room of shadows: the dim light came from thick fat candles scattered everywhere amidst a confusion of cushions, divans and sofas. Low tables held sweets, xocolatl, opium pipes, chess boards, books, writing implements, whips, chains, keys, leather gloves, goblets, feathered headdresses, totems, maps, compasses, brushes, plates of deboned chicken, roast beef, glazed potatoes, parsnips and devilled eggs. In one corner of the room stood a camera tripod, in another a Tesla set. The walls, she noticed, were covered in paintings of a kind she had last seen in Paris's Chinatown: Toulouse-Lautrec's writhing, almost alive joinings of flesh and machines.

Sade said, "Please make yourself at home." He went over to the Tesla set, twiddled the knobs, spoke quietly, listened, and turned back to her. "The Council has been notified. Wine?"

"Coffee, if you have it."

He made a gesture with his fingers. One of the silent nuns approached, already carrying a silver tray on which sat a silver coffee pot and china cups. "Cream? Sugar? Brandy? Allow me." The nun put the tray onto a table, sweeping away a map of the Arctic region, a phallus-shaped pipe and a plate of half-eaten duck. One remaining eye stared up mournfully at Milady. Sade waddled to a nearby sofa, sank down, and set to mixing brandy, coffee, cream and sugar. Milady watched, fascinated. Then she said, "You are a machine."

Sade laughed. "The original me died in this place," he said. "It seemed only fitting that the new, improved me should run it. I have been a good servant of the Republic, after all. And I am not entirely what you think I am."

"Oh?"

"Watch," he said. From one of the nearby tables he lifted a curved, long-bladed knife. The blade was dulled with dried blood. Sade raised the knife and brought it to his chest. Slowly, smiling and licking his lips, he pressed the blade against the material of his shirt, parting it. His flesh – if that is what it was – was the colour of rotten teeth. It was covered in a criss-crossing network of old scars.

Sade pressed the blade against his skin, parting it. He gasped, and beads of sweat appeared on his upper lip. Milady watched, horrified, fascinated: unable to turn away.

Sade's flesh parted easily. What lay behind it...

She had seen the inside of people before, more than she had wanted to. And she had seen the inside of machines. But what lay inside Sade...

She saw silver-coloured bones, the traces of a skeleton not entirely that of a human being. She saw intestines, organic glistening entrails and from inside the exposed belly came the harsh, sickening stench of rotting organic matter, and she saw a heart that was half-alive and half-machine, an enormous, engorged device beating steadily, circulating blood through that weird, internal landscape of metal and flesh... The blade was almost all the way down to Sade's waist now and his enormous belly flapped open and the stench from inside was suffocating and she said, "Enough. Please, enough."

The man's eyes were open and his face flushed and he smiled. He put down the knife. "Take a good look," he said. "I am something new. The Council needed volunteers, or conscripts, or both. I was both."

"What did they do?" she said – whispered – and then she thought – Viktor.

"They took my dying brain," Sade said. "My brilliant, lustful, delightful old brain, and they put it into a new vehicle, and they built me a new body, a human enough body to house a mind such as mine." His thick fingers reached for the open flap and pulled it closed. His thumb ran up the cut and, where it touched, the skin sizzled and hissed and the smell of it was like roasting meat. It closed where Sade touched, leaving a new, long scar. He gasped again as the last of the cut was closed, and the new scar stood dark against his skin, already fading to become just one more amongst the many. "I can assure you, all my parts are fully functioning." His eyes sought hers, and his tongue snaked out, fat and bloated. "All my parts, Milady de Winter."

A sense of unreality stole over her then: suddenly, it was all too much – her own changed body, the asylum, the bloated corpse that sat before her, talking, all the while looking at her with that hungry, terrifying look. Sade said, "Coffee?"

She took the proffered cup. The drink was sweet, laced with brandy, strong. It made her feel better. She said, "How long have I been… asleep?"

Sade shrugged. "A few months," he said.

"Months?"

He only shrugged again. She drank the coffee. It was very sweet. Sweet, and–

"You kept me sedated," she said, struggling to get the words out. Her body felt weak, unresponsive. The cup fell from her fingers, crashed on the thick heavy carpet without a sound.

"I had to study you," he said. "You fascinate me, Milady. I had to have you… for my collection."

Two of the nuns had materialised beside her. She had not felt their approach. "You never called the Council," she said, or tried to. Sade shook his head sadly. "Oh, no," he said. "I could not let you get away. You must forgive me, but–"

Her eyes, closing. Both her eyes. Mists behind her eyelids, and the whispering voices of the dead. The last words she heard were Sade's: "Take her to the examination room."

FORTY-SEVEN
The Sound of Drums

Flying through mists, her eyes throbbing – insidious green jade spreading through her brain, shoots of green taking root – she must have been dreaming, must have been asleep – drugged, she thought. Sade had drugged the coffee.

And yet she was awake – alive – and this was, somehow, real, and she was flying, flying through the clearing mists: they parted before her.

The air thrummed, a sound like a physical sensation invading her mind. Around her the dead whispered, talking softly of lives gone by. A silver river snaked down below – she was descending lower, above her a full moon cast silvery light. The air was humid, tropical. Two worlds juxtaposed, this one and the next – one seen through her remaining eye, and one through a haze of green jade…

The river fled ahead and joined another, and in the place they met a half-island rose like a green-shelled turtle, and on top of the shell was a city.

She saw a temple rise in the distance, its dome shining in the silver light of the moon. The sound – the beat of a drum – echoed inside her, a vibration of force running through her bones.

Flying over narrow cobbled streets, houses of dark wood and bamboo, lanterns hanging in doorways, shadows scurrying – going lower still, until she came to the gates of the temple.

Saffron-robed monks walking in procession – candles held before them, shaved heads reflecting the moon. Walking around the temple, slowly, while the drum beat – she raised her head and saw it, on top of a tower, a giant drum the size of an ox, beaten by two monks – with each beat the sound fled across the city, a human-made sound of thunder. The beat worked itself into her bones, her soul – the monks walked in silence, slowly, the candles held before them, a procession of lights.

Singing coming from inside the temple. She walked slowly across the courtyard, feeling like a ghost. Through a green of haze, the ghosts – silver strands and the white of mist and she thought – this is what it does, this thing, this device – it records the dead.

Why?

The sound of chanting, a reedy old voice singing inside, the drum beating, beating, and she climbed the steps up to the temple and stood a moment between the columns before going inside.

What – who – waited inside? She tensed, and it seemed to her that, back in the waking world, her body was shivering, and sweat was forming on her body, as if she were trying to fight an illness. She shook her head, and stepped into the hall of the temple.

Four elderly monks sitting cross-legged on a carpeted floor. It was very hot – a fat mosquito flew lazily in tracing figures of eight, as if drunk on the heat and humidity. The carpet worn from countless bare feet. A green jade statue rising ahead – a lizardine Buddha, looking at her with amusement.

She knelt down on the carpet. No feeling in her new leg but it obeyed her easily. The monks paid her no attention. The chanting continued, the air smelled of incense and sweat and gun oil.

Gun oil... she looked down at her arm and the Gatling gun shone silver in the light. She ran a finger, lightly, across her arm. Then she waited.

The drum beating like a heart – her heart. The ghosts of the dead whispered around her. She closed her eyes, giving in to the rhythm of the drums. She began to hear voices, babbling. Somewhere nearby. They said things like: Compilation of bio-data records approaching fifty percent and quantum pattern combination incomplete and attempt to locate source fail! and calibrating trans-dimensional gateway penetration routines and then another voice, a human one or mostly so, said, "Shut up!"

She opened her eyes.

Standing between the four elderly monks was a... was a man.

Mostly a man.

He was a grey armour, a hybrid of human and machine – complex shapes of silver darted across his skin, forming and re-forming, their patterns vastly complex, hinting at unsolved mysteries – his eyes were dark, his hair cut short, his hands were weapons. She thought – he is as beautiful as a gun.

The man, paying no heed to the monks, said, "Manchu!"

A hunched figure crawled to the man's feet. "Master," it said.

"Have you made the arrangements?"

"Everything is ready, Master."

She stared at the man, that beautiful, dangerous thing, like her a combination of human and machine. The Man on the Mekong, she thought. She stared at the jade statue of that alien, lizardine Buddha. The voices rose again, penetrating her mind: Geo-temporal relocation desirable – source of quantum burst unknown – entity nascent – trace patterns inconclusive–

A sense of sadness, a deep, ancient loneliness that almost overwhelmed her. The Man on the Mekong said, "Do be quiet. Manchu, prepare the boat for departure."

"Yes, Master."

The hunched figure slithered away. The man stood silently for a long moment. His eyes, dark as the heavens, were populated with jade stars. He raised his head, looked around, his face revealing sudden doubt. The monks continued their chanting, the drum continued to beat and Milady's heart beat with it.

She found herself looking into his eyes.

He took a step back, then held himself still. He was as still as a statue, as still as a gun waiting to be fired. He said, "Are you a ghost?"

She opened her mouth to speak, but no sound came out of her mouth. The voices babbled in the background about establishing contact protocols and rerouting physicality and lunar orbit station checksum negative, whatever any of it meant. The man said, "They are mad, you know."

She tried to speak again, but her voice was gone. "They send assassins after me," the man said. "Sometimes I wish they would succeed."

She stepped towards him, each silent footstep echoed by the drums. The ground seemed to shake beneath her. The monks continued to chant. Her eyes were still on his. His eyes were the deepness of space, and filled with the tiny, distant lights… "I am going from here," the man said, very softly. She stood close to him. When she reached out it was with her gun arm. His hand rose too, a metal hand, and clawed. They stood that way, not touching, not speaking, and the drum beat like a clock.

"Tell them…" he said. "Tell them that–"

Then his head moved back, his eyes shifting from hers, looking beyond her, and his eyes widened – "Get back!" he said, and then he pushed her, or at her, and she flew back from him, rising, dissipating like mist, through the roof of the temple, and for a brief moment looked down and saw the river alive with lights, an endless procession of candles floating serenely down the river, and a dark steamboat moored to a wharf–

She rose and the mists swallowed her and the drum beat and his voice echoed in her ears, a warning, and though she fought the pull it dragged her back, back into her body and she woke up, covered in cold sweat, in a dark red room, and an enormous, grotesque figure hovered above her.

FORTY-EIGHT
Escape from the Insane Asylum

Sade grinned, thick lips like overripe blackberries. In one hand he held a goblet, in the other a thin, surgical blade. A couple of the silent nuns were holding Milady, busy securing her to a rope hanging from a hook in the ceiling. She heard Sade say, "Hurry up, I want to start the examination–"

Milady let herself fall, her body becoming heavy and unresponsive. The two nuns faltered, reached for her–

She rolled, swept their legs underneath them. Her new metal leg rose, descended – crushed one of the women's kneecaps. The woman rolled on the floor, screaming, holding on to her leg – Milady aimed at the other woman's head, felt the nose smash. She rose, grinned, extended her gun arm–

Sade's smile faltered, then returned. "I did not expect you to wake so soon," he said.

She shot him. The Gatling gun barked, bullets smashing into the fat man's belly. Sade looked down, his smile gone, a confused expression on his face. Slowly, he reached down. His finger found a hole, pushed through. He brought it out again, smelled it, then put it in his mouth and sucked. He rolled his finger slowly in his mouth, then at last pulled it out, examined the nail for a moment, then let it drop. "I'm not that easy to kill," he said.

He picked up the goblet he had dropped. He took a swig of

wine. The wine flowed down his throat and out of the holes in his chest and stomach, staining his already-stained clothes an even darker red. Milady watched, repulsed, horrified. "Not the best vintage," Sade said. "Nevertheless, a shame to waste."

He threw the goblet at her. It hit her on the side of the head and her missing eye flared in green pain. She kicked, aiming for his kneecap, but he caught her leg easily, grinned, and made to break it.

She jumped, using his hands as leverage, rose high and did a back-flip. Sade said, "Impressive."

How did she do it? She didn't know. A new leg, a new arm – but was it Viktor's surgery or the jade in her body that did it? She didn't know and right then it didn't matter.

"Being a sportsman," Sade said, "I'll give you a head start." He turned away from her ponderously and, from a niche in the wall, picked up an enormous, ancient sword. He waved it experimentally, slashing the air with the dull-coloured blade, and laughed. "Oh, Milady de Winter!" he said. "You make me feel alive again."

She ran.

Sade roared behind her, booming out a laugh. She burst out of the room and found herself in a windowless corridor. Somewhere underground, she thought. She had to find a way up, to the surface. The corridor was dark. As she ran ghostly figures materialised at the end.

Nuns.

Nuns with guns.

She raised her arm, clenched the fingers that were no longer there, a half-turn as if turning a key in a lock, and the Gatling gun barked fire. One of the nuns dropped, the others returned fire. Milady threw herself on the floor, fired again. A noise behind her – Sade lumbering after her, the great sword swishing through the air. They put a madman in charge of the madhouse.

She rolled, jumped, was suddenly at the end of the corridor

– her foot lashing out, the Gatling gun arm slamming into heads, hands – the nuns dropped. Milady snatched up a fallen gun and kept running.

Stairs. She ran up them, into the dark level where Sade's quarters had been. Shouts behind her, gunfire, Sade's bellowing laugh. She should have gone up, but knew they would be waiting up there… She could hear the cries of the insane, agitated, carried down from their cells above.

She turned from the staircase, and once again entered Sade's quarters.

A sickly smell in the air, opium and hashish and candles and burnt wax and the sharp tang of cleaning fluids, though the place was a sty. A rack of pork ribs sat on a plate surrounded by glutinous sauce the colour of blood. Flies buzzed over the food. The same map of the Arctic region, the same cuffs and whips and glasses of old wine – she needed something, something she could use – but what?

From behind, snatches of conversation – "Where did she go?"

"She didn't come upstairs, we would have seen her."

"My quarters? The cheeky girl." That laugh again. She hated that laugh. She was going to choke it out of him if it killed her.

If she didn't die before she had the chance.

Searching the room, searching for weapons – a door half-hidden in the wall, unmarked. She tried the handle but the door was locked.

She kicked it open.

Darkness, the temperature a few degrees cooler. Behind her – "Milady! Yoo-hoo!" She shut the door behind her, waited for her eyes to adjust to the gloom. Nothing there – through the green jade that had become her eye she saw rough-hewn stairs cut into the stone, leading down–

"Where are you, my little bird?" – from behind the door.

Trapped.

She could make a stand right here, or she could go back down. She wondered what the stairs led down to, then decided there was only one way to find out.

When she followed them, the stairs led down to a hallway and three doors. The ground was the same rough stone. The air was cooler here. She looked at the doors:

Wine Cellar.

Operating Theatre.

Storage.

She'd had enough of wine and had no wish to go back to the second of the three.

She chose Storage.

"Leave my stuff alone!" a petulant voice, coming down the stairs.

Milady, looking at Sade's storage room, the jade casting a green glow over everything. "My, my," she said, quietly, and smiled. It felt good to be smiling again.

"We're not so different after all!" she called out. A heavy body crashing against the door. "Come out, little bird!"

"Not yet," she said, but quietly. Surveying the room, she felt like a kid on her birthday – though her birthdays had never been as good as this:

Machine parts, automaton parts – loose arms, loose legs, a brace of fingers – crates of bullets, a mounted cannon, curved and straight swords, a row of dusty books, miniature Tesla sets, knives, handguns, chemicals in vats, a few bottles of vintage wine, strange looking goggles, a medicine cabinet as large as a wardrobe, and there in the corner…

She said, "Beautiful," and went for the small crate marked Explosives.

"Ready or not, here I come!" Sade roared.

"Be ready in a moment, dear," she said, and helped herself to what she needed. She almost liked Sade then. He was a man of great appetite, and he kept a well stocked larder – for all eventualities.

When he burst through, roaring and waving the sword, she turned and shot him again, but it was little use, and he laughed. His bulk blocked the doorway. "Little bird," he said, "it's time for your medicine."

She needed to get past him. But how? He grinned, and came closer. She said, "Wait."

"Yes?"

Nothing came to mind so she kicked him between the legs instead – her new metal leg delivering a blow that would have felled a lesser man. But Sade was no longer a man.

He grunted, remained standing. The look he gave her was almost pitying. He reached one fat, meaty hand towards her, the fingers curling to grab her, and she almost screamed. Instead she pushed herself towards him.

They came together, her body against his bulk, taking him by surprise. She held on to him, one arm around his neck, and her gun arm snaked up and came to rest under his chin at an angle. "Want to dance?" she said. "Drop the sword."

He dropped the sword. "Careful now, little bird," he said. "Citizen Sade is not that easy to kill."

Her head was resting in the crook of his neck. She whispered, "But I don't want to kill you."

She felt him lick his lips. "What do you have in mind?"

"Let's step back out of the room," she said. "Slowly."

It was a precarious position and either one of them could change the balance in a single moment. She hoped he would go along.

He did. "I love to dance," he said. "And dancing with you, my lovely…" Slowly, bodies held together, they eased out of the room. "Turn," she whispered, and they did, until his back was to the storage room and hers to the staircase–

"My guards are waiting at the top," he said. "You won't get away. We can resolve this peacefully – I'll notify the Council–"

She felt his body twist even as he spoke – his hand, curling into a fist, caught her on the side of the head, rocked her away, and then a blade was flashing in his hand, a small surgical instrument that must have been hidden up his sleeve, and it came whispering towards her face–

She raised her arm to ward it off. It was the human arm and the knife cut through flesh. The pain burned through her – bright blood dripping to the ground, and Sade grinned. "I'll suck it right off your bones," he said.

She fled.

In her coat pockets the little birthday packages waited, and she dropped two down below and another when she reached the top, where the nuns waited. She fired, wondering how many rounds she had left. Not many. She hoped they would be enough. They fired back, and she had no choice but to charge through the open door, back into Sade's quarters, sending tables and chairs and maps and pipes and roast chicken to the floor, just trying to get away, get through the waiting nuns–

One came at her with a syringe and Milady turned and grabbed the woman's arm and broke it clean – a scream, and then she was out of the door and climbing the stairway to the cells.

Two more birthday presents in Sade's quarters, another one on the stairs – a bellow behind her – "No more games, Milady!"

The wails of the insane filled this floor. She passed locked cells and shot the locks, and the inmates of the Charenton Asylum came out of their cells and glared around them – the smiling man and the man who ate flies and the one who thought he was a wolf – and then the attacking nuns came into view and halted, and the released inmates, as if scenting blood, turned as one to look at them.

"Get out of here!" she shouted at them, but they only had eyes for the nuns. She didn't wait. She tossed more of the small packages into the emptied cells and when she reached the one that had been her own she went in. The window was still broken. A moon glared outside and a cloud of bats, frightened by the noise, were screeching as they flew over the roof. She kicked the bars.

Her new, more powerful leg, metal hitting metal, bent the bars. She kicked, again and again. Behind her, screams, gunshots, Sade's voice crying, "Animals! Back to your cells!"

Her smile was grim. She kicked, panting with the effort, and suddenly the entire panel of bars fell away from the window and crashed to the ground below. She went to the window, pushed herself up. The door behind her crashed open and Sade, bloodied and insane, filled the doorway. "Never!" he roared.

For a moment she was suspended on the windowsill, a dark shadow crouching, her head turned to him, her coat flapping in the breeze. They stared at each other. "They should have closed this place years ago," she said, softly. Then she smiled, and blew him a kiss, and as he came charging into the room she slid through the window and fell.

The ground came rushing up at her and she rolled with the impact, her breath knocked out of her. She rolled down the slope of wet grass and behind her the asylum stood, dark and forbidding and filled with screams. When she came to a stop she just lay there, for a long moment, getting her breath back. Then she stood up. Behind her the sound of gunshots and screams continued. She saw inmates come spilling out of the doors of the asylum. She heard Sade bellowing. Ahead of her was the gate, wrought iron, and beyond it freedom. She smiled and walked away from the asylum, her coat flapping in the wind, and as she did her hand reached into her pocket and found the Tesla transmitter she had picked up.

She pressed the button, still walking away.

Invisible waves travelling from her to the small packets she had distributed around the building... their own Tesla receivers picking up the signal, initiating a charge, and–

The heat of the explosion came rushing at her back,

throwing her forward, and for a moment she thought she was flying. Then the sound followed, multiple explosions joining into one giant booming wave of heat and sound and flame, and she rolled and came back to her feet and was through the gates, and when she turned the Charenton Asylum was a giant fireball on the hill, and dark shapes were streaming away from the fire and fled down the hill, and it took her a moment to realise they were rats, abandoning at last their ruined home.

She reached back into her coat pocket and brought out her shades, and put them on, and the flames reflected in the dark glass. Then she smiled, once, and walked away, towards the lights of Paris in the distance.

FORTY-NINE
The Return of the Phantom

Home was dark and cold, the gas lamps in the street outside whispering like grief-stricken relatives by a hospital bed. She let herself in, closed the door behind her, took a deep breath.

She was very tired.

In the fireplace, Grimm, dozing on long-dead coals. Milady knelt down, put the palm of her hand against the mechanical insect's head. The metal was warm. At her touch, Grimm's eyes opened. After a while Milady stood up.

She went to her bedroom. She undressed, went to the bath and ran the taps, adding salts and perfumes and soaps into the water until the foam threatened to grow out of control. While she waited for the bath to fill she looked into the full-length mirror. Slowly, she examined herself.

Scars, old and new. Without the eyepatch her eyes were mismatched, one dark, one a bright jade-green. She stared wonderingly at her new arm. The gun was light-weight, remarkably so. She looked at the place where her human arm ended and the machine gun began. The join was seamless.

The arm aroused strange feelings in her. With only five fingers she was clumsy – it was hard to grasp things, hard to dress, but the machine gun arm felt, somehow, as much a part of her. She stroked it with her remaining arm and decided she needed new rounds of ammunition to be put in.

Her leg, too, fascinated her. The same light material, with perfect joints, and somehow it obeyed her brain's commands – she raised it, kicking, then stood on it and pirouetted. She stood still and stared at her naked self in the mirror. Thinner, with a few new scars, her face gaunter than it'd been, but she was still herself, for all that. She was Milady de Winter, and she was still alive.

And she was armed.

Smiling faintly, she went to the bath and lowered herself slowly into the hot water. The water soothed her, bath salts at first burning, and then calming, her wounds. She closed her eyes – somehow that alien green jade could be controlled, which was another strangeness – and soon, without quite realising it, she fell asleep.

In the mist were the dead. Their voices called out to her. She saw Tom Thumb's face form in the mist, smiling at her sadly, puffing on a cigar. The smoke from the cigar rose and wreathed Tom's face and, slowly, it was Tom himself who became smoke, or fog, and blew away in an unseen breeze.

For just a moment the mists parted and she could see them, could see the dead: shambling corpses streaked with silver, snakes of molten silver-grey swirling across their bodies, and there was something beautiful about them, and precious, as if they were lives salvaged, not lost. They were walking along a river, but when she looked closer the river was merely a larger snake of the same silver-grey material and the dead were absorbed into it and it became a spiral that grew distant and at last disappeared...

Then there were cold stone walls around her and moss grew over the surface and she came to a door and she knew again where she was: this was the under-morgue, Containment Section: the place where they kept the most dangerous of their experiments, and those deemed too dangerous, by the Council, to ever be set free.

Iron Mask section – and suddenly she was afraid.

There was a sound coming from beyond the cell door. It took her a moment to recognise it as laughter.

The fear grew in her like a poisonous fungus, and for a moment she couldn't move. The laughter in the cell grew in volume and frenzy then, abruptly, stopped.

The silence was complete.

Containment Section, the under-morgue: she knew what lay beyond that door, though that was impossible – wasn't it?

She had killed him herself. She had watched him die – surely, surely she had watched him die?

Figures came walking down the corridor. Ghostly, they appeared, as if not quite real – Viktor, and three armed guards. When they walked past her it was as if she were the ghost. She realised they couldn't see her, and then thought, with some relief: This is just a dream.

Viktor went to the door and slid a small panel aside. He peered into the room, then brought out a small metal device from his lab coat. An Edison recorder, portable. He began murmuring into the device. "Subject shows extreme resilience. During the last week alone the changes in his physiology have been astounding. When first captured, subject appeared close to death, infected with the..." a pause, then Viktor said, with apparent distaste, "the so-called Grey Menace, at an advanced stage and shot through with Houdin's –" another short pause – "codename the Toymaker's experimental vaccine, delivered by means of a projectile weapon employed by Council agent de Winter."

The Phantom was alive.

She felt her throat constrict with bile. Her fingers curled into a fist and she wanted to put it in her mouth, to stifle the screams that wanted to come. Viktor said, "The subject's mind appears beyond repair. Yet his body, remarkably, is adapting. When first captured, subject had assumed an almost entirely inhuman appearance, particularly in the elongated shape of the skull and facial features, partially disguised by the subject by use of an iron mask. Now, however…"

Viktor paused again, and cleared his throat. There was silence from beyond the door. The three guards stood motionless. "Perhaps the effect of the Toymaker's vaccine helped to stabilise the subject's deterioration. But I suspect it is a foreign agent responsible for the change. The subject now exhibits a remarkable ability to alter his physiology at will, a mimicking as that evidenced in more primitive life forms… Physical strength is increased as well. As to the subject's mind, however…" Again, Viktor stopped. "Evaluation period extended by order of the Council, transferring subject to experimental sub-station Zero, Charenton Asylum." He pressed a button on the recorder, then slipped it back into his pocket. Speaking through the panel in the door, more loudly: "De Sade's looking forward to examining you, Tômas."

A growl from inside, then a burst of laughter. Viktor motioned to the guards. He put his palm against the door, waited.

The door slid open.

Milady stared, horrified, at the Phantom.

Gone was the mask, gone were the inhuman features of the face. The man who occupied the cell was handsome, brown-haired, and shackled to the floor and walls with heavy metal chains. "Viktor," he said. "It's good to see you."

Viktor made a jerking motion with his head. "Take him," he said. Milady watched as the three guards entered the cell…

The Phantom raised his head and looked directly at her. She took a step back, and he smiled, revealing white, even teeth. His eyes were the colour of green jade. Stop! she wanted to shout, but they couldn't hear her, couldn't see her. She wasn't really there. By inserting the fragment of jade into her eye, she suddenly realised, the Phantom had turned her into the lens of a camera obscura.

His eyes were on hers, and his smile became a leer, and she

could only watch as his skull began to shift and change, and teeth grew as his mouth extended–

Viktor, stop! but there was no one to hear her, and the guards were reaching for the chains and setting the Phantom loose when he rose, in one smooth, too-fast motion, and his hands had become talons, and he ripped the first man's face off and plunged his hand into another's belly before they even knew what had happened. The third guard raised his gun to fire... but the Phantom took it from him, like taking a toy gun from a child, and bashed him on the side of the head with the butt of the gun. He stood there, and his features slowly melted, the skull contracting, until the mild-mannered, handsome man he had once been stood there again – but this time he was unshackled and holding a gun, and a very frightened Viktor was backing away slowly as the Phantom advanced... The Phantom's jade eyes were on Milady's and he smiled, and said, "Sweet dreams, Cleo. I'll see you soon..." With one swift motion he had reached Viktor, and grabbed the scientist by the scruff of the neck. "Let's go, doctor," he said. "My ship awaits, and time and tide..." But she could not hear the rest, and the fog seemed to rise around her, flowing from the walls of the under-morgue, and the Phantom soon seemed a distant figure at the end of a white corridor, a cowering Viktor by his side, and then they were gone, or she was gone, and there was nothing but the mist, and the voices whispering far away about three-dimensional space-time constraints and quantum permutations scan and checksum errors and then they were all gone and she was floating face-down in a white, feathery sea, and it was rocking her, gently at first and then harder, and harder, until she thought she would drown and, crying out, opened her eyes.

FIFTY
The Message

"You look well," the Hoffman automaton said.

She had woken up from restless sleep and the sense of drowning, to see the hulking figure of her silent coachman standing above her.

Her presence was requested down below.

Now she sat before the Quiet Council. They were ranged before her like a shadowed fan; only the Hoffman automaton could be seen. How much do they know? she wondered uneasily. Her hand rose to her face, encountered the smooth leather of her new eyepatch, hiding the alien green jade below.

"We were very pleased with the outcome of the operation," the Hoffman automaton said. Milady, glancing down at her strange new arm, wondered which one he meant. "Most pleased."

She waited him out. The Hoffman said, "What happened at Charenton, on the other hand, is regrettable."

She couldn't hide a smirk. The Hoffman said, "De Sade's work for us is of a high importance. You destroyed–"

"I was kept prisoner!"

"You were kept safe," the Hoffman said.

"He wanted to experiment on me!"

"Be that as it may." The Hoffman sighed. "De Sade's…

enthusiasm sometimes gets the better of him. Nevertheless, his work for us is of the highest importance. The unfortunate incident you caused will set us back significantly."

"I didn't mean to burn down the asylum," she said, trying to sound contrite. "It was... an accident."

"Rebuilding Sade will take months!"

She shrugged. "Why bother?"

"Remember your place, Milady de Winter. I won't tell you again. There are secrets to which you have no access, schemes of the Council in which you have no part. De Sade is our tool – just as you are." The Hoffman waved a hand. Artificial eyes bored into hers. "Enough," he said. "We have use of you yet. Doctor Von F– tells us you are fully recovered?"

It took her a moment to realise he meant Viktor. Anger, so strong it threatened to render her mute, but she said, "I lost–"

"You lost!" Hoffman said. "What did you lose, Milady de Winter? A body appendage or two? A human is no less a machine than we are. Parts can be replaced."

She stared again at her arm. Her new arm. The metal glinted in the dim light of the cavern. "You performed the task set before you," the automaton said, "and you did it... well enough. Are you... unsatisfied?"

She stared at him, mute at last. She stared down at her arm, stroked it. The tips of her human fingers on the warm, light metal of this strange, deadly new arm... Six months, she thought. Six months in a hospital bed, the hospital in question being an old, secretive, insane asylum. No, she wanted to say. No, I am not bloody satisfied.

But she kept mum. Fragments of her dreams came back to her, teasing, green dead fingers reaching into her scalp... "Where is Viktor?" she said.

As if eager to answer her, the doors of the Council chamber banged open. The figure of a man lurched in, face bloodied, clothes torn. Viktor – and this sight of him made her the happiest she'd been for a long while. Viktor fell down to his knees. His long, bony face was raised, his eyes white, staring at the shadowed Council. "He's gone!" he said. His eyeballs seemed to shudder crazily, like a compass which had lost its bearings. "Tômas – he's escaped!"

Silence greeted his words. Milady, sitting in her chair, stroking her Gatling gun arm. She hadn't dreamt it after all. Before her, the Council seemed to draw deeper into the shadows. At their head, the point of the arrow, the Hoffman's face was impassive. "Explain yourself," he said.

"Gone," Viktor said. "Gone, gone! He killed the... he killed... the guards... and he took, he took..." He looked to Milady then, his eyes pleading. She smiled at him. There was nothing warm in that smile. "He made me take him outside..." Viktor whispered.

The Hoffman said: "And yet you live?"

She smiled again. She was, she realised, enjoying this. It was hard to tell if the Hoffman's question sounded incredulous, or disappointed.

"He told me... he sent me to... to deliver a message. Tômas said..."

"He is going after the primary object."

"Yes." Surprise in Viktor's voice. The Hoffman slowly nodded his mechanical head. "Leave us," he said.

"But... I don't..."

"Go."

Viktor stared at the automaton. His eyes shifted to Milady, found no sympathy there. Slowly, he nodded. "I need medical attention," he said.

No help was forthcoming. Slowly, the wounded scientist turned and began crawling towards the doors. Milady said: "Doctor, heal thyself..."

The look he turned back on her was full of hatred.

FIFTY-ONE
Onwards to Vespuccia

When Viktor was gone the chamber was silent. Milady, staring at the unseen faces in the shadows, said, "You let him escape."

The Hoffman said: "I beg your pardon?"

She said, "You wouldn't know how."

His silence was an answer in itself. She said – demanded – "Why?"

"Tômas still has his uses," the Hoffman said.

"I killed him! He should be dead!"

"He is not easy to kill. Neither are you, Milady."

"Why did you let him go?"

"He escaped."

"I want to know!"

"You will know what we want you to know," the Hoffman said, dispassionately. "But very well. A month ago we received a communiqué from the Man on the Mekong. He wishes to make the trade."

"With France?"

"With whoever bids the highest," the Hoffman said. "The primary object in his possession is a key, a thing of infinite value. While you were... resting, several expeditions were sent to locate the man in the hope of retrieving the object. We believe he was residing in a city deep in the Mekong Valley, in the lands of the Lao, named Luang Prabang. Unfortunately, such attempts as were made had... failed."

She thought of her dreams again, the giant drum echoing in the night, the thousands of lights floating down the river, and a man preparing to depart in a steamer, the jade statue of a lizard keeping guard... She said, "He is moving."

Was that surprise in the Hoffman's voice? "Yes," he said. "His message says he has decided to hold an auction for the primary. He has chosen the location well... He would not be easy to find."

"And so you let Tômas escape? You would use him to hunt the Man on the Mekong?"

"He is so very good..."

"I'm better."

"Indeed, Milady." A small smile played on the Hoffman's rubbery face, and then she understood: two sets of traps, one within the other – or was it two types of bait, thrown out on a single line?

"There is a ship waiting for you at the docks in Marseilles," the Hoffman automaton said. "You leave with the tide."

"Where?" she said, but something inside of her already knew, anticipated the single word that came, with the hiss of an old record, from within the Hoffman, as if she had known all along, as if her dreams already told her where the Man on the Mekong had gone...

"Vespuccia," the Hoffman automaton said.

INTERLUDE
The Lean Years

Then came the lean years. Years in which the statue waxed and waned, but mostly stayed quiet, its power exhausted. Years in which Kai no longer knew who he was – what he was. Somewhere, far behind him, lay a past, but it was distant and shrouded in mist. There had been a room full of steam, and the smell of clean clothes, and a warm breeze coming through the open doorway, carrying the smell of rain and falling leaves... The past was beyond the river, it was another, distant bank. The river was one that he couldn't cross.

In the long lean years the city was his to do with as he wished, but he kept himself hidden, still, after all the years, afraid. Others would come for him, he knew. They had come after him the night they killed his father and they would continue to come, never relenting, until they finally got what they wanted.

At night he read. He no longer needed candles. It was part of the change wrought in him, and though it brought him no joy, he was glad he could read.

Though he still read the wuxia stories of his childhood he increasingly turned to new books, and particularly to those tales of visitors to that wild and proud continent some called Vespuccia.

They told of a wide open place where the bison roamed

endlessly across the plains; of refugees from the Lizardine Empire, coming to the shores of that great continent in rickety ships, in waves, seeking shelter away from the lizards' rule; of the League of Peace and Power and of the Council of Chiefs and of the great cities that were being erected there, amidst the mountains and plains; of impossible machines, of Tesla sets and airships–

He loved stories of the mysterious pirates that were said to roam the seas (which he had never seen), of strange islands hiding ancient secrets, and most of all he thrilled reading about the entity called the Bookman, which may have been a man and may have been something else entirely. A secret assassin, like a being out of wuxia, who fought those strange lizards beyond the sea. A thing, in a way, like Kai himself, or so he thought.

In the lean years he began to weave his web of shadows, staying always in the dark. The Manchu was his messenger, his lieutenant, and through him others came, and his secret power grew, there in the city called Luang Prabang on the half-island, in the meeting of two rivers. The statue was very weak then, and he barely heard the voices.

Those were the lean years. Then everything, suddenly, changed...

PART V
The White Worm

FIFTY-TWO
Cargo

She woke up from uneasy sleep, dreams fading of a man travelling by ship through stormy seas. He'd been standing on deck and the green lizard statue was sitting in the prow and ball lightning danced around it as if the storm itself was in worship… She had stood on the deck and the man slowly turned and his eyes were on hers. He'd whispered something, but the wind snatched the words away.

She woke up to the motion of waves, the rocking of the ship. Rain outside, darkness beyond the small porthole. She lay still on the narrow bed. Listening.

Was that a rustle at the door? Was an unseen hand rattling the handle? Two days out of port and she'd been getting uneasy, listening out for the small noises in the night, the sounds that shouldn't be there.

Beyond the door, the boards creaked. Was that just the stress in the hull? Or were unseen feet stepping across the corridor? She pictured drowned corpses crawling hand and foot across the lower deck, dripping salt water, their skin bloated and pale.

She lay very still.

On the way to France, all those years ago, she had not been alone, but they still died around her, and in her dreams the lifeless corpses were still flung overboard. There had been ceremony at first, with each loss of life, but as the journey progressed no one said a prayer, and the bodies were simply disposed of. Her mother…

She closed and opened her eyes. Was that something fluttering against the window? A dark shape against the glass, or –?

She swung herself out of bed in one smooth motion and when she turned to the porthole there was nothing there. She raised her gun arm and tiptoed to the door and yanked it open–

Nothing beyond. She took a deep breath. The ship was working insidious fears deep into her mind, the way saltwater could drip, slowly, never stopping, until its touch became like acid, and it wore away body and mind…

There was nothing there. Nothing beyond the door but an empty corridor, and nothing outside but rain clouds, and a gale – and a deep watery grave underneath.

From Paris to Marseilles by train, and to the docks, where the White Worm waited: an inauspicious name for a ship.

"Woman on board brings bad luck," the captain said, and coughed out a globule of phlegm overboard, then laughed. "But this is a bad-luck ship."

Captain Karnstein: tall and wizened and wrapped in a too-long, dirty coat that hung loose over his frame. His forehead was lined, the lines like scars, and a thick, black beard grew over his face like a gathering of molluscs stuck to a rock. She said, "When do we sail?" and the captain spat again and jerked his head at the shore and said, "When the cargo's loaded."

She was going to say, What cargo? but just then a familiar figure appeared on the dock and she felt her gun hand twitch. Viktor stood down below. He had cleaned the blood from his face but still looked bad. There was a new vitality about him, she noticed uneasily. He practically shone. He looked bigger, bulkier than he had only hours before. When he raised his face his eyes met hers and she almost looked away. His eyes burned, and the smile on his face was ugly. The drugs, she thought. He must have used the Hyde formula – on himself.

And how long has he been doing that for?

Below on the docks, Viktor made a mock bow. "Milady de Winter!" he called up.

She said, "Viktor." Her voice was soft. "You seem much recovered."

"Rest..." his voice was like the rest of him – too loud, and at the same time brittle – "is always the best medicine."

"No doubt..." She raised her voice. "What are you doing here?"

"Supervising the cargo." His smile remained. Like Viktor himself, the smile stayed unpleasant.

Some things simply didn't change.

Behind Viktor, porters appeared. A grey mist lay over the docks, and the blowing wind was cold, easing frozen fingers through Milady's coat, touching her skin like the fingers of the dead. The porters were carrying long, heavy-looking casks. The solid wood was shut tight with iron. She took a deep breath, steadied herself. You could shoot Viktor, but you couldn't shout at him. She said, "What is this?"

"Nothing that need concern you."

Taking another deep breath, she walked down the gangplank to the wharf. "I won't ask you again," she said. Viktor took a step back. "Council orders," he said, sounding suddenly nervous. Good. She took a step towards him, and was gratified when he stepped back. "I have the paperwork!" Viktor said. "Here." He produced a sheaf of papers from a coat pocket and waved it at her. Around them, the porters swarmed, six men lifting one cask each, carrying it up the gangplank onto the dark ship. Milady was aware of Captain Karnstein's gaze from above. When she raised her head the captain only spat again, and the globe of mucus was swallowed by the sea.

"Give me that." She tore the papers from his hands. "Biological specimens – hazardous?"

"Nothing to be worried about," Viktor said reassuringly – which made her worry even more. "They're just samples for the research station on Scab. Send my regards to the countess, will you?"

"What?"

"Look!" Viktor said. "This is none of your concern. You're off to Vespuccia. Well, good for you." He grinned suddenly. "Did you know the lizardine court has asked for your extradition?"

That hit her hard. For a moment she forgot about the cargo or its mysterious destination. "What... what for?" she said.

"They said, and I quote: 'To assist Scotland Yard in their inquiries into the as-yet unsolved death of Lord de Winter'," Viktor said, and grinned.

"Why would they do that?"

"I sense that fat oaf Mycroft Holmes might have had something to do with it," Viktor said. "You seem to have a knack for making friends, Milady."

"Is that why..." she said, and faltered. "The asylum?"

"Keep you out of the way for a while, yes. The peace with the lizards across the Channel is fragile. They are too powerful for us to fight. What waits in Vespuccia could change that, however... which reminds me."

Around them the porters surged, the sealed casks disappearing one by one up the gangplank. "You are officially a fugitive from justice," Viktor said. "The Council will deny all knowledge of you. According to the information being sent to the lizardine ambassador as we speak, you broke out of Charenton, destroying the asylum in the process and releasing a horde of dangerous criminals into the streets of Paris. No doubt they are already well aware of the situation. That fire you started could be seen for miles."

For a moment she almost smiled. Viktor said, "You then

took the train to Marseilles, and there found a ship to take you away from the continent, destination unknown. You're a fugitive, disowned by the Council. In other words, Milady – you're on your own."

She shrugged, and said, "When has it ever been different?" The last of the casks had been loaded onto the White Worm. Viktor said, "Have a safe journey."

The fog thickened around them. She could barely see his face. "What's in the casks?" she said.

"Nothing," Viktor said. "They don't exist. And neither, any more, do you, Milady."

She reached out for him but he disappeared, moving quickly, with a sort of animal grace, into the fog. She had to feel her way back to the gangplank. The chill was beginning to settle into her bones. The research station on Scab?

And she was a fugitive, she'd have no support once she reached the Long Island, once she landed in Vespuccia. Well, that, at least, was something she was used to.

Do not touch Tômas, they told her, before she left. Your mission is to obtain possession of the object. For the benefit of the Republic, for the glory of France.

They wanted her to lay off the Phantom, but she had her own ideas about that...

From above, Captain Karnstein's scratchy voice punctured the night, with two words and a final stop ending, perhaps forever, she thought, her old life. She hurried up the gangplank, scrambling to get on board the White Worm.

"Tide's up," Captain Karnstein said.

FIFTY-THREE
The Unfortunate Death of Flies

Storm lashing the sea into rebellion; waves rising dark as empty houses; the wind howled, its anger beating against the ship. Milady thought: The ocean doesn't want us here.

She had lit a candle. Now she sat up, unable to sleep, every muscle tight with anticipation. The sounds of night scuttled through the ship like rats, and every creak and groan sent a shiver down her spine.

They were coming, and she was afraid.

On that long-ago journey to France, the hold was crowded with hot and sweating bodies. Babies cried incessantly. Flies, unwelcome emigrants who had jumped onto the ship, buzzed everywhere. We are going to a better place, her mother had said, whispering, holding her tight. But young Cleo still heard the unvoiced words that hung there, at the end of the sentence, like an empty noose in the breeze: I hope.

Hope was not a commodity worth buying. It died with her mother, died with the long voyage to the cold lands of pale-skinned men and plump, hard-eyed women and obtuse machines. It died on the streets of Paris, cut away from her soul with a sharpened knife. Hope was dangerous, the noose promising only one thing.

She had no use for hope.

She had been afraid on that long crossing and she was

afraid again now. Outside the porthole there was nothing but ocean, the Atlantic spreading out in all directions. The water was black and there was no moon, and the wind howled incessantly, like a dying baby.

They were coming for her – and there was no getting away.

The second night out of Paris she dined with the captain at his table. Karnstein was a dour, solitary figure. She rarely saw his men – the rat men, she came to think of them for, like the rats who infested the ship, Karnstein's men were sometimes heard, but seldom seen.

They were dining on chicken. A drumstick was wedged between the captain's lips, the grease running down into his thick black beard. The chicken tasted of cloves. Beside the captain's plate stood a tall glass filled with pure lemon juice. Every now and then he would pause, banish the chicken a short distance from his mouth, and take a long swallow of lemon juice. "Scurvy," he'd announce every time, a shudder making his face move as if a sudden earthquake had taken place across its tectonic plates. "Can't be too careful with Lady Scurvy. She'd eat you from the inside and make you bleed, every time."

Milady nodded, and tore a chunk of bread, and chewed it. It was floury and hadn't been baked long enough, and there were little black dots scattered through the dough that suggested the unfortunate death of flies. It made her think of the man in the cell at the Charenton Asylum. The captain said, "You're not eating! Eat!" and pushed the chicken carcass towards her.

"I'm not so hungry..." she said. The captain shook his head. "Eat every meal as it if were your last," he said, taking another deep gulp of lemon juice and shuddering.

If I eat this meal, Milady thought, it almost certainly will be my last. The meal had the feel of a last supper served to the condemned. The small dining-room was dim and gloomy, with thick tapestries hanging over the walls. She found herself studying them, noting scenes depicting – what?

Scenes of torture and battle; helmeted men with steel spikes attacking upright lizards whose weapons breathed flames; men dying with gaping, burning wounds; a captive lizard roasted alive above a fire; a flying machine mowing down soldiers with a hail of flying, metallic arrows; men running, lizard eggs captured, broken open; lizard young being stomped on; a castle, a siege; men hanging in rows from drab black trees. She said, "What is it?" and lifted a glass of wine to her lips. The wine had a slightly rancid taste.

"That?" Karnstein said, turning – with some surprise, it seemed to her – to the ancient tapestries. "Flights of fancy," he said, waving the drumstick bone at the images. "Things that never happened."

"It looks very... real," she said. The captain shrugged. "It's called The Battle of the Borgo Pass," he said. "An old legend from my homeland... fanciful, but it lends a certain élan to the room, don't you think?"

"Quite," Milady said.

It was hard to eat one-handed, though she was getting the hang of it, slowly. Her gun-arm rested on the table. She said, "Where is the cargo headed?"

The captain put down his drumstick with some sadness and reached greasy fingers to tear a chunk of breast from what remained of the chicken. "Closed orders," he said.

"Viktor mentioned a place called... Scab?"

A grim smile etched itself, the way acid etches itself on glass, for a brief moment on the captain's lips. "Closed orders," he said again. And – "You are to confine yourself to your quarters while cargo offloads."

"Where?" she said. "We're in the middle of the ocean!"

That smile again, and the chicken disappearing into it. She decided to change tack. "Aren't you worried about the cargo?" she said.

"Should I be?"

"It could be dangerous."

"The ocean's dangerous," the captain said and then, unexpectedly: "I hate the sea."

There was something wild and uncontrolled in the way he said it. His pupils, she noticed, had become dilated. His breathing grew heavy. She didn't speak again and, a short time later, excused herself from the table.

After that she took all her meals in her cabin.

And now they were coming. She listened out for their sounds. The tread of feet on boards, the ghostly whisper of an icy wind. The White Worm grunted and groaned all around her. She huddled on the narrow bed, her back to the wall. Watching the door.

Waiting.

For here, on the ship, she was no longer Milady de Winter. The years had been peeled away from her with a knife and what remained, in the small, dank cabin, was a small and frightened girl.

That same smell was in the hold of the ship when they had sailed to France… fear, sweat, bodies pressed together. "We're going to a new home," her mother had whispered to her. "A better place." Her mother's hope was like a candle. It had been easily snuffed. Or perhaps, she thought now, perhaps her mother never believed there was hope, but in pretending that for her daughter had tried to make it real, to wish it into being. Her body, like the others', was thrown overboard. By the time they arrived at port there were few enough of them left.

She rocked herself, hugging her knees one-handed, her gun arm useless by her side. The dead never truly went away, she thought.

She watched the door, waiting for them to come.

FIFTY-FOUR
Captive of the Waves

Sailing, with no land in sight, clouds in the distance assuming the shapes of imaginary continents, an entire alien cloudscape in the skies. Did someone live up there? Did cloud-women hunt amidst the grey-white landscape, did cloud-women fish from high above, dangling lines and hooks to snare a passing ship far down below? When she stood on the deck the air smelled of brine and tar and oil. It smelled cold, and she felt far away from home.

A whale in the distance, rising to the surface, blowing out a jet of water before the immense dark shape submerged into the water once more. A school of flying fish skittered over the surface like silver bullets. Steps behind her – Karnstein, wrapped in his dirty coat, a pipe stuck between his teeth: "Whales are the Queen's eyes, they say."

She didn't need to ask what queen he meant. In all the world there was only one that mattered.

She remembered Victoria. During the time of her second marriage she had often visited the Royal Palace. A tall, dignified being, her tail long and royal, her eyes hard. There were pools – swamps – in the Royal Gardens, and rocks for the royals to sun themselves on. The queen had a disconcerting habit of catching flies with her quick, long tongue... And she remembered the whales in the Thames. It was said they followed Vespucci's ship when it returned from Caliban's Island, bringing with it a strange new future…

"What's in the casks?" she said. Beside her, Karnstein chuckled. "You ask as if you already know the answer, Milady."

A clear grey sea, no land in sight… no other ships, no birds this far away from land. A desolate place – but this was only above. What lay below? The ocean had its own life-forms, its own geography, its own mysteries… ones she never wanted to know.

Somewhere deep down there, her mother–

"How much longer?" she said. Karnstein tapped his pipe on the railings. Ash and loose tobacco fell and blew away on the wind. "Making good time," he said grudgingly, then – "Might be a storm coming."

She left him there. Back in her cabin, the feeling of helplessness intensified. In the city, in the dark streets of Paris, she reigned supreme, but out here she was nothing but a prisoner, a captive of the waves…

She knew what was – what had to be – inside the casks. Biological specimens – hazardous. But she had to know for sure.

When she stepped out into the corridor there was no one there. She reached the stairs – nothing. There was no sign of Karnstein's rat men. Quietly, she began her descent towards the hold.

Why weren't they coming? She had seen them. She had made her way down into the hold. The smell of rot was strong, grew stronger the deeper she went. The darkness was near absolute – and yet, she could see.

Green jade shadows like cold shuddering flames… She saw not with her human eye but with the other, that foreign object lodged into the hollow socket of her missing eye. The thing in her skull responded to the shadows, writhing inside, and she bit her lip or she would have screamed with the pain. The jade fragment was alive, it was reaching into her brain, it was… it was excited, she thought.

Long wooden casks, bound in metal, were lined along the floor of the White Worm's hold.

But why lie? she thought. Call them what they truly were.

Coffins.

Viktor's research, the Phantom's gruesome job for the Council: the corpses of the infected, the bodies of those, like poor dead Madame L'Espanaye, who were touched by that alien illness that had entered Paris.

Though it was very dark in the hold, and the coffins were made of thick wood, she could nevertheless see them. Her jade eye showed her the interred corpses within their prisons. They were not still.

Restless, the deformed figures in the coffins writhed and fought to escape. Silver strands oozed across their dead and bloated bodies. A device, she thought again, recalling her dream, the temple on the Mekong, and the man who looked a little like her, who looked at her… a machine for recording the dead.

Or did they fail to understand it entirely?

There was a rustle in the shadows and she nearly jumped. She turned, heart beating, gun arm extended – jade-light showing her a bow-backed figure shuffling forward. Then a light flared, almost blinding her, and a gruff voice said, "Out of bounds, the hold is. What you doing here?"

In the light of the hurricane lamp the hold looked ordinary enough. There were coils of rope and fishing nets and sea chests, and the casks that weren't casks were silent and unmoving, as if they held nothing much inside. The speaker was one of Karnstein's dour rat men: whiskers grew out of his pale face and his figure was hunched as if from the weight of too many years at sea. His coat, like his captain's, was dirty, patched in places, torn in others. He wore a cap low over his eyes.

"Nothing," she said. "It was very dark, I–"

"Out of bounds," the rat man said. "Nothing to see."

"Perhaps if you could show me the way back–" she said, and then she paused.

For just a moment, the man had raised his face, regarding her through rheumy eyes – and at that moment she saw it.

A strand of silver-grey matter moving, almost sensuously, like a snake, across the man's skin.

FIFTY-FIVE
Infected

The same ocean, different skies… She was on the deck of the smaller ship and the man was there too, the man who was a little like her. Kai. Somehow she knew his name.

Kai.

The jade lizard sat in the prow, surrounded by candles. Incense wafted on the wind.

The man was leaning against the railings, looking out to sea. She approached him on soft feet. Above their heads the sky was a reddish-purple vista being slowly devoured by darkness. Stars were coming out, in ones and twos at first and then more and more of them, until the whole of the Milky Way was spread out across the sky from one horizon to the other.

"The sky was purple like a bruise, fading to black…" the man by the railings said. She noticed he was holding a book in one hand. He said, "I like that."

"Yes, Master," a voice said. She realised he was talking to his manservant, who was kneeling before the statue.

"I will be glad when this is over," the man said. He stared out across the sea, letting the hand holding the book drop to his side.

"Is it decided, then, Master?"

"They will not rest until they take it from me," he said. His voice was so sad... She had the urge to reach out and touch him, stroke his hair. "I will sell it to them, instead."

"For the right price, Master," the manservant said.

"Yes... my life," the man said.

He doesn't want it, she thought. He is a captive of this thing as much as I am. She went and stood beside him. Together they gazed at the field of stars.

"I don't understand it," the man said. He half-turned his head. Suddenly, she was aware of him looking directly at her. "I don't understand what it wants, what it does."

She stood very still. The man suddenly smiled. "My silent ghost," he said. "Or am I your ghost?"

"Master? Is something wrong?"

"It is nothing, Manchu."

She liked his eyes. She reached a hand, her human one, to cup his face, but her fingers left no impression on his skin.

"They are quiet tonight."

It was true. She could not hear the voices of the statue. "What do they expect to happen, when we reach Vespuccia?" he said. She tried to speak, to answer him, but no words came. "My silent ghost," he said again, and smiled, and then, as they did once before, his eyes looked beyond her and the smile melted from his face and he pushed at her–

Startled, she stumbled back, fell over the railings towards the dark sea–

She woke up with her hair damp against her forehead, her heart hammering in her chest. How could she have fallen asleep? The door to her cabin was ajar. A narrow band of light pierced through into the room. A dark figure standing above her, leaning down...

She saw a rat man and there were things crawling over his face, and silver-grey swirls moving in his eyes... Her gun arm rose instinctively, the muzzle almost touching the rat man's face. He paid it no attention, and his sick, dead eyes were fastened on hers, and now his hands, hands like claws were reaching for her and she–

She fired, her arm pumping as the bullets shot out, hitting the man at point-blank range in the face, blood and bits of skull flying everywhere. And now she could hear a cry rising through the ship – a communal, wounded screech that echoed eerily down the corridor, seeming to merge with the groaning of the White Worm.

Infected, she thought, horrified. She struggled to her feet, her naked toes almost slipping in the pool of blood. They were all infected. The rat man had fallen away from her and was lying on the floor. Half his face was gone. Still, he tried to rise, fingers scrabbling blindly against the floor.

She fired again, until he settled back and at last wouldn't move again. The silver-grey strands wove in and out of existence across his body, but as movement stopped they, too, were still.

She had fallen asleep in her clothes. She put on shoes and her coat, one-handed. The smell of the dead man was on her. Another howl, coming closer. They must be all over the ship, she thought.

And somehow, in there – amidst the fear and confusion – a sense of relief. It's begun. They are coming, at last.

She had warned the captain. After the incident in the hold, she had run back up to the deck, gone straight to Karnstein.

"A plague?" the captain said, hacking a cough around the word as if it were a sweet. "What's dead stays dead, Milady."

"Not any more," she said.

"Well," the captain said. He was rolling something in his mouth thoughtfully. She decided she really didn't want to know what it was. "We'll be reaching Scab soon enough. She'll know what to do."

"Who?" she said – shouted – at him.

"The countess," he said, as if surprised by her ignorance.

"So, nothing's changed. Remember to confine yourself to your quarters when cargo–"

"Is being offloaded, yes," she said. "But the cargo has already offloaded itself!"

A look of distaste crossed Captain Karnstein's face and he hawked onto the deck. She stared, horrified, at the little glob of silver-grey goo.

"It's strange," Captain Karnstein said, "but do you know, I've never felt better."

She watched the little globe stretch itself across the boards of the deck. Slowly, meticulously, it began to draw itself towards her.

She turned and ran.

Now she stepped over the still corpse of the rat man. The door, ajar. She reached, pushed it open, stepped into the corridor, gun arm at the ready.

But where could she go?

She was trapped in a place worse than any prison – for there was nowhere to go. Her warden was the ocean, and it was everywhere, hemming her in, offering no escape but a watery death.

Were they all infected? She needed the crew. She did not know how to pilot a ship. She had once piloted a plane – a small, fragile, dangerous thing, but at least the land was always close…

Here there was no land.

Trapped.

Stepping down the corridor, she silently cursed Viktor and the Council. The helplessness of her situation weighed her down. Stop, an inner voice whispered. There is no point in fighting any longer. This is how it ends – at sea, the way it had begun, so long ago.

Her mother waited for her, beneath the waves.

She decided to try to reach the upper deck. But when she

reached the end of the corridor they were waiting, three of them, rat men in their tatty clothes, and their faces were hungry.

They were very quiet. She said, "Please–" and raised her human hand before her, the fingers splayed. "You are sick. You need help."

Their mouths opened in tandem. Their teeth shone wetly. Silver strands like eels crawled across their arms and faces. She took a step back. "What do you want with me?"

They didn't answer. Together, they took a step towards her, gaining for themselves the ground she had ceded. "Who is piloting the ship?"

No answer. What did they want with her? Somehow, the infection in the casks must have seeped out, infected the men...

The statue. It was a mechanism of some sort, she knew that. A device for... she didn't know, exactly. All she knew was that it was spreading.

As if in response to her thoughts, she felt the alien entity in her eye socket awaken. Her hand rose to her head, pain jolting her. The approaching figures of the rat men were illuminated in a jade-green light, and she could see the entire spread of the infection on them. It was... responding. Responding to the alien shard lodged in her cranium.

They wanted the fragment of jade.

From somewhere, far, far away, whispering, insane voices: quantum encoding of data at tertiary levels, chrono-spatial scan proceeding, probe regeneration at full capacity–

Instinctively she raised her gun arm, fired, rounds of bullets emerging out of the Gatling gun, pounding into her attackers, these walking dead men, sending them back, breaking them.

She stepped through a storm of smoke and blood, gaining the stairs, running for her life.

FIFTY-SIX
Lights

Captain Karnstein, silhouetted like a bat against the sky. His rat men kneeling on the deck before him, mouths opening and closing without sound. Milady stopped, stood still. "They are coming!" the captain shouted. The silhouette turned, gazed on her without surprise. "Chrono-spatial scan proceeding!"

"Proceeding…" the rat men echoed in unison.

"Data-gathering approaching projectional capacity!" Captain Karnstein said.

"Capacity…" the rat man echoed.

No one at the helm. No steam rising from the boilers, the sails slack. The wind howled along the deck, and she felt herself shiver. Clouds in the distance, coming closer, a mass of darkness blocking out the stars.

She pointed, shouted – "There's a storm coming! We need to get the ship moving again!"

"Checksum error!" the captain said. "Checksum error!"

"Error…" the rat men murmured. "Error…"

She approached the captain. Her gun arm was raised, aimed. She felt herself shaking. "Get. The ship. Moving again," she said.

"The ships are coming," the captain said. "The fleet, the fleet is…" He faltered, fell silent. In the jade-green light of her foreign eye she saw them all, crawling with silver-grey worms. She said, trying to keep her voice steady: "Think of your ship. Would you have it destroyed?"

"The ship..." the captain whispered. "I have seen the ship... it was enormous, and yet as small as a speck of dust as it sailed amongst the stars..."

"Don't make me shoot you!"

His eyes rose, met hers. Was there a plea for help in those silver-grey orbs? The wind howled, making the captain's tattered coat flutter in the dark night like bat's wings. "Karnstein, please!"

But it was no use. If there had been understanding in his eyes, it died even as she watched, and the captain turned away from her. Lightning illuminated the skies, and an explosion of thunder came almost immediately after. Salt water spray stung her eyes. This is it, she thought. This is how it ends.

"Get her," Karnstein said.

Doom came on Lady de Winter like a settling of silk. Her back pressed to the railings, her gun arm raised, uselessly, before her, the band of crazed, infected sailors closing in on her, all seemed to signal an inglorious end.

And why not? she thought. Her earliest memories were of a ship, and death. It would be a fitting end...

The rat men's teeth shone in the flash of lightning. Thunder shook the deck. The rat men came for her, slowly, hands reaching out, mouths opened in hungry grins... silver snaked across their bodies, the back of their hands and across their cheeks. A wave hit the hull, spraying her with salt water, and for a moment she lost her footing.

The impact of the deck winded her. The rat men's hands were grasping for her and she fought them off, life returning as she realised she did not want to die – not here, on the stinking deck of a death ship, in the middle of a dark and hostile ocean. Cities she understood. But she would not die at sea.

With a scream of rage her gun arm came up and she shot the nearest rat man at point-blank range, the bullets slamming into the man's chest, tearing a hole clear through. For a moment the man was still, and she could see the night sky through his chest, a gathering of stars and a flash of lightning–

The man fell to the ground. His fingers twitched. His dead eyes opened, blinked slowly. Reaching out, his hand caught her ankle and would not let go.

Another flash of lightning, and another, and she tried to kick but he wouldn't let her go. She pushed herself up, one-handed, and stomped on his fingers with her artificial leg, hearing the bones in his hand break. Then she was free, and pushing away from the slow-moving sailors, backing away as she tried to make sense of what she'd seen.

For just a moment, glimpsed in the flash of lightning through the hole in the rat man's chest, she had seen something impossible.

She kept backing away, but now they were behind her, too, and she knew there was no escape.

Or only one...

Salt on her lips, rain and sea water falling down on her face. She raised her head, searching for the shadow in the dark.

A flash of lightning and–

There!

It wasn't possible – was it?

An enormous dark shape loomed above the ship, growing larger – growing closer, she realised.

What was it?

Did she imagine it? A flash of lightning again, the boom of thunder making the deck shudder, waves beating against the hull. In the light of the storm the sailors' faces were a pale sickly white, the silver strands oozing across their skins...

A city in the sky.

Towers rose high above the ship. Dark towers etched against the storm. A city moving on the waves–

She fired but the bullets did little to stop the rat men. And there came Karnstein, his coat flapping around him like the wings of a bat – coming for her.

Lightning hit close by, and one of the rat men shrieked. She smelled burning flesh, and watched as the man rolled on the deck, the silver strands flaming, melting, oozing off his skin... She blinked rain from her eyes. In the darkness she could no longer see the impossible city.

No one spoke. The burning rat man was motionless, a puddle of rain steaming around his body. Could electricity kill them? There was so little she knew about the infection. Hands reached for her, grabbed her. They had her gun arm now, and when she fired it was too late, the burst going wide, hitting nothing. She managed to release her arm but they had her by her coat and were grasping for her legs. She had only one chance–

She took it.

They were holding her coat when she tore herself out of it and ran for the railings. A flash of lightning again, an immediate corresponding boom of thunder, and the ship heaved, and she saw a dark, silent city rising out of the waves like a scab on the skin of the ocean. Memories of her mother returned, the corpses being hoisted off the deck, into the hungry sea... Still running, she jumped, and a howl rose behind her and was lost to the sound of the waves.

The water was cold, the impact took her breath away and threatened not to give it up. The waves rose and tried to smash her against the hull. She dived, trying to swim one-handed, knowing it was futile, and that she was going to die.

Eyes stared at her from the bottomless sea.

How long could she hold her breath? Desperately, she tried

to propel herself away from the ship, away–

Not eyes. Lights.

And now she knew she was hallucinating.

Lights like a cityscape down below the waves...

And something rising from the depths, something dark and gigantic, ebbing gracefully, ripples forming in the almost flat disc shape, and it was reaching for her... A tentacle as large as a hansom cab swept underneath her. Blind panic took her and she tried to rise, return to the surface, her lungs flaming in pain, but she no longer saw the surface, no longer knew where she was. Her next breath, she knew, would be water. She fought to rise and somehow, she didn't know how, her head burst out of the water and she gulped in air, desperately, and saw through a half-blinded eye the impossible city floating on the dark waves. I can do it, she thought, swim there, I can–

Something slimy and immensely strong grasped her legs, pulling her down, down beneath the waves, and the dark world disappeared, and she knew she was dying, and she must have been hallucinating again, too, because the last thing she saw was the head of a giant squid rising from the depths, with two giant, well-lit eyes like windows, and standing behind them was a woman, and she was waving.

FIFTY-SEVEN
Scab

Waking up was like pushing upwards through an undertow, a struggle for breath and light. She had not expected either.

For a moment she thought she was back in the ocean. Staring down on her from all directions were sea creatures. Two sharks glared at her while a dancing octopus hovered in what seemed like air, staring at her mournfully over its beak. Crustaceans scuttled to and fro on beds of sand, and a giant ray rippled majestically as a swordfish darted above her head.

Not the sea, she realised, relieved. Aquariums. And she was lying on a dry and rather comfortable bed, and the linen smelled of soap and laundry.

"You're awake," a voice said. "Good."

Startled, she looked around her, only then noticing the woman standing quietly beside the shark aquarium. She was a tall, graceful woman with an olive, Mediterranean skin burned darker by the sun, with long black hair tied behind her in a simple knot. There were lines around her eyes, which were a deep and startling blue. "I need you to sign this."

"Excuse me?"

"Receipt of cargo," the woman said, sounding a little impatient. She was, Milady realised, the same woman she had seen as she was drowning. It was all very peculiar.

"Here," the woman said, approaching her, putting forward

what was evidently the White Worm's cargo manifest, as well as a pen. "Sign here, here, and initial here and here – please."

"What?"

"Did you swallow more water than I thought?" the woman said. "Captain Karnstein is temporarily unable to fulfil his function as captain, which makes you, I assume, senior representative for the Council. Therefore, you're liable for the cargo. Therefore, you need to sign it over to me before I can take official possession of it." She glared at Milady. "I am Countess Dellamorte," she said, as if that explained everything.

"Where... where am I?" Milady said. Above the countess's head, the mournful squid blinked sadly.

The countess inched her head meaningfully at the cargo manifest. Sighing, Milady signed it, her gun arm clumsy as she tried to hold the paper in place while she put pen to paper. As soon as she was done, Countess Dellamorte snatched it back. "Excellent," she said. "Come."

Wordlessly, Milady stood up. Her clothes, she saw, were waiting by the bed for her, freshly laundered and ironed. The countess waited as she dressed, then motioned for her to follow.

They stepped out of the room into a hallway lined with more tanks: all manner of sea creatures slithered, crawled and swam inside. The countess trailed one hand against the glass as she walked. At the end of the corridor was an elevator. The doors opened soundlessly, and Milady followed the countess inside. The elevator began to rise.

When the doors opened, the light was momentarily blinding. Milady blinked, tears forming in her single eye. The jade fragment embedded in her other eye socket was still, for once. As her eye adjusted, however, details began to form around her: first the outline of walls, then the frames of massive windows set on three sides, and then, through the windows...

Down below her, hemmed in by the sea on all sides, lay the city she had seen in the dark. Yet not a city, she realised: they were standing in a tower that rose out of a giant platform that was, itself, floating, half-submerged in the water of the sea. There were figures down below, and rising towers and large box-like buildings. At the edges of the platform massive cranes rose into the air, and several smaller vessels were moored, bobbing in the water. Shafts, too, she noticed, were driven into the surface of the platform at several places, and she saw elevators descend and rise, and more tiny human figures entering or leaving them. The whole extraordinary structure, a thing of metal and construction, floated serenely on the sea, yet had no part of it, looking a little like–

"Welcome to Scab," Countess Dellamorte said.

"The specimens," the countess said, "are fascinating." It was a little later. They were walking along the platform. The sun was out and a pleasant breeze was blowing in from the sea. Heavy, house-sized containers stood everywhere, creating avenues and paths that turned and twisted and criss-crossed each other unexpectedly. Milady shuddered, trying not to think of the corpses in the trunks that had been on the ship. "What happened to the sailors?" she said.

"They'll live," the countess said, and gave a sudden snort of laughter. "In fact, that's the one thing we can expect for certain. This... plague that has infected them also seems to keep them alive. Come–" She led her through a narrow gap between containers and suddenly they were standing in the approach to an artificial harbour – and there was the White Worm.

Cranes hovered above it, offloading the coffin-shaped casks onto the platform. Small, steam-powered baruch-landaus were carrying the cargo away, driven by–

Milady couldn't help but stare. They were – women, yes, and men, but–

Were those gills? And did that short-haired woman driving a cargo cart have fins? She saw a burly man, with whiskers like those of a catfish, approach them. Were those gills, on either side of his neck?

"We are nearly finished offloading, countess," he said, giving the woman beside Milady a sharp salute. Milady stared at the man's hands.

Between his fingers – were those webs?

"Excellent," the countess said. "Section it in quarantine, McGill, for the time being."

"Of course, Countess," the man said and, saluting again, turned sharply back.

"Ex-military," Countess Dellamorte said fondly.

"Which military?" Milady said.

"Oh, several of them, I expect."

They looked at each other. And now Milady was finding the other woman's smile somewhat uncomfortable. "Please," Countess Dellamorte said, "do not worry. Scab, as you can see, is a scientific outpost. We study... life, here. My staff may appear eccentric, though that was not my work." She grimaced. "I'm afraid my predecessor, while a brilliant man, was also somewhat unstable. An Englishman, you see–" clearly expecting that that explained everything, which Milady rather thought it did. "But dear Moreau is no longer with us," the countess said. "It was decided he needed a sabbatical – a rather long one, in fact – and last I heard he had retired to some Pacific island, where the weather, it is hoped, better agrees with him. Regardless..." and she smiled again, "you are our guest. We don't, as you can imagine, receive many visitors."

Milady glanced around her, at that impossible floating structure, beyond which lay nothing but countless miles of open sea. "Yes," she said, "and though I'm grateful, of course..." She hesitated, and the countess said, "You were en-route to Vespuccia, and need to continue on your journey?"

"As soon as possible," Milady said.

"I shall see what may be arranged," the countess said. "Yet you and I have much to talk about before you go. It is not by accident I was sent the samples, you know." She made another of her head motions, indicating for Milady to follow her. "And I think my work here, and your mission, may well be linked. Before you depart, you should know what is at stake."

Milady nodded, unsure what the countess meant, and her companion smiled. "Come!" she said brightly. "Let us go and make study of the corpses."

FIFTY-EIGHT
Waldo

Behind glass walls, the sailors crawled... On hand and foot, they prowled, the rat men of the White Worm – all but their master.

With his tattered old coat the old captain looked more bat-like than ever. Silently, he peered back at them through the glass. Silver strands oozed across his large hands.

"My poor Karnstein..." the countess said, surprising Milady. She approached the glass, and laid her palm against the glass. On the other side Karnstein did the same. "Camilla..." he said. "Help me. Help us."

"I will," the countess said softly. Milady felt as if she were interrupting a private moment. She coughed, and the countess turned to her, her hand falling away slowly from the wall of glass. "Do you understand the nature of their malady?" she said, her voice sounding harsh in the quiet room. She glared at Milady, who did not reply. "I am well informed," the countess said. "The Council has been updating me on a regular basis as to the... events that took place in Paris. Events to which I understand you were central."

Behind the glass the rat men crawled pitifully. The countess said, "I know your nature, Milady de Winter. I have seen it in other agents of the Council–" Her tone made it quite clear she did not approve. "Single-minded. Determined – to a fault. I have met Tômas before, too, did you know that?" she smiled crookedly. "He was a handsome man in those days. Yet the same as you, Milady. The same as you. No conception of the larger canvas, as it were. Tell me, what do you think the nature of this malady is?"

Milady, thinking back to her vision of the lizardine statue, a thought recalled – she said, "It's a device, for recording the dead."

The countess's eyes opened wider – Milady, it appeared, had managed to surprise her. "You have a fragment of jade where you once had an eye…" she murmured. "What else do you see, Milady de Winter?" She tilted her head, looking at Milady curiously. "It is a good thing the Council sent you to me, to be studied."

Milady, her gun arm rising as of its own volition – "I am not yours to be studied."

"Ah, yes," the countess said, unperturbed. "The modifications are rather fascinating. Dear Viktor's work, yes? A darling man."

Milady had never heard Viktor referred to as anyone's darling, before. She bit her tongue and didn't answer. "A gun," the countess said, some amusement in her voice. "Always a gun is the answer to you, is it not? Tômas, he was the same. A weapon, you are. The Council's own guns." She sighed, and shook her head. "Guns do not think," she said, "guns are there to be wielded." She turned away from Milady, looked again through the glass. "Look at them!" she said. "A device, you said, for recording the dead, yes – or the living. A device for making impressions of organic life – would it surprise you to learn that I believe that had been rather a speciality of the lizards' science? No?"

She didn't wait for a reply. "Come," she said again – Milady was becoming seriously irked with the countess's manner – and walked away, Karnstein still standing with his hand against the glass, watching her. Milady, unnerved, decided to follow the countess.

"Yet you do not ask," the countess said, continuing a one-sided conversation as she stalked ahead of Milady – they were passing through a corridor and back out onto the open space of the platform – "you do not think to ask – why? You do not pause, in your endless chase, and ask yourself, not what it does, but why it does it? For what purpose?"

Milady, a small voice – "I have wondered–"

A snort from the countess. "You wonder. Indeed. Come. I will show you my work here."

They were approaching one of the shafts built into the bottom of the raft. Milady stared down into dark water. It was a wide, open hole into the ocean, and rising out of it–

She pulled back, her gun arm rising–

A giant creature, whose tentacles ebbed across the water–

"This is Waldo," the countess said, with some pride.

Milady stared at the creature. The head bobbed up to the surface and stayed there, and the wide body floated upwards, one of the tentacles rising into the air to come landing, extended, on the platform beside them. "I designed him myself," the countess said. "Come, come!"

A machine, Milady realised. And now the countess, quite unconcerned, was walking along the rigidly extended tentacle towards the head, where a mouth opened like a door. Milady followed her, afraid of slipping, and knew that, for the moment, at least, her fate was in this woman's hands. The thought did not make her happy.

She entered the mouth, found herself in a utilitarian room – the two eyes she had seen before were indeed windows, and just before them was a large control panel of polished wood and burnished chrome, two chairs before it. The countess sat in one and gestured for Milady to sit in the other. At the touch of a button, the door – mouth – closed and there was a hiss of escaping air. "We're now sealed in," the countess said. Another button – the countess's painted fingernail as polished as the controls – and the giant creature came to life. "And... down," the countess murmured. "Are you familiar with the poem by that fellow who was fond of laudanum? Down to a sunless sea..."

Milady shivered. Water began to rise over the windows as the vessel sank. In moments they were under the giant platform that was Scab. It was dark outside, and there was no illumination inside the vehicle. "It is dark," Countess Dellamorte said. "As dark as space, Milady de Winter. Think of space, Milady. Think of that vast unexplored region that lies just beyond our atmosphere. The universe is out there..." And now, moving the controls, she made the vehicle turn, and as it did Milady began to see lights coming alive down there, in the darkness, tens and then hundreds of lights blossoming in the depths of the sea.

"Stars, and planets, beyond count..." the enigmatic woman beside her said. "And who knows what manner of life dwells beyond our world?"

Milady wasn't sure she was expected to provide an answer. She stared instead, fascinated, at the approaching lights. A guage set into the control panel indicated depths, it seemed. They were sinking fast.

"You may have heard the theory expressed that those of the lizardine court –" a note of distaste in her voice – "have come from another world, beyond our own. That is, I can assure you, quite correct. Their technology far surpassed our own. Their race was able to build ships that sailed amongst the stars." She gave a chuckle that did not have much humour in it. "But technology fails – perhaps the first thing any practical scientist ever learns. Who knows what accident – if that is what it was – led to their being stranded here, on this world?"

"What are those lights?" Milady said. Countess Dellamorte shook her head. "You must consider the larger implications!" she said. "Like it or not, we are at war. Or will be."

"War?" Milady said.

"A few years ago, the Lizardine Empire successfully sent a probe into space. That probe was meant to study our neighbouring planet – Mars. But that was not its true function. What I am telling you, by the way, is highly classified. However, I feel I should be candid with you and, here on Scab, one is rather given more leeway... especially seeing as Scab itself, of course, does not exist."

"Of course," Milady said, and the two women shared a smile. They were both professionals, Milady knew. And as different as their positions were, their goals were the same – weren't they?

FIFTY-NINE
Descent

Waldo descended. Around the sub-aquatic vehicle the dark sea pressed, and Milady saw the dial of the pressure gauge moving slowly, continuously, in a clockwise direction. The darkness of the sea oppressed her. Who knew what lay below, deep at the bottom of the sea? Again she thought of her mother, all the others on that long-ago journey. Were they waiting for her, down below?

"Space," Countess Dellamorte said. Her voice seemed hushed, down here. "Look around you, Milady. I said my research involves life. More specifically, it concerns human survival in inhospitable environments." She gestured at the dark water beyond the glass. "The sea is my laboratory. Here, we work on the possibility that, one day, humanity will survive beyond the atmosphere. It is imperative that we do. The Lizardine Empire poses danger to us on Earth – but what unimaginable danger may threaten us from beyond the stars?"

"The probe," Milady said. The countess nodded. "It was a distress buoy, to use a nautical term," she said. "Sending out a message to – whom? That is what we must prepare ourselves for, why Scab was built, why funding can be found."

"But we have co-existed with Les Lézards for centuries," Milady protested. "Surely–"

"They have changed our history!" the countess said. "Changed our future, with their presence."

"We have peace–"

"Do we?" The smile the countess gave her was as cold as the sea. And now she could see the lights growing closer, illuminating–

There were structures in the sea, hazily visible through the murky water. Bubbles of hard matter anchored on an enormous chain, each bubble as large as a house. There were figures moving along the chain, human in shape, but only just. Suits, she thought. Some sort of outer layers protecting the divers. And long, elongated shapes like cigars moving in the water – submarines. They looked like tiny fish against the bulk of the chain and the never-ending sea.

"Krupp is developing a new kind of cannon," the countess said. "Krupp's Baby, they call it now – and Krupp's Monster, too. A cannon of the type the Lizardine Empire already possesses – one whose shot is so powerful it can penetrate the very atmosphere."

"A weapon?"

The smile played on the countess's face. "A weapon," she agreed. "For what can fire into space can also fire across vast distances right here. The future of war..."

"Who else?" Milady said – demanded. The countess nodded slowly. "Many others," she said. "All playing their own subtle game for domination. Chung Kuo, behind their secretive walls... the Council, the lizardine court, and others... It is said Lord Babbage himself is gathering power, and as for Vespuccia..."

Milady thought of the wide open spaces, the buffalo hordes and the cities of the migrants who came there to escape the lizardine dominion. The countess said, "Edison, Tesla, each gathering power. And as for the Council of Chiefs and their Black Cabinet – who knows what they think as they weigh and listen and learn and decide? They have the power of a continent in their hands. Do you expect them not to use it?"

As Waldo sank lower and lower the lights grew in brightness, and Milady's breath caught in her throat. Structures came into view, enormous bubbles tied together with a chain in complex patterns, and she realised she was seeing an entire city under the sea. Small figures and vessels moved between the alien structures, and she saw more of the bubbles were being added, as a swarm of vehicles converged over a half-built structure, and the chain was being extended. "What do you think the plague is?" the countess said. "This alien device – do you think it is the only one?"

"I… I don't know."

"Remnants of the lizards' technology can still be found," the countess said. "Objects of power far advanced from our own, fledgling technology. There are others, and more – what may we yet find beyond our own world? Did they litter our solar system with their machines, do you think? And are they sleeping? Or awake?"

Milady was growing uncomfortable of the countess's presence. None of this concerned her. Her objective remained the same. Scab did not – should not – exist. Talk of space seemed fantastical to her. All she truly knew was what truly mattered – she had a killer to catch, a job to complete. Regardless of the Council's instructions. The countess may have noticed her expression. "Guns," she said disgustedly. "You are fashioned so precisely by the Council that you can no more conceive of your true purpose than the objects you resemble. The object you are hunting, it is not a mindless sickness, a natural plague. It is a device, a thing created by a technology you cannot even imagine, Milady de Winter. And its purpose is clear."

"Not to me…" Milady murmured. The countess glanced at her sharply. "Then you are more dim-witted than I gave you credit for," she said.

Milady stared at the impossible city under the sea. What

manner of people would wish to live like this? she wondered. She saw it for what it truly was – a prison under the sea, the countess its warden. Peopled by those who could not live in society, exiles sent to live out their days on Scab. It was aptly named.

The countess, grimacing, took the controls. Waldo spun around, tentacles flowing gracefully. The countess pulled a lever, and the pressure gauge paused and then began to travel in an anticlockwise direction. "Enough," the countess said.

"It's a probe," Milady said quietly. The countess looked startled. Milady said, "That is your conclusion, isn't it?" She thought of the jade statue, of the insane, lonely voices babbling endlessly. "A device for studying a new territory, the way we send spies to learn the way for an… an invasion."

Countess Dellamorte looked taken aback, then, suddenly, pleased. "A gun that thinks," she said. "You please me."

Milady shook her head. She felt very tired, now. Her eyes threatened to close and she said, "Bring us up."

The thought that was forming in her head, the thought she did not bother sharing with the countess, was: What if it isn't what you say it is at all? What if it is lonely, and desperately seeking a way back home?

SIXTY
Glass Coffin

She had never been so glad to see sunlight again. Yet as she stepped away from the aquatic vehicle, a sense of unease permeated Milady's mind.

Something was wrong.

She couldn't tell what it was that disturbed her. "Come," the countess said, walking briskly beside her. "I want to take another look at the sailors in quarantine. And you need some food... something light on the stomach. I'll have McGill bring something over."

But she did not feel hungry. Her throat was raw and sore and there was a dull throbbing in her head. Staring at the countess, the alien jade in Milady's eye seemed to awaken and turn restlessly, hurting her. She hefted her gun arm, realising the Gatling gun had been reloaded for her while she was sleeping. It showed remarkable trust...

But then, where did she have to run? There was no escape from Scab, nothing beyond the platform but hostile sea. And below...

She didn't want to think of the experiments being carried out under the sea. The thought of people living in such conditions was insane – as insane as Dellamorte herself.

She followed behind the other woman, feeling tired and sluggish. Through the same aquarium-lined corridor, sharks glancing at her behind their cages.

Sharks... Dellamorte had called her a gun, but guns did not think, and Milady was thinking – hard.

A woman so bound by rules that she insisted on her signing over the ship's cargo – a pointless act of formality by any consideration. And at the same time, speaking freely to Milady, revealing at least some of the secrets of Scab... It did not make sense, not unless–

The room was dark and cool and behind the glass the rat men were motionless. She could not see Karnstein.

Did her gun work?

The countess spoke into a brass tube, then turned to Milady. "Food will be brought shortly. Please, make yourself comfortable."

Milady looked around but could find no chair. The only piece of furniture made her blood run cold: it was a glass coffin lying open, only missing an occupant.

"Karnstein?" The countess sounded worried – or perhaps irritated, Milady thought. "Karnstein, where are you?"

No movement behind the glass. The jade light flared in Milady's eye again, and she saw the shifting silver strands, and seemed to hear the distant voices murmuring, far away: Biological assessment routines reaching saturation point – quantum scan fail – adjusting error margin parameters – retry – retry–

She shook her head, trying to dispel the alien sounds.

"Are you feeling unwell?"

She raised her hand. "I'm fine."

"You are tired. Come, stand with me."

She did not appreciate the countess standing directly beside the glass coffin.

And now it occurred to her that she had not, so far, been offered food or drink.

She was weakened, unable to fight, with nowhere to run... suspicion waking fully, and she said, "I wondered why you are so open with me. You do not strike me as the kind of woman to break a code of secrecy…"

"I felt we could speak freely," the countess said. "Come, there is something I want to show you."

"I am sure there is." And now she raised her head, regarding the countess directly. "You do not intend for me to leave Scab at all, do you?"

"I'm not sure what you mean…" the countess said. Milady thought she detected a small smile playing at the corners of Dellamorte's lips.

"You can't imprison me," Milady said. She felt terribly weary. "I am an agent of the Council! I am needed elsewhere."

And now she could see the smile blossom fully. "The Council is a long way away," Countess Dellamorte said. "And you are a critical piece of the puzzle, and must be studied. Through you – through that alien object inserted in your head – I could reach the primary object, perhaps even initiate discussion with it! Who knows what we could learn!"

"I'll kill you first," Milady said quietly. The countess laughed. "I don't think you will," she said. She gestured with her head. Hands grabbed Milady on both sides. She had not even heard them approach. One was the man called McGill. The other was a woman with spots as of a leopard and sharp, canine teeth. "Put her in the coffin," the countess said. Turning to Milady – "Trust me, this is for the best."

She tried to fight, but they were strong, and more came in behind them. She felt something sharp touch her neck and then her body would no longer obey her. They carried her to the coffin and laid her down gently. Her eyes remained open. She could see and hear, but couldn't move. "I will begin by extracting the object," the countess said. "McGill! Record my observations. She will need to be carried to the surgical bay–"

A numbness spread through Milady's mind, a deep, terrible weariness. And yet, within it, a new voice whispered, and the thing in her eye socket moved restlessly, shifting against the bone and tender flesh, as if agitated. She was absurdly glad for the injection. She suspected that, if she was in full control of her faculties, the pain would have been unbearable.

Faintly, images rose in her mind. It was as if she and the jade have come to some sort of understanding, suddenly – a mutual, symbiotic relationship. It needs me as a host, she thought, appalled.

She felt them reach the coffin, bend down to lift it – and through the haze of jade became aware of the rat men behind the glass.

They were moving.

In her mind she could reach out, could feel them move – like marionettes, she thought, sickened. And yet she was controlling them. A shout above her, the coffin left untouched – "What are they doing?"

The rat men threw themselves against the glass.

"They're trying to break out!"

Countess Dellamorte: "Let them try."

Bodies moving soundlessly, not feeling the impact with the glass – and now she became aware of the silver strands, those strange, self-replicating entities crawling, studying – obeying the thing in her head.

Silver touched glass.

"That's not–"

The sound of breaking glass, erupting. A tall shape, a dirty coat around it, dark thick beard around a heavily lined face. The countess: "Karnstein... love..."

"Let her go, Camilla. She is my cargo."

"And you are mine..."

She couldn't see them. Trying to, through the rat men's eyes: two indistinct shapes facing off against each other, and she realised she was not controlling the captain. His words were his own.

"She knows too much now! She cannot leave."

"That is not your decision to make. You and I have chosen

to serve the Council. We obey."

"No! This is mine, not–"

"Camilla, she must go where she is meant–"

"Karnstein... I just wanted you to... I need you to heal."

"I've been through worse." A short, coarse laugh. In her mind, a contraction – the silver strands along the captain's body slithering as one, pouring down the man's face, his arms, gathering in one spot.

"She's controlling you!"

"No. She's helping."

Through the rat men's eyes: Karnstein and the countess, face to face, almost touching. "I will stay."

A flash of jade. The silver strands separating from the captain's body. Mists rising, the silver woven into strands of fog – the voices murmuring of Data transference initiated to primary core.

The countess, her arms falling to her sides – a weary voice. Defeated. "She would have to go as she is. I can ship her with the cargo bound for the Long Island..."

In the silver strands she saw the city beneath the waves, the whole of Scab, the platform, the docking bays, the shafts into the sea – numbers, graphs, fleeting words: Suspended animation, self-contained atmosphere, escape velocity–

"Milady de Winter."

A voice above her. The captain? It was getting hard to distinguish sounds. "You are safe."

"I must give her another shot. The acceleration would otherwise kill her–"

Beyond the broken glass, she made the rat men nod.

A cool touch against her arm. Above her, softly, "Thank you–"

The jade fading, darkness crawling over. Her last sensation was of the lid of the glass coffin, closing above her.

INTERLUDE
The New World

When he came off the ship it was into a new world. The harbour of the Long Island was a busy swarm of ships, from India and Mexica and Zululand, from Shanghai and Marseilles and even Portsmouth, in the heart of the Lizardine domain – entire fleets of ships disgorging passengers, cargo and exotic fauna. Amidst the smells of woodsmoke and cooking, of tar and salt and coal, amidst the hum of engines and the shouting of sailors a single feeling vibrated like a taut string, cutting across everything.

Excitement.

The Fair was coming.

And everyone was going to the Fair.

Kai stood on the railing and watched the throng below. Men were leading elephants off one ship – African elephants, the Manchu told him. They were enormous beings, far larger than the Asian type, and the males stalked and turned giant tusks menacingly. A troupe of Egyptian dancers; German acrobats dressed all in white; French automatons moving jerkily; Japanese swordsmen mingled with Italian knife-throwers, Indian magicians and Syrian horsemen. Beside him, the Manchu smiled, and said, "We will be lost amongst them as completely as if we were invisible."

"I have been invisible for too long," Kai said, but quietly.

The Emerald Buddha was quiet beside him, ensconced within a sturdy wooden crate. He thought then of the strange woman of his dreams, the one-eyed lady who evoked in him unfamiliar feelings – she reminded him, uncomfortably, of himself.

"Make me into a gun," he whispered, the words of long ago returning, and beside him the Manchu stiffened, and sent him a querying look. Kai shook his head, and the Manchu relaxed – just slightly.

Down in the harbour, young warriors of the Lenape kept order; a busy fish market was doing brisk trade; and beyond Kai could see fields of maize moving gently in the breeze. He took a deep breath, smelling this alien continent, this strange new world. Beyond the Long Island lay an entire continent, and they were going deep into it, following the buffalo roads into the lands of the Nations, and to the city the whole world, it seemed, was going to at once.

Shikaakwa. What the new settlers called Chicago, the black city. But a new city was rising there now, a new city to welcome the world…

And him, too. The Manchu was right. They would be all but invisible in the crowd, and safe – and the world would come and send its emissaries with it, to deal with Kai for the treasure he held. A treasure he never asked for, or wanted, but which was his burden nonetheless.

And as for the Emerald Buddha itself… Kai gripped the railings and looked out at the new continent, not seeing it, seeing rather the disturbing dreams he had been having, the dreams of pock-marked, cratered surfaces, of giant objects floating through space, and stars, so many stars…

The Emerald Buddha, he couldn't help but know, had plans of its own.

PART VI
The Black City

SIXTY-ONE
A Bowl of Hokkien Noodles

When she woke up she could smell something frying and her stomach growled, belly muscles moving in protest; her mouth tasted like a Parisian street sewer and her eye ached; everything ached. For a moment she was back on the White Worm, the deck rolling beneath her, the ghosts of childhood moaning beneath the waves. She felt hot, then cold. She shivered, her heart beating fast – too fast.

What had Countess Dellamorte given her?

She felt the green thing embedded in her eye socket move. For a moment she caught a flash of something far away – Kai riding a horse across a wild landscape, his cowl pushed back, his face, for just a moment, open in childish joy. His servant rode behind him. They were going towards–

She shivered again, and moaned. A voice above her said, "You should be dead, but aren't. Surely that is something to celebrate?"

She opened her eyes and glared at Ebenezer Long.

The elderly Mongolian was squatting on his haunches, looking at her with a smile. The ground was moving – no. It hadn't been the ship at all, she realised – she was inside a moving carriage. She could hear the neighing of horses, smell their pungent excrement, and beyond that–

The smell of smoke, of machines, of people – many people.

But those smells were in the distance and right here the air was dominated by cooking, just as her vision was obscured by the old Xia master. She said, "I guess somebody up there likes me."

"I doubt it," Master Long said, but he smiled when he said it. She said, "Where am I?" and tried to rise from the coffin–

Her muscles screamed in protest and again the shivering took her. Master Long said, "You are suffering withdrawal. As much as I can tell you have been injected with a powerful chemical compound distilled from opium. Water?"

He offered her a glass. She reached out with her human hand (it was shaking) and took it from him. She drank.

"Take deep breaths."

When she did her heart slowed, a little. She pushed herself up and looked around. There wasn't much to see. The carriage was covered – she could smell the not-unpleasant residue of the skins it was made of – and a small burner on the floor was heating up a pot which Master Long now returned to. He stirred the things inside with a pair of chopsticks.

"Soup," Master Long said, "is always the best cure at the end of a long journey."

"Eastern philosophy?"

"Mrs Beeton. Remarkable woman. Would you like some?"

"Maybe in a moment." Sitting up, she took another deep breath. "I do suspect you'd have been dead by now if it weren't for the object lodged in your head. Incredible. We spent so much time chasing it across Paris and here it is, after all that. I've told you once before, Milady: you are Xiake, a true warrior of Xia. Now more so than ever..."

"I did not ask for this thing," she said. Then, more quietly – "Is there any way to take it out?"

"Not without killing you, I suspect... Please, have some noodles."

Master Long lifted the pot from its little stove and dished out food into a bowl. Milady said, "What is it?" The smell rose around her, its fragrance overpowering – suddenly she could think of little else.

"Hokkien hae mee," Master Long said. "Or Hokkien noodles, if you prefer. A dish from Fujian that had undergone changes in Malaya – food, like people, must continue to evolve."

She took the bowl. She brought it to her lips and drank. Beside her, Master Long served another helping into a second bowl and sat picking at it with his chopsticks.

A flash of jade – a flash of fear that almost made her drop the bowl. She was no longer in the carriage, but elsewhere – in a dark, rectangular cavern. Beams held up the ceiling, and the ground was made of dark soil. She saw vats and barrels standing forlorn against the makeshift walls. A cellar.

Two things dominated the airless room. One was a steel-top operating table, of a kind she was well familiar with – too familiar with. It was empty.

The other thing was a kiln.

A flash of jade, and now a dark figure was moving in the cellar, lighting up a lamp above the operating table. It was approaching the kiln, setting to lighting it, and the flames began to rise, casting the room in shadows... The figure turned, sniffed the air, and Milady shrank back. "I can taste you..." the Phantom said. When he turned his face on her he smiled. "Do you like it?" he said. "Have you come to find me? I'll be waiting, Cleo..."

He turned away from her then, and walked back towards a door, and reached to open it. Milady dreaded the opening of that door. The movements of the Phantom were careful, fluid – theatrical, she thought. When he opened the door a gurney stood outside. Strapped to the gurney was a young woman. She seemed asleep. The Phantom began to pull the gurney into the cellar. "I cannot help the fact that I am a murderer," he said. "No more than the poet can help the inspiration to sing."

Milady raised her gun arm, wanting to shoot him, willing him dead, but already the scene was fading, the flash of jade gone, and she was back in the moving carriage and Master Long was regarding her quizzically, the chopsticks like weapons in his hand. "There is a great evil," he said, "in those with the power of Xia who fall from the path…"

"I saw him," she said. Master Long nodded, not speaking. "He's killing again. Here. He's close. And he won't stop – he won't stop!"

"Then you must stop him," Master Long said.

Somehow, the bowl of Hokkien noodles was empty in her hands. She stared at it – a simple clay bowl, burned in a kiln… "Teach me," she said. "Teach me how."

But Master Long shook his head. "I don't know," he said. "But you will–" He hesitated, then shook his head again. She said, "What?"

Instead of an answer he rose, and reached to the flap of the carriage's tarpaulin. "We're almost there," he said. Then he lifted the flap, and the world came pouring into the carriage.

SIXTY-TWO
The Black City

Tall, grey buildings rose high into the smoke-filled air in the distance. The ground itself seemed to thrum with the beating of unseen, enormous engines. From a distance the city looked like a malevolent maze, a trap closing in on the crowds of people and the passing of carriages and baruch-landaus. Two black airships hung suspended in the air above the city like silent carrion birds. Milady inhaled deeply, smelling the sharp tang of chemical waste, smoke, grease, blood and human waste. There was only one city in the world like it, and she knew it immediately.

Shikaakwa.

Chicagoland.

She had passed through there several times, with Barnum's circus, in the old days. The city had changed, she noticed: buildings grew taller, the streets darker, the mass of humanity greater – but the smell remained the same, the blood from the slaughterhouse district and the stench from the factories – the smell of human misery, the smell of a city–

In a strange way, the smell of home.

And now she could see the banners, flying everywhere, the flying streamers, the gay colours amidst the grey and black. All announcing the same event, the same momentous gathering: she stared at the approaching city, the carriage's progress slower now as it joined a stream of other vehicles and riders along the road. All going to the same place.

"The World's Vespuccian Exposition," Master Long said – and was that longing in his voice? He saw her look and smiled, embarrassed. "The World's Fair. They say it is the greatest show on Earth," he said. "An inexhaustible dream of beauty…"

"Have you seen the Exposition Universelle?" Milady said, civic pride offended. Ebenezer Long nodded, but the smile remained. "They say this will be grander," he said dreamily. Milady stared at the old Shaolin master. For a moment he seemed like the child he must have been, long ago, the one who went looking for relics in the desert. "Dreams can hurt you," she said, but quietly.

The Exposition Universelle took place in Paris four years previously. She remembered it vividly – the exhibits of shining new guns from Colt and Mauser, the demonstration of new police techniques given by the chief of Scotland Yard herself, Irene Adler, and that gruesome exhibition of explosives, cunningly hidden in books, that were authentic samples of the work of that most shadowy of assassins, known only as the Bookman… She had been particularly taken with a lecture on poisons, both ancient and modern, delivered by Dr Grimesby Roylott, a renowned authority in the field, who kept the audience riveted with his account of the deadly Indian swamp adder. Yes, the Exposition Universelle had been dazzling – and she doubted the Vespuccians could pull off anything quite like it.

"Not everything is a weapon," Master Long said, as if reading her mind.

She said, "But everything can be made into one."

Master Long did not reply. A young man – little more than a boy – was driving the cart, she noticed. She did not recognise his face. They were approaching the city, and she soon began to distinguish people in the seemingly endless crowd – local

Potawatomis, visiting Sioux, Iroquois, Shawnee and others, European immigrants, Chinese and Indians, Malay and Zulu – some escaping the growing lizardine dominance of their nations, some merely seeking out new life in this wide, remote continent. And amongst them all the visitors, distinguished by their dress and their air of faint unease as they navigated the unfamiliar roads of Chicagoland, drawn, all drawn like slivers of metal to a lodestone, all drawn to the World's Fair.

This is where he will come, she knew. The Man on the Mekong, the man from her dreams. This is where he was heading, to sell or trade or buy his way away from that alien statue, the one that dominated them both and bound them both. The two of them, and a third: for the Phantom, too, had come to the black city. She thought of her vision again, the sight of him in that cold, dark cellar, the wheeled gurney and the woman strapped to it, drugged and asleep... He would wake her up, she knew, before he began. He would want her to know what was happening, alive with fear for every single second, until the end.

How many had there already been? He must already be in the city. Like a shadow, like a phantom, he could be impossible to find – but he would want her hunting. She knew that, somewhere in that black city ahead, a message would be waiting for her: a message from her Phantom.

"How did I get here?" she said, turning away from premonitions of dread. She turned to Master Long. "Last I remember I was..." she hesitated, then said, "far away, on the ocean–"

"You were delivered," Master Long said, "to an unregistered naval station on the Long Island, by means, I believe, of a sub-aquatic vehicle. A very rapid device, and the Council agent in charge sent a query through – shall we say, unofficial channels – to my people. It was decided that, since our objectives are closely linked with the Council's –" she noticed he didn't say they were the same – "I shall assume temporary responsibility for your well-being. As I said, I am glad to see you're not dead."

"Thanks."

"Don't mention it."

"What are your objectives?" she said. "Out of curiosity."

"The same as yours," he said – which left it ambiguous.

"Mine, or the Council's?"

"Are they not the same?"

She had no answer for that, and Master Long smiled, and said nothing. The carriage rode towards the black city.

SIXTY-THREE
The Message

A man came through the door with a gun.

Midnight in the black city: Milady de Winter's accommodation a boarding house for gentlewomen on Tecumseh's Road. Starlight breaking through grimy windows, the floor creaking with heavy steps – she was ready.

"Drop it."

His smile lit up his face. The gun disappeared, like magic, into its holster. She stared, said, "Cody?"

"Cleo!"

She lowered her gun hand. The man's gaze travelled down, examined it. When it rose up it took in her eyepatch. He raised his eyebrows. Milady shook her head. Cody grinned.

"Good to see you're still alive," he said.

"You too," she said. His grin widened. "You didn't expect me to be," he said – not a question so much as a statement of fact.

She shook her head. He said, "Sorry to disappoint."

"Not at all."

The grinned at each other, and suddenly Milady de Winter was gone, as if she had never existed, and she was Cleo again, Cleopatra of Dahomey, The Amazon Queen! And he was…

"Damn you, Bill Cody," she said. "How did you find me?"

"Aren't you gonna ask me in?"

She swept her hand. "Sure."

Buffalo Bill came into the room. He took off his wide-brimmed hat. His eyes hadn't left Cleo's. "Heard you married an Englishman."

"It didn't last."

"Never does," he said, "with the British."

"How's Lulu?"

His grin was a little abashed. "She's fine," he said, scratching his beard. "You know."

"She didn't come with you?"

"She prefers to stay at home these days."

"You mean you prefer her to stay at home."

He shrugged, smiled. "So many ladies…" he said.

She stared at him. He was older than she remembered, stockier. The beard had strands of white and grey. Buffalo Bill Cody: ranger, rider, showman first and foremost. "I didn't realise you were part of the Fair."

"We're not," he said. "I offered to pay, but they turned me down. So we set up just outside. Eighteen thousand seats, Cleo – and we fill 'em every night. We get paid – and the Fair doesn't. Their loss. You got any drinks?"

"This is a ladies' boarding house, you know," she said.

"You ain't no lady, Cleo," he said, and she had to laugh. "I am now," she said.

Buffalo Bill shook his head. "Now ain't that the darnest thing," he said. "What was his name?"

"De Winter."

"Sounds chilly. Whatever happened to him?"

She didn't answer, and his smile widened again. "Poor feller," he said, his hat clutched to his chest. She shook her head, went to the dresser, and uncorked a crystal decanter. Pouring two glasses, she carried them over, handed him one. They clinked glasses and both downed their drinks. "Damn, that's better," Buffalo Bill said.

"Damn, Cody, why are you here?" she said.

"I told you. I heard you were here." But he wasn't smiling any more.

"Heard how?"

"We're the main attraction of this World's Fair," Buffalo Bill said – modesty, she thought, had never been one of his strong points. "Nothing much gets past my people."

"Who, specifically?"

For a moment he looked uncomfortable. "Elderly Asian gentleman, in fact. You should see the Chinese pavilion in the White City, Cleo. It's something. Though I'm not sure he was Chinese..."

"Why did he tell you where I am?" then, seeing his face – "Cody, are you in some sort of trouble?"

The smile had gone completely from his face. And now she saw that his face was pale, and that the hand holding the empty glass was – though it was barely noticeable – shaking.

"Tell me," she said, feeling an urgency rise inside her like a physical force, and Buffalo Bill said, "I'd better show you."

"What is the meaning of this?"

The man was clearly agitated. He was young, barely past twenty, yet his authority was obvious. His dark, expensive suit sat on him uneasily, as if the man was too restless to let the signs of money on him rest. Cody said, "That's Bloom. Sol Bloom. He's the head of concessions for the Midway." His smile was crooked. "In other words, he gets to pick the shows."

They were standing outside the White City. She had not been prepared for it. She tried to block out the rising skyline, but impressions kept flittering through.

The giant pyramid at the hub of the Fair...

The white electric Tesla lights bathing the scene...

That giant, ever-moving wheel, crackling with a sort of eldritch tension...

She said, "But you're not part of the Fair."

"Sol was appointed too late to sign us up. One of the things he vehemently regrets..."

There was a crowd. There was always, she began to realise, a crowd in this place. There were horse riders and belly dancers, knife throwers and clowns – grim-faced Potawatomi warriors reinforced with federal troops – she saw Mohawks and Sioux and Lenape amongst them – tried to keep the crowd away.

But it was impossible. The press of bodies, even here, outside the White City itself, was showing no sign of abating. She heard shocked whispers, excited conversations muted by the glare of electric lights. When she raised her head those tall, impossible buildings rose above, and the wheel turned, and turned...

She took a deep breath through her mouth and tried to focus.

She had seen something like this once before.

She had seen it, every day, in the mirror.

She bit her lips until she drew blood. Her gun arm twitched.

But there was no one to shoot.

"This is an atrocity!"

Sol Bloom, hands waving. "We cannot let this sort of thing go on!"

From the captain of the guards – "The chiefs must hear about this."

"They must not!" Bloom's face was turning red. "The president himself is coming to the Fair! I will not present Sitting Bull with a, with a..." his hand, waving, took in the gruesome scene. Then Bloom deflated. "I don't feel so well," he said. Cleo watched him hurry away. A little way back, Bloom was loudly sick.

Cleo couldn't blame him.

She knelt down and examined the corpse.

SIXTY-FOUR
Winnetou

"I saw it…" Cody swallowed. "Her, when I came out after the show. I–"

She cut him off. "Do you know who she is?"

"No." He shrugged. "Do you have any idea how many people come to the Fair every day?"

She could imagine. Above her the White City still rose, immense, dominating – an urban space erected in the span of months: a city of the future.

She stared at the corpse.

The young woman had Cleo's dark skin, though she was shorter in stature, and younger. A visitor from one of the African nations? Or a transplanted Vespuccian?

She had the feeling it didn't matter. Who the girl had been in life was not, she felt, a factor for the killer.

But who she resembled in death…

She had to turn away, for a moment. But she couldn't look away. When her gaze returned it took in the hole where the woman's eye should have been, and the amputated arm was nowhere to be found. One of the woman's legs, too, was missing.

"Tômas…" she whispered, and didn't know what the feeling that rose in her was – was it anger – or fear?

The Phantom, her Phantom, had left her a message, a letter

signed in innocent blood.

"Word will be out all over the city by daybreak," Sol Bloom said, groaning. Then, as if noticing her for the first time – "Who the hell is she?"

Cleo didn't answer; and Bloom, taking in suddenly the similar appearance of the corpse to this strange woman, turned white. "Special agent for the Quiet Council," Cleo – no, it was Milady de Winter speaking, now – said. "This murder relates to an ongoing investigation."

Bloom didn't ask for her papers. "Is this – is this official, then?" he said.

Milady shook her head. "The Council likes to keep things… quiet," she said. "Your people no doubt wish to do the same."

"Sitting Bull is coming to the Fair and how do you think this will look?" Bloom said. He glared accusingly at Cody. "This isn't even a part of the Fair proper," he said.

"I offered to lease space in the Fair grounds–" Buffalo Bill began–

"You know perfectly well I was not yet in place–"

"Gentlemen!"

They quietened at her voice. Their argument sounded like a long-rehashed one. "Please."

The local force, she noticed, had not yet made a move other than to secure the perimeter of the scene. Neither did the federals… Waiting, she thought. Who were they waiting for?

The answer became apparent when a new man came marching into the arena.

He was dressed in comfortable clothes the colour of trees in autumn. On his feet, moccasins made his movement silent. He wore a gun in a shoulder-holster, and a single white feather in his hair.

At a signal from him the local force began to push the crowd of onlookers away. He strode forwards, then knelt down beside the corpse. When he rose again his face was expressionless. He said, "I want the man who did this."

Milady nodded. She said, "I'm Mi–"

"Lady de Winter, yes. I know who you are." For a moment his eyes softened, and there was a pull of amusement at the corners of his lips. "I watched you, long ago, when you were with Barnum's show. You had a different name, then."

"You can call me Cleo," she said – surprising herself. The man did smile, then. "Winnetou," he said.

She nodded. The Vespuccian signalled to his men. Four hurried over and lifted the young woman's body off the ground. "We'll do this your masters' way," Winnetou said. "Quietly."

"Is she the first?" Milady said. But the Vespuccian did not reply.

In under fifteen minutes nothing remained of the crime scene. A relieved Sol Bloom declared he had full faith in Winnetou's authority and left, accompanied by an Egyptian belly dancer. Buffalo Bill, told to keep word of the event to himself, muttered there was nothing to worry about on his side and departed too, giving Cleo a parting look she found hard to interpret. In under fifteen minutes the crowd had been dispersed, the body removed, the blood washed away – and Cleo was left alone with Winnetou, who said, "We need to talk."

White electric light illuminated the night.

The White City rose above them, alien structures above an ancient shore. Suddenly she missed the smell of sawdust and paint, the shouts as the heavy canvas tent was raised every night… There had been torches, then, burning against the dark.

It all seemed a very long time ago.

She said, "Then talk."

He looked around. Was anyone watching them? she wondered, uneasily. Would the Phantom be watching, making sure she got his message? He would enjoy it, she knew. Winnetou took her arm. She followed him, feeling relief as they drew away from the scene of the murder. "The World's Vespuccian Exposition," Winnetou said. "Millions of visitors, and a handful of police. What's one corpse amidst the multitude?" Even at this hour, even outside the White City itself, the streets were thronged with people. A gaiety in the air, excited voices raised, the smell of candy… a gaiety neither of them shared.

"How many?" she said. He shrugged. "Who knows?" he said.

She pictured it in her mind. The visitors came streaming to this place, this city of the future – whole families, single men looking for work, single women… and the sharks who always circled in the sea of humanity, scenting weakness, scenting fresh blood… How many young women came to the Fair and disappeared in the sea, never to be seen or heard from again?

"The letters keep coming," Winnetou said. "'Have you seen my daughter? She went to Shikaakwa to see the Fair. She came looking for work. She came looking for a husband. She came looking.'" He sighed, a long shudder of air, and said, "She'd seen too much. She'd seen–" His hand gestured in the air, towards the place they'd been. "She'd seen that, and that was the last thing she'd seen."

Dread rose in Milady like bubbles from the depths of a dark sea. How many others? She had seen the Phantom's sanctuary, that windowless cellar, dominated by a kiln… she, too, had seen too much.

Yet she was still alive.

"He has to be caught," she said. Winnetou nodded. When he turned to face her, his expression was ferocious. "He will be," he said. "But you will not get involved."

She said, "Excuse me?"

He sighed. They paused under a street light. A pool of white electric light fell over them, its edges cast in shadows.

He said, "Milady – Cleo – I have the highest regard for you. You must know that. Your masters have communicated with mine. I have seen your dossier. What you went through… it must have been terrible."

She looked into his eyes, waiting. He seemed reluctant to continue. At last she said, "But–?"

"But you will not involve yourself in this investigation," he said.

"That's unacceptable," she said, and he almost smiled. "Let me put it in plain words," he said. "This is my case. Make sure you stay out of my way."

She took a step back. After a moment, she nodded. This was not her jurisdiction. She had no power here, and he did. "I don't want you to get hurt," he said, and she said, "It's a little late for that."

His smile was rueful. "Enjoy your stay," he said. "Really, you must visit the Fair. They tell me it's spectacular."

And with that, like a shadow, he was away – a lone, long-legged man with a feather in his hair and a gun close to hand. Lawmen were the same, she thought, wherever you went in the world. Like cab drivers…

"Let's see who gets there first," she whispered, and a small smile touched, unexpectedly, the corner of her lips.

SIXTY-FIVE
Top of the World

He was close, she knew. Somewhere nearby… he would set himself up close to the Fair. Like her, he was bound to the statue, changed by it. They were linked, the way the Kai man was, that lonely man she had only seen in her dreams… all three of them, bound by that alien statue and those terrible, insane voices that emanated from it. The Phantom would want the jade statue but more than that, he would want to be close to that sea of humanity, seeking out those vulnerable, lonely souls floating within. He would stalk them, slowly, patiently. He would isolate them, charm them, bewitch them and finally, when they least expected it, put an end to them. He was close – he could be watching – watching and waiting.

Well, let him watch. They would meet again, and soon – and it would be Tômas who would scream for mercy then.

She walked without hurrying, the streets alive with humanity, the outline of that strange, white city rising above the black. Mohawk and Sioux and Lenape mingled with English and Romanian, Zulu and Sotho, Egyptian and French, Chinese and Siamese and Indian – for the world had come to the World's Fair. They had named it for Vespucci, the man whose ill-fated voyage from Europe to the New World had brought back with it the awakened Les Lézards. Now the lizards sat on the green throne of England, ruling an empire over which, it was said, the sun never set. The machines, the old and patient machines ruled France, and in the Middle Kingdom the secret societies of the Wulin schemed to get back the power they had lost, and an Empress-Dowager ruled behind the throne...

They had all come here, to this Chicagoland, and to the free continent where the Council of Chiefs ruled by consent of all. They had welcomed in the new immigrants, given them land to set their cities on, and kept a wary eye beyond the shore, fearing Victoria and her get.

This is the future, they seemed to say. A human future, in a place you do not rule. When you come, come as guests.

And yet the lizards, too, had come to the Fair. She saw a black hansom cab go past and as it did a curtain twitched, and she caught sight of the elongated skull inside, and alien eyes caught, for just a moment, hers...

They had plans, she thought. Long, patient, ancient plans. What did they really want? Where had they come from?

And she thought – perhaps the jade statue could answer those questions...

Pain.

It came on her without warning. It ran down her arm and into her stomach and she doubled over. In the empty place of her eye the thing moved, that foreign presence, a beetle grasping, and she almost screamed.

Pain. The taste of bile in her mouth, and her breathing came out ragged and short. She felt a shiver go down her spine, the hair rising on her arms, the back of her neck.

A flash of jade, the pain arcing through her like electricity–

Then she was gone, the street disappearing, and she was standing somewhere high up, looking down at the White City.

A balustrade of green metal – the lizards' metal, the stuff they had made Notre Dame out of, and their Royal Palace.

The pyramid, she realised – the great pyramid that dominated the White City, towering above the white buildings, casting its shadow over the Midway. It was a not-so-subtle message. The Fair may have been the world's, it seemed to say – but the world belonged to the creatures who had, centuries before, cast their power over it. An exhibition space, in truth: displaying the power and glory of the Lizardine Empire, in rising levels – and she was somewhere high up, near the pinnacle, and looking down–

It was quiet there, and the wind blew hard and cold, and black clouds came drifting from the lake. It smelled of coming rain, and cold.

And in the voice of the wind she heard those other voices.

They sounded excited. Impatient. They spoke of Ninety percent completion rate and electrodynamic properties readjustment and spatial alignment and the jade in her head shifted and turned as if it, too, was excited, and the pain throbbed through her and she screamed.

She was not alone up there, she realised then. Down below, the mass of humanity, illuminated by the harsh white light, seemed as insignificant as an anthill, as featureless. What did a single ant signify? She was not seeing them with her own eyes, she suddenly knew. When she turned her body was a thing of metal and flesh, and the jade was everywhere in it, and her mouth opened and whispered, "Kai. My name is Kai."

She saw herself reflected in the green alien metal. The face that stared back at her was his face, the Man on the Mekong, who was no longer on the distant Mekong river – he was here, on the top of the world, looking down at his own reflection. The sadness in his eyes arrested her.

An image in her mind – a giant wheel, turning, a flash of lightning – then it was gone. She saw her hands – his hands – close over the balustrade as if trying to rip them apart. The pain arced through her again and she thought –

It is his pain I am feeling.

"Kai," she said, and the lips that weren't hers moved with her intent.

Then they said, "Help me–" and the jade flared through him, through her, and the pain burned and they were severed.

When she opened her eyes again she was lying on the ground, beyond the walls of the city, where she had fallen. A small crowd had gathered to watch. From down here they were not ants, she thought. Each one was different, each one an agent of his or her own fate. She raised her head, looking up at the pyramid. Lights spun in the air above the Fair. The giant wheel kept moving, carrying passengers in its hanging cars. Did they, too, see only ants? she wondered. She pushed herself up, trying to ignore the crowd. A carriage with black windows was parked on the other side of the street. As she stood up lightning flashed in the black sky overhead, and rain began to fall.

SIXTY-SIX
The Monsignor

"Milady de Winter."

The voice was chilly, the voice of a long winter. She knew it well, from another time, another place…

Hated it, feared it – respected it, too.

She wished someone had told her it would be the Monsignor.

They had picked her up when she was still trying to recover from the flash of pain. Two of them, out of the black carriage, expressionless mannequins, coming to her aid. When they closed on her, one on either side, she knew who had sent them.

Now she was sitting in the moving carriage, the silent man-shaped automatons on either side of her, and the Monsignor before her.

One of the oldest of the Quiet Council… modelled on a man who had lived long ago. His robes were dark purple, his eyes lifeless. The voice was old, scratched, and came slowly. The voice said, "Need I remind you of your obligations?"

She didn't reply. A bald head, a scratch running down one side. The semblance of humanity was fleeting. He was one of the oldest, with a skin of yellow rubber and jerky motions, primitive technologies patched and haphazardly upgraded over the years… She said, "You are the resident agent in charge?"

He snorted. "I am the Council," he said, the words each of them, those secret masters of France, said when they took their place. All for one, and one for all – she remembered that, too, from another time and place. It was cold, and she was wet from the rain. On either side of her the Monsignor's mannequin bodyguards were motionless.

"I have not been told–" she said, and his voice exploded out of the unmoving lips: "You are not meant to be told! You are meant to listen!"

"I'm listening," she said. A pain in her head. Dim jade light bursting and fading in her field of vision.

"I doubt it," the Monsignor said. "You were told to secure the item," he said. "Do you have any concept of its importance?"

"To France?" she said.

"To all of us!" the Monsignor said. "Humans, machines – anyone on this tiny, fragile world. In the wrong hands it could end us all."

"I am working on locating the–" she began, but he cut her off. "No," he said. "Do not lie, Milady. Do not lie, not to me."

"Locating the Phantom…" she said, almost whispering.

"Yes…" the ancient automaton said. "Truth, now. A rare and precious ingredient in our mix of spices, is it not? And so refreshing…"

She said nothing. Could machines taste? Could they smell? Did they really comprehend what spices were, or what they meant? She did not intend to ask. The Monsignor said, "You will not pursue Tômas."

Tension knotted in her stomach. She raised her head and stared directly at the automaton. "He is killing people. Women."

"The lives of the few matter little," the Monsignor said. "The lives of everyone living now and still unborn are in danger. Tômas… can be useful. You will not pursue him."

It was said with a finality she could not abide. She said, "He can't be allowed to remain free!"

"Tômas will answer to the Council in due course," the Monsignor said, sounding amused. "As will you. For now, you must seek out the item and secure it. There are many, here, in both the black city and the white, seeking, searching – and it is close, Milady, is it not so? Can you not feel it?"

And as he spoke she saw it – a tiny glimmer of jade as the Monsignor's head moved. So there had been other fragments. "Sometimes I believe I can hear voices..." he said. "Speaking too softly for me to understand. They do not use Tesla waves nor light nor anything I understand, and yet they speak, and the world shakes... It is a machine, Milady. A very dangerous machine, held by a very dangerous man. They must both be contained."

She wanted to shake her head then, to explain – about Kai, about being trapped by the statue, about having no choices – but it was the Monsignor before her, the Cardinal, they once called him, and he had no mercy – none of them ever did.

I am the Council, she thought, and shuddered, and the cold seeped deeper into her.

"You are wet," he said. "Unwell. Return to your quarters, dry, rest. Leave Tômas... to me. And find the item!"

The carriage stopped. The door opened, by itself. The bodyguard on the left stepped out, scanned the area, gave a tiny nod.

"Goodbye, Milady," the Monsignor said. "Remember our conversation."

Outside, puddles of water on the grimy street, and fog curled in the air around them. Gas lamps burned here, yellow flames fighting the night, not the blinding white of the Fair. This was the old city, the black city – and they had deposited her outside her boarding house.

The bodyguard returned into the carriage. The door closed. The carriage moved away and shortly disappeared into the fog, and she was left alone.

I should do what he says, she thought. I should go back inside, and wash, and rest, and tomorrow go hunting for Kai. I could find him, too. He is nearby, and the voices have plans...

She nodded. When she clenched her phantom arm the gun it had become wanted to fire. Soon, she thought. She looked up, at the closed doors of the boarding house. Then she thought of the dead mutilated girl left for her to find.

SIXTY-SEVEN
Holmes

She thought of what Master Long had told her, all that time ago, beneath the Seine, in that dark half-world of the under-city of Paris.

The code of Xia, he had said.

There was a code, she thought. It was not something you could put into words, as such. It was not set down in writing, not signed, not displayed. It was a... a feeling, a sense of right and wrong.

She had been told to follow the statue, and let a murderer go free.

And she knew, then, that she couldn't do it.

It was not a matter of choice. It was simply what she had to do, the path she had to follow – against orders, against sense, perhaps. There was a choice, the Monsignor had told her: of saving a world, or saving a handful of lives. But she could not quantify one against the other. Perhaps it was too big for her, too incomprehensible – a world was a hazy concept, ill-defined: but a murdered woman was a murdered woman, and a killer was a killer.

She turned her back on the boarding house. It was raining again, and the streets were dark. It suited her. The flames of the gas lamps cast yellow light that shivered over broken cobblestones. This was a place she understood.

She ran her fingers over her gun arm. The Gatling gun was fully loaded, she knew. She felt awake then, alive. She walked down the streets and watched the shadows, and they watched her back, and knew her for one of their own. People disappeared in the black city. The river washed corpses away. It was a place of profound change, this Chicagoland. For here, the city of the past met the city of the future, and yellow light gave way to white. It was a dream-future, dreamed up by humanity, a shiny, alluring future – but was it real?

There would always be killers, she thought. And there would always be people like her, to try and stop them. Nothing more, nor less, than human. There were no eternal champions, no guardians of the ages at the end of time... there were only the laws, the kind humans made, and the guns they made to keep them.

And so she went, to keep the law. She knew the Phantom would be somewhere nearby. He would stay close to the white city, to the future city, but not within it. He would prey on the unwary, the dreamers, those who came to see the future, to be mesmerised by it, and forget this was still the old world, and predators lurked in it – not in the dark but in the light, with charming smiles and pleasant words...

A boarding house, she thought.

A shiver ran down her. Her hair was a dark halo in the gaslight. Did she guess it, intuitively, or did she sense it, through that fragile link that joined her to the Phantom? He would open a boarding house, and welcome in those lonely, trusting souls, those visitors to the great Fair. A boarding house near enough to the white city, and cheap enough – for the right boarder. For there would be a different price to pay...

She prowled the street, restless, her gun arm ready at her side. Though he had not been so easy to kill, the last time...

But then, neither was she.

•••

She tried something then. The same way it had happened on Scab: she reached inside herself, reached for that alien thing lodged in her empty eye socket, wakening it. The pain tore through her, worse than ever. The thing shifted, and she imagined the groan of bones and flesh as the jade moved in her head like a living thing. Jade flashed, inside her head or outside, she didn't know. The pain was terrible, and she was bending over, bile rising in her throat again, through her and onto the street. She blinked away tears. Flashes of jade, and she tried to control them, tried to direct them.

Dead... the dead were all around her. She could sense them, in that other world – quantum representational matrix, data storage, the voices seemed to whisper – minds trapped, studied, analysed, and stored, like victuals. There was a body floating down the river, and silver snaked across its skin. There was a body in a cart, being driven to a hospital – two men in the front talking of the price it would fetch, not aware that, behind them, underneath the tarpaulin, the corpse was twitching, moving... and beyond, beyond, pushing through the pain: searching for him.

She was retching, blind now, on her knees, but still she pushed, still she searched – voices coming from afar: Ninety-five percent lockdown, opening sequences checksum correct!–

And then she saw him.

He stood before a tall mirror. He was changed again – Tômas with his thousand faces, dressed now in a respectable black suit, his face different, a pleasant countenance – but she could see the silver strands run like eels down his arms, beneath the cuffs of his ironed shirt. He was smiling at the mirror, practising. Did he know she was there? Did he know she was watching through his eyes?

"How do you do, Mr Holmes?" the Phantom said to his mirror-self. He bowed, then reached out and put on a tall beaver hat. "How do you do, Mr Holmes?"

Holmes, she thought. It was the name of a well-known

British detective. Had Tômas taken on the name?

"A pleasure to see you again, my dear."

She startled back, thinking he was speaking to her. But no – he was still practising his patter – like a magician before a show, she thought. The pain throbbed through her. She didn't know how long she could keep watching. "I have missed you, terribly. I trust you enjoyed your visit to the Fair?"

Mimicking again – a girl now. "Oh, it was wonderful! The lights, the buildings! How do they build them so tall?"

"A marvel of the age–" Tômas again, a charming smile. "But come, I have a surprise for you."

"You do? Oh, how wonderful! What is it?"

"It's a secret," he said. "I will have to show you..."

"Is it far?"

"It is right here... in my cellar," he said.

Then he chuckled. Staring at himself in the mirror, his face changed again, the silver flowing into it, the skull elongating, teeth growing. His eyes shone with jade. "You will like it there," he said.

SIXTY-EIGHT
The Phantom's Maze

Coming out of the vision, her skull burned with pain. Her eyes were holes poked through with sharpened sticks dipped in acid. The fragment of jade, full of jagged edges, burned like a star in her eye socket. Retching, nothing came out, and she wondered when she had eaten last. The taste in her mouth was of the sour drink she had given Wild Bill.

Coffee, she thought. She needed strong, black coffee.

Wrapping herself more tightly in her long coat, she strode across the dark streets. The pain receded, slowly, but did not go away. She wondered if it would always be there, now – growing in strength slowly, the closer she approached its source. Somewhere in the city the statue waited, and planned. The voices were always there now, just on the edge of hearing, growing stronger all the time. They said only one thing she fully understood.

Their time was coming.

She should be going after the voices, after that thing that somehow scanned and briefly animated the dead – the thing that was patiently gathering information, patiently planning something terrible–

And yet the voices sounded so lonely. It was hard to feel the urgency, even when the fragment sent shards of sharp pain into her mind, even when the voices spoke of ninety-six percent completion and initiation procedure checksum correct, even as the percentages grew closer and closer to a hundred–

It was the Phantom who worried her, who scared her. The Phantom she hated – for what he did, for what he had become: for what she had become, perhaps.

Holmes. The name kept reverberating in her mind. Now she had a name to put to the phantom in her mind. A name, and a place: a boarding house, close enough to the white city, yet on the edges of the black.

In an all-night diner she ordered coffee and grimaced as she sipped it. Staring through grimy glass windows at the rain outside… the place was awash in smoke and flickering lights, and sawdust covered the floor. A newspaper lying on the next table spoke of Sitting Bull arriving for the presidential visit at the Fair. She picked it up and leafed through it. There was a feature about the wheel. A man named Ferris had built it. A notice about a picture show. The newspaper was full of nothing but the Fair. She sipped her coffee and turned the pages until she reached the Classifieds section. Staring at it, she realised she could not even read the words. She needed to eat…

She ordered a meat patty in two slices of a bun. It came slathered in tomato sauce, with cold, greasy fried potatoes on the side, a portion of coleslaw – it was the best thing she had ever tasted.

Wiping her lips with a paper napkin, she felt better. The voices had quietened somewhat, sank into the edge of hearing. Inside the dark diner no one paid her any attention. A Buddhist monk sat alone in one corner, his back to the wall, peacefully asleep. Two Africans were playing cards with a cigar-smoking Cossack. It was quiet, and she was just another alien, here.

She picked up the paper again. Classifieds. Pages and pages of ads. She went through them.

Prof. A. Huff, Practical Phrenologist. Examinations and delineations of character and talents with marked chart to your fancy. Students taught this noble science.

Colling's Electric Belts will cure all diseases that flesh is heir to; my belts run one year without refilling which can be done by anybody, or I will make them as good as new for nominal sum. Send for pamphlet.

Mrs W. Weir, Telegraphic medium, controlled by the late Mrs Breed of Austria, the wonderful rapping medium, sittings daily; also a powerful magnetic healer, treats all kinds of chronic and acute diseases successfully. Every day except Sunday.

All of which were unhelpful, to say the least.

Lists and lists of advertisements for accommodation. She scanned through them, her eye hurting as she tried to make out the small type in the smoky darkness of the diner. Jade pulsed behind the other, the eye that was no longer there.

Yet at last she found it. For a moment her fingers touched the rough paper almost lovingly, the tips stroking the newspaper edge. There, it could only be the one she sought: Dr H.H. Holmes is offering a place of quiet refuge in the bustling city. Close to Fair and all amenities, gaslight in every room: perfect for the single visitor. Long- and short-term accommodation available.

Dr Holmes?

But people always trusted doctors. Didn't they?

She stared at the advertisement, at the address printed below. And she thought – could it really be that easy?

Englewood, the streets dark and quiet, shops shuttered, street-lamps glowing like fireflies, casting little light. The air was cold. It had stopped raining, but the puddles lay heavy on the ground, and mud splattered Cleo as she walked.

Too easy, she thought. Too easy.

And yet she could not turn back. There is a path we must

follow, she thought. Beyond reason, beyond law. Her gun arm twitched. Behind her eye the jade fragment twisted and turned, sending short, sharp shocks of pain into her head. Restless. It was sensing the Phantom, she realised – the proximity of one jade fragment to another.

And so he, too, must know she was coming.

She had little doubt he had anticipated this, was expecting her.

Let him.

She stood across the road from the building and knew that soon she would kill a man.

What could be said of that place, of Dr Holmes' castle? It was a dark, imposing two-storey building. On the ground floor were shops; a Chemist, Holden's; a sign advertising Used Jewellery; another for Jobs Available: For Young Ladies of Suitable Skills. Where the ground floor had display windows the first was a façade of dark stone.

Cautiously, Cleo approached the closed doors.

She smashed the window with her gun hand. Shards of glass fell like tears on the floor. She pushed her way in then, up dark stairs, and onto a long, cold corridor. Doors lined it, all closed. Nothing stirred. There were no windows. She kicked open the first door.

A girl lay in the bed. Young, she slept peacefully, or so it seemed at first. When Cleo approached her the girl didn't stir. She put two fingers to the girl's neck, cautiously. A weak, too-weak pulse. She tried to shake her awake, but the girl did not open her eyes.

Something was making her slow. Dimly, she became aware of a sound, a hiss of air. She scanned for it. A hidden nozzle, high above her. Gas, she thought. Gas was being pumped into the room.

She picked up the girl, dragged her across the floor. Once in the corridor she shut the door behind them. Her head slowly cleared. She shook the girl again, and this time she opened her eyes.

Milady's gun arm was pointing directly at the girl's head. The message she wanted to get across could not be subtle. She said, "Get out of here."

"The doctor..." the girl whispered.

"What?"

"You won't hurt the doctor...?"

"Get out of here! Now!"

Not waiting for a response, she moved to the next door and kicked it open. Another sleeping form – approaching it she knew it was too late. When she put her fingers against the girl's neck there was no pulse, and the skin was cold.

"Get out!" she shouted now and, running down the corridor, fired into the air. She kicked open doors, dragged semi-conscious girls out to the landing. "Run!"

He wouldn't be up there, she knew. Where she found windows she burst them open, and the cold air washed in like medicine. The girls finally began to go, some running. Two more asked about the doctor, pleaded with her not to hurt him.

And two more never stirred from their beds. The last one had been dead longer than the others, she saw. When she opened the door there was no hiss of gas, but the air smelled of a rotted sweetness. The corpse on the bed had been dead for a while. She watched the silver strands move like eels across the girl's skin. The girl's eyes opened, then, and stared at her.

And the corpse smiled.

She fired before she was conscious she was doing it, and the girl's head plopped back against the pillow, and her eyes closed. The smile faded, and the girl looked sad now. He had been gaining power, she thought. She raced out of that room, looking for a way down, knowing it would be concealed, all the while the alien fragment in her skull thrashing and the pain echoing through her bones, a pain that was a part of her now.

A maze... he had built himself a maze, and she was trapped inside it. Doors led nowhere, corridors twisted and turned and opened back on themselves. She knocked on the walls, searching for hollows, found a secret passageway, followed it, but it terminated in a brick wall. She retraced her steps but somehow the path was different now, and a door led into a new room, and as she stepped into it the door closed behind her with a clang. The room was windowless, bricked-up on all sides. The door was metal. There was no lock.

Stupid! Stupid! she thought. The gas was pumping into the room. Behind her eye, the jade fragment moved. Use it, she thought. Exhaling slowly, she reached within herself, and out–

Into a cellar crawling with shadows, the kiln burning, and the Phantom, raging – a keyboard of wood and chrome was before him and he worked at it, pulling levers – a map of the building stood before him like a screen.

A puppet-master, she thought. But his puppets were running away, and there was little he could do.

Looking at the map through his eyes, as the Phantom closed and opened doors and sealed exists, turned on hidden pumps of gas, rooms in which the walls seemed to close in, and there–

A chute, she saw. One of many. The building was such that some rooms had a hidden chute built into them – leading directly to the cellar...

He could kill in a locked room and the corpse would simply disappear.

Later, the kiln would do the rest...

She pulled back. On her hands and knees now, no air remaining, but she found it, a hidden lever in the wall, and when she pulled it the empty bed tilted forward and a trapdoor opened in the floor.

Not waiting, not wanting to think, she lowered herself through the trapdoor and let go.

SIXTY-NINE
Qinggong

"Cleopatra."

There was venom in the voice.

She said, "Tômas."

The fire burned between them.

She had come down shooting. The bullets echoed in that closed, dank chamber.

But he had been ahead of her.

She had landed heavily, rolled – only then noticing the overwhelming heat, the open door of the Phantom's kiln.

"You shouldn't have come."

"I'm beginning to think you are right."

He moved like shadow. Conventional bullets could not harm him. The room was small, her eye stinging – but she could see him clearly through the jade, a figure made monstrous by the shadows.

And yet, this time, she wasn't afraid.

They met mid-room. The Phantom leaped into the air, tracing a parabola as he soared high, bouncing off the wall to come at her. But she too was ready now.

She was no longer human, she knew that now. The jade had changed her, shaped her, that alien machine with its own, unknown purpose working through her. She flew to meet him, sailing through flames, and her hand caught his throat as he came for her.

Squeezing, and he landed a fist like a metal globe on her chest, but she held him still as they both fell. No guns, no bullets, but person to person, in single unarmed combat. She smashed her gun arm against his skull.

He twisted – impossibly – his legs rising to meet her face. She had to let go, pull back to avoid the full brunt of his attack and, laughing, he was free again, bouncing gracefully from a wall to come back at her, all the while the fire burning, burning in that room of death.

"I've killed your like in this room more times than you can imagine," he said.

"You've been a busy boy," she said.

"I've been a bad boy," he said, and laughed. Had he always been insane? Once he must have been a valuable agent for the Council. Once…

And now?

"I will kill you," he said, "and then go for the statue. I know what it does. I know what it wants. I have been listening to it for a long time."

"What does it want?" she said. He came for her, through the air, but she was no longer where she was, turning and catching him from behind with a kick that sent him flying at the wall–

His face smashed into the bricks. When he pulled back she could see the indentation in the wall, but the Phantom was unharmed.

"It wants this world," he said. "The world and everything in it."

"For itself?"

"For its masters… and when they come, I shall be rewarded. I shall rule!"

"They should have put you in Charenton a long time ago," she said.

"But they put you in the asylum instead," he said, smirking.

She watched that hungry, elongated skull, and knew he was insane, and had to be stopped.

"You shouldn't have listened to the voices," she said, coming at him. He leaped up and they met in mid-air, and this time his kick found purchase and she felt the air going out of her as she sailed back and smashed against the wall near the door.

The door!

It was getting hard to breathe in the room.

"They were lonely," he said. "They'd been lonely for a very long time."

"And now they have you?"

But she knew he was wrong. The voices did not care about Tômas, did not care about her. She thought of the Shaolin, keeping the statue for countless years, of old, lonely Master Long and the child he had once been. She thought of the corpses animated, however briefly, by that alien machine. She thought of the voices.

They were barely aware of them as individual entities, she realised. They had been some sort of information-gathering machine and, awakened, they studied the world. Everything that happened was just a by-product of that impersonal, detached survey – the Phantom and she were insignificant particles in that great schema of the machine.

She went low then, and he went high, and she grasped his leg and yanked him down from the air, bringing him crashing down hard on the floor, and then she put her gun arm to his head and fired, at point-blank range, and heard him scream.

When he pulled away his fist lifted her off the ground and, too quickly, he turned. His skull was ruined, and his mouth opened in a scream of rage, but no sound came. Her back hit the wall. She lifted her gun arm again, trying to aim but, too quickly, he whipped around. No! she tried to shout, but he had opened the door and was gone through it – too quickly!

She heard the lock close from the outside.

It took her a moment to realise she was trapped in the Phantom's cellar.

She rose slowly to her feet. She hurt in numerous places. She felt ravenously hungry, too, as if her body had been expending energy beyond its natural ability, and now needed to compensate for it. And she knew she was no longer the woman who had first met the Phantom, there in the under-morgue of Paris, in what seemed a lifetime away.

For it had been a lifetime. And she was a different person now, a different thing.

She went to the kiln. And she pushed it.

She had never had such strength, but her conviction lent her power, and her desperation drove her. She knew this place could not, should not exist. She kicked the metal with her artificial leg and again she pushed, hearing the strong foundations groan, the heat burning her–

But she would not burn.

With the last of her energy she jumped, flying at the wall, leaping from it, back at the kiln. The impact jarred her body, and she fell numb to the floor–

But the great, obese, obscene object had succumbed. Slowly, it toppled over.

And the fire burst out.

Blinking tears, she pushed herself up, feeling as if she were drowning. Her gun arm shook as she pointed it at the door. She fired, through the flames, watching wood fly. When she kicked the door it fell back. Cold air rushed inside, touching her cheeks like a mother's hand. She ran, and the fire pursued her.

SEVENTY
Dismissed

"You're a fool."

Winnetou's voice, like cold water. She had come crawling out of the burning building, soot and ash over her and the taste of fire in her mouth. Arms dragged her away. She sat, propped against a wall, and watched the building burn.

Confused girls in a gaggle outside, throwing her strange looks. Wrapped in firemen's coats, feet naked in the cold. But the fire warmed the night.

She knew he was still nearby. But not pursuing, any more. He was her prey now, and their roles had changed. She felt his fear, and it warmed her.

Winnetou, above her, his face angry. His men ringing the building – too late. The killer had gone but some of his intended victims, at least, had survived.

"I did what I had to do," she said. Speaking quietly, her throat raw from the smoke.

"I told you not to get involved."

"I told you, I was already involved."

He turned away from her. She let him go.

Run, she thought, aiming her words at a misshapen figure running through mists. Run, Tômas. I'll catch up with you soon enough. She felt tired, so tired... and yet, strangely, at peace.

She knew it wasn't over. But she had done what she had to do. Master Long had been right. Sometimes it's the best we can do, she thought.

And sometimes even that's not enough.

She saw a familiar black carriage come to a stop. She expected the two automatons to come out of it. Instead, it was the Monsignor himself – itself – who came to meet her.

The ancient automaton glided across the hard ground. His robes hid his means of movement. She did not think he had legs... The carved face looked at her expressionlessly. "You have disobeyed my orders."

There didn't seem anything to say to that. She didn't. He raised his hand. A figure stepped out of the carriage. Two others followed behind it, like obedient shadows.

"Dellamorte..."

The countess, at least, was courteous. "Milady de Winter," she said, nodding. "I trust your journey was not unpleasant."

"I am much obliged," Cleo said, "for all your courtesy."

"It was the least I could do."

They stared at each other. A small smile played at the corners of the countess's mouth, was answered. "I trust Captain Karnstein is well?"

The countess inched her head. "He is recovering," she said.

"I'm glad."

Hovering without a need for an answer was the question: What are you doing here?

She already knew.

She recognised the two figures behind the countess. McGill, and the leopard woman, from Scab.

So they did not trust her to do her job.

"I am to be relieved of my duties," she said – not a question. The countess looked elsewhere. The Monsignor's face, of course, did not change expression. He said, "My colleagues in the Council think highly of you. So do I. However..."

"You planned it all along," she said. "You had to, for them

to have arrived so quickly–"

"You were to be detained on Scab," he said – the same scratchy, even voice, the recording of a long-dead human. "Countess Dellamorte, alas, let her emotions get the better of her–"

"Karnstein," Cleo said.

"We are not so different, you and I," the countess said. And was that apology in her voice?

"You are unstable," the Monsignor said. "You would have been more useful being studied. I cannot allow you to run free and interfere. There has been a communiqué... The auction is set to commence. I shall bid – for the Council. And whether I win, or lose... we must have it. The countess's team shall supervise the retrieval of the item. You are not to interfere." He coughed, the sound as artificial as the rest of him. "Am I clear?"

"You were never clear," she said, or thought she had. She felt so tired... Let someone else take the burden for once, and let her sleep, and be at peace... she had done what she could. One did not expect thanks in the service of the Council.

"Take her back to her lodgings," the Monsignor said.

McGill and the leopard woman approached her. Wearily, she pulled herself up to her feet. "I'll walk," she said.

"I don't think–" the countess began, then subsided. Milady inched her head, and the countess nodded. "Very well," she said.

The fire still burned. It lit up the night, sending showers of sparks and embers floating on the wind. Sunlight was gradually touching the sky on the horizon, drawing a panorama of colour above the black outline of the city, and it merged with the fire so that it seemed the sky itself was coming alight. She began to walk away then, following the still dark, empty streets. Dawn was approaching, but to Cleo it felt far away.

INTERLUDE
Moving Pictures

In the white city, Kai sat in the darkened space of the Zoopraxographical Hall and watched the silent screen.

Moving pictures. They were like the shadows that flitted behind his eyes, those glimpses of another world. Cigar smoke curled up into the air and was illuminated by the beams of light from Edison's new machine. A hush in the packed hall, and he knew that, amidst all those people, he was truly alone.

They were looking for him, everywhere, across the black city and the white. He had seen their silent watchers, in the Midway Plaisance, in the Electricity Building and the Manufacturers and Fine Arts building and around the lake. They looked for him inside the pyramid...

But of all the buildings, of all the tall, impossible buildings of the White City, it was the Electricity Building that frightened him most.

Tesla's building.

The Fair was lit up with electricity, Tesla's alternating current, and the statue was in love.

The statue needed the electricity.

Craved it, with a hunger that frightened Kai even more than this entire alien city did, with its strange people and displays, its masses of humanity, its bustle and noise and commerce. He was frightened, and he could tell no one that he was. Only here, in the darkened room, did he feel some safety. Safety from the voices, safety from the watchers. Safety from himself.

Images flickered on the screen and the audience was spellbound. There was no musical accompaniment, nothing but the changing images on the screen. Kai hugged himself, drawing himself into a ball in his chair. I could hide, he thought. I could hide here forever, and pretend none of this was happening. Pretend I was someone else, somewhere else.

Once, he had wanted to be a wuxia hero. In the books the heroes were never scared. They fought, bravely, for a just cause. They faced the dark. But Kai was not afraid of the dark. It was the light outside that scared him, and only in the darkness did he find some comfort, some escape.

He thought of the woman he had seen in his dreams. A strange woman, darker than the mountain people who lived high above Luang Prabang, a woman who was fashioned into a weapon, much as he himself had been. He wished he could go to her. He wished she could help. But there was no one who could. The voices were in a cacophony of excitement, whispering that the time had come. He thought of their plan and shivered. He stared at the screen and rocked in his seat, lost just as he had been all those years before, when he left his father's shop and ran into the forest, clutching a strange statue in his hands. He wished he'd thrown it away, then. When he had the chance.

He rocked in his seat and watched the pictures flickering across the screen, and waited, alone in the dark. It would not be long now, the voices promised.

PART VII
The End of the World's Fair

SEVENTY-ONE
The Magician of the Fair

She woke up clutching her head, the jade flaring in her eye socket, the pain coursing through her like a green turbulent river. The voices whispered, Ninety-eight per cent complete, ninety-eight point one per cent complete… they whispered Quantum sequence identified, locked and origin point identified and Rerouting power to accelerant device in progress, making her want to scream.

She rose up, washed, dressed, loaded her gun arm, ate a cold breakfast in her room and thought.

And realised she was still being played.

The Council was like the vast mind of a chess player, and its pieces were alive. It did not like its pawns to know the grand design, used them unsparingly, sending them off with as little information as possible – or the wrong information. Watching them follow a trail, whatever the cost.

And she had not been taken off the board, she realised. Dismissed, the Monsignor had said. But chess pieces were never dismissed. They were eliminated, or used. And she had been sent back unharmed…

The old machine, the entire power of the Council at his disposal, still needed her. The countess would be watching the auction, yes, and her strange, misshapen creatures with her – but the Council had a suspicious mind.

Did they expect a ruse?

The main game would take place without her. That was certain. But what if the main game turned out to be a lie?

She watched herself in the mirror, her hair like a dark globe around her head. She touched her fingers to the eyepatch. The pain was with her always now. Would it ever stop? Soon, she thought, thinking of the voices, counting the rising percentages… one way or the other it would end.

She looked at herself, and finally smiled. A young, unfamiliar woman looked back at her from the mirror. They nodded to each other.

Go, her reflection seemed to say. You and I must follow the path we've chosen long ago. Wherever it leads.

She turned away from the mirror, knowing what she had to do.

She took a tram to the white city. It was late in the afternoon. She came to the gates of the World's Vespuccian Exposition. The white city could be seen from a distance, the outline marred only by the lizards' pyramid, that enormous structure dominating the centre of the Fair. The lizards' alien green metal shone wetly in the sunlight. Look at our power, it seemed to say. Though we let you play at being builders, at being free, we are still the true power in this world, now. The Everlasting Empire of Les Lézards is named thus for a reason. Come and see our glory.

She paid the entrance fee and walked in.

The white city. Already the sun was setting, and the electric lights were coming alive, illuminating the white buildings. Massive searchlights mounted on the Manufacturers and Liberal Arts building swept the grounds. There was light everywhere, white electric light, and the buildings, huge, cavernous, seemed to grow out of the very ground, rising high into the air. She walked along the Midway, heading for the lagoon that lay nestled between the buildings. There were so many people...

And watchers.

The sensation stole on her slowly, but would not go away.

Watchers in the crowd, waiting, calculating... she passed an Egyptian village and a troupe of Russian Cossacks, an orchestra, a miniature zoo, getting lost in the mayhem, not heading anywhere in particular... She paused when she came to a giant cannon. "Krupp's Monster," she heard someone say. She turned and saw a woman speaking, apparently dictating into an Edison recorder. "A fearful, hideous thing, breathing blood and carnage, a triumph of barbarism crouching amid the world's triumphs of civilisation." The woman glared at the giant cannon, then said, "End quote," crisply. But Cleo rather liked the weapon.

Or was it a weapon? Or was it as the countess had told her, that Krupp, and others, were looking to – what? Send people into space?

Well, it was not her concern. She kept going, pausing now and then, checking her reflection, turning abruptly – but there were too many people. She could not tell who, if anyone, was following her.

There were fire-eaters and belly dancers, displays of cheese making, a display of scalping, phrenologists with human skulls marked by areas, Mongolian archers, food-sellers, photographers carrying their bulky equipment this way and that, machines that spun sugar, booksellers extolling the virtues of Scientific Romances and imported Penny Dreadfuls, Bedouins riding camels, chess-players hovering over a board the size of a town square, where the pieces were all automatons...

She passed a crowd of surging people and saw the flash of lightning beyond them. Curious, she pushed forward. A man was standing on a stage, and – impossibly – lightning danced around him, but he was not harmed. The man raised his arms and smiled at the audience. There were gasps, and cheers. The lightning flashed on and on. Nikola Tesla himself, she realised. She watched, repulsed and fascinated, then turned away.

The city rose all around her. She passed jugglers and sword-swallowers and a fortune-telling machine. The wheel was always in sight, turning slowly, turning, cars loaded with people hanging from its frame. Ferris's wheel. She passed a short, straight, smooth path that led up to a ramp, and stared: a machine with delicate wings rushed along the road to the ramp and, instead of falling, launched from it and soared slowly into the air, a steam engine belching steam in the tail. A man was sitting in the small cabin between the giant wings. The crowd gasped and cheered – it was a sound she was getting used to.

The magic of the Fair…

The sign said, Du Temple Monoplane and, below: Félix du Temple, Proprietor. She stared at the monoplane. She'd used one once before, during the Robur Affair…

More flying machines, most on the ground. She checked out the signs. Stringfellow's Aerial Steam Carriage. Wnek's Gliders. L'Albatros artificiel. One sign towering above the rest: The Montgolfier Brothers: Dominating the Skies Since 1783.

But it looked as though they'd found some competition.

She turned away again. Somehow she had found her way to the lagoon. An island rose in the middle of the water, overgrown with wild growth of flowers and trees. The roof of a temple peeked out from behind the vegetation. Electric boats hummed their way across the surface of the lagoon. She watched the water and saw stars beginning to blink into existence, faint at first but growing larger and more luminous. When she raised her head she realised she had been wrong, and she smiled. They were lanterns, hundreds of floating lanterns rising slowly into the air.

At that moment the place felt bewitched. The white city

was reflected in the calm water, bathed in unearthly light. And a voice beside her said, quietly and unexpectedly, "Night is the magician of the Fair."

She turned, slowly, and was not surprised to find Master Long standing beside her. In his hands he held a lantern – a thing of bamboo and thin paper. As she watched he lit the small candle underneath the canopy of paper and, after a moment, gently let the lantern go. It hovered in the air between them, as if uncertain. Then, gracefully, it began to rise above their heads, and soon joined the others, becoming another bright star in the skies above the Fair.

Cleo shook her head, as if trying to dispel the moment. "Night's not the only magician at the Fair tonight," she said. Master Long followed her gaze and then smiled.

A young man – almost a boy, Cleo thought – was sitting cross-legged on the ground a little distance from them. He was brown-skinned, wore robes, and a hand-painted sign beside him said: The Amazing Indian Yogi: Showing Miracles and Wonders from the East. As she watched the young yogi spread earth over the mat before him and began to chant. "Goly, goly, chelly gol," he sang, waving his hands over the earth. "Goly, goly, chelly job, chelly job!" he said.

Cleo almost laughed. "It's coming, it's coming!" the young yogi said. He covered the naked earth with a red cloth. A companion, as dark as he was, was playing a lyre beside him. The yogi waved his hands over the cloth – and when he lifted it, two small sprouts of green appeared out of the brown earth.

His small audience gasped.

The yogi smiled – revealing white, well-cared-for teeth – and covered the earth again. The next time he lifted his cloth, two miniature mango trees had appeared where the shoots had been.

The audience clapped, and the lyre player collected the money given, and the yogi said, "Chelly gol, chelly gol."

Cleo laughed, and said, "That is some of the worst acting I've ever seen."

"Do not underestimate our young friend," Master Long said, and this time he wasn't smiling. "Mister Weiss has not, perhaps, found his true role yet, but he is skilful. He's been following you for some time..."

"Weiss?" She stared at the young yogi, who looked back at her now, still smiling, a challenge in his eyes. Wash the paint off his skin, she thought, and you'd get–

"I believe he goes by the stage name Houdini, most often," Master Long said. "After your own illustrious Robert Houdin."

The Toymaker. She thought of the man, alone in his dark workshop, with only his machine-child for company, and grimaced. She let it go, said, "Vespuccian?"

"One of the immigrants who came here as a child," Master Long said. "It is my belief he is here, unofficially, on behest of the Black Cabinet."

The Council of Chiefs' intelligence service. She looked at the boy with new eyes. He rose up slowly, then, gracefully, bowed. She had to laugh. "At least he has style," she said.

"Yes," Master Long said. "I foresee great things in his future – but you must know he is not alone in the white city tonight. The auction is set to commence, and who shall gain the ultimate prize? They all want to get their hands on the statue, but its power is too great to be controlled."

The young magician, meanwhile, had given her a last smile and – along with his companion – disappeared into the throng of humanity. Still, she could feel invisible eyes gazing at her – and knew the Black Cabinet of the Vespuccians was the least of her worries. "Where is the auction held?" she said, and saw Master Long smile. "You are the last of my pupils," he said. "Not Wudang, or Shaolin, but a follower of Xia nonetheless. Perhaps the last, if you are successful..." He was no longer smiling. She thought of the Monsignor's prohibition and pushed it away from her mind. "Tell me where it is," she said.

SEVENTY-TWO
The Auction

She could no longer sense the Phantom. She could no longer sense Kai.

Something was changing.

The voices said, Ninety-eight point eight per cent, ninety-eight point nine. The pain was still with her, but she couldn't see.

The auction was at the Zoopraxographical Hall.

She staked it out. Waiting for the players to arrive, the Phantom, Kai. She couldn't go – the Monsignor's orders were very specific.

She watched Dellamorte arrive. McGill and the leopard woman were with her. They fanned out, found observation posts. She saw her signal – more of the Scab people were already in place.

Master Long had left her. She was on her own. She knew he had his own operation going – she thought she saw Mistress Yi on the roof, but she was gone before Cleo could be certain.

So many watchers and she was watching the watchers. She wondered who was watching her.

The voices said, Ninety-nine point one per cent and something was wrong, but she didn't know what.

The buyers began to arrive.

She didn't recognise the Sioux chief, but she did recognise

the Empress-Dowager's emissary. She entered the building with her escort: ushers on the door searched everyone for weapons. Madame Linlin bore it stoically.

More faces she didn't know – a short black man who may have represented Zululand, a tall one who may have been Dahomey. A fat white man had to be helped from his carriage and she stared at his face: it had to be Krupp, the industrialist.

A delegate from Siam, then an Aztec, then another familiar face: Mycroft Holmes, puffing on a cigar. They kept coming, these sole representatives, while their people watched from outside and had the entire building under lockdown. There was no way out of there. Kai had no way of escaping… She knew they would all bid, but who would actually get hold of the statue depended on later, on who had the superior firepower.

Ninety-nine point two per cent. And something still wasn't right.

There were no windows. Inside was a machine that showed pictures. Is that what they thought the statue was? Pictures of another world… She shuddered, feeling suddenly cold. She was sitting in a coffee shop on a roof opposite the building. She wondered how many of the other diners were watching too, waiting as she did.

All of them, she thought.

She saw a tall turbaned man come to the Zoopraxographical Hall. His face was familiar – Prince Dakkar, she thought. She had once seen his dossier… A delegate from the empire of the Mexica next, followed by a tall pale man – one of the Nordic countries? – and another, and another. The Monsignor's black carriage arrived. His two bodyguards helped him down. They disappeared through the doors.

More delegates…

Last one, unexpected: she saw Master Long.

Before he entered he turned his head, for just a moment. Did he see her?

He disappeared inside. The ushers followed, and the doors closed.

The auction was set to begin.

And something still didn't feel right.

She knew then that she had to get inside.

She saw him before he saw her, she was sure of that.

Tômas, a shadow moving against the wall.

She left money on the table and was gone. She was on the street and running, and the alien energy coursed through her. Someone tried to grab her – McGill. She broke his wrists and kept going. Someone high up took a shot at her. She rolled and kept going. The Phantom turned, saw her chasing, grinned.

He leaped up into the air, found purchase on the wall, climbed. She followed.

So this is what it felt like, long exposure to the statue, she thought.

She could do impossible things.

They leaped on and off walls, street lamps. Gunfire zinged past them. But the watchers couldn't come any closer. The terms of the auction were strict... and the prize too valuable to risk.

For anyone but the Phantom and her.

He found a side door and burst it open as if it were paper. There were guards inside and she arrived a fraction of a second too late. He'd killed them neatly and kept going.

She followed.

Into darkness and smoke–

The Phantom disappeared, too quickly to catch. She stood very still.

A light flickering, a beam crossing a cloud of smoke. Moving pictures: figures moving through mist, haltingly, grey figures with the faces of the dead. The mists seemed to part, but didn't – something behind them she had to see and couldn't.

She was standing to one side of the screen, hidden by a pulled-back curtain... an audience of faces looking up. They were all seated, and on the stage a man was standing before a podium, and a jade statue of a cross-legged lizard sat on a velvet cushion in a glass display cabinet beside him.

But it was not Kai.

She could still not see him. She could not feel the Phantom...

Ninety-nine point three per cent. Initiating gateway transfer protocols. Checksum routines engaged.

She had seen the man before.

Kai's servant.

The Manchu.

There was excitement in the audience. The images flickering on the screen were hypnotising. Could they not see what was happening?

Mycroft Holmes: "Ten million."

Madame Linlin: "Fifteen."

Dakkar: "Sixteen."

Krupp: "Twenty million."

She stared at the statue, felt nothing.

The images kept flickering on the screen. Pictures of the dead, the mist almost but never quite opening...

Not yet.

The Sioux chief: "Twenty-three."

Krupp: "Twenty-five million."

Holmes: "Thirty."

She saw several of the delegates shake their heads. She knew the real bidding would be between a handful of people. But it was wrong!

And where was Tômas?

She spotted him. He had moved around the audience, a shadow in the dark, was approaching the stage on the other side from her. He grinned at her, his face barely human, then his gaze turned towards the statue and remained there.

She couldn't put the audience at risk. On the stage, the

Manchu said: "Ladies and gentlemen, for this once-in-a-lifetime offer, please let us move past the courtesy round. Do I hear fifty million?"

But it was all a charade. Couldn't they see it? The statue was worth any amount they could throw at it, but Kai and the Manchu could not possibly hope to get out alive after the sale–

And where was Kai?

Ninety-nine point four per cent, whispered the voices, from far away.

Madame Linlin: "Thirty-five."

Holmes: "Forty million."

Images flickering on the screen. The Manchu waving an auctioneer's hammer – she looked for the Phantom again and couldn't see him–

Then a roar, and the Manchu dropped his hammer–

Shouting in the audience – she saw Master Long turn his head – their eyes connected – a message in his eyes she couldn't decipher. He shook his head – no.

The Phantom had leaped onto the stage. The Manchu drew back his hand, sent a fist into the Phantom's face–

Tômas extended claws, tried to rip the other man's throat out–

The Manchu laughed in his face.

Shouts, the bidders rising from their seats in a panic – on the screen the mist rolled on. The voices of the statue said, Ninety-nine point four five per cent complete. Transference protocols initiating. Primary power source hooked up to origin-point mechanism.

The Manchu had Qinggong, she realised: long-term exposure to the statue gave him strength equivalent to that of Tômas.

With a bit of luck they would kill each other.

And no one was minding the statue...

She dashed onto the stage, broke the glass of the display case and grabbed it.

SEVENTY-THREE
The Wheel

She had expected pain. There was none. The jade fragment in her eye socket remained motionless. No visions, no flashes of green – the statue was inert in her arms.

She ran.

They were trashing the stage, the Manchu fighting Tômas against a background of moving pictures. Screams were muted – everything was muted.

And something was still very wrong.

She carried the statue one-handed. It felt too light. Bursting out to the street outside – it was chaos. The security forces of more than a dozen nations descended on the building. A familiar face – Mistress Yi running, Ip Kai behind her–

"Milady, no!"

The leopard woman tackled her. She had claws for hands. She missed Cleo's eye, left bloodied gashes on her face. Cleo kicked – the woman came at her again, hissing.

She shot her.

Her gun arm had a life of its own. She shot half a dozen attackers but there were too many of them and it was hard to fight holding the statue...

Wrong. All wrong.

She ran – they followed. Bullets missed her – mostly. One hit her artificial leg, sent her sprawling. The statue rolled away–

The voices kept whispering in her mind, but they were too far away.

And Kai was never in the building, she realised.

Mistress Yi, a light shadow – "I'll distract them."

She grabbed the statue, jumped – onto a street lamp and going higher, trying to scale the roof of the next building. People ran screaming down the road – innocents caught in the crossfire of politics.

Cleo was ignored – they were all pursuing the statue and she'd lost it.

Construct the sequence of events, try to overlay some logic. The auction was a diversion, Kai had other plans–

He still had the statue, and it was nowhere near the Zoopraxographical Hall.

Which meant the statue on the stage had been a decoy.

Which meant–

She ran.

She tried to reach him, through the fragment – reached into the jade light, forcing it.

Met resistance. It was pushing her out – the pain spread through her so quickly she couldn't even shout. Glimpses, nevertheless: Tômas bloodied, the Manchu holding him down – the inside of the Zoopraxographical Hall was a mess, the stage had collapsed – Tômas rolled, bit down on the Manchu's arm. She heard bones breaking, heard the Manchu laugh.

Was pushed away – the jade a viscous liquid. Where was she? Running blindly, the lake on her left, searchlights criss-crossing the white city – lanterns floating in the air.

She stopped, took a deep breath, held still.

Tried again.

Ninety-nine point five per cent. Primary power source engaged.

And all over the white city the lights dimmed and died out at once.

All around her, uncertain silence.

In the darkness only one thing remained alight.

The Ferris wheel. It shone with a blinding white light – too strong.

There were gunshots in the distance…

Someone screamed.

The silence broke – the screams rose from multiple directions. She tried to hold her ground – people pushed against her, running now, trying to get away.

The magic was gone from the white city.

She pushed into the jade. A picture resolved – slowly, and it hurt when it appeared. Kai against a background of stars – he seemed to float in mid-air.

Kai: "Help me…"

She saw the statue beside him. It was burning, engulfed in cold flames.

The Ferris wheel.

Once again, she ran.

Screams.

They cut through the night, voices wafting down from on high. Trapped in the moving cars of the giant wheel: thirty-six cars and up to sixty people in each – and it had been busy every day since it had opened for business.

Two thousand people trapped above-ground – the wheel kept rotating, faster and faster. It was a streak of white light in the night, a blur of motion.

She looked up – no way to climb, Kai somewhere up there – electric cables snaked towards the base of the wheel. When she stared up the air inside the wheel seemed to shimmer.

"Master Long says you must stop it." A voice beside her – Mistress Yi materialised, minus the fake statue. Blood covered her face, one arm was bent at an unnatural angle. She was breathing heavily.

Milady: "How?"

Mistress Yi: "You have to climb up there."

Milady: "Up where?"

But she already knew.

Flashes of jade – Kai wasn't in a passenger car. He was at the centre of the wheel, on the axle itself. He was fastening the statue to the spider's web of spokes. Electric cables ran up there, too. The statue glowed. The air inside the wheel shimmered and looked like a mirror.

Mistress Yi: "Use Qinggong."

Milady: "Are you insane?"

The girl shrugged. "Then it's going to succeed."

"What is it doing?"

"What it must."

A key. A key was for opening doors…

And this one led to another world.

Ninety-nine point six per cent. Initiating quantum hookup.

Kai, distant: "Help me!"

Screams from the cars. The wheel was moving faster and faster. Darkness over the Fair – torches offered sporadic illumination.

The wheel was almost three hundred feet high. There was no way up there.

Unless…

She said: "Stay here. There was one way to get up there–

She ran.

The plane was where she'd last seen it. There was no one around. The Du Temple monoplane, looking like a moth, wings too delicate to work, the body tiny–

But it did work. Thirteen metre wingspan, a light carriage weighing a mere eighty kilograms – she had to add her own weight, hope the ramp was high enough – but she'd seen it fly. A flash boiler–

It was loaded – the pilot must have expected to make another flight. She lit the flame, climbed into the seat – the engine came alive behind her. Steam burst through a network of tubes, compressed water heated by the flame – no time to think now, no time for anything but–

A jet of pressured steam came roaring out of the engine and the plane glided forward, gathering speed–

She flew down the ramp. Wind and smoke stung her face. The roar of the engine filled the night–

The plane reached the end of the ramp and flew over it–

The ground came very close and missed her.

The plane rose.

She coaxed it, talking to it – she rose, slowly, slowly – the ground grew distant. She turned, swerving – saw the plane's reflection in the lagoon. She found a pair of aviator glasses and put them on. Circling, the wheel rising impossibly high, the air inside it changing now, the mirror becoming a lens, through which she saw...

The voices said, Quantum signature verified. Opening entanglement channels. Handshake protocols response correct! Correct!

And – Ninety-nine point seven per cent. Ninety-nine point eight.

She could feel their elation. She took the plane in a wide circuit, the Manufacturers and Fine Arts building rising on one side, the lizards' pyramid on the other, and she flew the monoplane straight–

She could no longer see the spokes of the wheel. The structure of the wheel was no longer there, or – not exactly.

It was overlaid. She saw through jade – Kai huddled on the main axis, the statue bathed in flames – the sky behind them disappeared and was replaced with–

The voices said, Ninety-nine point nine – triumphantly. Behind her the air was full of steam. She aimed for the centre of the wheel–

Where there was a deep blackness, filled with stars.

SEVENTY-FOUR
The Gateway

The size of the thing did not make sense. And the engine had begun to splutter, and she was losing power – rapidly. The monoplane could glide – but she did not fancy her odds.

And something was climbing, inhumanly fast, from one hanging car to another.

Take things one at a time…

Inside the wheel, the universe.

Stars glared at her. A field of stars brighter than any that could be seen in the sky. They shone bright, were overwhelmed by–

An immense structure floated in space. A sun rose, a ball of fire almost blinding her, and in its light she could see the ring.

It was enormous, ancient – strange. Its surface was pockmarked with the scars of countless impacts. It turned – slowly, rotating not unlike the Ferris wheel itself. Imagine a Ferris wheel lying on its side, floating in space, backlit by stars. Turning – she saw flecks of light rising from it and somehow realised they were craft, related to her monoplane the way ants were related to humans. The voices babbled, Contact initiated! and transferring informational matrix to source and home!

Flashes of jade – every dead person the silver streaks have ever touched was somehow still alive inside the beam that she was piggy-backing: memories, dreams, knowledge, all going through that hole punched into space, going towards that impossible structure no human could have built–

The engine, faltering. She was high above the axis and now she glided down, knowing the monoplane could only go one way now–

Sensing rather than seeing the movement of the thing climbing the wheel – the Phantom roaring rage, shouting: "Mine! Mine!"

The flecks of lights from the other side of the screen came closer, became ships – if ships could sail in space. They were growing closer in this Camera Obscura, coming towards the lens–

One hundred percent.

She screamed – "No!"

The engine died. She glided – down.

Tômas had reached the axle. For a moment he tottered, for the first time aware of the gulf of space lying inches away. He made a grab for the statue–

Kai fought him. She watched through goggles, half-real sight, half-jade. The statue was falling apart – the jade peeling, a machine unbending inside, opening translucent wings, ready to take flight–

An alien fleet approaching, closer and closer, tiny against the ring behind it, yet each craft easily the size of the white city itself. The plane was on a collision course – she raised herself from her seat, cursed–

Kai and Tômas below her, fighting on the axle–

She jumped.

The moment stretched, forever.

She was lost in the darkness. The space inside the wheel seemed to expand, spread out until it blocked out the entire sky – became the sky.

Perspective shifted–

A sun, rising, and in its light she saw not one ring but

hundreds. They revolved around the sun, a ring of rings. Each must have been hundreds of kilometres across. Ships travelled between the rings, strangely shaped vessels, a cloud of moving lights.

Voices: Unidentified communiqué on antiquated frequency – identify, identify!

The statue: Probe reporting completed survey – emergent life form identified–

Milady: Emergent life form?

A stream of confused images: memory/images/data – the city of Oxford, a signal from deep below – the statue awakening, initiating ancient, lumbering instructions – searching.

For what?

Voices: Identify – sounding confused.

Images – they were a recollection: a ship moving through space – planets, rings around them – she thought them beautiful but they passed too quickly – a dead, pock-marked world – it must have been the moon. Something dropping from the ship – she watched it fall and crash into the lunar surface. Emergency procedures initiated. Prepare for crash-landing.

A green-blue world, beautiful. And the ship was falling, falling, through white mist, clouds, a great blue sea opening below, a speck of land just visible amidst the blue – an island the dying ship was making for…

There had been an explosion…

Voices: Thought lost – unimportant. Emergent life form class identify?

The statue: Not enough data.

Voices: Sending investigatory fleet. Stand-down for gateway expansion.

The lights growing closer – a fleet of ships approaching, the space inside the wheel growing, expanding–

She said, "No."

•••

She fell, landing on the axle – hard. Pain flared through her.

The plane sailed above her head, almost grazing it–

It hit the membrane of that non-space inside the wheel–

The air shimmered – the plane passed through and tumbled through space against a brightness of stars.

A frozen tableau: the Phantom, Kai – herself. She stood up, righted herself.

She said: "We have to close it."

The statue was shedding jade flakes. A machine inside, unfurling – a delicate thing like a monoplane, spreading wings.

The statue: Initiating target parameters. Stand by to receive.

She blasted it with her Gatling gun arm. Kai shuddered as if the bullets were piercing him. Tômas, screaming: "Mine!"

He jumped – putting himself between her and the statue. She and Kai locked eyes – his said, Do it.

Voices: Gateway open. Coming though–

She kicked Tômas, her artificial leg lending her power – the impact made her lose her balance. She tottered on the axle – the ground was a long way down.

Tômas screamed. Cleo felt herself falling–

A hand reached and caught her.

Kai, pulling her up. She watched–

A whoosh of hot air, scorching her face–

Something immense and dark burst out of the space inside the wheel, just as–

Tômas, flying – her kick had sent him at the statue and he grasped it in his arms, like a lover–

Momentum kept him flying–

Through the space inside the wheel and out the other side.

Cleo watched–

Tômas floated in that other space against a background of stars, still holding the machine to him – like a lifebuoy.

Voices: Gateway sequence interrupted! Explain!

Tômas screamed, but no sound came. He rolled through

space – his mouth opened and closed without sound. Their eyes met, for just a moment–

Gateway linkage shutting down.

The statue: No!

She did a last kind thing. She didn't think she would. She fired, the bullets travelling through the distorted surface and through it to the other side.

They swarmed, silently, through space, and found Tômas.

SEVENTY-FIVE
Lights

The wheel turned, slowing down. The image in the space inside faded, gradually. Sun, rings, ships – had they ever really existed? Tômas's twisted features growing darker – the light in his eyes going out – the monoplane was a piece of discarded junk floating in space, its engine dead. The alien stars were fading. The babble of the voices was gone.

She stood by Kai on the axle of the Ferris wheel. A last shudder of air, like a breath, held too long, at last being exhaled, and the images flickered into nothingness, and comforting, familiar stars shone through the wheel.

It was quiet.

She watched the world below, the white city of the future coming alive all around them. Lights were flickering back into existence, bathing the white buildings, the lagoon, the wooded island in their soft glare. Screams from the hanging cars of the wheel turned to jubilation, then quietened down altogether.

She stood high above the ground as the wheel turned, and watched the lights. She said, "It's beautiful–" There was something in her hand. It took her a moment to realise it was Kai's hand, and it was warm.

He said, "It's over–" There was a terrible weariness in his voice, but something else, too, something that must have been new to him – relief? hope?

People swarming down below – they stopped now, turned their gazes upwards, a sea of humanity welcoming the new daylight. The wheel turned behind them, sedately. She could see rescue parties forming below, beginning to offload passengers as their cars came into station.

She said, "For now–"

Kai looked up – following her gaze. She felt his hand tightening in hers.

A dark saucer hovered in the air above the Fair. It rotated gently, gave nothing away. Then, like a blinking eye, it shot up, and away, growing smaller and smaller in seconds until it was gone into the night skies.

"For now," Kai agreed. Then, abruptly, he smiled. Cleo smiled back and squeezed his hand. They stood, on top of the world, the wheel turning at their back, and watched the city, bathed in light.

EXTRA! EXTRA!

READ ALL ABOUT IT!

FROM THE LOST FILES OF THE BOOKMAN HISTORIES

In the chronicle which you have just read, the worlds of east and west meet as the mystery of our lizardine masters deepens. What does the future hold for humanité? That, not even those great and secret machines which slumber deep under la Ville Lumière can truly know. More may be learned of the ending of that glorious century under her lizardine majesty, Queen Victoria may-she-live-forevermore, in the follow-up dossier titled The Great Game, *yet those seeking answers may find ever more questions being raised as to our place in the cosmos.*

The following journal is presented without comment as to the veracity of its claims. Its story is set some two decades after the events depicted here.

Beware, gentle reader, the lure of darkest science, and pray that you may never have reason to journey upon the wild seas on board :—

TITANIC!

10 April 1912

When I come on board the ship, I pay little heed to her splendour; nor to the gaily-strewn lines of coloured electric lights, nor to the polished brass of the crew's jacket uniforms, nor to the crowds at the dock in Southampton, waving handkerchiefs and pushing and shoving for a better look; nor to my fellow passengers. I keep my eyes open only for signs of pursuit; specifically, for signs of the Law.

The ship is named the *Titanic.* I had purchased a second-class ticket in London the day before. I had travelled down to Southampton by train. I had packed hurriedly. I do not know how far behind me the officers are. I know only that they would come. He had made sure of that, in his last excursion. The corpses he left were a mockery, body parts ripped, exposed ribcages and lungs stretched like Indian rubber, he had turned murder into a sculpture, a form of grotesque art. The Japanese would call such a thing as he a *yōkai,* a monster, otherworldly and weird. Or perhaps a *kaiju*. I admire the Japanese for their mastery of the science of monstrosity, of what in our Latin will be called the *lusus naturae*. I have corresponded with a Dr Yamane, of Tokyo, for some time, but have of course destroyed all correspondence when I escaped from London.

And yet I cannot leave him behind. I had packed hurriedly. A simple change of clothes. I had not dressed like a gentleman. But I carry, along with my portmanteau, also my doctor's black medical bag; it defines me more than I could ever define myself otherwise; it is as much a part of me as my toes, or my navel, or my eyes; and inside the bag I carry him, all that is left of him: one bottle, that is all, and the rest were all smashed up to shards back in London, back in the house where the bodies are.

I present my ticket to the steward. There is no suspicion in his eyes. He smiles courteously, professionally, already not seeing me as he turns to the ones behind me; and then I am on board. Perhaps infected by the other passengers' gaiety, perhaps just relieved at my soon to be escape, I stand with them on the deck, against the railings, shouting and waving at the people we are soon to leave behind. My heart beats faster; my palms sweat; I am eager for us to depart, for our transatlantic journey to begin. I long for escape.

At last it happens. The horn sounds and the gangplanks are raised and we are off! I sigh with relief; I had not realised how tense I had been. But fear had taken its hold on me, in all the long years of living with him; his presence is my life had made me fearful; the day he would get careless, or go too far, and leave me to be captured.

No longer!

England is a cesspit of corruption. It is too small, too confining. It looks not to the future, but to the past, it is rigid and unyielding. It is time for me to look elsewhere, to the New World; where a scientist may work in peace, where there is space to grow... and where he, too, could roam more freely, for it is a vast land and people may disappear there more easily; and never be seen again. Yes, he could be controlled, there. But for now he is dormant within me. He will not emerge on this voyage. Not unless I will it.

A near-accident. Our huge bulk causes waves in the harbour. We nearly drown two smaller ship: The SS *City of New York* and the *Oceanic*. I watch them rise on the waves, thinking of the size and power of the *Titanic*, like the power that I, myself, hold within me. It is a power all human beings have; yet I alone have found the means of liberating it. Only in Japan, perhaps, is there science greater than mine – but that land is far and their experiments have taken them in a different direction to my own. No, I am confident in my heart, my potion is unique; and I, a true original.

The passage out goes without a further hitch. The two

smaller ship are not harmed, and I feel neither satisfaction nor disappointment. I stand on the deck and watch the harbour recede from view for a long time. I watch England grow smaller in the distance. I cannot wait for it to disappear.

11 April 1912

Cork.

How I loathe the Irish!

The docks swarm with these Irishmen and their equally squalid women. They come on board, several obviously drunk and singing riotously. I stand on the deck and smoke a cigar. A man of middle years and a somewhat stooped posture engages me in conversation. "You are a doctor?" he says, on noticing my black bag (I do not dare part with it. These Irishmen may steal a doctor's bag as easily as they would slit a man's throat!).

"Yes, yes," I say, "what is it to you?"

Instead of taking offense he chuckles good-naturedly. "I myself am in the medical profession," he says. I say, "Oh?" and roll the cigar in my mouth. "Yes," he says, "I am a purveyor of the snake oil cure, are you familiar with that panacea?"

"*Enhydris chinensis,*" I say. "It is a medicine of the Chinese people, is it not?" I do not tell him I had studied it intensively, my research has increasingly taken me to study the obscure and arcane sciences of the East.

"Yes," he says, "it is a marvellous medicine, a cure-all."

I make a dismissive gesture and his moustache quivers at that. "Do you not agree, sir?" he says.

I tap my cigar and watch the ash blow in the wind. Will the ship never leave? I am unsafe as long as we are in these European waters. Have the bodies been found yet? Has Hyde been implicated? He is well known to the police. "Excuse me," I say. "I meant no offence."

His good humour returns. He gives me his calling card and asks me to call on him once in New York, promising me a bulk discount on his stock. It is of the utmost benefit to any doctor, he assures me. I am glad to be rid of him. At long last the ship departs. There are thousands of us on board.

12 April 1912

At last, the open sea!

The ocean is calm. The weather is mild. A sense of wild freedom grips me. The New World beckons! I have successfully avoided pursuit, capture. In New York I could start again, and the name of Jekyll will be forgotten. I pat my bag, thinking of the bottle it holds. Already I am craving it. In America I will make more of the potion. He wants to get out, I can feel him, pushing.

13 April 1912

A cold front. Strong winds and high waves. Nevertheless I brave the deck. I find being confined below excruciating, the press of people is repulsive to me. I take in the sea air but my attempts to light a cigar prove futile.

Last night I tossed and turned, the need burning inside me. I could feel Edward leering inside me, pushing to be let out. I find myself regarding women with Hyde's eyes, with his hunger. I see men and think of the blood coursing through them, and of the glint of knives. More than two decades ago when my experiments had just began he and I were sloppy. Jack, they had called him then. I had less control of the formula then. The cold air revives me. Anticipation of the New World soothes me. I feel as though I have been given a second chance.

14 April 1912

The sea is very calm, but there is a chill in the air. It is a fine morning. I have spoken to no one. It is a lonely life, sometimes. But I have him for company, always. The presence of the bottle in my bag reassures me. It will not be long now.

14 April 1912

An ungodly crash!

I had just been climbing up to the deck when the entire ship groaned and creaked as if hit by some vast and monstrous hammer. I fell but found my balance. My black bag was with me and I assured myself the sample inside was intact. I hurried up stairs, finding the decks in a confusion of people. What could this mean?

"Sir?" I hear an officer speak near me, and I find myself pushed to the front, and realise the man replenished in magnificent uniform further ahead is the Captain. "Sir? We've hit something!"

"It is an iceberg?" the Captain says, his manner outwardly calm.

"No, sir," the officer says. "It isn't an iceberg. It's a—"

Someone screams. It is a high pitched scream, but I cannot tell if it is made by a man or a woman. "Look up! Look at that – that thing!"

As if on cue the ship's powerful spotlights come on at once, piercing the night, momentarily blinding me. I hear a terrible sound, a roar as of a thousand engines cranking up to their utmost power and beyond their breaking point.

"It's a... it's a–!"

My God, I think, awed. How could anyone mistake this for an *iceberg*?

It towers over the ship, and the *Titanic* looks like a toy

in comparison. An enormous, beautiful monstrosity, like a cross between a gorilla and a whale: it opens its mouth and roars, and a lizard's giant claws land with a defeating roar on the deck of the *Titanic*, splintering wood and cutting deep into the underlying levels. I hear screams, and see a man's head explode like a wet red balloon where the monster had crashed it in its wake.

"It's a–!"

"It's a *daikaiju*," I say, though they do not hear me. I breathe out. A giant *kaiju*! The scientist in me is enthralled. The beast within me is hungry. Hyde responds to the creature like a drunk, he bangs against the walls of his prison, to be let out. Screams rise into the air. The monster, angered or afraid, lashes again at the ship. Its powerful tail slams into the side of the ship and the deck tilts alarmingly. Bodies fly through the air.

"Abandon ship! Abandon ship!" Panic takes over the *Titanic*. "To the lifeboats!" A press of bodies as the ones down below attempt to climb up to the open deck, to find escape. People shove and push each other in their panic. I see a woman trampled underfoot. I, too, try to make my way to the life boats, but the swell of people is too strong, and I am old; and panic rises in me as I am side-lined, pushed, shoved, hurt, and all the while the beast roars above our heads, lashing with talons and tale at the *Titanic*, ripping it slowly apart.

"To the boats!" and there they go, while, unbelievably, the ship's orchestra *plays on*, at least until the beast, annoyed, perhaps, by the noise, slashes at them with its claws and the music stops abruptly with a clatter of panicked notes. The ship tilts: we are sinking. I hear the boats dropping into the waters, hear a gunshot ring as officers attempt to control the manic passengers. "Children and women first!"

And something breaks in me. Something that has no name, no label I could easily affix to it, like to a specimen bottle, or a beaker of potion. I can escape, I realise, and yet...

"Doctor!" I hear the cry. "We need a doctor! Please, help!"

A woman lying on the deck, holding an injured child in her arms. Her face is panicked. There is blood on the deck.

I still tightly hold my black medicine bag. Now I open it. All of a doctor's requirements are there. I could help them...

I reach inside and find the bottle.

The potion. My life's work.

I could help the child, I think. Or I could let out Mr Hyde.

I stare at the bottle in my hands. To swallow its contents would liberate me, would Hyde me, would allow me to fight my way to the lifeboats, and to escape, to live.

I had lived half my life a monster, I realise; and that had led to my eventual ruin, and my disgrace, and finally my exile.

I look up at that titanic being towering over the ship. It is frightened, I think. Monstrous, yes: but also beautiful. And I am glad I have lived long enough to see one.

I look at it for a long moment, and then I look at the bottle in my hands.

"Please! Help him!"

I could live, a monster, I realise; or I could die a man.

I stretch my arm as far back as it would go, then back, in one smooth motion, and throw the bottle as hard and as fast as I can into the roiling sea.

THE END

FLEX
FERRETT STEINMETZ
THE FLUX
FERRETT STEINMETZ
FIX
FERRETT STEINMETZ

GRAFT
MATT HILL
THE SINGULAR & EXTRAORDINARY TALE OF
MIRROR & GOLIATH
BY ISHBELLE BEE
THE CONTRARY TALE OF THE
BUTTERFLY GIRL
BY ISHBELLE BEE

THE FLOATING CITY
CRAIG CORMICK
INFERNAL DEVICES
K.W. JETER
MORLOCK NIGHT
K.W. JETER

"A delight, crammed with gorgeous period detail, seat-of-the-pants adventure & fabulous set-pieces."
The Guardian

THE BOOKMAN
LAVIE TIDHAR
The Jerwood Fiction Uncovered Prize & World Fantasy Award Winning Author

IS THERE NO END TO THIS SCANDALOUS SUCCESSION OF OUTRAGEOUS VOLUMES?